Council of Fire

THE ARCANE AMERICA SERIES

THE ARCANE AMERICA SERIES
Uncharted by Kevin J. Anderson & Sarah A. Hoyt
Council of Fire by Eric Flint & Walter H. Hunt
Benjamin Franklin: Wizard for Hire by Peter J. Wacks and Eytan Kollin (forthcoming)

BAEN BOOKS BY ERIC FLINT

THE RING OF FIRE SERIES: *1632 • 1633* with David Weber • *1634: The Baltic War* with David Weber • *1634: The Galileo Affair* with Andrew Dennis • *1634: The Bavarian Crisis* with Virginia DeMarce • *1635: The Ram Rebellion* with Virginia DeMarce et al • *1635: The Cannon Law* with Andrew Dennis • *1635: The Dreeson Incident* with Virginia DeMarce • *1635: The Eastern Front* • *1636: The Papal Stakes* with Charles E. Gannon • *1636: The Saxon Uprising* • *1636: The Kremlin Games* with Gorg Huff & Paula Goodlett • *1636: The Devil's Opera* with David Carrico • *1636: Commander Cantrell in the West Indies* with Charles E. Gannon • *1636: The Viennese Waltz* with Gorg Huff & Paula Goodlett • *1636: The Cardinal Virtues* with Walter Hunt • *1635: A Parcel of Rogues* with Andrew Dennis • *1636: The Ottoman Onslaught* • *1636: Mission to the Mughals* with Griffin Barber • *1637: The Polish Maelstrom* by Eric Flint •*1636: The China Venture* by Eric Flint & Iver P. Cooper • *Ring of Fire I-V* • *Grantville Gazette I-VIII*

The Assiti Shards series: *Time Spike* with Marilyn Kosmatka • *The Alexander Inheritance* with Gorg Huff & Paula Goodlett

With Alistair Kimble: *Iron Angels*

With Dave Freer: *Rats, Bats & Vats* • *The Rats, The Bats & the Ugly* • *Pyramid Power* • *Pyramid Scheme* • *Slow Train to Arcturus*

With Mercedes Lackey & Dave Freer: *The Shadow of the Lion* • *This Rough Magic* • *Much Fall of Blood* • *Burdens of the Dead* • *Sorceress of Karres*

With David Drake: *The Tyrant* (General Series)

The Belisarius Series with David Drake: *An Oblique Approach* • *In the Heart of Darkness* • *Belisarius I: Thunder at Dawn* (omnibus) • *Destiny's Shield* • *Fortune's Stroke* • *Belisarius II: Storm at Noontide* (omnibus) • *The Tide of Victory* • *The Dance of Time* • *Belisarius III: The Flames of Sunset* (omnibus)

Joe's World Series: *The Philosophical Strangler* • *Forward the Mage* with Richard Roach

Mother of Demons

With David Weber: *Crown of Slaves* • *Torch of Freedom* • *Cauldron of Ghosts*

The Jao Empire Series: *The Course of Empire* with K.D. Wentworth • *Crucible of Empire* with K.D. Wentworth • *The Span of Empire* with David Carrico

With Ryk E. Spoor: *Boundary* • *Threshold* • *Portal* • *Castaway Planet* • *Castaway Odyssey* • *Castaway Resolution* (forthcoming)

With Mike Resnick: *The Gods of Sagittarius*

Edited by Eric Flint: *The World Turned Upside Down* with David Drake & Jim Baen • *The Best of Jim Baen's Universe I–II*

Eric Flint Story Collections: *Worlds 1• Worlds 2*

Books by Walter H. Hunt
The Dark Wing • *The Dark Path* • *The Dark Ascent* •
The Dark Crusade • *A Song in Stone* • *Elements of Mind* •*Harmony in Light* •
1636: The Cardinal Virtues with Eric Flint • *Council of Fire* with Eric Flint

To purchase any of these titles in e-book form, please go to www.baen.com.

Council of Fire

THE ARCANE AMERICA SERIES

ERIC FLINT AND
WALTER H. HUNT

COUNCIL OF FIRE

This is a work of fiction. All the characters and events portrayed in this book are fictional, and any resemblance to real people or incidents is purely coincidental.

Copyright © 2019 by Eric Flint & Walter H. Hunt

A Baen Book

Baen Publishing Enterprises
P.O. Box 1403
Riverdale, NY 10471
www.baen.com

ISBN: 978-1-9821-2415-1

Cover art by Tom Kidd
Maps by Michael Knopp

First Baen printing, November 2019

Distributed by Simon & Schuster
1230 Avenue of the Americas
New York, NY 10020

Library of Congress Cataloging-in-Publication Data

Names: Flint, Eric, author. | Hunt, Walter H., author.
Title: Council of fire / Eric Flint & Walter H. Hunt.
Description: Riverdale : Baen Publishing Enterprises, 2019. | Series: The
   Arcane America series
Identifiers: LCCN 2019029168 | ISBN 9781982124151 (hardcover)
Subjects: GSAFD: Alternative histories (Fiction) | Fantasy
Classification: LCC PS3556.L548 C67 2019 | DDC 813/.54—dc23
LC record available at https://lccn.loc.gov/2019029168

Printed in the United States of America

10 9 8 7 6 5 4 3 2 1

Dedications

Walter: I would like to dedicate this book to my wife Lisa, who has helped me see with new eyes.

✤ ✤ ✤

Eric: Well, I was planning to dedicate this book to hideous gruesome monsters, who fill the pages of the novel and are such a never-ending comfort and delight to scribblers, but . . .

In light of Walter's dedication, it seems more fitting (not to mention prudent) to dedicate this book to my wife Lucille, who has also helped me see with new eyes.

(As for you, hideous gruesome monsters, suck it up and stop whining. You're supposed to be *monsters,* not crybabies. I'll dedicate something else to you. In the fullness of time.)

North America
as of March 1759

Gulf of St. Laurence

St. Laurence River

Acadia

New France

Fort Beauséjour · Louisbourg

Halifax

Annapolis-Royal

Atlantic Ocean

Quebec

Trois-Rivières

Montréal

Crown Point · Fort Carillon

Salem

Boston

Fort Johnson

Onondaga

Albany

Canajoharie

New York

Philadelphia

Fort Venango

Logstown

Fort Pitt

Michael Knopp

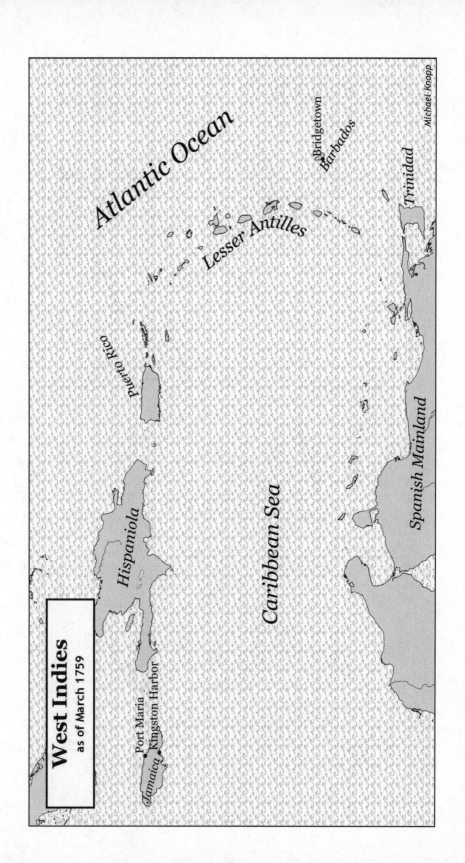

West Indies
as of March 1759

Atlantic Ocean

Bridgetown
Barbados

Trinidad

Lesser Antilles

Puerto Rico

Spanish Mainland

Hispaniola

Caribbean Sea

Port Maria
Kingston Harbor
Jamaica

Michael Knopp

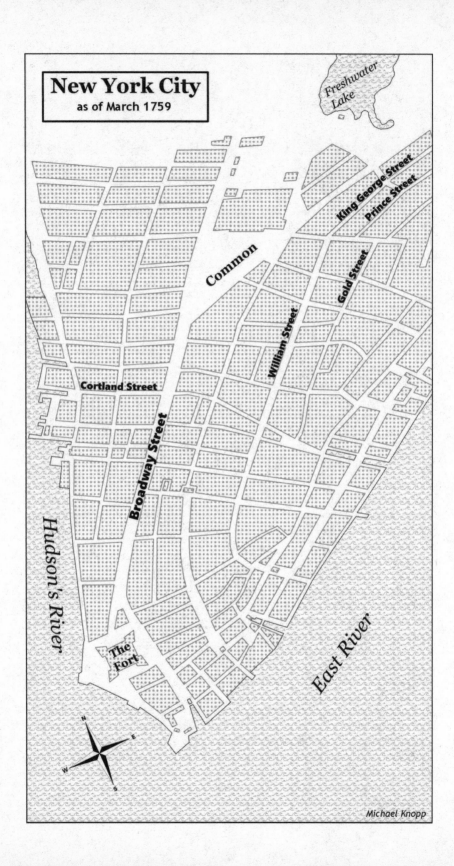

New York City
as of March 1759

Freshwater Lake

King George Street

Prince Street

Common

Gold Street

William Street

Cortland Street

Broadway Street

Hudson's River

The Fort

East River

Michael Knopp

Council of Fire

THE ARCANE AMERICA SERIES

Cast of Characters

The number in parentheses is the first chapter in which the character appears. Historical characters are in **bold**. Fictional characters are in ***bold italic***.

✢ ✢ ✢

ENGLISH (and ENGLISH-accompanying)

Absalom (b. 1725). Free black man, a chandler's apprentice in New York. (39)

Alexander, James (b. 1691). A lawyer and savant in New York. A Jacobite in his youth, he came to New York in the 1720s and became a loyal Whig. (35)

Amherst, Jeffery, General. (b. 1717) Commander in chief of His Majesty's Forces in North America. Led the attack on Louisbourg in 1758; intended to renew the campaign against Fort Carillon in 1759. (18)

Baker, George (b. 1731). Lieutenant and acting commander of *Magnanime*, originally under the command of Sir William Howe. (8)

Bartram, John (b. 1699). Perhaps the most famous botanist in North America; he traveled throughout the continent gathering samples and categorizing species. (21)

Biggin, Josephus (?) Merchant factor, located at Bridgetown, Barbados. (11)

Boscawen, Edward, Lord (b. 1711). Admiral of the White. Commander of *Namur*; en route to the Mediterranean at the time of the Sundering. (4)

Coffey (b. 1742). A free black woman, living in New York. She is close friends with York. (39)

Cotes, Thomas, Vice-Admiral of the Blue (b. 1712). Appointed to the Jamaica station in 1757; friends with Boscawen. (21)

De Lancey, James (b. 1703). Governor of New York Colony; in full authority from 1753-55, and again since the departure of Sir Charles Hardy in 1757. A *patroon*, well connected in New York and English society. (35)

Dunbar, William (b. 1718). Major in His Majesty's service; commander of the 40th Infantry, aboard *Magnanime*. (8)

Equiano, Oladuah ("Gustavus") (b. 1745). Igbo. Slave, owned by Michael Pascal. Wrote a famous biography later in life, one of the earliest literate black men in America. (5)

"Fayerweather," Charlie. (Charles Evan Toombs) (b. 1723). Ship's captain in the Caribbean. Originally from Salem, Mass. (13)

Grant, Robert. (b. 1714). Merchant factor, under contract to the Royal Navy in Halifax. (8)

Gridley, Richard (b. 1710). Commander of Massachusetts militia. Freemason. (42)

Haldane, George, Hon. (b. 1722) Scotsman. Governor of Jamaica from 1756. (20)

Hanover, Edward Augustus, later Duke of York and Albany and Earl of Ulster (b. 1739); Brother of George, Prince of Wales, and grandson of King George II. Officer in the Royal Navy since 1758. In the Navy he is called "Mr. Prince" or "Commander Prince." (1)

Hughes, Edward (b. 1720). Captain of *Somerset*. (6)

Johnson, Sir William, Baronet (b. 1715) Superintendent of Indian Affairs for New York Colony. "Chief Big Business." Molly Brant is his common-law wife. (6)

Jupiter. (b. 1736) A slave blacksmith. (39)

LaGèndiere, Catherine (b. 1737). Woman of gentle birth, daughter of a colleague of Messier. (11)

Leacock (b. about 1730?) Able seaman, rigger aboard *Namur*. Scotsman. (4)

MacArran, Kenneth (b. 1737). Subaltern in the 40th Regiment of Foot, stationed at Fort Pitt. (29)

Marshal, William (b. 1724). First mate of *Namur*. (4)

Messier, Charles (b. 1730). French astronomer, in the employ of M. Delisle, the French Royal Astronomer. Caught in the Sundering, comes aboard *Namur*. (11)

Minerva (b. 1717). "Mercy." A free black woman, living in New York. (39)

O'Brien (b. about 1740?) Unrated seaman aboard *Namur*. (4)

Pascal, Michael Henry (b. about 1725) Lieutenant aboard *Namur*. Owner of the slave Gustavus (Oladuah Equiano). (4)

Perry, Francis (b. about 1720) Boatswain aboard *Namur*. Cornishman. (4)

Pinfold, Charles (b. 1712) Governor of Barbados. A "placeman." (11)

Pownall, Thomas (b. 1722). Governor of Massachusetts Bay Colony. (9)

Prideaux, John (b. 1718). Brigadier-General; fought at Dettingen with the 3rd Foot Guards. From 1758 commander of the 55th Regiment of Foot. Promoted to general after the Battle of Fort Niagara in 1758. (19)

Revere, Paul (b. 1734). Silversmith, artillery officer. He served Massachusetts in the French and Indian war. (42)

Ranford (b. about 1730?) Able seaman aboard *Namur*. (4)

Rogers, Robert, Major.(b. 1731). Frontiersman and colonial officer. Commander of "Rogers' Rangers," a "special forces" team. (19)

Saunders, Sir Charles (b. 1713); Admiral, commander of *Neptune*. Given charge of the fleet sent to subdue Quebec in 1759. (1)

Washington, George (b. 1732). Colonel of Virginia militia. This is just at the time of his marriage to Martha; thus, he is recently come into wealth. It is after he has helped set off the French and Indian War in 1754. (34)

Wolfe, James (b. 1727). Colonel of regular troops at the taking of Louisbourg during the 1758 campaign, given overall command of the Quebec expedition in 1759. (1)

York (b. 1743). Slave in New York, apprentice to a blacksmith along with Jupiter.(49)

FRENCH

Bigot, François (b. 1703). *Intendant* of New France. An intensely venal and corrupt man. (2)

Briand, Jean-Olivier (b. 1715), Vicar-General in Québec for Pontbriand. (62)

D'Egremont, Olivier (b. 1739). Third son of a minor nobleman, in New France to make his fortune. (17)

"Georges." A French deserter from Carillon. (3)

Lévis, François-Gaston, Chevalier de (b. 1719). Second-in-command to Montcalm, army colonel. (2)

Montcalm-Gozon, Louis-Joseph de, Marquis de Saint-Veran ("Marquis de Montcalm") (b. 1712). Brigadier General, in command of all French troops in North America. (2)

Pontbriand, Henri-Marie Dubreil de, (b. 1708) Archbishop of Québec. (62)

Récher, Jean-Félix, Pére (b. 1734). Parish priest at Notre-Dame de Québec. (15)

Vaudreuil, Pierre de Rigaud de, Marquis de ("Marquis de Vaudreuil") (b.1698) Governor-General of New France. Top civil authority in the French colonies. (16)

NATIVE AMERICAN

Brant (b. 1710?) Mohawk chief, stepfather of Joseph Brant (Thayendanegea). (3)

Brant, Joseph (Thayendanegea) (b. 1743) Mohawk warrior, Wolf Clan. (3)

Brant, Molly (Degonwadonti) (b. 1736) Mohawk woman, common-law wife of Sir William Johnson. Sister of Joseph Brant. Wolf Clan of Mohawks; her father was from Turtle Clan. (6)

Donehogawa (b. 1734) Cayuga warrior from Ichsua. Scout. Surrenders to Amherst's army to provide information. (46)

Fourth Sparrow (b. 1695) Onondaga wise woman. (33)

Guyasuta (b. 1725). Seneca leader, relocated to the Ohio Country. (26)

Kaintwakon (b. 1750) Brother of Sganyodaiyo. (26)

Karaghiagdatie (b. 1700) Mohawk Wolf Clan sachem. Present at the Treaty of Five Nations in 1748 (26)

Neani (birth date unknown) Clan-mother of the Cayuga. (48)

Osha (birth date unknown) Clan-mother of the Heron of the Oneida. (10)

Red Vest. (b. 1710~) Seneca warrior. Related to Guyasuta. (14)

Sganyodaiyo (Handsome Lake; pronounced "Kenyodaiyo") (b. 1735) Son of Gahonneh, Turtle Clan, Seneca. Shaman. His brother is Kaintwakon. (26)

Shingas (b. about 1720) "Half King" of the Delaware, relocated to Ohio. Allied to Guyasuta. (26)

Skenadoa (b. 1706). "John Skenadoa." Born a Susquehannock, adopted as an Oneida when he was a teenager, a chief by 1759. (10)

Tacky (Takyi), (b. about 1730?) Leader of a rebellion on Jamaica. An Akan, from west Africa, enslaved several years before the rebellion. (21)

Tadodaho (birth date unknown) Spiritual leader of the Iroquois Confederacy. (10)

Tekarihoga (birth date unknown) Mohawk chief sachem. (3)

Tiyanoga (b. about 1740) Mohawk warrior, named for the famous Tiyanoga (Hendrick). (3)

SUPERNATURAL

An-De-Le. (d. 1759) The leader of the Jo-Ge-Oh ("Little People"). (54)

Campbell, Duncan, Major (b. about 1720?; d. 1758) Scottish soldier with the 42nd Regiment of Foot (Highlanders). Along with many of his regiment, killed during a frontal assault on Fort Carillon (Ticonderoga) in 1758. Bears a strong resentment against James Abercromby, who ordered the attack. (17)

Ciinkwia. "The spirits of thunder and storm." Usually depicted as a tall man and woman. The man has a tomahawk and a bow; the woman a staff shaped like a sheaf of wheat. (16)

Prologue

In reconstructing history, as historians tend to do, it became quite obvious that Newton knew. At the time that the comet passed, in 1682, he was deeply ensconced at Trinity College—not yet Master of the Mint, not yet even Sir Isaac—and as he worked on mathematics and how it mirrored the God of Nature, he was also obsessed with the study of the chimerical art of alchemy. In his writings, in the few published letters that survived, in the Waste Book that scholars were able to peruse after his death, it is clear that the effects of the 1682 transit were much on his mind.

Halley knew as well, or at least suspected; in an addendum to his seminal 1705 work, sometimes included in the published edition and most times not, he warned of the ill effects of what the vulgar called the "broom star." He speculated—again, many editions of the *Synopsis* did not include this disturbing, rambling afterword—that the 1682 passage had fundamentally affected many people, making them more sensitive to the effects of the æther. The afterword was the source of much derision in the Royal Society; one reason it was so frequently omitted. In a rare act of human courtesy, Sir Isaac (for he had been so honored by that time) simply excised it from future editions and never spoke of it again. But as Halley lay on his deathbed at Greenwich, he told a story to his future biographer concerning a discussion he and Sir Isaac had had, in private, away from prying eyes and mocking lips, many years before. He feared what might happen when the comet returned, its orbit ever so slightly perturbed by its passage through the Solar System, a nudge

9

from Jupiter here, a nudge from Saturn there. But that was still in the future when Edmund Halley traversed the gates of the infinite in 1742.

If others knew of the effect of the comet's passage, or feared its next return, they did not speak or write of it. This was God's work, and God allocated to each man only three score and ten years, be he John Plowman or Sir Isaac Newton. From the lowest to the highest, every man dies, and leaves worries and concerns to those who come after.

And as for doomsayers: every event and every phenomenon brings them out, armies of them, so that no one expected anything more to come from it in 1759.

After all, there were many far more mundane things to worry about.

Part I: Transit

March, 1759

Dr. Halley observed . . . how much greater irregularities must not a comet be liable to, which at its remotest distance gets near four times farther from the Sun than Saturn, and whose velocity in drawing near the sun needs but a very small increase to change its elliptic into a parabolic curve.
—Charles Messier,
A Memoir, containing the History of the Return of the famous Comet of 1682, Phil. Trans., Jan. 1765

Chapter 1

The sea giveth and the sea taketh away

Aboard HMS *Neptune*
North Atlantic

A few minutes after three bells Sir Charles Saunders, Admiral of the Blue, set his quill aside and rubbed his eyes, unsure how he should continue writing the account of *Neptune*'s current situation. It was all for posterity, of course; it would be transcribed into an Admiralty book and placed upon some dusty shelf somewhere, to be reviewed sometime by someone.

Lord Anson had told him years ago when they were circumnavigating the Earth in *Centurion* that, as much as every captain—or, for that matter, every admiral—dwelt on the exact words he might use to convey the account of his travels, in the long run they were largely ignored. *But it doesn't mean you don't write them nonetheless,* Anson had told him.

He wondered whether now that Anson himself was First Lord, he took the time to read what was written in ship's logs that found their way back to London—as opposed to the ones that were lost, destroyed or neglected.

Saunders took his hat from its hook and left the cabin to go abovedecks, hoping that there might be some inspiration there.

Middle watch belonged to his executive officer. *Mr. Prince* they called him in public: Prince Edward Augustus, third child of the late Prince Frederick and younger brother of the Prince of Wales, was certainly the socially highest-ranking officer in His Majesty's Navy.

It had taken some negotiation and discussion between Whitehall and the Admiralty to settle the delicate point of address—but the Prince: *Mr. Prince*—was junior on board to the Master-before-God commander of *Neptune*.

Saunders walked up onto the quarterdeck, offering only the slightest of nods to each salute. He reached into his sleeve and withdrew his glass, turned to face east and focused on the horizon. There was light all along it; it looked a great deal like sunrise—but the new day was hours away.

"Mr. Prince. Tell me what you make of that."

He snapped his glass shut and gestured toward the eastern horizon.

His executive officer stepped forward to stand beside him and took out his own glass and raised it to his eye.

"I have no idea, My Lord. Maybe it's the comet."

"The comet? That should be over there." Saunders gestured toward the northern sky, which was muddied with low clouds. "But *that*—I don't know what that is."

Commander Prince closed his own glass and tucked it away. "Perhaps we should ask the general."

Saunders snorted. "I do not think the general has anything much to say."

"Still hasn't managed to get his sea legs," Prince said.

"He doesn't have sea-guts," Saunders replied. "Apparently he has always had this . . . weakness. I expect he goes queasy when he strolls across London Bridge."

"He is quite capable on land, My Lord Admiral. His bravery at Louisbourg several months ago led to the capture of that fortress. I trust that you are not questioning His Highness' choice of commanders."

Saunders cocked his head and smiled. "I don't usually tolerate that sort of insolence from my officers. But, of course, only one of my officers is a Prince of the Blood. So let me assure you that I mean no disrespect to His Highness by my remarks."

"And I mean no disrespect to you, My Lord Admiral. Indeed . . . I am somewhat disheartened that General Wolfe has never accustomed himself to travel by sea, since he seems to have done so much of it."

James Wolfe was only recently elevated to the rank of general as a part of this expedition. As a colonel the previous summer, he had seized an important post on his own initiative during the British assault on the French fortress of Louisbourg—their present destination, a few weeks away. He would be in command of the next step in the war against the French; this time, instead of seizing some jumped-up fortress in Godforsaken Acadia, there would be an expedition along the Saint Lawrence to drive the French from North America once and for all.

"We each have our assigned roles, Mr. Prince," Saunders said. "When we reach Louisbourg I am certain he will . . . rise to the occasion."

Prince Edward nodded. "He is a very brave man."

"He—" Saunders began, but stopped. He looked up at the masts. The sails were rippling with a sudden and strong change in the wind.

He shouted orders; Commander Prince touched his cap and headed for the main deck. Saunders opened his glass and looked east.

In the pilothouse Saunders studied the barometer. He had been at sea for all his adult life and a few years beforehand, and he had never seen it drop so fast. A storm was coming—not just the stiff wind that had already led *Neptune* to haul its sails tightly before it, but a stronger, fiercer one; and it was blowing from the east.

The horizon was aglow with a yellow-gray haze that he could not adequately describe. What he and Prince Edward had noticed on deck early in the watch had become a—what had the young royal called it?—a *phenomenon*. The sea was rough now. It had been nearly an hour since *Neptune* had been able to make out any sort of flag from the other ships in his squadron, and Saunders was worried.

The sea giveth and the sea taketh away, he thought. Mastery of the oceans had made his country great, but the roiling Atlantic was still greater, and easily capable of swallowing them all up. Spithead was far behind, and Nova Scotia far ahead—it was as if they were alone, with the hostile sea all around them.

"There is something unnatural about this."

Saunders looked up from his barometer to see the pale face of James Wolfe. It was a far stretch from handsome—angular, with close-set eyes, a prominent nose and a receding chin that always seemed to be jutting upward. He looked drawn, as if merely standing erect was an effort—which, under the circumstances, it likely was.

"It's just a storm, General. Nothing unnatural about that."

"And the bright light on the horizon? What might that be, my Lord?"

"I wish I knew. Please feel free to give me your thoughts, sir. I am sure you will do so whether I solicit them or not."

Wolfe appeared ready with an angry response, but seemed to bite it back. "I am concerned for the welfare of the royal person we carry aboard," he said. "I assume that you are doing whatever you can to get us away from this storm."

"I have only so much control," Saunders said. He wanted to add the words *as you know*, but concluded that Wolfe probably had no idea what was involved in making an Atlantic crossing—he likely spent most of them hurling his dinner over the side or collapsed on his bed. "And the *royal person* is an officer of this ship. A valued *senior* officer who, despite his youth, has more than proved his mettle."

"Nevertheless, if anything were to happen to him—"

"I fail to see where this discussion is going, General. Perhaps you will be so kind as to let me attend to my business."

"If I can be of assistance—"

"You can stay out of the way, sir. And for pity's sake try not to be washed overboard. I might be court-martialed if I lost His Highness, but if I were to lose *you* it would be endless paperwork."

The storm blew harder and harder. General Wolfe bravely stayed abovedeck, but out of the way of the sailors and well back from the railings—*which was just as well*, Saunders thought; four able seamen were washed overboard as *Neptune* pitched and struggled at waves and in wind he had never seen in any Atlantic crossing—or anywhere at sea, ever in his life; not rounding the Cape of Good Hope, not circumnavigating the globe with Lord Anson in *Centurion*.

And unlike any storm he had ever known, it was cast in an unearthly pall of yellowish-gray light that dominated the eastern sky from the horizon to forty degrees azimuth—like a huge sun that gave no warmth. There was no point in trying to raise signal flags, since there was no one in sight to spy them.

There was no dawn—at least none to be seen from the decks of *Neptune*—but when the ship's chronometer recorded a time a few bells after sunrise, a cloud of glowing mist gathered aft of the ship, emanating—so it seemed—from the glow at the horizon. *Neptune* was making a remarkable headway, a steady eight knots due westward by the compass. The cloud moved considerably faster, overtaking the ship and cloaking it for two to three minutes, making sight nearly impossible and smothering sound.

Saunders was unwilling to stray very far from the pilothouse. He could not even make out his own quarterdeck. As he looked out across the main deck, though, he thought he made out a familiar figure-a tall man dressed in a uniform of antique style, who gazed sternly back at him.

"My God," he said to no one in particular. "Admiral Wager—I—"

He began to move toward the figure but nearly collided with Wolfe, who looked more gaunt and sick than usual, but his eyes were frantic. In total violation of decorum or protocol, he grasped Saunders by the shoulders.

"It's Neddy," Wolfe said. "My Lord Admiral, why is Neddy aboard this ship?"

Then, suddenly, Wolfe seemed to realize what he was doing and let go of Saunders. "I'm—I'm sorry, My Lord. I beg your pardon. But look—" he gestured toward where the admiral had seen his long-dead superior, Sir Charles Wager, Admiral of the White.

Now he saw nothing at all. "What are you talking about, man? And who is *Neddy*?"

"My . . . my brother, My Lord. My brother Edward. But . . . he died. Long ago, in Flanders, when we were both on campaign with the Pragmatic Army."

Wolfe looked away, then back at Saunders with a fierce expression. "But I *saw* him so clearly—dear old Ned—"

Saunders had a sickening feeling in the pit of his stomach. *He* had seen someone as well: Sir Charles Wager, sixteen years in the grave. It made no more sense than Wolfe's vision of his dead brother.

"Pull yourself together, General," he said after a moment. "The fog—this blasted fog is playing tricks on your eyes. And if you are seeing things, everyone else might be as well.

"Mr. Prince!" he called out. "Mr. Prince, are you on deck?"

From somewhere in the murk he heard an answer—something inarticulate, between a cry and a shout.

"Mr. Prince! This is the admiral. Report, sir!"

Prince Edward seemed to stagger out of the fog, like a man who hadn't gotten his sea-legs—*or*, Saunders thought, *like a man who had seen a ghost*. The prince stopped and straightened, offering a smart salute—but Saunders could see some pain, or perhaps fright, on his face.

"Reporting, My Lord," he said.

"Call the roll of the watch, Mr. Prince. See to it that the men are all accounted for. At this speed we'll come out of this fog shortly, and I'll want us to be properly manned and the sails correctly trimmed."

The prince hesitated for only a moment and then said, "Very good, sir." He saluted again and turned, vanishing into the fog.

"You saw something," Wolfe said quietly. "You saw someone. And so did *he*."

"We'll discuss this later, General," Saunders said, pushing past Wolfe and out of the pilothouse.

Fifteen hours after it began it began to subside, with *Neptune* still making headway westward—but there was no other means of determining their location other than to note that the ship was beset with ice floes, suggesting that they had been driven far to the north. *Neptune* was alone in a partially frozen sea, with a leaden sky above and choppy, icy water beneath.

There was no other ship in sight.

The sea giveth and the sea taketh away. But it was unclear just then what the sea had given them.

Chapter 2

Do you believe in omens?

Québec
New France

The Upper Town was at the top of a steep hill that overlooked the St. Lawrence. It was like a great ship, with the waters parting and then rejoining around it. When the marquis stood on the platform behind the Battery of St. Louis and looked downstream, he felt as if he was at the aft end of that ship, watching the water pass into the distance as he moved upstream.

But it was an illusion, just as the robust defenses around the city of Québec were an illusion. True, it would take a mighty assault to wrest it away; but the British were coming. They had taken Louisbourg, and they were assembling a force to traverse the Hudson River toward Lac du Champlain, and there would be another thrust toward Oswego . . . they were *determined* now, and they controlled the seas, and New France—whatever its natural defenses—was no match for the enemy that would soon invade.

The intendant and the governor remained supremely confident, at least in public; at least in the hearing of any *habitant* who might question the ability to defend against the coming storm.

But to Louis-Joseph de Montcalm-Gozon, Marquis de Saint-Veran, commander of the military forces of His Most Christian Majesty Louis XV, it was a fiction that was not at all comforting. Vaudreuil and Bigot: the detested governor and the corrupt, diseased worm of an intendant—they would be playing at this game until the enemy's standard waved over Cap-Diamant Redoubt; and maybe even after that.

He heard someone clearing his throat behind, and turned to see Lévis standing there, looking a trifle uncomfortable to have interrupted him.

"François," he said, smiling. "How long have you been waiting?"

"Only a minute or so." Lévis looked up at the royal banner snapping in the stiff March wind. "You seemed deep in thought."

"I could drown in it. But it would not get me away from here."

"The battle will be here, Monsieur," Lévis said, coming up to stand beside him. "Probably not until the summer. But it will be here."

"I know my duty."

"Of course," Lévis said. The man was seven years his junior, but they were close friends. They had served together on the continent, and the younger man had agreed at once to accompany him as his aide when he had come to New France in 1756. In the two and a half years since they had gone from success to success, most recently at Fort Carillon—when the English general Abercromby had thrown away the lives of his Scottish Highlanders in a frontal assault against the fort's abatis.

But Lévis, like Montcalm, understood what was on the way this spring and summer.

"I dreamed of Candiac last night, François. My beloved home . . . but it was empty and lifeless. I went from room to room, calling the names of my children and my dear Angélique; but all I heard was echoes. From my bedchamber I could see the gardens, but they too were neglected and vacant. What do you suppose it means?"

"It means you digested your dinner poorly, Monsieur," Lévis said, smiling. "Or there was a bad lump in your mattress, or a draught from a window."

"Or it is an omen."

"My dear Marquis," the Chévalier de Lévis said. "We are soldiers. Whenever we go to battle there is the possibility that it could be our last day on this earth. If we let ourselves be chased by omens and haunts, we will be consumed by them."

"So you don't . . . "

"Really. Do you believe in omens? I wonder what His Eminence the bishop would say about *that*."

"What he says about everything, François. Which is not very much."

"If you want to take something as an omen, tell me what you make of this much-heralded comet. If we had a clear sky—which we never seem to do—we could gaze upon it. The common folk fear it, but it's just a . . . well, it's just something in the sky, whatever it is. Once in a lifetime, and then it's gone."

"Strange that it should come now, in this critical time."

"It was predicted, *non*? Every, what, seventy-six years it comes into the sky once and twice, and then disappears into the dark, not to be seen again by the same eyes. At least *I* don't expect to see it again."

"Assuredly not." Montcalm looked out at the St. Lawrence again as it rushed below. "And I don't expect to see Candiac again either."

"Melancholy ill becomes you, Monsieur. Especially when you are to meet with the governor."

"I suspect he does not hold with omens either."

"I do not think I would mention it, Monsieur."

"No. I do not think the subject will come up."

The governor was waiting for Montcalm and Lévis at the Intendant's Palace, a rambling old structure in the Lower Town. Regrettably, it meant that the meeting would also include the presence of François Bigot, the *intendant* of New France. If there was one man in North America whom Montcalm detested more than Vaudreuil, it was Bigot—not just for his scarcely-disguised venality, but for his physical presence.

Montcalm sometimes thought that he might rather face a concerted cavalry charge than to stand close to Bigot. He suffered from a disfiguring affliction: what was called *ozène*, a sort of infection of the nose; he was constantly dabbing at it with a lavender-scented handkerchief, but the odor penetrated the cloying perfume. It was unpleasant enough that the Marquis avoided the odious little man as much as possible.

The Intendant's Palace was damp and chilly as the two men walked through the entrance. A servant was there to take their hats and walking-sticks and beckon them toward the stairs. Montcalm found Vaudreuil at a large table, with Bigot hovering close by. He could smell the man's perfume at a distance and did his best not to wrinkle his nose.

"So good of you to come on short notice, Monsieur," Vaudreuil said, offering the slightest of bows. "I require your advice."

Montcalm looked from the governor to the intendant and back. "On what subject?"

"There appears to be some sort of panic among the savages. They view the transit of the comet as a particularly evil omen."

"It was viewed as an evil omen in London and Paris in 1682, and I am sure each other time it has passed near to the Earth. What of it?"

"You seem to take the matter lightly, Marquis," Bigot said, dabbing his nose. "Surely the participation of the natives is critical to our strategy."

"That does not mean I listen to everything they say. And you know well, Monsieur Intendant, that they often do as they please regardless of what *I* say. But say on, Governor. What do they make of this omen?"

Vaudreuil seemed to be contemplating his response, and Montcalm remembered the question he had asked Lévis on the fortifications. *Do you believe in omens?*

"You know that their shamans perform what they call 'medicine,' in which they make an augury for the future. One of them—an Onondaga, I believe—made some dire predictions which were repeated to a *courier de bois*. The ones he particularly made note of were that the comet—the 'broom star'—would 'come to earth,' leaving a path of death and destruction; and that something, or someone, would extinguish a council fire—whatever significance that might have."

"Did the ranger say those precise words? The Council Fire?"

"Something to that effect, yes."

"Is he still in Québec? I would like to ask him myself. If he heard those words, Governor, it is an ill omen indeed. I can imagine why the natives were so upset."

"I fail to understand," Bigot said.

"Obviously," Montcalm said, which drew a sharp look from the intendant. "If the man spoke of the Onondaga Council Fire, then having it be extinguished is *highly* significant. You are native to New France, Governor: you must understand."

Bigot arched an eyebrow; Montcalm glanced back at Lévis, who said nothing and kept his face impassive.

"Our native allies to the south—the Six Nations—are centered on the lands of the Onondaga, Monsieur Intendant. There a fire is kept continuously burning at the Onondaga Long House. It is the place that the various tribes and chiefs bring their burdens and their disputes. If the fire went out it would portend the end of their confederation."

"We might deal more easily with them in detail," Bigot said. "Their bargaining power would be reduced."

"Some of them would defect to the English," Montcalm snapped back, almost adding, *you idiot*. "And even those who were still our allies would be unreliable. It would be a disaster."

"It is no more than a primitive omen, Monsieur," Vaudreuil said. "It means nothing."

"I am not so sure. And you are not sure either, Governor, or you would not be taking my time to discuss it. The English must have heard the same rumors and will act accordingly. Now is the *courier de bois* still in Québec?"

"I really have no idea."

"Then I shall go and see. If this is the substance of his report, we should be very concerned indeed."

The storm came in the pale, overcast morning, like a bank of fog that rolled westward up the St. Lawrence, first wrapping itself around the lower town and then drifting upward along the cliffs to *Vieux Québec*.

The Marquis de Montcalm was walking along the landward-facing wall that overlooked the plateau west of the old city, the so-called *Heights of Abraham*. They were apparently named for a riverboat pilot of the last century—for his good works, or some such thing, he was granted the valuable tract beyond. The name had become enshrined in local geography.

He stopped for a moment to imagine what a battle might look like there. Assuming an enemy army—a British army—could somehow make the ascent from the river, they would have to deploy out there, crouching behind the hillocks and the gradual rises. Infantry only, of course—there'd be no horsemen and certainly no cannon. It would be muskets and bayonets . . .

The fog drifted across where he was standing. Not the usual damp fog that was native to Québec, but a pale, almost luminescent one that carried the slightest odor of . . .

. . . *Of gunpowder*, Montcalm realized. *It smells like a battle.*

From across the plains, he thought he heard gunfire and shouting . . . and the rolling thunder of artillery.

They're firing on us, Montcalm thought: *the Austrians have us in their sights, and we're in a bottleneck. This is not where we are supposed to be—and Maillebois must know it. We were to deploy to the north of Piacenza.*

They found out. Somehow Count Browne must have found out what we were doing and moved against us . . . and now they have our range.

We will have to charge them. The only way out is through the Austrian lines. The only way . . .

The fog swept across the battlefield, and Montcalm led the Bourbon cavalry against the Austrians. There was no way but forward.

The sun peeked through the clouds of the setting sun, and a shadow crossed them. Montcalm looked up to see Lévis standing over him, bending down slightly, looking concerned.

Montcalm blinked. "Bin ich jetzt in Verhaftung?"

"I'm sorry . . . Monsieur, what did you say?"

He looked around him. He was reclining—quite comfortably, actually—against the bole of a large tree. In the near distance, across uneven, rolling hillocks, he could see the landward wall of the old city of Québec. Not Piacenza . . . Québec . . . and it was not 1746, but rather 1759.

No, he thought. *I am not a prisoner. That was long ago.*

"Why am I here, François?"

"I would ask you that question myself, Monsieur," Lévis said. "No one has seen you in hours. I have looked all around the Old Town, and down in the lower town . . . and no one has seen or heard from you since mid-morning. I was a bit worried."

"Monsieur Chévalier," Montcalm said, getting slowly to his feet and brushing off his clothing, "I have been a soldier for His Christian Majesty for most of forty years. I fought in the Polish war, against the Austrians—"

"I remember, Monsieur; I have been in service about as long. They took you prisoner at Piacenza. *Verhaftung.*"

Montcalm looked at him curiously. "I hadn't realized you had much command of German, François."

"You asked me a question in German just now, Monsieur."

"I did no such thing."

Lévis looked away, the sunset light etching his profile.

"Did I ask you something in German? Why would I . . . "

Piacenza, Montcalm thought. *I was back at Piacenza—I was leading the charge against the Austrian cavalry . . . and at the end of the day I was a prisoner of the Austrians.*

"Can you tell me what happened today?"

"It is . . . hard to say. But one thing is certain: if you look at the sky—" he pointed upward. "The comet is gone."

Chapter 3

One word over and over

Lands of the Six Nations

The night of the Change had been still and cold, with no hint of the coming spring. But still, there had been something so odd that no one, not even the oldest among those at Canajoharie, could remember anything like it. A wind swept across the settlement, bringing with it a strange fog that seemed to contain dancing lights—it came and went in less time than it took the moon to climb from between the tall trees to above them. The next day the shamans and many of the women reported evil dreams—of lands rising from the water, and the scourging of the people by ancient, terrible creatures . . . but the sun still rose in its usual place and people went about their usual tasks.

Brant and his stepson sat on two tree stumps, watching the white stranger converse with another warrior. The white man seemed nervous, looking around as he talked.

"What do you make of that?"

"He's a soldier," Joseph said. "He stands straight and has his hands ready."

"I wonder if Tiyanoga knows that."

"He went with the war-band last year. He would see the same things I do."

Brant stretched and yawned. The stranger noticed the movement, his eyes darting toward the two natives sitting on the stumps. But he did not otherwise react.

"He's not dressed as a soldier, but rather as a trader. I wonder why."

"No single soldier would come into the Mohawk lands," Joseph said. "Neither British nor French trust us . . . not to be *savages*."

His stepfather laughed at that, and again the stranger's glance went to them.

"Let's see what this *trader* has to say for himself," Brant said, standing. His stepson joined him, and they walked to where the conversation was taking place.

The white man turned his attention completely to the newcomers. He looked around and noticed that there were several others nearby, watching the exchange.

"I think I would best be on my way," he said in English—but it bore an accent that suggested that it was not his native tongue.

"I think our *Tekarihoga* would like to sit with you, Brother," Brant said. "So you will remain with us for a while."

The man looked up at the sun, well into the afternoon. "I have far to go before dark—"

Brant laughed. "A trader who does not wish to trade? No, you will stay." He gestured at the little crowd that had gathered. "Too many to fight, and you cannot run fast enough—my son has the feet of a deer and will catch you. You will make the right choice to sit and smoke a pipe with us, won't you?"

"I am a Scottish trader from Albany," the man said, sitting cross-legged in the house of the *Tekarihoga*, the chief sachem of the Canajoharie. A small group of other warriors, including Brant and Joseph, sat in a circle, listening carefully.

The sachem took a long pull on his pipe and handed it to the white man. "You are not a clever liar, Brother."

The man held the pipe for a moment before drawing on it, then letting the smoke escape his mouth. "I don't know what you mean."

"You are neither trader nor Scottish man. You are French, and a soldier."

"Why do you say that?"

"Because my eyes and ears are open. Why are you here, French soldier? This is far south for one such as you to come, and no trader moves on without trying to do business. Yours is a poor disguise.

"Tell me the news. We may have traveled the warpath with the British last summer, but their war-bands had strong arms and legs but a weak head. We watched them die, and then we went home to wipe away the tears of those families who had to mourn their own dead. So we mean one Frenchman no harm, even for sport."

The man who called himself George—or Georges—took a few moments to consider, then spoke. "I was a soldier at the place you call Ticonderoga, in the fort we named Carillon."

"War-bands of our people were there. Go on."

"Some days past there was a strange cloud, like a shining fog. It passed over the fort and down into the valley, and soon after . . . things began to happen."

"What sorts of things?"

"We began to hear music. The bagpipe mostly: that strange instrument the Scotsmen—"

"The *real* Scotsmen," Brant said, and the Mohawks laughed, as the white man reddened slightly.

"The one the Scotsmen play as they march," Georges continued as the laughter subsided. "Even though there were no enemy soldiers in the valley we could hear the bagpipes play. And then we began to see them: spectres or shades, rising from the mist; ghosts of those Scotsmen who had charged the *abatis* last summer. Even in daylight we could make them out. Some of them had huge gaping wounds from bayonets or musket balls—some had no heads, some had heads but no faces . . ."

His voice trailed off, and the horror was obvious in his face.

"I thought the white men did not believe in *ghosts*," the *Tekarihoga* said. "Does your Christian book not say that everyone goes either to the Plentiful Country, or into some pot of boiling fire to be cooked forever for the pleasure of the Great God? There is no place for ghosts."

"I know what I saw, honored one," the white man said. "They are still there. You can look for yourself."

The *Tekarihoga* nodded. "We will, we will. So you ran away from the ghosts?"

". . . Yes. We all did."

"What do you mean, you all did? Are there no more servants of the *Onontio* at Ticonderoga then?"

"No. It is abandoned. No one can stand the sights or the sounds—the bagpipes, and the ghosts of the Scotsmen repeating one word, over and over."

"And that one word?"

"*Abercromby.*"

A party of Mohawk warriors—the sachem Karaghiagdatie and two young warriors, Tiyanoga and Joseph—traveled by canoe and by foot for three days to reach the French fort. It would have taken a white man far longer, but they did not know the woods and roads like the natives. As they moved toward the sunrise, there was a feeling of dread on the ground and in the air that made them shiver. Of the three, Joseph was the most sensitive: he was a born tracker, who as much *felt* as *saw* the signs on the trail, and the closer they came to the French fort the more it affected him.

When they reached the lake, they could see no smoke rising from the chimneys of the fort. It seemed that the French trader who had come to Canajoharie was not the only one who had abandoned Carillon . . .

And when they pulled their canoes onto the shore, they could see the ghosts by the hundreds milling around the base of the hill.

Chapter 4

The keepers of the house shall tremble

Aboard HMS *Namur*
In the Atlantic Ocean

If he had been able to sleep that night, Admiral Edward Boscawen might not have survived the experience. Of such things is history made; the whim of chance, the roll of dice on the backgammon-board, the choice of this path rather than another.

But sleep had not come that night and he instead found himself on the quarterdeck of HMS *Namur*, bound for the roadstead of Toulon, where he would command the squadron charged with bottling up De la Clue's fleet and preventing its escape from the Mediterranean into the Atlantic. It was a post with distinction, but not without its perils; after all, not two years since, a colleague—Byng—had been hanged on his own deck for being less than ardent in his pursuit of the enemy.

Boscawen accepted the assignment without comment or complaint. Hawke would have made his displeasure known—but Boscawen was not Hawke. Brilliant as he was, the man had a pernicious skill in raising his fellows (and his superiors) to anger.

The province of the quarterdeck is customarily sacrosanct, a private refuge for the master of a vessel. A captain, or an admiral, would hardly expect to be disturbed in his contemplations save in the case of some weighty matter that could not be handled by subordinates. But Admiral Edward Boscawen was unusual among his peers, and his crew knew it; thus, when he heard the polite clearing of a throat, he was not surprised or upset. He turned from his contemplation of the ocean to see Francis Perry standing at the top of the stair. The boatswain immediately saluted.

"What is it?"

"I beg your Lordship's pardon," Perry said, tugging on the brim of his cap. "I would not disturb you, sir, but . . . "

"No matter. Come over here, boy, the deck isn't on fire."

Perry stepped tentatively onto the quarterdeck and crossed to stand before his admiral. He had the look of someone who indeed expected the quarterdeck to burst into flames if he stepped on it.

"All right then. I assume you've been given the dog watch for some reason, Perry, and I'll not inquire. What demands my attention?"

"You told me to keep you personally informed of all that happens belowdecks, My Lord. I wanted to let you know that the men are about ready to keelhaul young O'Brien."

"What's he done now?" O'Brien was a young lad, younger than Perry, who had been impressed at Dublin a year ago. Boscawen recalled what he knew of the boy. He was not given to thievery and had not taken up his race's propensity for drunkenness—indeed, he had served well in attending to the officers' mess and seemed to be learning his skills as an able seaman.

"It's the dreams, My Lord. He cries out in his sleep and disturbs the men that are on watch."

"I should make them work harder so that they sleep more soundly. Go on."

"It's not just the noise, beggin' your Lordship's pardon. It's what he says."

"And what does he say?"

"He talks about . . . " Perry looked away from Boscawen, and cast his gaze toward the southwestern horizon, beyond the bow of *Namur*, where the apparition of the comet was clearly visible. It had become brighter in recent days, even more than had been predicted. "He talks about the comet."

"And what of it? It's a natural phenomenon. It is nothing unusual, merely the passage of an object through the heavens. Nothing to be afraid of."

"That's not what he says, sir. He says that it will strike and change the world."

"Nonsense. It is a once-in-a-lifetime event; every seventy-odd years it returns, passes through the sky once as it heads for the sun, and once as it heads away—and then it is gone, not to be seen until our grandchildren's time."

"I know that, Admiral, and you do too—but O'Brien says otherwise."

"Perhaps a few lashes will change his mind."

"Sailing master has already given him a taste of the cat, beggin' your Lordship's pardon. It didn't change his tune a whit, sir."

"How long has this been going on?"

"Since we left Portsmouth, My Lord. Whenever *it* was visible in the sky. A few nights there were clouds, but otherwise . . . " Perry let the sentence trail off, like the strands that extended from the tail of the comet.

"Where is the man now?"

"Ranford and Leacock are keepin' him company aft, My Lord."

Ranford was an able seaman from Cornwall; he'd sailed with Boscawen for a dozen years. Leacock was a Scotsman with a foul temper, but one of the most agile riggers aboard *Namur*. Both good men, for what they were.

"Have O'Brien present himself to my cabin at once. We'll not make a spectacle of this—but it's not to go any further. Understood?"

"Loud and clear, sir. And—My Lord—"

"What is it, Perry?"

"There can't be . . . I mean, there's no chance that there is any possible way . . . "

"No," Boscawen said. "It's the fever-dream of a homesick Irish lad. This is the last you'll hear of it."

While he waited for the lad to be brought to him, Boscawen drew a thin volume from his writing desk and opened it. It was a copy of *A Synopsis of the Astronomy of Comets*, Halley's 1705 work, a gift from Frances at his departure from England. The book was even more remarkable because it was a first edition, including the strange afterword that had been absent in later printings.

Make of it what you will, his wife had told him. *It might be a load of rubbish, dear, but . . . one hears things.*

Halley had already become the secretary of the Royal Society by the time the work was published; he was rational and logical—the narrative, tables and diagrams were remarkably clear and well thought out. But the last four pages diverged from that rationality and logic.

In ye passage of 1682/3, Halley wrote, *the sublimation of ætheric patterns insinuated itself into the minds and hearts of those subject to such effects. It might be, or might have been, that the eye of the Eternal God was turned away, allowing those things that He might not sanction to enter into the mortal realm . . .*

Load of rubbish, Boscawen thought. His wife was most insightful in that way—indeed, in all ways.

Boscawen's reverie about Frances was interrupted by a rapping at the door of his cabin. The young Irish cabin boy stood outside, his cap in his hand; he managed some sort of salute and stepped into the admiral's inner sanctum, looking around him as if it was a sort of place he'd never seen.

"Close the hatch, if you please. O'Brien, isn't it?"

"Yes, sir. My Lord," he added hastily.

"Very good then, O'Brien. Tell me what it is that is causing such ire belowdecks."

Boscawen was using his best admiral's voice; he kept his face stern, looking straight at the lad. That usually made seamen and even junior officers glance down, or at least away—but O'Brien met him gaze for gaze.

"The comet, an' it please your Lordship," O'Brien said. "The comet is coming."

"Anyone can see that—"

"Nay, my Lord," O'Brien interrupted. "'Tis *coming.* 'Tis almost here. And when it arrives the world changes; the old powers will rise."

The fact that an unrated seaman interrupted an admiral was singular enough—but the intensity of the boy's expression made it a striking moment, one that Boscawen would remember much later.

"Where are you from, O'Brien?"

"Ireland, Admiral, sir. Connemarra."

"And where you come from, O'Brien, do they believe in the true and living Creator?"

"Aye, sir," he said, crossing himself in the Roman way. He smiled for just a moment, then returned to his former serious intensity. "Of course."

"And in Connemarra do they teach the Bible?"

"Aye, sir."

"I do not recall any discussion of the rising of 'old powers' in Scripture, lad. The coming of the Saviour swept all of those 'old powers' away, did it not? And the comet—it is no more than an apparition, a body moving through the heavens. What effect could it possibly have?"

"It will change the world, my Lord."

"That is no answer. I think you have not accustomed yourself to life at sea, young O'Brien, and you have an ague or a fever."

"I beg to disagree with your Lordship," O'Brien said. "I am hale and quite settled. I am learning the skills of an able seaman."

"And yet you speak nonsense. How . . . how do you know of these 'old powers'? Your foolish nightmares?"

"My mum was a water-finder, My Lord. She is a wise-woman. So is my Gran. 'Tis a family gift, since the comet's last coming."

Sublimation of ætheric patterns, Boscawen thought, *Rubbish.*

"I cannot affect your thoughts, young O'Brien," Boscawen said. "It is not in my power. But your actions are subject to my orders. Your comments on this matter are disrupting the sleep—and work—of the other crew, and it is my order that they cease. Do you understand?"

"I cannae control my dreams, my Lord."

"Then you shall sleep on deck, away from others. As long as the comet is in the sky, until it passes—as it ultimately will—you shall make your bed in the lee of the pilothouse."

"Under the open sky."

"That's right. Then you can bay at the moon and pray to the comet if you like."

"Thank you, sir. I should like that very much."

Boscawen raised an eyebrow. "We will see if your tune changes the first time we have heavy weather. But you will be sure to secure your hammock well so that the storm does not toss you overboard."

"I will see to it, sir." He saluted again, a sloppy job, but at least it showed effort. "Thank you, sir," he repeated.

"See to it at once," Boscawen said. "Dismissed."

And that, as far as Admiral Boscawen thought, would put an end to the disturbance.

✣ ✣ ✣

There was heavy weather almost at once. A few days later *Namur* was sailing close-hauled; the wind was coming from the northeast, pushing them further out to sea. The Spanish coast was not in sight. Indeed, very little was in sight—except the comet, further up in the sky than it had been, and brighter, its light pushing eerily through the storm-clouds.

O'Brien did not seem the least discomfited by sleeping on the deck, under the overhanging shelter aft of the pilothouse. No complaints reached the admiral's ears; but while he was making his rounds of the deck, bundled in his greatcoat, he paused to speak to the lieutenant of the watch.

"Pascal, isn't it?"

"Aye, my Lord." Lieutenant Pascal touched his cap, looking away from his black servant—or slave, he wasn't sure which—who was coiling rope beside him.

"Have you heard anything regarding the Irish boy sleeping on deck?"

"O'Brien, sir?"

"Yes. That's the one." Boscawen tilted his head more upright; since an injury in battle some years before, he had a tendency to hold it sideways. "Has there been any complaint from the watch?"

"Complaint? I don't know of any, my Lord. He talks in his sleep, but no one pays him any mind." He glanced—just for a moment—at his boy, then returned his attention to the admiral.

It might have been to check on the work, but Boscawen sensed that it might be more than that. "Boy," he said to the servant. "Does he speak English?"

"Quite well, sir. Gustavus, give your attention to the admiral."

The black let go the rope and stood upright. He was young— probably no older than the Irish lad—but unlike many of his race, he held his head respectfully but not especially subserviently. Some in the Service might have thought that an insult, particularly if he was a slave; but Boscawen was neither affronted nor particularly interested in others' reactions.

"*Gustavus* is your name?"

"Yes, it please your Lordship, that is the name I have been given."

"I thought it an unlikely name for a black."

"I am named for a great king, so 'tis said, sir. I take it with pride."

"What is your actual name, may I ask?"

"My mother named me Oladuah, My Lord, which means 'well spoken' in my native tongue. I have been called Michael, and also Jacob. But I answer to Gustavus just fine."

"What do you know about O'Brien?"

"O'Brien, sir?"

"Now answer the admiral, Gustavus," Lieutenant Pascal said. "You know what he wants to know."

Gustavus—Oladuah—looked from his master to the admiral, and then said, "He is a seer of the future, my Lord. He has seen the coming of the fiery star."

"You mean the comet."

"Yes, my Lord."

"He told me that the comet is going to change the world. Do you believe him then?"

"Of course, my Lord. It is the signal of the end of days. The return of the Saviour, as is taught in the Scriptures."

"That's not exactly what O'Brien told me," Boscawen said. "Is this some belief among your tribe?"

"I do not hold to the beliefs of my own people any longer, my Lord," Gustavus said. "I have been blessed and baptized as a servant of Jesus and follow Him. Surely the signs of His return are evident in the heavens?"

"The comet has come and gone many times, Gustavus. This time is no different."

"I . . . fear to dispute with you, sir," Gustavus answered. "You asked what I thought—and I am honored to be asked; but I risk your anger by giving you an answer you do not want."

"You are well-spoken for a . . ."

"A slave, my Lord," Lieutenant Pascal said. "I bought him in Virginia Colony. And he is very bright; not just for one of his kind, but even when compared to many whites."

"Truly," Boscawen said. "Gustavus, how do you disagree with me?"

"I do not wish to anger your Lordship."

"You do not. Answer my question."

"You say . . . you say that the fiery star has come and gone, and this time is no different. But truly, *each* time is different—last time and this time. There is a legend among my people that divine spirits came out of the fiery star and began to walk among them, and that when the star came again, they would be reunited with the God-above-all. When I received the Gospel, I heard those words repeated in a different form. Now I know it to be true."

Gustavus raised his eyes toward the sky, where the comet seemed brighter and closer than ever.

Boscawen followed his gaze, and then looked down and across the main deck of the ship. The sky had grown dark and the wind had picked up; many others had stopped their work and were looking toward the heavens.

"It comes," said a voice, somewhere aft, in an Irish accent.

Father Frederick, the ship's chaplain, stood near the foremast; he caught Boscawen's eye. He looked frightened.

"Pascal . . . " Boscawen began, then turned on his heel and walked rapidly, with as much dignity as he could manage, to *Namur*'s pilothouse. Above him, the sails began to flutter as the ship drifted into the wind. Pascal and his slave followed behind.

Inside the little cabin, the officer of the watch was trying to maneuver the ship's whip-staff with the change in the wind. Boscawen gestured the young man aside and took control of it himself.

The wind had begun to blow hard, and the sky was filling with an eerie yellow light despite the dark clouds. Boscawen had been on the sea for most of his adult life and had crossed the Atlantic a number of times—a perilous undertaking even in good weather—but this defied description. The swells had grown deep, and *Namur* was gradually giving way, being blown this way and that; even under his steady hand, the ship was beginning to become unmanageable.

Pascal and Gustavus appeared at the pilothouse doorway.

"Hail the crow's nest," Boscawen said, not looking away. "Tell me what he sees."

There was some shouting between the lieutenant and the lookout. Pascal put his head inside the doorway.

"It's like nothing he's ever seen, My Lord. The sea—the sea—"

"Out with it, man."

"It's parting, sir."

"*Parting?*"

"Yes, My Lord. Like the Red Sea. Almost directly due north and south."

"That's impossible. It must be three hundred fathoms deep."

"As you say, sir. But it's happening. It's almost as if the rays of the comet are—are dredging up the ocean."

"And dropping us into it?"

"It seems so."

Boscawen could hear Father Frederick shouting over the din. He was quoting Ecclesiastes. *In the days when the keepers of the house shall tremble . . .*

"Parting," Boscawen repeated.

Pascal was white-faced, but to his credit he stayed at his post. Gustavus stood beside him, unmoving.

Boscawen tilted the whip-staff as far to port as he could manage, turning the ship to starboard. As it slowly came about, the scene came into view: an unbelievable sight—the ocean parting, one half cresting to the east and another to the west, revealing dark indigo depths below. It was as if *Namur* was somehow climbing a great wave, higher and higher, the sea carrying it up into the air, and the motive force causing the waves to part was a cascade of yellowish light, looking very much like the tail of a comet.

It was impossible, but it was happening—and it was carrying *Namur* further out to sea.

"The wave—" Boscawen gestured. "That wave would have hurled us against a lee shore. If we manage to survive this, we'll have to beat our way back toward land. And when it hits—"

Pascal opened his mouth to answer, then closed it again. He could not seem to find words to describe it.

It was difficult to tell when day ended and night began, and it was impossible to imagine how *Namur* remained upright. In the face of impossibility, the crew responded to the commands of the officers, shortening sail and keeping the lines from fouling. The swells broke the jib and the winds shredded the sails on the foremast, but somehow *Namur* remained seaworthy.

And sometime during the ferocious afternoon someone made Father Frederick stop praying aloud—and at some point, the young Irish cabin boy, along with two other crewmen, disappeared from the deck, lost in *Namur*'s struggle to keep from being swallowed by the impossible sea.

Finally, *Namur* was becalmed, the waves settling and the clouds parting above, revealing the tiniest sliver of a moon. An exhausted Edward Boscawen, who had never left the pilot's cabin nor given up the whip-staff to another, gathered his officers in the wardroom after issuing a double ration of rum to everyone aboard.

When everyone was settled and the appropriate salutes had been offered, he spoke. "Gentlemen," he said. "I invite your comment."

No one answered for several moments, exchanging glances. At last Commander William Marshal, *Namur*'s second-in-command, cleared his throat. "Admiral, this is uncharted water for all of us."

"It is a very unusual situation, to be sure."

"No, My Lord, more than that. I have received the report from topmast lookouts—and it truly *is* uncharted water. Land has been sighted eastward—it is very sharply defined, like a range of mountains."

"Where do you think we are?"

"In the North Atlantic, sir, but somewhere in the tropics. The star sightings put us between 13 and 15 degrees north latitude." As Boscawen began to respond, Marshal continued, "Begging the Admiral's pardon, sir, I know that seems ridiculous—we had not even passed Cape Finisterre last night, but the stars are—the stars."

"We rode an impossible storm, Commander. 15 degrees north would put us . . . near the Cape Verdian Islands, I suppose."

"It doesn't account for the mountains, My Lord," Lieutenant Pascal said. "We looked at the charts, and while there are peaks on the islands, they don't correspond to the sightings."

"We'll see what the lookouts report in the morning."

"The sightings were made before night fell, Admiral," Marshal said. "The man knew what he saw."

Boscawen gave his executive officer a stern look. "What do you recommend, then, Commander?"

"At the very least, My Lord, we should investigate."

"Without charts and soundings? If this truly is unknown water, I don't think I relish the idea of running aground."

"It will be a good exercise for the crew, sir. Something to take their mind off—the comet."

Boscawen considered this, then nodded. "Very well. We are in open ocean, with no convenient anchor; we will come about and begin to tack northward with shortened sail. In the morning we will . . . carefully . . . investigate this coast. In the meanwhile, I suggest we all get whatever rest we can."

Chapter 5

This is the end of the world

Aboard HMS Namur

The coast was more visible in the morning, with the seas calm and the wind scarcely blowing—the best sort of weather for a survey. It became gradually clearer that this land was not the Cape Verde Islands, but was some land hitherto unknown. What at first was taken for snowcaps turned out to be the pale color of the land itself. It was stark, almost like the Dover chalk-cliffs, bare of vegetation.

Boscawen summoned the slave Gustavus to his quarterdeck. Once again, he was impressed with the young black man's poise and lack of fear. Unlike Perry, the boatswain, he seemed to have no inhibition to tread upon the private area of the ship's commander.

"Gustavus," Boscawen said. "Do you recognize this coast?"

Gustavus looked out at the pale mountains; Boscawen took his spyglass and handed it to Gustavus, who took it and placed it to his eye. After a moment he lowered it, his face showing alarm.

"What is it? Do you know this place?"

"It . . . O'Brien spoke of this, My Lord."

"O'Brien? The Irish lad with the dreams?"

"The seer, My Lord. Yes. He called this the Place of Bone."

"That's rather ominous." Boscawen reclaimed his spyglass and surveyed the land—which did seem to have the pallor of a bleached skeleton. "He dreamed of this, I suppose."

"It was in his visions, sir."

"You seem to be making very careful distinctions, Gustavus. You *are* well-spoken. Take care that your tongue does not become too clever."

"I apologize if I have given offense, my Lord."

"No." Boscawen snapped the spyglass shut and secured it at his belt. "Tell me what the unfortunate lad said of this 'Place of Bone.'"

"He said . . . that it would rise out of the sea at the time of the fiery star, and that it would form a boundary between this world and the next."

"A boundary?"

"That is what he said, my Lord."

"That is very interesting. I think that we should have a closer look at this 'Place of Bone,' don't you think?"

Gustavus' face registered surprise, and even fear. "Oh, no, my Lord, no! We should not go to that place, no, never!"

"Even if I order it?"

"I . . . would take many lashes for defying you, my Lord, but no, at the peril of my soul, no!"

"What makes you so fearful?"

"I . . . do not know."

"You know very well indeed." Boscawen grabbed Gustavus' shoulder and turned the young man to face him. "What is it, boy? What do you fear? Ghosties and ghouls?"

Again, the slave surprised the admiral by looking directly at him, seemingly without fear.

"Will you punish me if I say yes, my Lord?"

Boscawen took out his spyglass and scanned the horizon, looking from north to south. As far as he could make out, the bone-pale mountains lay ahead—where no mountains should rightfully be.

If he was going to return *Namur* to home waters, he would have to find a way around them. If there was, inexplicably, no way, then he would never see England, or Frances, or his children again.

"No, Gustavus," he said at last. "I will not punish you for being afraid. For I am afraid as well." He lowered the spyglass to his side and looked at the young black man. "But if you will come with me, I shall be less afraid."

The sailing-master cast the log and determined that they were in shallow enough water to counsel against coming closer to the shore;

accordingly, Boscawen caused his barge—somewhat battered by the storm, but still intact—to be lowered. He chose Lieutenant Pascal and six able seamen, as well as Gustavus, to accompany him, leaving Marshal in command of *Namur*. All, other than Gustavus, were armed with cutlass and pistol.

They rowed slowly into the shallows. From a distance, Boscawen made out a figure on the beach, sitting atop a large bone-pale rock; it was a young man, sitting with his knees drawn up in front of him.

Through the spyglass, the admiral recognized the figure as the Irish lad, O'Brien, who had gone over in the storm.

Another impossibility, he thought. As the barge came aground, Gustavus—and some of the landing party—recognized O'Brien as well. He looked drawn and tired, but his eyes seemed to give off an unearthly glow.

None of the others seemed the least interested in setting foot on the shore. Boscawen waited for a moment, then stepped into the shallow water, taking a few steps on to the shore. At his gesture, Gustavus joined him, remaining slightly behind and to his left.

O'Brien straightened out his legs and dropped on to the sand. He was wearing what remained of his cabin-boy's uniform, lacking a cap or shoes; the jersey and trews looked as if they had been dragged through the ocean. He did not seem to notice.

"Stop," he said, holding out his right hand, just as Boscawen stepped onto the land. The word seemed to echo up and down the beach.

"I beg your pardon?" Boscawen said. "We—"

"This is not your place, Admiral," O'Brien said. "This is our place now. You have no business here."

"Explain yourself."

"You were kind to me," the young man answered, his voice returning to something like its normal timbre. "I remember that. In courtesy to you, I will offer what explanation you can understand.

"The world has changed, Admiral Edward Boscawen. The comet has changed it in a great way, just as it once changed it in a small way. Things are beginning to awaken. This is the end of the world. It belongs to us now, and you will be best served by going the way you came—and not returning."

"What is this place? What are these mountains?"

"This is the Place of Bone, Admiral. This is the end of the world. There is no land beyond." He gestured behind him, at the pale-colored ridge, and when he turned back to face Boscawen, his eyes were glowing crimson. All around them, in crevasses and shadows formed by the piled-up rocks by the shore, Boscawen, Gustavus and the landing party could see other pairs of crimson eyes looking out at them—first a few, then a dozen, then hundreds.

"I tell you this in return for your kindness," O'Brien said. "But if you do not go now, there will be no way to stop those who wish you ill."

"What of you? We feared you were dead."

"I am not dead," O'Brien said, and the fearful tone had returned to his voice. "I am born anew. Now go, Admiral. And do not return."

Boscawen thought of what he might say; he exchanged a glance with Gustavus, who might have been terrified, but remained close by. Then, with the dignity born of gentle birth, and courage beyond what he knew he possessed, Admiral Edward Boscawen turned and walked away into the shallow water, leaving O'Brien and the Place of Bone behind.

Chapter 6

An enjoyable way to start the day

Fort Johnson, Colony of New York

As she now often did after realizing she was pregnant, Molly Brant rose earlier than usual and spent some time just wandering through her new home. You could hardly call it a "house," in the way white people normally used the term. The edifice her Anglo-Irish husband Sir William Johnson had built a decade earlier in the town of Amsterdam was called "Fort Johnson"—and for good reason. The large two-story stone building served Johnson as a combination home, trading center and office for his various affairs, and was surrounded by wooden fortifications.

Fort Johnson had soon become the center for British relations with the Six Nations, especially the Mohawks. During the Crown Point expedition in the summer of 1755, Johnson and his Mohawk allies defeated the French at the battle of Lake George, during the course of which he received a wound from which he had never fully recovered, since the musket ball which lodged in his hip couldn't be safely removed. The injury stood him in good stead, however, since it added a certain luster to his martial reputation—which had hitherto been nonexistent. Although the battle at Lake George had not been a decisive victory, the war had been going badly that year for the British and they needed a hero.

Enter, William Johnson. King George II made him a baronet and Parliament voted to give him £5,000 as a reward for his services. Much more importantly in terms of the future, in January of 1756 the British government made Johnson the Superintendent of Indian Affairs for the northern colonies. This position was a military one, allowing him to report directly to the government in London—which meant he would not be subject to the rulings and restrictions imposed by provincial governments, which so often hamstrung the activities of officials assigned to deal with the native inhabitants.

Between the new post and his longstanding existing relations with the Six Nations, Johnson rapidly became one of the most powerful political figures in the colony of New York. And that position also led to his marriage to Molly Brant.

Johnson had been in a longstanding common-law marriage with a German immigrant by the name of Catherine Weisenberg, with whom he had three children. She had died recently and given his changed position in life; he'd sought a new wife among the Mohawks.

His interest and attention had soon settled on Molly, since he'd been friends with her stepfather Brant Kanagaradunkwa, a Mohawk sachem belonging to the Turtle clan, for years. She was quite a bit younger than he was—in her early twenties compared to his mid-forties—but neither of them saw that as an obstacle. Both the English aristocracy and the Iroquois approached marriage as a practical matter, not a romantic one.

Her Indian names were Konwatsi'tsiaienni, her birth name, and the name Degonwadonti, given to her as an adult. But as was true of many Mohawks by the middle of the eighteenth century, she was a Christian and usually went by the name of Molly Brant. The surname came from her stepfather.

Between her Christian faith, the literacy she'd acquired from the schooling her stepfather had provided for her at a British-run school—her penmanship was excellent—and her position as the stepchild of a sachem, Molly made a suitable match for the ambitious Johnson. And the match was quite acceptable to Molly because the young woman was ambitious herself. She understood full well that her position as the wife of Sir William Johnson, Superintendent of Indian Affairs, would give her far more influence than anything she could achieve on her own in Mohawk society.

Johnson was an influential figure among the Iroquois as well as the British, especially the Mohawks. He spoke their language and they had adopted him into the tribe and given him the name of Warraghiyagey.

Soon after settling in with her new husband in Fort Johnson, Molly became pregnant with her first child. And found herself wandering through her new home early in the morning, both to admire the structure as well as to consider her now-greatly-expanded prospects in life. All in all, she found it a most enjoyable way to start the day.

Perhaps a bit less enjoyable than usual, this particular day, because both her husband and her younger brother Joseph were absent. Johnson had left some days earlier to visit the Onondaga. Her brother and their stepfather had gone to Canajoharie, also known as the "Upper Castle," one of the two major towns of the Mohawks.

She missed her brother more than her husband, if the truth be told. Molly's relationship with Johnson was friendly enough, to be sure. But she felt little of the personal attachment to the older man that she felt for her teenage sibling. She and Joseph had always been close; closer than most brothers and sisters.

She worried about him now more than she had in times past. Joseph had not reached his full manhood yet, but even at the age of sixteen he was more physically powerful and adept than most adult men. Molly thought that made him reckless, at times; not so much because he overestimated his own prowess and skills but because he underestimated those of his opponents, be those adversaries human or animal or—perhaps most dangerous of all—inanimate forces. Be a man or boy ever so strong, he was hopelessly outmatched if he fell into a swiftly moving river headed toward rapids or a waterfall. Or slipped on a wet rock at the edge of a precipice. Or—

She broke off that train of thought. There was no point to it. Joseph would do whatever he would do, and although he heard her advice that didn't necessarily mean he listened to it. Or the advice of his stepfather or anyone else, for that matter.

She left the big house and entered the compound formed by the palisades which surrounded and protected that building. That building—and several others. Johnson had a sawmill and a blacksmith shop within the walls also, and the quarters for the slaves were in a detached building against the eastern wall of the stockade.

Johnson owned four slaves at the moment: a middle-aged man, along with two younger women, one of whom had a three-year-old son. The two women worked in the house, one as the residence's cook and the other as an all-purpose maid who helped Molly maintain the place. Cumberland, the man, operated the sawmill and was a skilled blacksmith, although the compound's smithy was fairly primitive. He regularly badgered Johnson to invest more in it so Cumberland could use his skills to their full extent.

He could get away with that unseemly pestering where most slaves wouldn't dare because Cumberland had been with Johnson for many years. The two women, Hany and Ruth—Ruth was the cook, and the mother of the child—for only five years or so. Johnson had bought them at the same time. They were cousins, as slaves reckoned these things.

Molly was fairly certain that Cumberland was the father of Ruth's boy, but she'd never inquired. Whatever the relationship might be between Cumberland and Ruth, there didn't seem to be any trouble associated with it, so Molly figured the details were none of her concern.

As Johnson's wife, Molly also held the title of his "housekeeper," which meant that she was in overall charge of the household and served as its hostess for all public occasions. She also supervised the slaves and the servants; though, of course, not Fort Johnson's resident lawyer, doctor, and her husband's personal secretaries. Those were under Johnson's own management.

Partly because of her innate temperament and partly because she thought it was stupid to do otherwise, she tried as much as possible to rule the household—slaves and servants both—with a light hand. And she'd never seen where being friendly and courteous to subordinates did anyone any harm on either side.

It took her no more than twenty minutes to complete her circuit of the compound. Very few of the servants and none of the slaves were up yet, so Molly was engaged in fewer conversations than she would be later in the day, and the ones she did have were mostly brief. Not much more than simple greetings and well wishes, except for the one she had with Hosea Dowling, who served as Fort Johnson's chief teamster and hostler. That conversation ran on for several minutes, not because Dowling had anything of any significance to report or discuss but simply because he was a garrulous man by nature.

Molly didn't mind, and listened patiently to Hosea's largely aimless musings on the new day and its likely developments. Why not? She could spare the man a few minutes of her time; it wasn't as if she had any pressing concerns of her own that day.

Eventually Dowling finished. She returned to the house a bit reluctantly, because her footsteps sounded hollow to her—which was a bit silly. Between the comfortable moccasins she was wearing and the fact that she was light-footed anyway, she was barely making any sound at all, even on the stone floor which covered the first level of the house.

The "hollowness" was a product of emotion, not hearing. She missed her brother; and, albeit to a lesser degree, her husband. The worst of it was that the nature of their journeys made it very uncertain when either of them would return.

So be it. She'd always had an independent spirit, since she was a little girl—and she reminded herself that her new position in life gave her plenty of responsibilities to keep her busy.

Part II: Awakening

April, 1759

The change came not like a wave but like a creeping fog: it took time for men of all kinds to realize what had happened, and why their world would never be the same.

—John Quincy Adams,
The Time of the Change: A Chronicle, 1814

Chapter 7

You are the man you have always been

The Maritimes

The days had been long. The nights were longer, it seemed; they sailed close-hauled, avoiding ice floes bigger than *Neptune* itself—it was as if some great sheet of ice had separated itself and crumbled into giant pieces, and was now floating southward like a fleet of ships looking for an enemy to engage. Collision with the smallest of them might tear the ship apart.

To Saunders' surprise, the young General Wolfe spent a considerable amount of time on deck, showing little sign of the terrible seasickness that had plagued him before the awful fog had passed over *Neptune*. Wolfe was reserved and aloof most of the time but had spoken forthrightly about his vision on the night of the fog— he had seen his brother Edward, with whom he had served in Flanders during the Pragmatic War a decade and a half earlier.

"I saw my old mentor Admiral Wager," Saunders had told him, in a moment of disarming honesty that Wolfe seemed to appreciate. "And Mr. Prince told me afterward that he had seen his father, Prince Frederick."

"Yet none of that can be," Wolfe had replied. "Ned died in 1742, and His Highness in 1751—"

"And Sir Charles Wager in 1743. No, sir, you are correct—these are impossible visions. But they are hard to dismiss. Each of us saw someone who was dear to us. And it was not only the officers. I have heard many accounts of visions by other officers and crewmembers—it's a wonder that we were able to hold the course and keep the ship in order."

"Words fail me, Admiral. I do not know what to say . . . but it is reassuring to think that it was not only me. I scarcely feel myself to be the same man."

"Are you the man who led the assault on Louisbourg last year?"

"Yes. Yes, of course."

"Then you are the man that you have always been, General Wolfe. I daresay that is enough for the king . . . and his great-nephew."

There were numerous things that troubled Saunders during their navigation through the ice-strewn waters. His charts were scarcely adequate, though the skills he had learned through the years served him well. But accounts of North Atlantic currents and winds were useless, either due to their position or—he scarcely wished to admit it—because something had fundamentally *changed* while they were making the crossing.

Just as surely as the comet was no longer in the sky, it was clear that the distant land had changed. Saunders and Prince made a series of careful observations on clear days with calm seas and mapped a range of jagged mountains to the north and northeast, almost at the limit of their vision. Prince climbed the topmast to confirm what they saw from the quarterdeck—a scene which was probably not foreseen at the Court of St. James when he was added to the expedition; but he came safely down at least. They marked the mountain range to lie well west and south of Iceland—where no such terrain was known to be.

At last, with provisions beginning to run low, they sighted land to westward; the northern extremity of Newfoundland, which seemed just as rocky and inhospitable as he remembered it. That placed them at 51 or 52 degrees north latitude, at least four hundred miles north of their intended destination . . . and of the other ships in the squadron there was no sign.

The ice persisted as they traveled southward, enough so that they were unable to reach Louisbourg harbor until two weeks later. It was still iced in, as it had been the previous year. This was not lost on Wolfe, who had hoped to be a part of an expedition against the great

French fortress of Québec, had the season not already been too far advanced to make it practical.

1759 was not 1758, however; and regardless of the weather, Louisbourg was now in His Majesty's hands, and the gateway to the St. Lawrence was open.

It took another two days to reach Halifax on the southern coast of Nova Scotia. Both Saunders and Wolfe hoped to find other ships waiting for them that had somehow survived whatever event had occurred out on the ocean. Instead there was only one, which they identified at a distance as the 70-gun *Somerset*, a part of another squadron sent to meet them in the Maritimes.

"Do you know this officer, sir?" Prince said to Saunders, as they watched the boat row across from *Somerset* to *Neptune*. The commander of *Somerset* was clearly visible; he was a stout, stern-faced man, who sat in the middle of the boat, holding his hat to his head against the stiff wind—the only seeming concession to the chill inclemency that seemed to be characteristic of the area.

"The captain of *Somerset*? Not very well," Saunders said. "I know he has been in His Majesty's service since an early age and was advanced by both Vernon and Knowles—which speaks well of him."

"Not to mention the ship he commands now."

"*Somerset* is a third-rater, but it's a fine vessel nonetheless," Saunders said. "I believe it was here at Louisbourg, so I am sure General Wolfe knows the gentleman."

The Prince did not answer. It was clear that the admiral and general had become cordial during the last few weeks aboard, but he still found Wolfe distant and haughty, even when paying his respects to a prince of the blood.

"Why is *Somerset* here in Halifax, My Lord?"

"He was attached to Admiral Knowles' squadron, which was intended to rendezvous with us at Louisbourg. That his ship is the only one here does not bode well. They were to have transported a portion of the troops intended for the Québec expedition—and if they are not here . . . "

"I don't need to observe, sir, that the rest of our ships are absent as well."

"I don't need to be reminded of that," Saunders snapped back, and immediately thought better of it. "Yes. Yes, of course. And now there is an impossible range of mountains in the ocean. I wonder if . . . they had a similar experience to ours."

"I assume you'll ask him yourself, sir."

"I expect we'll both have questions that require answers."

Hughes was piped aboard with all due ceremony. Wolfe was present to greet him, though he seemed to have no particular regard (or, for that matter, disdain) for the captain of *Somerset*. After formal greeting and review of the honor guard, Saunders led Hughes, his executive officer and General Wolfe to his own cabin.

"Is *Somerset* the only ship of Holmes' squadron on station here, Captain?" he asked when the four men were settled.

"I regret to say that it is," Hughes said. In person he was a substantial man, still relatively young—though Wolfe himself was several years his junior—Captain Hughes more than filled the sea-chair he was assigned. "We were separated in the Atlantic during the crossing. There was . . . "

Saunders saw a troubled expression on Hughes' face, but wanted to hear the man's firsthand account. "Please proceed, Captain. What happened?"

"It is almost impossible to believe, my Lord. I was in flag distance of *Devonshire*, a ship very slightly larger than my own; we were in a heavy blow, somewhere near the thirtieth degree of west longitude. I had just given the order to close haul when something began to happen."

Once again Hughes paused for several seconds, as if gathering his thoughts. "There was a cloud, rather like a bank of fog—except that it was glowing. Eerie, really: like a river mist filled with tiny lights. I lost sight of *Devonshire* in the fog—and when it cleared, I caught sight of it again—and it was as if it had been lifted in the air, a hundred feet or more."

"Out of the ocean?"

"Yes—yes, sir. And it looked as if it was caught—I don't know quite how to describe it. It was as if a shoal of rocks had come up out of the ocean, and *Devonshire* was caught on them, a hundred feet in the air, and then it fell crashing into the sea.

"A great wave, the like of which I've never seen, sir, drove us away from the spot, and it was the last I saw of *Devonshire* or any of the rest of the ships of the fleet."

"A shoal of rocks in the middle of the ocean?" Saunders said. "Are you sure, Captain? That is an extraordinary tale."

"I swear by Heaven and by my oath as an officer in His Majesty's Navy, My Lord, that it is true. I'm not sure, but I believe we were able to make out the shoal a day or so later when the weather cleared. But it wasn't just a shoal then, it was like a mountain range."

"In the ocean."

Hughes nodded.

Saunders exchanged a glance with the prince, then stood and walked to his chart-table; he picked up the annotated chart of the North Atlantic and brought it to where the portly captain was sitting.

"The mountains extend northward well above fifty-three degrees latitude, Captain. We have observed them as well. If your observations are correct, it suggests that we are—in some way— separated from Europe, perhaps permanently."

"Permanently, My Lord? How could that possibly be?"

"How could there be a mountain range in the ocean, Hughes? Which begs the question—what has happened to Knowles' squadron, and to mine?"

"And the troops intended for the assault on New France," Wolfe said. "What of them?"

Hughes did not respond, but all the men knew the answer.

"Without resources, Admiral, it will be impossible to carry out His Highness' orders here in America. Without troops, there is no possibility of investing Québec."

"Without a way home," Saunders said, "we may have to decide our own course."

He looked directly at Mr. Prince, who appeared uncomfortable with the scrutiny.

"Are you suggesting that we abandon our orders, Admiral Saunders?" Wolfe said quietly. "Because if so, you are jumping to a rather sudden and unsettling conclusion. I'm not sure I am ready to go along with that, not just yet."

"We will have to take stock of our situation, General Wolfe," Saunders replied. "It is not merely a matter of force projection. Our ships' support—stores, sails, every tot of rum and coat-button— depends on contractors based in England and supplies coming across the ocean. If that chain is cut, more than war planning is affected."

"Obviously," Wolfe said.

"I assure you, sir, it is more obvious for those on whose shoulders responsibility falls."

"Are you suggesting that I—"

"With due respect, sirs," Mr. Prince interrupted—a presumption that would never be accepted from anyone of lesser status—"I don't think anyone is suggesting anything. We have an extraordinary situation, and we must think of the welfare of our ships and our men in view of what has happened and what is happening."

Wolfe considered the words, and the man who had made them, and settled back into his chair without further comment.

Chapter 8

This might be a matter of our own survival

Halifax

If there was any doubt regarding the changed circumstances of the expedition, it was resolved two days later when HMS *Magnanime*, a 74-gun warship, reached Halifax harbor. Even to an untrained eye, it looked as if it had been through hell: its sails were patched and it had a badly-damaged foremast; Wolfe and Saunders could see that the mainmast had been restepped as well.

Magnanime was in good enough order to pipe the admiral and general aboard in proper form, but the commander waiting for them at the top of the gangplank wore a first lieutenant's uniform.

"Lieutenant George Baker, My Lord," he said, offering a perfect salute.

"I was expecting Captain Howe."

"It would have been his great honor to receive you, sir," the young lieutenant said. "But it is a stroke of fortune that any of us have come safely to harbor."

"I'm sure that your skill contributed to that effort, Lieutenant."

"It is kind of you to say so, my Lord," he answered. "If you and General Wolfe would care to review the honor guard?"

Once the formalities were accomplished, Baker accompanied Saunders and Wolfe ashore. They had established a temporary headquarters in the offices of Robert Grant, the Royal Navy's contractor at Halifax; it was certainly comfortable enough but had an air of the civilian about it. Saunders sent word to Captain Hughes and Prince Edward to join them, and shortly they were gathered around a set of charts and bound books from *Neptune*.

"When we left England, we had three squadrons and almost forty sail," Saunders said. "Now we have *Neptune*, *Somerset* and what is left of *Magnanime*. Durell has ships in this theater, though God knows whether something has happened to them. Very well, Captain Baker—give us your story."

Baker did not respond for a moment to the title—he had been given a promotion on the spot, it seemed—but regained his composure. "We were about three weeks out from Spithead, My Lord, when we encountered calm seas and a thick fog the likes of which I have never seen. Captain Howe had been signaling the flagship, but the visibility became too poor, so he ordered us to sail close-hauled, hoping we would come out of the fog."

"And did you?" Saunders asked.

Baker looked pale and did not respond for a moment. His face held an expression that suggested he was experiencing a painful memory.

"Something happened to Captain Howe," Hughes said quietly, glancing at Saunders, who nodded.

"Out with it, man! We've all been through something singular, the likes of which we can't quite understand."

"We came out of the fog and were aimed bow on to a . . . "

Saunders began to speak, but Prince Edward raised his hand slightly, and for a second time in a matter of less than a minute Sir Charles Saunders yielded to a subordinate—though in the second instance, the subordinate was of royal blood.

"Take your time, Captain," Mr. Prince said. "This is the fate of Captain Howe you are about to describe."

"Yes, Your Highness."

"Commander or 'sir' will do, Captain. Please tell us what happened to Captain Howe."

"It was a creature—something of legend. A sea-monster, a—a *kraken*, if the admiral pleases. A huge thing, as big as *Magnanime*, maybe even bigger. One moment we were in the fog, and the next . . . it was pulling men off the deck into the sea. There wasn't time to prepare a broadside, though I managed to heave the ship to and get off a few shots with the stern chasers. We lost our foremast and the rigging was fouled on the other two—I don't know how we managed it, but we drifted back into the fog and the thing lost sight of us."

"One of the men pulled off the deck was Captain Howe," Saunders said, his voice flat and emotionless. Howe was one of the most experienced and talented ship-captains in His Majesty's Navy; Saunders had argued strenuously with Lord Anson to have him included.

"Aye, sir. One of the very first. Three other officers senior to me were also lost. I didn't even realize I was senior man aboard for the better part of an hour. We drifted for two or three bells, staying in the fog bank in case the thing was still out there. I kept the men busy working on the rigging and sails, but they were terrified. I don't mind admitting, my Lord, that I was as well."

"And you finally cleared the fog, I take it. Did you see any of the other ships in your squadron?"

"No, sir. Not a one."

"I was originally to have sailed with *Magnanime*," the prince said. "Richard Howe was a good man, one of the best." He smiled faintly. "It was decided that the . . . delicacy of the situation required that I be in the officers' complement of an admiral."

"General Wolfe," Baker said. "I have the honor to have had Major Dunbar's 40th aboard *Magnanime*, and the men acquitted themselves with great skill in assisting what remained of my crew. I promised myself that if we reached shore, I would commend them particularly to your attention."

"I will include that in my dispatches," Wolfe said. "Though it isn't clear when they might ever be delivered." He glanced at Hughes, who had sat silently through the entire interview.

"What are your orders, Admiral?" Baker asked.

"For the moment, Captain, see to your men and your vessel. Whatever you need to requisition from the contractor, you may do on my account."

"Yes, sir." He stood and saluted. "Thank you, sir. I will have a written report—"

"In due course. Attend to your duties, sir."

He saluted again and took his leave.

"That is a very brave officer," Wolfe said to Saunders.

"It seems to me that all of our officers will need to be brave. We have damn few of them." He shifted in his seat; he had been sitting in proper military posture, and he saw no need to continue the practice. "If all we have is three ships and a few hundred troops, General, there is no possibility of an expedition against Québec. So let me ask you: what do you intend?"

"I'm not sure. I have been seriously considering the matter for the last few days. There is one thing that reassures me: if we are cut off from support from home, the French likely are as well. Our plans will have to be . . . less extensive, I daresay; but there is no reason that we should not undertake something."

"You still want to attack New France."

"You seem surprised, Admiral. Isn't that why we're in North America? They *are* still the enemy, are they not?"

"They are—unless mountains rising from the sea and great and terrible krakens are our enemy."

"I'm not quite sure I take your meaning, My Lord."

"I think I have some insight," Prince Edward said. "If I may."

"Please," Wolfe said.

"Consider the ancient war of the Persians against the city-states of Greece, General Wolfe. When Xerxes, King of Kings, gathered together his army of a million men and built his bridge of boats across the Bosporus to invade the Greek lands, he would certainly have fared much better if those states continued to war with each other. Instead, though they had many differences, they put their feuds aside to face the common enemy.

"If we are now in a time when krakens erupt from the sea and mountains rise to cut us off from our home, perhaps we should reconsider whether it is the best time to prosecute a war. This might be a matter of our own survival. The French might well come to the same conclusion."

"What do you suggest?"

"I would not presume to offer strategic advice, General. But if we are indeed facing . . . otherworldly forces, it might be time to take stock of the situation before planning any military campaigns. And in due course, it might be prudent to send an emissary to our French rivals to determine, under these circumstances, if they are indeed still our enemies."

Chapter 9

Convulsed with madness

The Atlantic Coast

It would have been more to Admiral Saunders' liking to sail to New York himself, with Prince Edward on his own deck; but in the absence of Admiral Knowles and most of their two squadrons, he was obliged to remain in Nova Scotia and in command of what was left.

There was no reason, however, to detain the prince there. It was unclear what his role might be, but without question he was the man with the highest social rank on this side of the ocean—he might even be able to speak with his grandfather's authority, if it came to that. Accordingly, he was seconded to Baker's vessel, and after a careful examination by *Neptune*'s ship's carpenter, he issued orders to *Magnanime* to sail to New York with General Wolfe and the 40th to rendezvous with General Amherst, who had overall command of land forces.

What lay before them, God only knew. Saunders knew that he did not.

George Baker was a very capable seaman, even lacking the charts that the prince would have thought were vital given the number of obstacles, crosscurrents, contrary winds and hidden perils that lay along the coasts between Nova Scotia and New England.

There was no problem finding something to do aboard *Magnanime*. Baker had been in His Majesty's Navy since he was twelve, and was honored to have had a chance to serve with Richard Howe; but he could not run the ship without officers, and Prince Edward had learned more in the last few weeks with Admiral Saunders than in the previous three years elsewhere. Baker took a little time to accustom himself to having a royal prince under his command—the business of addressing him as "Mr. Prince"—but Edward made a point of following his orders to the letter, as an example for the others.

The attack on the ship was frightening, but the loss of Howe—which had happened before Baker's eyes—was worse, because it was a personal loss. He presented a veneer of authority and confidence, but when *Magnanime* passed into a fog bank off Maine's southern coast Edward saw the fear in his eyes return. But there were no monsters in the fog, and none when they emerged.

Instead, there was a new peril, something else that, much later, he realized could be attributed to—blamed upon—the event that had changed the world.

"Heave to!" Baker ordered, and Mr. Prince repeated it. *Magnanime* turned toward the wind, giving way before the strong westerly, allowing the other ship to approach. It was flying a warning flag and approached only close enough for communication.

"What news?" he shouted through his speaking-trumpet. The other vessel, a small coaster, came alongside at a distance.

"There is illness in Salem," came the response. "Don't approach."

"What sort of illness? Typhoid? Cholera?"

It took some time for the other to respond. "No, nothing like that. We're . . . we're not sure."

"There must be symptoms. What ails the people of Salem?"

"You are from the home country, sir, aren't you?"

"Why does it—"

"This is Salem, Captain. We . . . there are things you do not know about Salem. About our history."

"What about your history?"

"It has come back to haunt us, Captain. Years ago we, the town, committed a heinous act. We had thought it was behind us—but it is not. It is best that no one be exposed to it."

"Is there a contagion?"

"There is no way to know. We cannot prevent you from entering our harbor—but we implore you to stay away."

Baker exchanged a glance with Prince.

"We will sail for Boston instead," Baker said. "Do they know what you have just told me?"

"There is a train band deployed on the turnpike between Boston and Salem, Captain. They know what is happening in Salem—they know very well."

They knew in Boston.

Magnanime was too deep draught to come all the way into Boston harbor; they anchored beyond Castle Island and Baker took a party ashore. After the encounter at Salem, he decided that a jolly boat was too small. It wasn't clear what he might encounter, so they hoisted the gig into the water and Baker took two ensigns and twelve men from the 40th as an escort, leaving Prince in command—with orders to keep station and repel any intruders. General Wolfe chose not to accompany him but remained in his cabin. He had not suffered much from seasickness—perhaps some effect of the change—but he saw no point in coming ashore.

Before the gig came in sight of Long Wharf, the most prominent feature of the town's harbor, two other boats came out to intercept them. The army subaltern in command of the soldiers looked at Hughes, who held his hand up.

"What's your business, sir?" someone shouted from the nearer boat.

"I didn't realize I needed permission to come ashore," Baker answered. "I am Captain George Baker, in command of His Majesty's ship *Magnanime*. We are en route to New York but intend to lay over in Boston. I'd like to pay my respects to Governor Pownall."

The man scowled. "You have quite an escort to *pay your respects*, Captain. We don't take kindly to press gangs in Boston."

"This isn't a press gang."

"It's about the right size for one," the other answered. "We had an admiral come here a dozen years ago trying to fill out his crew. We sent him on his way."

Baker tried to imagine what it would mean for a colonial town to send an admiral in the Royal Navy on his way but couldn't manage it. Impressment wasn't his intention in any case.

"I should like to visit the governor, sir. Is it your intention to keep me from doing so?"

There was an extended pause; the spokesman consulted with the other men in his boat. At last he said, "No, do as you please. But we'll be keeping a sharp eye on you, mark my words."

The ensign turned his head away from the view of the Bostonians and said, "Begging your pardon, Captain, but I think this rustic needs to be taught a lesson in manners."

"I agree," Baker said. "But this is neither the place nor the time. Take us in," he said to the coxswain, and the oarsmen pulled for the docks.

Governor Thomas Pownall placed a glass of port in front of his guest and settled into his own armchair. The governor was a stout man, clearly accustomed to his creature comforts.

"I will confess that I am not surprised by their behavior, Captain," the governor said. "This is how they are here; independent, willful, discourteous to a fault. It is as if they consider allegiance to the king an option, rather than a mandate."

"What have you done about this insolence, sir?"

"What can I do? Only so much." Pownall sighed. "Massachusetts Bay is a *chartered* colony. While the royal writ conveys some power to the governor, there is considerable authority given to the assembly—the Great and General Court, if you please. Theirs is the power of the purse."

"That does not excuse their behavior. Or their hostility to His Majesty's Navy."

"That derives from an incident that took place several years ago. Admiral Knowles sent press gangs ashore and took a number of tradesmen aboard. It led to a riot. The admiral had at last to relent.

"Years before that, the citizens of Boston took a royal governor *prisoner* out at Castle William and sent petitioners to London to request the respecting of their rights under their existing charter. If not for the overthrow of King James, I think that those messengers— and the ringleaders here in America—would have wound up swinging from ropes. Instead they were granted a new charter, that remains in force today." He sipped his port. "Now *there's* insolence for you."

"I have no desire to interfere with, or complicate, your colonial politics, sir. Let me ask a different question." Baker picked up his glass, then set it back on the tray beside his chair. "Have any ships from Europe come into port recently?"

"We have scarcely emerged from winter. Not too many vessels of any sort have come into the harbor."

"But none from Europe."

Pownall frowned, thinking. "Yours is the first in some time. I hadn't considered the matter until you just mentioned it. Still, it is just past winter, and . . . " Pownall paused, his frown deepening. "You do not ask this out of idle curiosity, Captain Baker. What is your point?"

"You may not see any vessels arriving from the mother country for some time, Governor. Perhaps never again. Something has happened—something inexplicable. I fear we are on our own; what is taking place up in Salem may be a part of it as well . . . they said that the past has come back to haunt them and denied us entry to their port."

"*Denied*? I hardly think that they could stop you."

"They implored us to stay away. There was no explanation other than that. Can you enlighten me on the subject, Governor?"

There was another long pause before Pownall said, "What makes you think that I know anything of this?"

"There is a train band on the road between Boston and Salem." Baker reached for his hat. "Governor, my sincerest thanks for your hospitality, but if you do not wish to be honest with me, I will make my report to General Amherst that something is amiss in Massachusetts-Bay and he can decide what to do with it himself."

He began to stand up, but Pownall held up a hand.

"No. Wait," Pownall said. "Very well. You seem to be well-informed. Salem . . . Captain Baker, what do you know about Salem?"

"Please enlighten me." Baker kept his hat between his hands in his lap, as if he was willing to put it on and depart at any time.

"Several decades ago there was a series of trials based on accusations of witchcraft. I know that it's hard to imagine in our modern time, but not terribly long ago the people of Massachusetts Bay Colony were obsessed with the actions of the Devil. They were convinced that despite their precautions, despite their *purity*, the Evil One walked among them.

"A number of men and women were accused of performing acts of witchcraft. There were trials, very sensational trials, and public executions. It was a horror—and there is every suggestion that the accusations were false, and the accused were innocent. Even the presiding judges expressed remorse . . . long after the fact, of course.

"A few weeks ago, reports came to me that there had been sightings: ghostly figures, spectres—if you can believe it—claiming to be the victims of those trials. They called for retribution and justice. I sent a trusted member of my council there to investigate."

"What did he say?"

"I have had no report from him," Pownall said. "Two men and one woman arrived from Salem three days ago. One of the men— the only one barely coherent—told me that the town was convulsed with madness. It is no wonder that they did not want you to approach."

"What does that mean? *Convulsed with madness*?"

"I don't know." Pownall rubbed his eyes and pinched the bridge of his nose. "I cannot venture to say. I have assigned a train band to watch the road. Coastal vessels have reported seeing fires. That's all I know."

"What do you intend to do, if anything?"

"For the moment, nothing. I intend to wait and see if this passes. Ultimately, I shall have to send the train band north to investigate. God alone knows what they may find."

"That seems to be the paragon of indecision," Wolfe said when Baker related the interview to him.

"He was frightened, General. Genuinely frightened. I can only assume that this, like everything else we have seen, is an effect of the world's change—and it's unlikely that he knows about all of that."

"An outbreak of madness in a small village—"

"A range of mountains rising from the sea. Monsters appearing out of the fog. And—spectres of long-dead men and women executed for witchcraft. Irrational things. Supernatural things.

"Tell me, General Wolfe. What are we to make of this? What are *any of us* to make of this? What will you tell General Amherst?"

"I don't know."

"Forgive me for speaking so plainly, sir. But I told Governor

Pownall that we are on our own." Baker grasped the arms of his chair. "I think I told him the exact truth."

"Captain Baker, I want to know what that means. I embarked from England with a mission, thousands of capable, veteran soldiers, and the confidence of His Highness the King. Now I have . . . a few hundred soldiers, a few ships—enough to carry them upriver to Québec, but not enough to take the city from the French. What should I do now? What would you suggest that I tell Sir Jeffrey when we reach New York?"

"General, I—"

"No. With all due respect, Captain Baker, I am eager to hear what you have to say."

"I've only been a captain for a few weeks, General Wolfe."

"And I've only been a general for a few months. Neither of us is a seasoned veteran in his current position. We are, both, in positions we never expected to be. So I ask you, Captain-for-only-a-few-weeks Baker: *what should I say to Jeffrey Amherst*?"

"Tell him . . . what I told you. What I told Thomas Pownall. *We are on our own*, General Wolfe. I don't know what is ahead of us, sir. But what is behind us—the world that is behind us—is out of reach."

Chapter 10

The world is changing

Lands of the Six Nations

A steady walk from the sachem's house at Canajoharie to the Onondaga Council Fire might be five, or even six, sunrises. But Joseph of the Wolf clan would do it in three.

"Go quickly, my son," his stepfather had told him. "The elders must know what we have seen."

He ran by day, as far as his legs would carry him, and rested so that he could walk by night. Rain and wind were no obstacle—Joseph was young and strong. The Wolf clan of the Mohawks was well known even outside of their lands, and anyone close enough to loose an arrow or throw a spear would see the markings and know that he descended from sachems and war-leaders, and was not to be harmed.

And as for the trail, the markings stood out to Joseph, day or night, as if they were etched in starlight: where to turn, or cross, or descend. It was said that he could travel from one place to another as quickly and as quietly as any Mohawk warrior, from the youngest and most nimble to the strongest and most experienced.

He would speak of what he and his father Theowaghwen-garaghkwin had seen a hand of days earlier at the great fort of the Onontio, at the place they called Carillon, and the tribes called Ticonderoga . . .

He ate sparingly and slept little; the elders of Wolf clan would have clucked and talked about how the young can live on nothing but sunshine and stiff breezes. But he did not feel weak—the urgency of the mission kept him running, alert to trail sign, hearing every forest rustle and bird call as he traveled toward the sunset, toward the Council Fire of the Haudenosaunee, the Six Nations.

And then as he was crossing a field of tall grass toward evening, three arrows thudded to the ground in front of him, missing his right moccasin by the span of two fingers. He dove to the ground, rolling onto his side and drawing his bow as he had been taught.

All of a sudden, it was disturbingly quiet. A flock of blackbirds had taken flight as soon as the arrows struck. Joseph tried to be as still as possible, listening for footfalls.

He could hear his heart pounding in his ears and willed himself to be calm.

There. Two, or perhaps three, sets of feet approaching from the direction of the sunset. They were trying to be stealthy, and it was almost good enough.

He carefully drew back his bow, aiming chest-high in the direction of the footfalls as they drew closer . . .

A figure appeared—a very tall figure, dressed richly as a chief, his hands held out in front of him, his eyes seeking the place where Joseph crouched.

"Peace, young warrior," the chief said. "You know me. You know my face."

"Skenadoa," Joseph said, still not moving. "If you are with those who shot at me, know that I demand honor be satisfied."

"It will be," Skenadoa said. "You are the son of a Mohawk sachem, who stands to defend the eastern door. I know your voice. Now show your face."

"Let the others show themselves first."

Skenadoa looked directly at where he lay hidden, his face unmoving. After a moment he nodded and shouted out a command. Joseph heard rustling from not far away: two, and then two more sets of footsteps approaching. He slowly got to his knees and then to his feet, never letting go of his fully drawn bow, which was pointed directly at Skenadoa's chest.

"There is no feud between us, young Joseph, nor with your clan, nor with the Mohawk tribe."

"I was shot at."

"They missed you," Skenadoa said. "Be assured, young warrior. If they wanted to harm you, they would not have missed. And if they wanted you to be dead, you would be dead."

Joseph thought for a moment and then lowered his bow.

"Come to the longhouse," Skenadoa said, gesturing toward the sunset. "There is something you must see."

It was almost completely dark when Skenadoa and Joseph reached the longhouse of the Onondaga. He had been there before, attending with his father's escort. This was the place of the Council Fire of the Haudenosaunee, the center of the Confederacy. For centuries, members of the Five—and now Six—Nations had brought their petitions and their disputes before the *Tadodaho*, the spiritual leader of the Nations. Graves were covered, hatchets buried, and conflicts were resolved before the Council Fire.

Skenadoa was not a talkative man, but he seemed unusually silent as the traveling party came to the sacred grove on the lakeshore, where the great old longhouse had stood for centuries. Joseph remembered the scene from earlier visits; even from a distance it was easy to pick out the longhouse and smell the fragrant smoke from the constantly burning Council Fire. But he could see nothing but shadows and smelled nothing but the forest and the nervous sweat of his companions.

"Something has happened," he said to Skenadoa, who said nothing in return but led him to the longhouse. He stepped inside and in a darkness interrupted only by a pair of hanging oil-lamps, he saw a very old chief—the *Tadodaho* himself—and a familiar white man sitting opposite on blankets spread on the floor.

The rest of the longhouse was vacant, except for three old women sitting off to the side, which was itself unusual—both the vacancy as well as the presence of the women under these circumstances. Joseph recognized one of the women—her name was Osha, if he remembered correctly—and she was the Clan Mother of the Heron clan. He assumed the other women represented two of the other clans.

The clan mothers occupied a very powerful position among the Iroquois. They presided over the longhouses, they controlled land use, and they had the right to choose the sachems of the various tribes.

"Hello, Joseph," the white man said, turning his head but not rising.

"Sir William," Joseph answered. *Joseph* was the white name he had been given by Sir William Johnson, the white *sachem* who had become his patron a few years earlier; Johnson seemed unsurprised to see him. "What has happened to the Fire?"

"Put out," Skenadoa said at last. "Something has extinguished the Council Fire."

"When?"

"A few nights ago. When the great broom-star fell," the *Tadodaho* said, his thin, old voice sounding like rustling paper. "It is as foretold. The world is changing, young chieftain's son."

"And where is everyone now? Where are all the *sachems*, honored *Tadodaho*?"

"They are out," the old man replied. "They are watching for enemies."

Joseph was ready to ask another question, but Johnson rose slowly from his seat and took him by the elbow, leading him to the doorway of the longhouse.

"You are looking well, young Joseph," Johnson said, placing his hands on Joseph's shoulders. "Why have you come? The news of the Council Fire cannot have reached Canajoharie yet."

"My father sent me. Something else has happened—a few hands of days ago we witnessed the spirits of the dead in the mists near Ticonderoga. They call for *Abercromby*."

"What sort of spirits?"

Joseph was surprised that Johnson seemed unfazed by the idea of spirits in the mist. The Englishman—his patron in the world of the Europeans—had always been pragmatic and rational, respecting but never quite believing in the stories of the shamans of the Iroquois.

"They were Scotsmen, Sir William. General Abercromby sent them to their death against the French in their hill-fort. I remember. I watched it happen. The English general threw their lives away, throwing them at the French defenses."

"Highlanders." Johnson looked away. "Abercromby ordered the soldiers of the Highland Brigade against the abatis. The brave men were too proud to withdraw and too soldierly to refuse the order. And now . . . they are returning to walk the earth?"

"Excuse me, Sir William, but don't you find that—strange? I would not have expected you to just accept the account as anything but a tale by a . . . "

"A savage."

"Yes. The *Tadodaho* would accept this as true, but not a white man. I did not think you believed in such things."

"Since the fall of the comet—the broom-star—I have come to believe many things. I was here the night it happened, a few sunrises before you saw your apparition. We were gathered around the Fire and suddenly there was a cloud of light, like mist. In an instant the Fire was snuffed out as if it was covered with a great dark blanket. The *Tadodaho* said that there had been an omen about this: a shaman had predicted that it would happen."

"What else did he predict?"

Before Johnson could answer, they heard a cry from outside. Joseph hesitated for a moment as Johnson went to the door of the longhouse; the *Tadodaho* waved at him, indicating that he should go.

When he came out into the clearing, Joseph could see an apparition at the edge of the trees. Floating up near the upper branches was a hideous glowing object, shaped roughly like a large head. It had fiery eyes and long, tangled hair; its mouth was a rictus filled with sharp teeth, and it was muttering words that he could not understand.

"*Konearaunehneh*," Joseph whispered. "But—what has brought it?"

"It hardly matters," Johnson said, coming up beside him. He had a musket in his hand and had picked up a powder-horn. "It means us harm."

"I don't know if a musket-ball will do anything to it," Joseph said. "That is a creature of evil dreams."

"It doesn't seem to be affected by the warriors' arrows," Johnson said, pointing toward the two warriors shooting at it a dozen yards away.

Joseph squinted, looking at the hideous apparition in the bright moonlight. He could see—barely—a tendril of something, like a spider's web but somewhat thicker, trailing from the bottom of the head toward the ground.

"What about that?" he said, pointing toward the trailing tendril.

"What?"

"The string. It hangs down from the head."

"I don't see anything."

"I do," Joseph said, and began to run toward the place where it seemed to trail on the ground.

He could hear Sir William Johnson call his name as he ran, and caught a glance of the two archers, who turned aside to see him, pausing in their attacks.

He could see the tendril clearly in front of him, and he reached out to grasp it—

It was as if he was looking at the world from a great height, like a huge mountaintop. The world was a long oval, extending from fields of ice in the north to steamy jungle in the south; it was ringed around with ridges of mountains rising from the sea. Far to the north and west was a great waterfall, taller than any he had ever seen; there was another far to the north and east, dropping off the edge of the world.

Sir William, and other whites, talked of a land from which they had come, across the eastern ocean. But it was not there: beyond the mountains in the sea there was nothing, only blackness. The world came to an end, and there was no more.

"He is stirring."

Joseph opened his eyes to see Skenadoa sitting next to him, smoking a long clay pipe. Sir William Johnson was beside him, now bending down. The sky was deep blue above; Joseph was lying in a rope hammock.

"I—" he began, and coughed; he lifted his right hand to his mouth and found it covered in a bandage.

"I'll fetch you some water," Johnson said, and moved out of Joseph's field of vision, then returned with a gourd. He helped Joseph to sit up and drink from it, but the world was full of blue spots and he fell back to lie flat.

"What happened?"

"I could ask you the same, young Joseph," Skenadoa said, taking the pipe out, scowling at it, and tapping it against his boot. "You ran under the Flying Head and made some medicine. There was a bright flash and it floated away. When we reached you, your hands were burned and you had gone to sleep."

"I saw something. I saw . . . "

"What did you see?" Johnson said.

"I think I saw the whole world, Sir William. I don't know how that could be. But I could not see the land of your people, of the white people. The mountains are the edge of the world. There is nothing beyond."

"I don't understand."

"You may not be meant to understand, Warraghiyagey," Skenadoa said, using Sir William's Iroquois name—*Chief Big Business*, the *doer of great things*. "But if there is no more land of the whites, then things have changed for all of us."

"It might have been just a vision," Sir William answered.

"I trust this one's sight," Skenadoa said. "But we will have much to consider. It is well that we are at peace—for now."

Chapter II

They sound more like demands

Barbados

It took five days against adverse winds and with inferior charts for *Namur* to make its way to Bridgetown, the capital of His Majesty's crown colony of Barbados. The tiny island was one of the richest bits of real estate in the British Empire. Its economy was based almost entirely on the production of sugar, for which there was an endless demand, and its location—south of most of the Leeward Islands and eastward of all of them—made it the first stopping-place for ships bound from Africa.

Except that Africa was no longer reachable, as it lay beyond what had been named the *Place of Bone*.

Most ships approaching Bridgetown along the southwestern coast of the island came from the north and west, using the highlands on the island's north side as a means of navigation, or from the north and east, making the middle passage from the slave coasts. *Namur*, however, came upon Barbados from the south. If they had not located it, the next landfall would be more than a hundred miles further—a strain on the ship's stores, unforeseen when it set sail for its original destination in the Mediterranean.

Bridgetown was a neat little town, showing evidence of the wealth of its inhabitants. *Namur* was unopposed and unchallenged as it entered the harbor. There were two large, armed merchantmen visible at dock—both in excess of three hundred tons, Boscawen guessed, as he surveyed the scene through his spyglass.

"The war hasn't made too many stops here, I'd wager," he said, lowering the glass and turning to Pascal. "I'll have to go ashore and speak with the governor regarding victualing. You'll prepare a list of what's lacking so that I can present it to him."

"Very good, My Lord. I don't know if the purser will have enough funds, however."

"The victualer will take a note of hand, then. I'll not have *Namur* under provisioned; given what we've seen, it might be some time before we see England again."

"If we ever do," Pascal said.

"That, sir, is a conjecture you will keep to yourself. The men have seen . . . " *a great deal,* he added to himself. "The men have been through an ordeal, but they will not want to be told that they will never go home."

"It will have to be discussed sometime, My Lord."

"Yes." Boscawen tilted his head slightly; his expression was stony. "But not at *this* time. Do you understand, Lieutenant?"

"Yes, sir. Of course."

"Good." Boscawen walked toward the main deck. "Have my barge prepared, along with an escort. I'll go ashore at once."

"Forgive me, my Lord, but that is out of the question."

Charles Pinfold, governor of the colony of Barbados, was a portly man of middle age—*a placeman*, Boscawen thought: the sort of bland political appointee who had found a comfortable place as a result of some powerful patron. He didn't know to whom Pinfold might be answerable—and it might no longer matter.

"You will *not* provide me what *Namur* requires?"

"If you need to refill your water-casks, by all means. But provisions—I have a strict and particular allocation, my Lord. Our contractor provides us only what we require, and no more."

"Only what you pay for."

"Just so."

"I will not eat into your profits, Pinfold. I am prepared to pay for the victualing—"

"I am certain you are willing to offer me a *promissory*, Admiral. But that will not be sufficient for those who arrange the supplying of other ships here in the Caribbean . . . which leads me to ask, if I might be so bold: why are you here at all? I did not think that *Namur* was assigned to this squadron. I had thought that you were based in home waters, or in the Maritimes . . . "

"There was a change in plans."

"And are you in command here, my Lord? Have you been assigned command in this theater?"

"Whatever position our king has elected to assign me, Governor, let me assure you in terms that brook no disagreement or contradiction that I outrank you, sir, and that I expect compliance with my requests."

Pinfold didn't respond for several moments; he had been sitting at his ease while Boscawen stood at parade rest, his hat tucked under his arm. The governor stood and walked to a side-table; he removed the stopper from a cut-glass decanter and poured a small amount of liquid into a matching glass. He didn't offer a drink to Boscawen.

"They sound more like demands," Pinfold said, and swirled the drink in his glass. "And I am not accustomed to responding to demands, Admiral. I might even be inclined to say that I find such things offensive." Boscawen opened his mouth to respond, but Pinfold held his hand up. "And I find it so even if it comes from the son of the Viscount of Falmouth and a Member of Parliament.

"Our provisioning and supplies are designed to account for the requirements of the squadron based here and elsewhere in the Leeward Islands. It is calculated based on the number of ships, the number of days at sea, and so forth. I am sure that you are familiar with the method and with the precision with which His Majesty's contractor, Mr. Biggin, must determine our needs—down to the last ha'penny. It leaves no room—"

"I am extremely familiar with the—"

"It leaves *no room* for the addition of another ship, particularly one with the tonnage of *Namur*." Pinfold tossed off the drink. "So . . . requests or demands, as they may be, will have no impact."

"You are refusing me," Boscawen said.

"By all means refill your water-casks, Admiral. But otherwise . . . yes, that is what I am saying."

Pinfold set his glass carefully down. His face darkened. "If you elect to *take* what you are not *given*, My Lord, you should expect that there will be a letter directly sent to Rear-Admiral Cotes, and one to

Mr. Biggin's agent in Jamaica, and one to the Victualing Board in London—"

"You may do as you like with regards to Thomas Cotes and—this contractor, Biggin?—but as for the Victualing Board, I wish you luck, sir. I do not think there will be any ships sailing for London."

"Whatever do you mean?"

Something about the way in which Pinfold asked the question struck Boscawen as odd. The man stood there, his drink within reach and yet left untouched, his attitude just as defiant. But the absurd idea that there would be no ships leaving Barbados for Europe did not seem to be coming as a surprise.

The man *knew* something. Boscawen was an excellent judge of the intentions and motivations of his fellow man—it was an integral part of command. He was no mind-reader, but he could tell when something was being held back.

"Why don't you tell me what you are not telling me, Governor."

The governor of Barbados held his gaze for another few seconds, then looked away.

"There are limits to what I can provide, Admiral . . . but if you will consent to solving a problem for me, I may be able to assist you."

"Problem? What sort of problem?"

Pinfold sat down behind his wooden desk—in a rather undignified, unmilitary way, to Boscawen's eye. He picked up a little bell and rang it. After a moment, a young clerk opened the door; some unspoken communication passed between them and the door closed.

Pinfold gestured to a seat; Boscawen considered the idea of continuing to stand, to hold the weather-gauge in the room, but wasn't sure how long he might be forced to wait. He took the offered seat, placing his hat in his lap.

"I would inquire, but I assume that all of this will be made clear in due course."

"Just so. May I offer you refreshment?"

"The sun has passed the yard-arm somewhere, Governor. But it certainly has not done so here."

The governor shrugged and drank from his glass. It seemed to have a small salutary effect, as he sat a little straighter—unless that was in response to Boscawen's own upright posture.

Within a matter of a few minutes a knock came at the door.

"Come," Pinfold said, and the clerk appeared once more, ushering a middle-aged man and a young woman into the office. The man held—clutched, really—a small wooden box in his hands.

Pinfold and Boscawen both rose at the lady's appearance, and Boscawen offered her his chair, which she took with a silent acknowledgement of the courtesy.

"Admiral Boscawen, may I have the honor of presenting Monsieur Charles Messier, and his companion Mademoiselle Catherine LaGèndiere. Monsieur Messier is an astronomer and has . . . recently come here to Barbados."

"I see," Boscawen said, though he did not see at all. "Are the gentleman and lady your prisoners?"

"In a strict sense, yes," Pinfold said. "But I would not characterize them thus. They have been my guests for the past several days."

"We were shipwrecked here," Messier said, in slightly accented English. "After we were hurled across the ocean." He looked down at the box and then at Boscawen.

"I'm not sure, sir," Boscawen said to Pinfold, "exactly what this has to do with *me*."

"We have been waiting for you," Messier said before Pinfold could answer.

"For me?"

The young woman looked up at Messier, then directly at Boscawen. "I am a great admirer of your lady wife," she said. "And I have been eager to meet you in person."

Boscawen answered with a slight bow. "I am honored, dear lady, to make your acquaintance. But I fail to understand why."

"If I may," Messier said. Pinfold nodded and moved a stack of parchments from the least-crowded part of his desk. Messier placed the box on the desk and unlatched the top; he lowered the two sides so that they lay flat, revealing a curious instrument of glass and wood. It was rather like an hourglass, braced at each corner by a brass fitting to hold it in place, with a finely marked measuring gauge at the front. The oblong glass formation in the middle held a dull gray liquid—quicksilver, Boscawen supposed—that seemed to undulate up and down.

"It is because of this instrument, Admiral," Messier said. "It has led us to *you*."

"What do you mean?"

"This is an . . . alchemetical compass. It has not been finely calibrated, but I had attuned it to measure certain aspects of the recent comet, which I had the honor to have discovered—independently of Herr Palitzch, I might note, and despite the reluctance of my employer to take note of it."

"He is jealous of your brilliance, Monsieur," the young lady said.

"Yes, yes, that is as may be," Messier said. "Whatever the case, I had taken this instrument out to sea to be free of certain interference inherent to measurement on land. We had just begun our nightly observation when something began to happen."

Pinfold leaned back in his chair, steepling his fingers. "I will be interested to hear what you make of *this*, Admiral."

Boscawen ignored the governor. Instead, he leaned down to examine the apparatus that Messier had placed on the desk. He reached his hand toward the glass vessel—and as he did, something curious happened: the liquid content seemed to move forward, as if it was attracted to the admiral's fingers.

"What the devil?" Pinfold said, leaning forward and half-standing.

"As I said," Messier said quietly. "It is attracted to you."

"I . . . assumed you meant this *metaphorically*, Messier," Pinfold said. "What is the meaning of—"

"Governor, if what you wish is for me to take Monsieur Messier aboard *Namur*, I accept. Monsieur, Mademoiselle, if you will make yourself known to my purser, we can prepare to accommodate you."

Chapter 12

What has happened to the world I knew?

The Caribbean

The crew and officers of *Namur* were surprised by the appearance of the Frenchman and his young lady companion but asked no questions as the admiral came back aboard. He left Mademoiselle LaGèndiere in the care of Father Frederick, and escorted Messier to his private cabin. With the hatch secured, he directed Messier to place the unusual instrument on his chart-table. With the sides opened, Boscawen reached his hand toward the glass with the same result as before: the gray liquid climbed the side of the vessel to follow the movement of his fingers.

Boscawen settled himself into his chair, leaving the Frenchman to stand, slightly hunched, in the cramped cabin.

"I require an explanation, Monsieur. Who you are, what this—instrument—might be, and why you are aboard my ship."

"You invited me—"

"Do not try my patience, Monsieur Messier. I beg to remind you that your king and mine are enemies, and our nation is at war. I suspect that you have knowledge that I need, and there is some reason that Governor Pinfold is eager to send you packing. Now, out with it, sir."

"I am an astronomer," Messier began. "I am formerly in the employ of Monsieur Joseph Delisle—"

"Formerly?"

"I believe that employment ended a week ago, Admiral, when we were deposited on this side of . . . whatever the comet has wrought."

"Pray continue."

"Monsieur Delisle is the astronomer of the Navy of His Highness King Louis. I had the honor to be in his employ for several years, during which I applied myself to the discovery and cataloging of comets. I had a particular interest in the one that was predicted to return this year."

"You said that you discovered it in the sky, Monsieur."

"Yes . . . with the assistance of Mademoiselle LaGèndiere and her instrument."

"Ah, so this peculiar device is something of *her* invention? Then perhaps we should send for her to join us."

Messier shook his head. "She is generally reluctant to discuss the device. Partly, I think, because she got the inspiration for it from her father and—" He broke off, shaking his head again. "Her family situation is . . . ah, difficult."

Boscawen frowned. "Her family . . . Is the lady married?"

"Yes, but—ah—her husband chose not to accompany her on the voyage. As I said, the situation is difficult." Messier's expression made clear that he did not wish to pursue the topic any further.

There was some mystery here. Boscawen had gotten no sense at all that the relationship between the French astronomer and Catherine LaGèndiere was in any way an amorous one. Yet why was she traveling unaccompanied and under the title "Mademoiselle"?

But there seemed no need to investigate that now, so the admiral decided to acquiesce to Messier's clear desire to avoid the topic. "Tell me more about this alchemetical compass, then. And why it seems attracted to *me*."

"As to the latter question, I cannot say, except that she assured me that it was you to whom we would be guided. The device detects the . . . patterns of the earth and aligns itself to them. It was particularly active during the period just before the arrival of the comet, and as I told you earlier, it was necessary that we distance ourselves from land in order to properly calibrate it. While we were at sea, the event happened.

"Our ship was hurled against a rocky shore, and only a few of us survived, thanks be to God—" Messier crossed himself piously— "Mademoiselle LaGèndiere and I were among them. And we were able to save one of our three instruments. The others . . . " he made a dismissive gesture.

"The rocky shore was Barbados, I presume. This must have come as something of a surprise."

"Not to Mademoiselle LaGèndiere. She assured me that it was Divine Providence that had guided us to this point, and that we need merely present ourselves to the governor of the island and inform him that we were waiting for you to appear."

"Governor Pinfold was then *expecting* us?"

"Expecting *you*, Monsieur Admiral."

"I still fail to see why . . . why me."

"I cannot answer that question, as I told you."

"Then perhaps you can explain to me what we have experienced, and what has happened to the world I knew."

Messier looked around the cabin; his eyes fell on a small piece of round shot, perhaps three inches in diameter. He picked it up and drew out a pocket handkerchief. He took the ball and draped it in the handkerchief, then held it at arm's length. "Imagine this is the comet, a heavenly body of some sort: a rock like a lump of coal. This object flies through the heavens, and when it gets close enough to the Sun it catches fire and streams the result behind it." He moved the shot about so that the handkerchief fluttered. "This is the tail. As it swings around the sun, more and more material streams out; when it falls away and back into the void, it eventually cools enough that it is no longer afire."

"Why does it not all burn away, then?" Boscawen asked. "And why isn't it smaller the next time? You would think that, after several trips around the sun, it would be all consumed."

"I don't know. In any case, the comet is usually at some remove from our terrestrial globe." He removed the handkerchief. "But imagine now that this ball is the Earth." He moved it to his other hand. "And *this* is the cometary tail." He waved the handkerchief. "I think that somehow we passed *through* it this time, instead of watching it go by." He moved the handkerchief past the ball, letting it brush the surface. "I don't know how that could be, but I do think it's happened."

"Wouldn't that mean that this lump of coal has changed its course?"

"Yes. In fact, I think that already happened—the last time it came this way in 1682. There is a book about the comet's motion, written by the esteemed Dr. Halley, which was originally published with an unusual essay—"

Boscawen held up his hand. He leaned over and unlatched a sea-chest, from which he drew a slim volume, which he handed to Messier.

The Frenchman took it and leafed through the last few pages with an almost mystic reverence. "Yes, yes—this is the first edition. It was largely suppressed by Newton, when he was head of the Royal Society, as a courtesy to Halley. Have you read this book, Monsieur Admiral?"

"Yes. It was a parting gift from my wife. It is a load of rubbish about ætheric patterns and mystical awakenings. It is no wonder that Newton removed the essay. It would have destroyed Halley's reputation for all time."

"Be that as it may, Monsieur, there have been a number of incidents and tendencies that suggest strongly that the transit of the comet in 1682 began to awaken latent abilities among those disposed toward them. It is no accident that individuals like my companion have what I might generously term 'attunements.' Unusual things. Visions; clairvoyance; that sort of thing."

"There are places in the world—including your native land—where one could still be burned at the stake for exhibiting that sort of ability."

"Quite true. But if the 1682 transit awakened a few latent abilities—perhaps even what might be taken for witchcraft—in the past, what would a more serious interaction bring about this time?"

"This is all speculation." Boscawen looked from the French astronomer to the alchemetical compass. For a moment, the liquid seemed to move of its own accord, rising on the side of the glass nearest him.

Messier moved the handkerchief across the surface of the ball again. "As you say. But whatever this material is—fire, or gossamer, or æther, or something completely unknown—for it to fall to earth could do more than simply change one man or another. It could change all of us. It could remake our image."

"I don't know what that means."

"Nor do I, Monsieur, but if Divine Providence has placed us here, I would assume that It has some purpose for us: myself, you, my companion.

"You asked me what has happened to the world you knew. I cannot say except to suggest that it is gone forever."

With exaggerated care, Messier placed the round shot in the place from where he had picked it up and tucked his handkerchief back into his vest.

There was a compromise. Pinfold wanted to send *Namur* packing, water-casks full but otherwise not reprovisioned. Pascal was in favor of seizing both *Achille* and *Lady Ann*, the two cargo ships in Bridgetown Harbor, to supplement the ship's stores. Instead, Pinfold let *Namur*'s purser gather the most important items—flour, sugar, pease and rum, primarily—and they left the rest for the other ships in the squadron. Pinfold's letter went off to Admiral Cotes; there was no ship bound for London to take his complaints to the Victualing Board—he would wait for the next supply ship to take it back. Messier and his female companion remained on board *Namur*, no longer the problem of the governor of Barbados.

Boscawen did not expect another supply ship—not in the next few weeks; perhaps never again. And he didn't care what Thomas Cotes said—if there was no way to contact London, the chain of command would be confused enough. Two days after arriving at Barbados, *Namur* set sail for Jamaica. Whether or not there was a personal conflict ahead, Admiral Boscawen was expecting to reach Kingston before Governor Pinfold's letter. Whether his voice would be louder remained to be seen.

The charts Boscawen was able to obtain told him in detail what he already knew: that the trade winds blew more steadily from north to south. Ships departed Jamaica for Barbados and Barbados for Europe—going in reverse was more of a challenge to sailing.

"But sail it we must, and shall," he said. "Mr. Pascal, I should like to see wind filling those sails."

"We are making—" Pascal checked his watch and looked up at the topmast—"a bit over four knots, my Lord, and we are sailing four points to port."

"And Saint Lucia is well behind us." Boscawen looked out to sea, watching the waves. "I wish I was more comfortable with this."

"My Lord?"

"Over my career, Pascal, I have prided myself on preparation and planning. I had specific orders for my ship and the other vessels in the squadron—the *Mediterranean* Squadron. We are not fitted out for this assignment. The men are improperly clothed, our hull is not properly proofed against boreworms. I have inadequate charts."

"With due respect, my Lord," Pascal said, "Whatever the circumstance, we are *here*, and not at the bottom of the ocean, or shipwrecked on the . . . what was it O'Brien called it? The *Place of Bone*. I agree that the situation is not ideal, but we are officers in His Majesty's Navy—as I am sure you would tell me yourself if I were making such observations."

Boscawen fixed his junior with a stare that had caused many a junior officer to wilt. "You are being extremely forthright, for a lieutenant in His Majesty's Navy, sir."

Pascal did not look away. "My Lord, do you think we will ever see England again?"

"I don't know."

"Nor do I, Admiral. And if we never do, then I daresay that the social order to which we both have become accustomed will be severely changed. Our place in it will depend on our own will. I . . . have no reason to tender you anything but obedience and respect while aboard *Namur*, sir, but there are assumptions that are likely to be challenged."

"Such as?"

"I should think that would be obvious. Sir."

Boscawen considered a response, but just as with the governor at Barbados, he wasn't sure what the point of it would be. The man was right; all the polite veneer that constituted military discipline, not to mention civil society, would be upended if this was their world—if the realm and the King were out of sight and inaccessible.

And for now, there was nothing but open ocean—at least several hundred miles of it—before they reached Jamaica.

"Pascal," Boscawen said. "Look at the waves."

The lieutenant looked out to sea, away from the bow. "Waves, Admiral?"

"Look ahead, a few points to starboard. Something is interrupting the waves. Ask the top if he sees any land."

"Aye, sir." He shouted the order to the sailor in the topmast. "But we are unlikely to find an island out here—"

"I do not trust our charts. It's possible that something was overlooked."

Pascal touched his cap and nodded, walking back toward the pilothouse. Boscawen looked through his spyglass again, in the direction from which the cross waves were coming. There was something . . . a small formation, like a tiny island, several hundred yards away . . .

. . . And as he watched, he saw it begin to move.

"Beat to quarters!" Boscawen said. "Division officers, prepare all guns to fire! Come about—" he called out a heading that took them in the direction of the formation.

It takes only a few minutes for a well-trained crew to prepare and run out the guns on a warship. *Namur* had an exceptionally well-trained one—Boscawen had picked most of them himself, including a fair complement of Cornishmen loyal to their Cornish admiral.

The ship's gun crew was separated into six divisions, each under the command of a junior officer. *Namur* had two decks of guns as well as bow- and stern-chasers. The process of preparing the main broadsides was a demonstration of the well-oiled machine: loading the cartridge, pricking it open through the touch-hole, loading the shot, applying the rammer, rolling the gun carriage out through the port, and waiting for the order to pull the lanyard to set off the gunlock on order so that the entire broadside was fired at once. The recoil from the discharge pulled the gun carriage back inboard, where it was stopped by the breech rope. Then the cannon was swabbed, and the process was repeated. A good crew—and *Namur's* crew certainly qualified—could do all this three times in the space of five minutes.

Boscawen assumed that the object he saw was another ship—and in mid-ocean, it was as likely to be an enemy as an ally. The guns could always be hauled back in if he spied a Union Jack.

Namur's sails caught the wind, and its smooth bow cut smoothly across the crosscurrents generated by the other ship—except, as they approached the target, it became apparent that it was no ship. The dark form that Boscawen had seen was the top of a head that slowly rose from the waves, water washing off the skull, and then the torso, of a great, fanged, tentacled *thing*—a creature from nightmare, a sea-creature. A more lyrical person, like his beloved Frances, might have called it something like a *kraken*.

It loomed up, fifteen or twenty feet in the air—which suggested to

Boscawen that there was likely a great deal more of the creature submerged nearby. It was not an island or a ship—it was some terrible enemy.

In the face of a thing he had never before seen, in the middle of an ocean he had never before sailed, Admiral Edward Boscawen had only one thought.

"Gun-captains! All guns—*fire!*"

The *kraken* was a terrifying thing, but the gun-crews were too busy to see what they were firing at, which was just as well. Even his brave Cornishmen might have hesitated in the face of the impossibility of it. They fired on the roll, after *Namur* turned to present its broadside; after two cannonades, the being—which, for all Boscawen knew, had never encountered round shot before— retreated beneath the waves.

When all was quiet again, and the guns were secured, Boscawen stood for a long time at the rail of the quarterdeck, holding it tightly as he gazed overboard into the dark, choppy sea below.

What has happened to the world I knew? he asked himself once again. But from the wind and the waves there came no answer.

Chapter 13

There's been some sort of working

The Caribbean

"Tell me what you make of that."

There was no sea-monster this time, but a single ship—a merchantman, cutting steadily through the chop; sunlight reflected cheerily from its metal fittings. The strange thing was that *Namur* was sailing in rough water with a dark, overcast sky, several hundred yards away.

"I think it's flying a Jack, Admiral," Pascal said, lowering his spyglass. "Of course, it could be a ruse."

"It doesn't appear to be a man-o'-war. But . . . "

"The weather. I have no idea, sir. I cannot explain it. Of course, I can't explain mountains in the sea or sea-monsters either. I don't know if we can catch her, given the weather we sail under."

"We shall try," Boscawen said. "Turn us about to follow."

The other ship might have been able to outrun them but seemed uninterested in making it a chase; it put on no extra sail as *Namur* approached, but rather changed its point of sail so that the two ships were on the same heading, a few dozen yards apart. There was a cheer from the main deck when *Namur* broke out into sunlight. It was the first blue sky they'd seen in several days.

"Welcome aboard His Majesty's ship *Namur*, Captain Fayerweather," Boscawen said. "Your name is quite apt."

"Well, sir," the man replied. "It's a *nom de guerre*, of course. Real name is Toombs. Charles Evan Toombs, of Salem. My honor to meet you, sir."

Boscawen tilted his head. "I see." He gestured to a seat in the cabin. Pascal remained standing in the doorway.

Fayerweather was almost the perfect image of a prosperous sailing-man; his hair was cropped fairly short and clubbed into a queue, his clothes were plain and well-worn but of decent quality, and he had donned a dark-blue coat and a beaver hat, holding it in the crook of his arm in deference to the station of the man who now entertained him.

"My lads started calling me Charlie Fayerweather some years ago, Admiral, because where I sailed the weather was usually fine. Of course, that's the sort of thing that can get you burned as a witch back in my hometown."

"Still? I thought that practice was long since abandoned."

"I've not been back to find out." He smiled, showing a fine set of teeth—too perfect, perhaps not his original set: curious, given the expense of such a thing. "I mostly ply the routes down here, carrying this and that, and making a decent living."

"And always under fair skies."

"Aye, most times. I know most of His Majesty's vessels in these waters, Admiral, and I confess I've never seen you here; but I do know your name."

"I am gratified," Boscawen said. "We only just arrived."

"From Europe."

"That's right."

Fayerweather sat back in his chair. "Well, now, sir, that's interesting; because I had heard that we'd not be seeing much traffic from the old country anytime soon."

"Why would that be?"

"Things have changed, Admiral Boscawen. There's been some sort of working, I'm certain of it." He lowered his voice. "I saw when I came aboard that you have a blackbird in your crew. You'd be best served to get him off your ship as soon as possible, if you value your safety."

"A . . . 'blackbird'?"

Pascal cleared his throat. "I think he means Gustavus, My Lord."

"A black man," Boscawen said.

"I'll not have them on my ship. The blacks have a secret cult," Fayerweather said quietly. "Particularly on Saint-Domingue up north. The cult has a lot of names, but the most common one is *vodou* . . . They want to kill all the slaveholders and have a special hatred for whites. They called on their demons and spirits, and—something happened. They all know it. They can feel it in their souls."

"Our Gustavus is a Christian," Boscawen said. "And as far as I know he has not been in contact with the slaves in Saint-Domingue."

"They all *know*," Fayerweather hissed. "This isn't something benign like my little knack—though *that*'s become much more reliable since the change. This is much, much bigger, Admiral. You'll see. Put that blackbird in a little boat if you must but put him off your ship."

"I don't take kindly to being given orders, Captain," Boscawen said angrily. "And I don't believe in vast plots involving people who never met each other and are involved just because of their race."

"I didn't issue you an order, sir. Just a piece of friendly advice, one crown's subject to another. But I can see I'm not wanted here, so I'll take my leave—unless you're looking to detain me."

Boscawen waited for long enough to see the man's smirk begin to disappear, as if he suspected that he'd gone a bit too far with a Royal Navy officer; then said, "No. Get off my ship."

"I would have offered to give you good sailing toward Jamaica," Fayerweather said. "But I can see you can take care of yourself." He stood and picked up his hat; the cabin was too low for him to put it on. He turned and found Pascal in the doorway.

"Pardon me, sir," he said. Pascal hesitated, and then stepped out of his way. He exchanged a look with the admiral.

"Let it go, Lieutenant."

"Aye, sir. I'll see him off our deck, if I may be excused."

Boscawen nodded. "And send Gustavus to me."

"Admiral—"

"Attend to your duties, Lieutenant. Dismissed."

I'm not going to throw him overboard, Boscawen thought. *I just want to ask him a few questions.*

His thoughts went to Frances again, wondering what she would make of any of this. At home, there would begin to be word of this . . . *sundering*, he supposed it might be termed; on the other side of the barrier they would wonder what had happened to the Americas.

Unless there is nothing on the other side of the barrier.

He tried to grapple with the idea that they weren't cut off from Europe, but that Europe had somehow ceased to exist. Was there a difference? Frances would know—the abstract was much more her province than his. He would rather deal with wind and tide than symbol and idea. And something—something *physical*, he assumed—had brought about the sundering of the New World from the Old. Perhaps it was the comet, or perhaps it was something else. But he was damned if he was going to believe that a group of black slaves pulled down the sky and broke the earth.

"Admiral, sir?"

Gustavus was at the door of the cabin, silhouetted against the bright sunny day outside; but not far beyond Boscawen could see the storm-clouds that surrounded Fayerweather's island of good sailing.

"Come in, boy. Come in and sit down."

The young man came in and sat tentatively at the edge of a chair. "Sir."

"Tell me, Gustavus. What do you know of *vodou*?"

"Begging the admiral's pardon—"

"It's all right, Gustavus. You can talk to me without fear. I am not angry with you."

"It is not that, my Lord. It's just . . . *vodou* is a white man's term. It comes from *Bon Dieu*, the French words for God. It is not what it is truly called."

"Pray enlighten me."

"In Barbados and in Virginia, Admiral, the black people do not call their religion by the white man's word. They call it by the name *obeah*. It is from a word used among my people—my *father*'s people, where I came from—for the man who made the talking charms and cured the people of their illnesses. That is the word that the slaves use for their practices, though only among themselves."

"Apparently Captain Fayerweather does not know that word, Gustavus."

"That man is not a good man, Admiral. I know I can be beaten for speaking ill of a white man, but he is a *diabelero*, a carrier of evil. I can smell it on him, and I am no trained *obeah*-man."

"He is very afraid of blacks. He told me to throw you overboard—" Gustavus started back in fear, and Boscawen reached forward and patted him on the knee. "No, no, boy. You must not be afraid. I told him to go back to his own ship, though I had some thoughts about more drastic things. Something worse."

"He is a bad man, Admiral."

"Yes. Yes, I know. I smelled it too." Boscawen smiled and laid a finger beside his nose. "He told me that the blacks, particularly the ones on Saint-Domingue, made the change in the world."

"They are very powerful, sir, but I do not think that even the greatest of the *obeah*-men of Saint-Domingue could do . . . what we saw." Gustavus closed his eyes for a moment, as if remembering the event.

"I did not tell him what we saw. As far as I know, only we and the people at the Place of Bone know how the ocean was torn apart by . . . "

By whatever did this, Boscawen thought. *By whatever sundered the world.*

After a brief silence, Gustavus said, "then you will not throw me into the sea."

"No. Of course not. But I require you to tell me whatever you can about this *obeah*, and what it *can* do. There was a time not so long ago that I would not have believed a single word of it; but I think that time has passed."

Chapter 14

Hates men, hates the light

Québec

They had been streaming into the low town for a few days: traders, *couriers de bois*, even missionaries, finding their way from Upper Canada and the wild lands of the Far Indians, seeking the safety of Québec.

The rivers and lakes had become dangerous. It didn't make much sense to Montcalm, but after the event that had drawn him onto the Heights of Abraham—the strange confusion that had drawn him back to the battle at Piacenza a dozen years earlier—he was not sure what made sense.

A few weeks after that incident, he received a message from François de Lévis, requesting his presence in the low town. It was a chilly, overcast day; there had been a cold rain the night before, leading to the sort of damp that creeps into the bones—*the sort that makes you feel old*, he thought as he made his way down from the promontory.

Lévis was at the wharf with a native that he did not know. The dock was strewn with some sort of wreckage, and the two men were examining it closely. When Montcalm approached, Lévis stood and saluted. The Indian remained crouched, holding a long, jagged sliver of what might have once been the keel of a *bateau*, a flat-bottomed boat common on the St. Lawrence. He looked up at Montcalm with some emotion that was difficult to read but seemed mildly hostile.

"Monsieur," Lévis said. "This is Red Vest. He is a Seneca—a warrior and guide, well-known among his people."

The native offered a slight nod, but his expression did not change. "What is all this?"

"A *bateau*—or what was once a *bateau*, at least. It floated downstream this morning. Something attacked it."

"Something or someone? It looks as if it has been torn apart."

"Red Vest has a possible explanation," Lévis said, gesturing to the native. "He thinks that it was attacked by a . . . "

"*Maneto*," the native said. It was the first word he had spoken, and it came in a deep, resonant voice that carried along the dock; several other people stopped and looked at him as he stood upright, still holding the jagged piece of wood in his hands.

"What, or who, is *Maneto*?"

"What," the man answered. "*Maneto* is a snake, a great serpent that lives at the bottom of the lake. Some call it *Kichimanetowa*. It waits for boat to pass over and then—" He snapped the wood fragment in two and tossed the pieces to the dock. "Hates men, hates the light."

Montcalm looked from Lévis to Red Vest. "Why have we never heard of this before? We have traveled across many lakes and rivers here without being attacked."

"Servant of *Onontio* knows the answer to this," Red Vest said, folding his arms in front of him. "*Maneto* sleeps for many years, but now has woken up. *Maneto* hates all men but has most hate for white men."

"How can it tell?"

"The smell," Red Vest said. He turned his head and spat. "*Maneto* can smell white flesh."

"You will show courtesy to the Marquis," Lévis said, taking a step toward Red Vest. "What do you mean, the smell?"

"Whites have no medicine," Red Vest answered. "Red men have medicine, and *Maneto* is careful with them. Among my people, when we fish from lake we always give one back to *Maneto* so he is satisfied, so he sleeps. But white men fish and take every one.

"But there is more. The wind has changed, and *Maneto* feels the change. He knows that white men have taken all the fish, and he is angry and *hungry*." Red Vest gestured toward the remains of the boat scattered on the dock. "White men should stay off the rivers."

"That's not practical," Montcalm said. "Tell me, Red Vest, why don't the red men—or the white men—just kill all the *Maneto*?"

"Kill *Maneto*?" Red Vest spat again. "They are at the bottom of the lake—"

"Not when they come up and attack."

"Their hides are as tough as old trees, and they have great horns and teeth, *Marquis*," the Indian said. He gave the title an angry intonation. "They are hard to kill, and even if you could, another would grow in their place. *Maneto* only fear one thing."

"And what is that?"

"*Ciinkwia*," he said. "The spirits of thunder and storm. If they choose, they take the forms of men and stride across land and water and put the *Maneto* to sleep."

"That's what he told me, Monsieur," Lévis said. "The Miami shamans are calling on the *Ciinkwia* to come and put down the *Maneto*. Meanwhile . . . " he gestured toward the scattered remains of the *bateau*.

"Please give Red Vest his reward, and then attend me," Montcalm said to Lévis, and turned away from the Indian without another word.

By the time Lévis caught up with Montcalm, he had walked into the lower town. Most of the recent arrivals did not trouble the marquis as he passed; they had their own concerns.

"Tell me about Red Vest."

"He is as he seems, Monsieur," Lévis said. "A trader and guide. He thinks very little—" A group of roughly-dressed traders stepped around Montcalm with scarce courtesy. "He thinks very little of whites."

"And these are the savages we consider to be our *friends*," Montcalm said. "What do our enemies say about us?"

"They do not stop to converse, Monsieur," Lévis said. "They use other means to communicate."

"Then why am I inclined to believe that this wise, white-hating *trader and guide* is not spouting nonsense about man-eating snakes and thunder spirits that walk on water? I think our Far Indians may have gone to the warpath, François, and driven our people from the lakes and rivers, and the Miamis and our other friends among the natives may be too weak, or too afraid, to do anything about it."

"So you do not believe his story," Lévis said.

Montcalm took Lévis by the elbow and led him out of the street to an alley overhung by the eaves of a small warehouse. "I do not completely discount it," he said, lowering his voice. "There are strange things afoot. But I am not inclined to give credence to rumors that will frighten large numbers of people."

"That seems to have already happened." Lévis gestured to the nearby street. "Many of these people were travelers or settlers some distance from Québec. They are afraid of *something*, Monsieur, and I don't think it's just Far Indians."

"I grant that. But I will not feed the fears of the *habitants*, François."

"Then what do you propose to do, Monsieur?"

"I need you to pick a few dozen men—*brave* men, François, not just time-servers. They should be good marksmen, and if possible, they should be tolerant of the savages. Find me a priest who will be willing to accompany them. We are going to travel upriver and see just what there is to this *Maneto* story.

"And if they exist, for some reason, we are going to kill one and bring it home and plant His Christian Majesty's flag in the middle of its ugly, scaly back. That should show the people—and the savages as well—what sort of power the *Onontio* possesses."

Chapter 15

People become frightened, Monsieur

New France

A twelve-gun sloop was hardly a man-o'-war, but it was significantly more impressive than a *bateau*. Loaded with two dozen soldiers and a few Indian guides, *Soleil* looked solid and safe. Montcalm expressed his confidence that he was equipped for a *Maneto*—or anything else that might come his way.

In his private thoughts, with the shore slipping away and Québec's promontory shrinking in the distance, he was far less assured.

Above Québec, the Saint-Laurent meandered west toward the settlement of Trois-Rivières, beyond which it widened into Lac Saint-Pierre. According to Red Vest—who, after some convincing, agreed to board the ship and act as a guide—there had been no sightings of *Manetos* along the river, just in the larger, more placid bodies of water; if there was to be a sighting of the creature that had frightened so many, he expected it to be there. If there were no monsters to be found, *Soleil* would continue another ninety or so miles upstream to Montréal, where the falls would block their further passage.

"It will be spring soon, Monsieur."

"*Père* Récher, you are a stubborn optimist," Montcalm answered, turning away from the view upstream to face the younger man. Jean-Félix Récher, parish priest of Notre-Dame in Québec, had been a last-minute addition to the expedition, pressed on Montcalm by Bishop Dubreil de Pontbriand. He wasn't sure what Récher had been instructed to do, but it would have been impolitic to refuse

Pontbriand—and besides, he considered the elderly bishop a friend, who shared his disgust for the corrupt intendant.

"God provides."

"Yes, He does. But sometimes Man must make his own provision."

"I'm sure Monsieur *l'Évèque* would take issue with that statement, but I shall let it pass." Récher folded his hands in front of him and smiled. "He is a Jesuit, of course, and I am not—they feel it is their duty to argue about *everything*."

"What has His Grace said about the lake monsters?"

"He doesn't believe in them, obviously," Récher said. "Do you, Monsieur?"

"I saw what they did to the *bateau* on the dock."

"You saw a *bateau* on the dock, and you heard tales of monsters. A savage drew a line between the evidence and the stated cause, but you did not witness the latter."

"But I gather that a fair number of *habitants* did. Am I to disbelieve all of their stories?"

"People become frightened, Monsieur. Especially simple people, especially when they face the perils of winter, of war, and of savages living right nearby. My lord bishop asked me . . . well, *told* me—" he smiled again. ". . . to accompany your expedition to lay the rumor of monsters to rest, and to assure the *habitants* that they do not exist."

"Because, I assume, they would sooner take your word for it than mine."

Récher fingered his clerical collar. "It helps to speak with the voice of spiritual authority, Monsieur le Marquis. But please do not take it as an insult. I believe that the bishop wants this business laid to rest as much as you do—perhaps more. It is better for the *habitants*—"

"The 'simple people.'"

"Yes. It is better for them to live in their own settlements, to enhance the glory of God throughout New France, than to huddle as refugees in the low town of Québec."

"But you must admit that they were truly frightened by *something*."

"Of course. But what is to say that it was not something other than this—mythical beast?" Récher turned at a sound, and saw Red Vest emerging from the lower deck. He inclined his head at the native; the other scowled at him and turned his head, spitting.

"*He* says," Montcalm said. "And while I appreciate your rationality, *Père*, I cannot simply dismiss what he has said. Honestly, while I hesitate to admit it loudly and publicly, I think there are creatures of some sort lurking in Lac Saint-Pierre. My hope is that they will find that canister shot is not to their liking."

With a slight bow, Montcalm excused himself and walked across the deck to where Red Vest was looking at the riverbank.

"So," the native said, spitting over the side. "What does the scarecrow have to say?"

"You mean *Père* Récher? He doesn't believe in the *Maneto*, or that the people should be afraid of it."

"His cross-God doesn't seem to have done much to protect them," Red Vest said. "The spirits of the earth are very angry since the broom-star fell. The servants of the *Onontio* offend them less than those of the English; but all the whites will have to learn new ways."

"We'll see."

"You seem very sure of yourself, Marquis. Are you sure that your people's power is great enough?"

"I'm obliged to believe it, Red Vest. It has served us adequately so far."

"That is arrogance, Marquis."

"Really. Now tell me, Red Vest: you are a Seneca, is that not correct?"

"Yes. Guyasuta, the great chief of the Onondowaga, the Keepers of the Western Door, is my mother's uncle. What of it?"

"There was a rumor that something had happened to the Council Fire of the Iroquois. Is that true?" It was only a rumor of a prophecy, but it would be an interesting reconnaissance in force.

Red Vest did not reply immediately, but Montcalm could see that the question had struck home—the native was visibly upset. He frowned at Montcalm and began to answer, then clenched his jaw and looked away at the riverbank again. He gripped the taffrail with white knuckles.

"So it is true."

"Almost no one knows of this, Marquis. Some red man's tongue wagged."

"Something like that. What does that mean? Are the spirits of the earth unhappy with the people of the longhouse as well? Are we all in this changed world together?"

Red Vest did not answer.

"The *Onontio* counts the Seneca people as friends, Red Vest, and would count all of the people of the longhouse as friends if they wished it. If these earth spirits are angry, but more so at the English, isn't it time for our people—the people of New France—and your people to make common cause against the English? I know that it has become quite an artful thing for you to remain balanced between the two European nations to maintain your power, but I think that whatever change has come over the world may force you to choose."

"I do not make decisions for the Onondowaga, Marquis."

"But you are a respected man among them." *Or you are no more than a provocateur and a poser,* Montcalm thought. *We shall see.* "After we are done with this expedition, perhaps you can take a letter back to your chiefs, so that I may learn on what terms we can . . . "

"Make 'common cause.'"

"Just so. That is, if the Iroquois are still a confederation after the difficulty with the Council Fire."

"Whether the Council Fire still burns or has gone out is of no consequence to the Onondowaga, Marquis." Red Vest still gripped the rail, and still did not look directly at Montcalm. "The league may have lived too long as it is."

"And your chiefs . . . "

"*Our* chiefs might say the same, Marquis." He let go of the rail and turned to face Montcalm, his face returned to its hostile expression. "But it will be up to them to say."

"I will be interested to hear their answer."

"I am sure," Red Vest said. "If any of us survive the *Maneto*." Without another word or courtesy, Red Vest walked away from Montcalm, leaving him alone with his thoughts.

Chapter 16

Maneto likes the rain

New France

Soleil cast off from Trois-Rivières in pouring rain. It would have been prudent to wait a day or two for the weather to clear; but Red Vest made it clear to Montcalm that he did not believe that the weather was mere circumstance.

"*Maneto* likes the rain," Red Vest said, standing under the overhang aft of the pilothouse.

"I like the rain as well," Montcalm told him. "It is a gift from God."

As with so many other things, the native's response to the comment was to spit on the deck and turn away.

Soleil ran out its guns. The gun-captains did their best to keep the powder dry and the gunlocks in proper order—but that was easier if the ship was in an actual battle, with a target in sight and the "clock running." As with so many things in the navy, it was long periods of boredom interrupted by moments of sheer terror.

Soleil's intended course was across the lake southwestward, toward the place where the river narrowed again. It was a maze of crosscurrents; the wind wasn't cooperating either, requiring the ship to make frequent corrections in course.

Then, without warning, the choppy water they were passing through went calm and flat. Red Vest took his rifle in hand; Montcalm did so as well.

There was still a breeze enough to partially fill *Soleil*'s sails, but it was otherwise whisper-quiet, with the occasional interruption of a bird call from the shore. Even the ship's crew had gone largely silent, giving the scene an eerie feel.

And then, just as suddenly, something erupted from the water less than twenty feet away. It was a horror from nightmare: something like an octopus, pallid green and grey, with a distended head containing pupilless eyes and a ragged mouth, a huge, dark torso shedding water and long, ropy tentacles extending out from its sides. *Soleil* was almost bow-on to the creature, but the ship's captain showed presence of mind by bringing it about to present a broadside; the gun-captains were already issuing orders, preparing the six starboard guns to fire.

With a movement almost too quick to notice, one of the tentacles lashed out toward *Soleil* and wrapped itself around Red Vest, who stood only a few feet from Montcalm himself. It lifted him off the deck and into the air.

Before Montcalm could react or bring his weapon to bear, the ship's guns fired with a deafening roar, hurling canister shot over the short distance between *Soleil* and the *Maneto*. It caused the creature to recoil; the tentacle that held Red Vest straightened and stiffened, and Montcalm thought he heard the native cry out. But as he watched, Red Vest took careful aim with the rifle he still held and took the one shot he would be able to take.

The captain of *Soleil* was bringing the ship about, preparing for a port broadside. Montcalm took aim with his own rifle, as did several others on the deck of the ship, and fired, but the pitching and turning of the vessel made them ineffective. At the same time, though, there was a bloom in the creature's right eye, causing it to utter an unearthly sound. The tentacle relaxed, and Red Vest was hurled into the now-roiling water, still clutching his rifle.

While the rifle shots from *Soleil*'s deck were fruitless, the cannon fire found its mark. Large pools of dark blood spilled on the waves and the *Maneto*, still howling, sunk into the water just as the other broadside was launched.

Montcalm rushed to the rail, looking for some sign of Red Vest, who had just performed the single bravest act he had ever witnessed. The muddied lake was disturbed by the now-underwater thrashing of the *Maneto*, making visibility difficult. There was even the possibility that some part of the two broadsides had struck Red Vest, or that he had been pulled under by the creature. He began to take off his coat, preparing to dive overboard to try and locate him, but one of the crewmen pointed at the water and shouted, "There he is!"

Montcalm sat with Red Vest in his cabin. The native was draped in two heavy Indian blankets. Most of his outer clothing lay nearby, stained with the creature's effusions that had mixed with the lake-water. The rifle, also badly soaked, lay on the deck before him, partially stripped. He had never let go of the weapon, and Montcalm could scarcely blame him—it had given him excellent service in a moment of extreme danger.

"I have never witnessed such a feat," Montcalm said.

"Your ship guns did far more," Red Vest said. But he nodded and even favored Montcalm with the slightest of smiles.

"There is something I do not understand."

"What is that, Marquis?"

"Of all the men on the deck of the ship, it was *you* that the creature chose to grapple. Why was that?"

"A simple answer," he answered. "I asked to be chosen."

"You *what*?"

"Marquis, you are a brave man. But you do not understand what has awoken. You needed to be shown. I asked the *Ciinkwia* to choose me."

"But—but certainly I did not need to be shown by you risking your life in that manner. I already believed in the threat."

"Believing is not understanding, Marquis. The scarecrow *believes*. You *believe*. But you believe in the cross-God. But if you ask the scarecrow what he thinks about the *Ciinkwia*, he will say that they are made up, the stories of primitives. Of *unbelievers*."

"Yes. He would say that."

"He would believe in the *Ciinkwia* if he was brought face to face with them."

"Face to face . . . "

"We will go to the shore, Marquis. I will speak to the *Ciinkwia* and they will tell me more of what I must do."

"This is insane," Récher said, shifting from foot to foot, his steps making a squelching sound. "What did that savage say to you?" he whispered.

Red Vest was a dozen feet ahead, up a little hill. He turned; it was unclear whether he had heard the priest's comment.

"This demonstration is partially for your benefit, Père. He intends to show you something that you will refuse to believe."

"I am prepared to believe—"

"Oh, spare me, Père. You have trained for a lifetime in the finest institutions of Christian education and traveled thousands of leagues to this unknown frontier to save lost souls. You have not come here to open your eyes to new experiences and new . . . "

"New what?"

While they spoke, Red Vest had raised his hands toward the rain-filled sky, and a bright glow had begun to form around him.

"I hesitate to say," Montcalm said, not looking at the priest.

"What am I watching?"

The glow was forming into two human figures—one vaguely male, the other vaguely female, made of rain-spattered light.

"Red Vest called upon these beings and asked them to choose him to fight the *Maneto*. They honored his prayer."

"And when you say 'prayer,' Monsieur, you imply that he . . . worships these beings? He considers them gods?"

Montcalm did not answer.

"No," Récher said. "No. This cannot be. This shall not be."

"I don't think you have much choice in the matter." Montcalm felt rooted to the spot. The two figures had almost completely materialized now: a man and a woman, in traditional native attire. They were very tall. The woman held a staff shaped like a sheaf of wheat; the man had a bow over his shoulder and held a tomahawk.

"There is always free will."

"You must not interfere with this," Montcalm said. He placed a hand on Récher's cassock, but the priest shook him off.

Récher took his pectoral cross in his hand and walked slowly up the hill. From Montcalm's view the priest's steps were sluggish.

"Père, please—"

"*No*," the man-figure said, glancing at the woman-figure. "*Let him approach*."

Red Vest did not lower his hands but glanced over his shoulder. Montcalm saw an expression on the native's face he had never seen: terror and . . . something else.

Rapture.

"Exsurgat Deus et dissipentur inimici ejus," Récher said, gripping his cross and holding it in front of him. "Et fugiant qui oderunt eum a facie ejus. Sicut deficit fumus deficiant; sicut fluit cera a facie ignis, sic pereant peccatores a facie Dei."

Let God arise and let His enemies be scattered, and let them that hate Him flee from before His Face. As smoke vanisheth, so let them vanish away, as wax melteth before the fire, so let the wicked perish at the presence of God.

The two figures remained silent and motionless while the priest spoke the Latin phrases.

"How dare you?" Red Vest said, turning to face Récher. Rain streamed down his face, but his eyes were filled with the light that streamed from the two figures above him. "Your cross-God has no power against—"

"My God has power *everywhere*," Récher shouted, "and power against *everything*! Begone, creatures of Satan! I rebuke thee, I reject thee, I consign thee to the nethermost hell!"

Red Vest raised his hands, and they too glowed with the light from the *Ciinkwia*. "Say only a word, and I will do your will."

"You cannot hurt me," Récher said.

"And you cannot hurt us, white man's priest," the woman-figure said. *"We have slept for many seasons, but we have awakened. We extend our open hands to protect our people—and we close them to smite those who are our enemies."*

As they watched, the beautiful faces gradually changed—it was as if they shed their skin to reveal horrible grinning skulls, glowing with an inner light.

"Do you call yourself our enemy, Priest?"

"If you know me," Récher said, not lowering his cross, "you know the power of My Lord, and you know that I cannot turn away."

"It is time for you to turn back," the man-figure said. *"Beyond the place you call Montréal belongs to the tribes. We will summon the Maneto and Oniate, we will command the Stone Coats, and they will not trouble your people any further."*

"How can I know that you will keep your word, demons?"

"You doubt our word?" the man-figure answered. *"Your tribe has broken every promise ever given to our people. We have gazed into the future and seen other times—and your promises will be broken then as*

well. You have no *assurance from us, Priest. You must accept what we are telling you—and know this. As sun follows sun and moon follows moon, we only grow stronger."*

"Go," Red Vest said. He moved his palms toward each other, and as Montcalm watched, Récher began to move backward, one agonizing step at a time.

"Red Vest—" Montcalm said, but the native did not spare him a glance.

"Consider yourself fortunate that you leave here with your life, Marquis," Red Vest said. *"Go."*

They left Red Vest behind, not that there was a choice in the matter. He did not appear to have any interest in returning to *Soleil*; he had achieved some rapport with the luminous beings. Récher and Montcalm had no interest in remaining to debate the matter.

The priest was visibly shaken by the encounter—he gladly accepted a drink in Montcalm's cabin as *Soleil* stood at anchor off the shore. He positioned himself in a seat that gave no view of the glowing scene visible through the porthole.

"You were brave in that encounter, Père."

"I sounded more brave than I felt, Monsieur." He sipped at the drink. "During the confrontation I felt . . . I thought for a moment that I would be destroyed by the savage spirits. One more step—one wavering thought—and . . . " he visibly shuddered.

"Your faith is unshakable. Or so I would have thought."

"You must not speak of this to the archbishop, but I felt their power—and could scarcely feel my own. I felt small and weak, and sensed a mightiness that I was unable to combat."

"Nonsense. You rejected them with the power of the Holy Cross you bear."

"I would like to think so, but I don't really believe it. I dismissed all thoughts from my mind in the moment. But there was a presence, one I have never felt, not in the most consecrated holy place I have ever visited."

"What sort of presence?"

"A *divine* presence, Monsieur. I think . . . I think we have encountered a pair of gods. My faith protected me at that moment, but I am not sure it would do so again."

"You underestimate your fortitude, my friend. This is merely a test, and you passed it."

"I suppose you are right."

Récher did not continue the thought; he smiled faintly and sipped again at the drink. But Montcalm, accustomed to be a leader of men, saw the tremor in his hands and the fear in his eyes and knew that the priest did not believe it to be true.

Chapter 17

This is all the world there is now

New France

"I would prefer to wait until the marquis returns from upriver, Governor," Lévis had said; but Vaudreuil had not seemed interested in that line of argument. Indeed, the chevalier was reasonably certain that the governor of New France was giving him the order precisely because Montcalm was not in Québec to countermand it.

Instead, Vaudreuil had insisted: "There is no time for delay, Chevalier. You and a company of soldiers—of your choice" he said, as if he was according Lévis some great honor by giving him discretion—"will embark at once, and determine just what sort of foolishness caused His Majesty's men to flee their duty at Fort Carillon."

"Shall I take some of those who did so?"

"I daresay they would be the most unreliable. Of course, I am not a military man, so perhaps your judgment in this matter is better than my own."

Perhaps your judgment . . . Lévis had felt like striking the governor with his fist but had thought better of it.

Instead he had given a salute and departed the Intendant's Palace, to assemble his company and to locate *couriers de bois* who could transport them across Lac St. Sacrement to the fortress that had been abandoned a few weeks earlier.

He took a dozen of the hardiest, most stalwart-looking soldiers who had come back to Québec to tell of the apparitions at Carillon. Only a portion of the garrison had even come to Québec—at least half of the men had scattered elsewhere—and Lévis' choices weren't from the best; but he wanted to have some people who had experienced what they were about to see.

Spring in New France is a tug of war. Nature wants to display her riches and beauties everywhere, while the cold hand of winter wants to strike them down. In the best of circumstances it becomes an uneasy truce; cool, crisp sunny days and chilling, frost-filled nights taking their turn until well past the solstice time. Lévis' company dressed for the cold: there was no particular need for crisp parade uniforms or ceremonial attire. Instead they dressed like their guides—homespun and buckskin, fur vests and stout boots. Anyone observing the group would likely not take them for soldiers in service to the king of France.

It took ten days overland to reach the head of the lake, carrying their *bateaux* with them as they moved through the forest. Lévis was amazed at how the trackless wilderness yielded to the knowledge and experience of the *couriers de bois*, following trails and paths that he never would have been able to find. Still, when they emerged from the woods and put their boats in the water at the north end of Lac-Champlain, all of them breathed a sigh of relief.

On the first night ashore, Lévis sat with his adjutant, a young officer named Olivier D'Egremont who had come to New France the previous year. His was a typical story—third son of a minor nobleman, with no land or title waiting for him in the home country, obtaining a commission and service in North America as a way to make his own fortune.

"This is a beautiful country, Monsieur," D'Egremont said, leaning back against the bole of a great old tree at the corner of their camp.

"Isn't it? A shame that we may have to give it over to the English."

"Why?"

"I didn't think I needed to explain why. There are ten Englishmen for each Frenchman, D'Egremont. They have control of the seas, and are finally—*finally!*—ready to make the commitment to fight us here on land. The loss of Louisbourg was just the beginning—there is more ahead."

"Then what is this about?"

Lévis smiled. "Which 'this'?"

"This expedition, Monsieur. If we are bound to lose, why bother to reoccupy Carillon? Especially given the stories . . . "

"What have you heard?"

"I . . . " D'Egremont smiled. "I have been listening to the men who left Carillon and came to Québec. They have some interesting stories."

"They haven't spoken a word to me. They—they scarcely meet my eyes, to be honest."

"They are ashamed, Monsieur, and it is hard to blame them, since they abandoned their post. But it is also hard to blame them for having done so in the first place."

"There was talk of ghosts. What do you make of that?"

"I am not a father, Monsieur, but I am an uncle, and I have watched my older brothers and their wives in dealing with their children. When there is a dispute among them, they ask each to tell their story in private—and then the adults compare what is said. I would believe that much of what our men say is a fabrication, except that each of them tells the same story: what they heard, what they saw.

"What I don't understand is how this could possibly be happening. There are folk tales of ghosts—but this seems more than that, and more frightening than that. What do *you* make of this?"

"Something has happened, D'Egremont. The marquis thinks that it might have to do with the comet, which has now disappeared from the sky; but that does not truly explain how there could be ghosts in the woods and monsters in the lakes. I confess that I am at a loss. I will be interested in hearing what the marquis has learned when he returns."

"And when we return."

"That depends on what we find."

"Do you have any idea what it might be?"

"I hesitate to speculate. But I know that the governor would like us to find nothing, and that seems unlikely."

Approaching Fort Carillon and the town below it brought back memories for Lévis. The previous summer had been a great French victory in which he had taken part, commanding one flank against the British army that had come up to besiege the fort—but it was more a result of the needless slaughter of the enemy's troops, hurled against the bastion without even the benefit of artillery. As a Frenchman, he could rightfully thank God for a stroke of fortune that halted the enemy's threatened advance toward the heart of New France. But as a soldier, he decried the loss of life among the brave soldiers ordered to their deaths by an incompetent general.

The fort was still there; the banner of His Most Christian Majesty still flew over it. But from his vantage, at the front of one of the lead *bateaux,* Lévis could see that the lower town was lifeless—indeed, it was shrouded in a low-hanging mist that was a stark contrast to the sunny vista and crisp air out on the surface of the lake.

And in the mist, there were human figures moving to and fro, and even at a distance they could hear the occasional skirl of the Highland bagpipes, providing an additional eerie aspect to the scene.

He had two of the Carillon veterans in his boat, and though they sat upright and rigid he could see the terror in their eyes. The scene troubled him as well, but Lévis knew that he could show none of it; he was the commander and, as such, could show no fear.

Still, it was hard to keep a calm face as his *bateau* came close to the dock where three ghostly figures stood, awaiting the boat's arrival. The figures were substantial, but not completely opaque: the town's buildings could be seen behind and through them. All wore the distinctive Highland dress, and each bore the evidence of having sustained terrible wounds. One had a face with a gaping hole— probably a musket-ball discharged at close range; the other had a horrible chest wound, visible through his tunic; and the leader had a round bullet-hole directly above his left temple—the shot that had felled him.

Before Lévis' boat bumped up against the dock, the leader lifted his left hand; his right arm hung at his side, the sleeve empty below the elbow. A breeze kicked up at just that moment, blowing into the faces of the Frenchmen.

"This is no longer your place," the man said in English, of which Lévis had a good command, unlike most of the men who accompanied him. "Turn back, while you are still able."

"I have not come this far to turn back," Lévis replied. "I am François de Gaston, Chevalier de Lévis, and I am here in the name of the governor and intendant of New France, and His Most Christian Majesty Louis, King of France."

"I know who you are," the ghost replied. "My name is Major Duncan Campbell. Your men killed me and mine here, in this place, last summer. I saw you on the battlements, on the French right flank. You were a prominent target," he added, touching the bullet-wound on his temple. "But your marksmen were more proficient than ours."

"I am unaccustomed to speaking to dead men," Lévis answered. "Major Campbell, your time on this earth is done. You . . . died as a soldier, in service to king and country; as a fellow brother of the sword, I honor your sacrifice. But you must yield to the living."

"And why should I do that?"

Lévis was unsure how to answer. "I ask in return," he said at last, "why your spirit is unquiet."

"Abercromby," Campbell said, and Lévis—and the others in the French boats—heard the name echoed, over and over, from out of the mists. "*Abercromby*. The general who ordered us to our deaths. We seek our revenge against him. Bring him to us, Chevalier, and we shall retire to the Beyond and give you back this cursed place, for all that it does you good."

"Abercromby."

"Aye. Tell the British commanders that if he does not come to us, we will come to him, and nothing shall stop us: not wall, nor musket, nor cannon."

"What about an ocean? We understand that General Abercromby was recalled to England. He is not here any longer, Major Campbell. It is not possible for you to exact your personal revenge here in the New World."

The expression on the face of the shade of Major Duncan Campbell did not change as he said, "Abercromby is gone."

"Back to England. Unless you are prepared to cross the ocean—"

"That is not possible, Chevalier. That route is closed."

"What do you mean?"

"This is all the world there is now, Frenchman. You should go back to your land and tell your governor and intendant that news."

"This land is our land as well."

"No, Chevalier. It is not. This land belongs to *us*. The unquiet spirits of those who died here, killed by the cruelty and incompetence of a *Sassenach* general who sent the Highlanders against your fortress. But it is your fortress no longer."

"My governor will not welcome this news."

"I have no dispute with you, Chevalier. But do not doubt that I— and my many, many countrymen—will fight you if you come ashore. We can hurt you . . . but we are beyond hurt.

"But . . . " Campbell looked aside at his two companions, then back at the Frenchmen. "But you are a fellow soldier, and a man of honor. You ceased to be an enemy when I ceased to draw breath. Out of respect, we will permit you to go safely to the fortress above and take down your flag. You can take that back to your governor and explain to him how you came by it. But you may not reinvest Carillon—that the Indians call Ticonderoga—nor can the English, and neither can the natives. As long as we remain in this world, this place remains ours."

"You . . . will guarantee my safety."

"Yes. You only. Your soldiers remain on their boats."

"I would like to take my aide," Lévis said, gesturing toward D'Egremont, who stood in a *bateau* just a few feet from the dock.

Campbell hesitated for a moment and then said, "Agreed. But you will go up to the fort and return by nightfall; after that I cannot speak for the other Highlanders. Their pain and resentment run deep, and they may not forbear by night what is ordered by day."

Lévis and D'Egremont walked in silence through the deserted lower town; later Lévis would remember it as the strangest, most eerie experience of his life. Ghostly figures watched their progress, sometimes quiet, sometimes murmuring something inarticulate or indistinguishable. The bagpipe sounds faded in and out as they walked up to the open gate to the fortress proper.

When they came into the *place des armes*, where no Highlander was in sight, Lévis turned to D'Egremont.

"You have some command of English."

"I had a tutor," the young man said. "He taught me dancing and English. Beastly language, but my father thought it might come in useful."

"And so it has. How much did you understand of my conversation?"

"Enough to make my knees shake, Monsieur. But I am here."

"Good man." Lévis squinted at the sky; the sun was visible from here, clear of the mists below, and it stood at midafternoon. He did not want to stay much longer than necessary, but there was at least time to take a look around.

"Are you going to take the flag and return?"

"I think that I am left with no other choice, D'Egremont. Even if I believed that there was anything that could damage or destroy ghosts, I don't think most of the men would stand and fight."

"Why did you bring me along, Monsieur?"

"I wanted at least one other person to see whatever I saw, to corroborate my story. It will be difficult enough for them to believe as it is. Come on, then. Let's get the flag down and make our way back."

On the highest bastion of Fort Carillon, with all of Lake Champlain and the vista of the New York wilderness spread out before them, the two French officers slowly lowered the flag that had flown over the fortress since it had been erected a handful of years earlier. When it came into their hands, they carefully and respectfully folded it in the correct manner, so that it was a small blue triangular bundle with the Bourbon *fleur-de-lys* marching across it in gold.

"We will be the last of His Majesty's soldiers to take in this view, Monsieur," D'Egremont said, leaning on the battlement in front of him.

Lévis was not sure he could see that deeply into the future. Instead of answering his young aide, he merely took in the view, wondering about what Campbell had said.

This is all the world there is now, Frenchman.

Looking down at the bundle he held in his hands, he tried to imagine what that meant.

Part III: Concentration

May, 1759

It is not so easy for a bellicose nation to turn its back upon war.
—Sir Charles Saunders, *Memoirs*, 1778

Chapter 18

Every place will have its haunted past

New York

George Baker wanted to pace. It was *his* quarterdeck, damn it, and it was one of the few places aboard *Magnanime* that he actually *could* walk any distance without exchanging salutes, ducking his head or running into something: rank had its privileges.

But it would not do to turn his back on a Prince of the Blood, even if he was of an inferior naval rank. That was especially true when he was asking permission for something that, truthfully, he could have chosen to do without Baker's consent.

"You don't need my permission, Your Highness."

"I know that, Captain. But it seems inappropriate for an officer and gentleman to choose a course without at least consulting his senior."

"My seniority is tenuous at best, especially now."

"I actually would have thought the opposite." The young man allowed himself a slight smile. "If England is now no longer part of the world we occupy, I don't see why we should be treated any differently. Of course, what I want to do flies in the face of that pragmatism."

"I don't think General Amherst will have any hesitation in dealing with you as befits your rank, Your Highness. Whether England is a few weeks' or a few years' sail away, you are a prince of the realm—and that counts for a great deal."

"He is more than twice my age, Captain Baker. He was a soldier with my grandfather when I was soiling my small-clothes. What's more, his country *needs* him."

"Your country needs *you* as well, Prince. In fact, it needs you very much—and I am very concerned that you might be exposed to unnecessary danger."

"From General Amherst?"

"No, no—good God, not from the general. But these are the colonies. Untamed lands, unruly places. We were told what is going on in Massachusetts-Bay as a result of the event, but who knows what awaits us in New York?"

"Salem is a singular case—the witch-trial events linger on—"

"I beg your pardon, Your Highness, but *every place* will have its haunted past. New York had a revolt against His Majesty's Government at about the same time as the witch trials: a man named Leisler led it. He was executed for treason. And less than twenty years ago, about the time Your Highness was learning to walk, New York suffered a violent slave revolt. What if the—what if the event has stirred up memories from those events? Who knows what awaits us in New York? I am hesitant that Your Highness' person should be subjected to such risks."

"So I am to be kept safely aboard *Magnanime*, away from all danger? How do you propose to carry that out, Captain? It is neither practical nor sensible."

Baker did not answer. He resisted the temptation to turn and pace, but instead stared past Prince Edward out at sea, where the southern coast of Long Island lay against the horizon.

"I beg your pardon, Captain," the prince said. "It is improper for me to speak thus to my commanding officer."

Baker couldn't decide what made him more uncomfortable, the junior officer's tone or the prince's apology.

"As an officer under my command, General Amherst has no reason to take your counsel—or, indeed, even to receive you. But as Prince Edward of England, he cannot fail to do so. As it is necessary for him to be impressed with the earnest of our situation, you are much more important in the latter role than in the former.

"I grant permission, of course," he said. "And while I would prefer that you and General Wolfe meet with General Amherst aboard *Magnanime* for your own safety, I agree that since you are my junior officer, you could not represent the Crown properly without going ashore."

"Thank you, sir."

"Don't thank me for that, Highness. From what little I know of General Amherst, he will not take kindly to being *summoned*."

If it had been up to him—as he had said at various times, in the appropriate company—Jeffery Amherst would rather have been holding a plough at his family's estate at Riverhead than receive all the honors that had been given him in the New World.

By the limited standards of America, New York was fine enough. One of the great "cities," along with Philadelphia, Boston and Charles Town, but a world away from London or even Bristol or York. It was scarcely more than a town, compared to Paris or Madrid or even Edinburgh. But it was his headquarters; he had spent the winter here, trying to pick up the shattered pieces of the 1758 campaign, which—other than their triumph in the Maritimes—had been an utter disaster. He had come to that conclusion after touring the battlefield near the French fort of Carillon the previous October; Abercromby had made a hash of what should have been a straightforward campaign—he had not only failed to take the key strongpoint, he had wasted good, capable men in doing it. Scots, admittedly, not the most reliable sons of the Empire, but hard, veteran soldiers all the same.

Amherst had reviewed the troops who remained at Halifax and then returned here to New York to prepare for the coming campaign, now confirmed as commander in chief of His Majesty's Forces in North America. There had been nothing for it but to wait for reinforcement; though instead of good old Edward Boscawen, the Admiralty had informed him that the new expedition would be led by Admiral Saunders . . . and would include James Wolfe, who had sailed back to England in late summer in what Amherst could only describe as a *huff*.

And now . . . word had come from Halifax, and reports had arrived from sea, indicating that *something* had happened—some terrible storm, or irruption, or—a variety of other things that Amherst discounted as seamen's imagination. There were apparently no reinforcements for his planned campaign up the Hudson River, and none to force their way up the Saint Lawrence toward Québec. He was expecting to get an accurate report from Wolfe. What he was not expecting was a demand (disguised as a "request") to present himself to a young prince who was part of the Halifax expedition.

There was no alternative but to appear in his best dress uniform and to offer his politest bow and sharpest salute. And then there would be a more *detailed* discussion.

Amherst and his staff were waiting as the carriage halted outside Fort George. A dress-uniformed lieutenant opened the door and held it as Prince Edward and General James Wolfe disembarked. Salutes were exchanged, and the two visitors turned toward the gate of the fort. Two staff officers stepped down to the cobbles on their own.

To Amherst, the prince looked composed and calm, showing considerable dignity for a young man his age. Wolfe's angular face was tilted, his nose pointed upward as if he was sniffing the New York air. It seemed almost rude—about what he would have expected from the younger officer.

The visitors approached and the prince and general offered Amherst smart salutes.

"Your Royal Highness," Amherst said. "You honor us with your visit." And to Wolfe, he nodded and said, "General."

Wolfe looked ready to respond, but wisely waited for the prince to speak.

"I wish we were here under more auspicious circumstances, General Amherst," Prince Edward said. "General Wolfe and I are eager to apprise you of current events." He paused and looked from Wolfe to Amherst. "But perhaps first . . . one of your subordinates could give me a brief tour of this excellent fort."

Amherst took a moment to respond, then beckoned to the lieutenant who had received the carriage. "Show His Highness our disposition, if you please," he ordered, which shortly left him alone with Wolfe.

"General," Wolfe said.

"General," Amherst answered. "I suppose I should congratulate you on your advancement."

"Does it trouble you, sir?"

"Does it matter whether it troubles me or not? I confess to being surprised, Wolfe. I would have thought that your rather abrupt attitude regarding my strategic decisions would have kept you from being considered for *any* sort of advancement."

"Apparently others disagree," Wolfe sniffed. "But in any case, it hardly matters now. We had our chance to defeat the French last summer, General, and that was our last opportunity. The world is fundamentally changed now."

"I don't take your meaning."

Wolfe explained, in the simplest terms he could manage, what they had seen and heard since the crossing of the Atlantic several weeks earlier, including their experience aboard *Neptune* and the accounts given by the men of *Magnanime*. It was given in a tone that stopped just short of insolence; but Amherst listened intently. Wolfe was headstrong, impetuous and dismissive of those with whom he had disputes, but he was also intelligent, brave and had no reason whatsoever to dissemble.

"This is . . . very disturbing news," Amherst said at last. "An extended breach of contact with home will certainly affect our ability to defeat the enemy."

"By which you mean the French."

"Of course. Who else do you consider the enemy, General? Aren't we here in America to fight the French?"

"Yes, of course. But I don't know how we should be expected to proceed. We assumed that this year we would have several thousand troops to prosecute the war—here in New York, in the Maritimes, and wherever else. Those men are *gone*. They are either beyond the new boundary or have drowned in the Atlantic. Whatever we do, whatever we wish to do, will have to be done without them."

"And what, if anything, do you advise?"

"I think we have two choices, sir. We either use all of our forces to prosecute the campaign right away. After all, the French will be as isolated as we are, and we have the advantage of numbers."

"And the second alternative?"

"Though it pains me to say it, General Amherst, the other choice is to seek an armistice."

"Our king has not authorized us to negotiate anything of the sort."

"Our king . . . " Wolfe looked away toward Prince Edward, who was carefully examining a field piece in the company of a young lieutenant. "General Amherst, from the time the event occurred, I believe that the mantle of kingship descended upon that young man. We may never see our sovereign again—but in the meanwhile, we have someone who may have to take his place."

✣ ✣ ✣

If Amherst were of a different character, it might have rankled him to think that Wolfe was right about the stark choice presented by the events the younger man had described. But personal animus, he knew, must always bow before pragmatic necessity.

With staff assembled and at least some of the stiff parade-ground uniform dispensed with, he outlined the situation in detail for Prince Edward.

"We have half a thousand Blues from New Jersey, and about a quarter of the promised five thousand provincials from Pennsylvania. I would have none of them, of course, if I had not threatened to withdraw garrisons from their Ohio forts—the Quakers would rather stand by and watch their colony be overrun than take a musket in their hands and defend their hearth.

"In addition, there are nearly two thousand New Yorkers, with another thousand currently encamped near Albany, and a thousand men from Connecticut. The promised troops from Massachusetts have not arrived. I expect that the events in Salem you describe—" Amherst gave the slightest of nods to Wolfe—"have delayed, or possibly even prevented, their departure."

"What about regulars, General?" the prince asked.

"The 17th, 27th, 53rd and 55th are at Albany, along with some artillery and rangers."

"Rangers?"

"Irregular forces, Your Highness," Amherst replied. "Under the command of Major Rogers, an . . . unusually skilled woodsman. They are used for scouting and special missions. Invaluable man, though his methods are somewhat unorthodox."

Wolfe looked uncomfortable at the idea—whether it was due to the described method of warfare, or the fact that the man was a provincial, Amherst wasn't sure. Wolfe had made some extremely uncharitable observations about Americans during the previous summer's campaign.

He'd best get used to them, Amherst thought. *They are our countrymen and neighbors now.*

"In any case," Amherst continued, "I do not know when these forces will be ready to embark. My supplies are not yet prepared, and I do not have most of my American troops in camp."

"If I may ask," Wolfe said archly, "what is your best estimate of an embarkation date?"

"Mid-June, perhaps."

"That is nearly two months from now," Prince Edward said quietly. "With respect, General, many things may have changed by then."

"With respect, Highness," Amherst answered, "if General Wolfe's conjectures and observations as well as your own portray the situation correctly, then this is the only army I am likely to have. As he has pointed out to me, the circumstances of our isolation apply equally to the enemy. There is no reason to deploy our forces prematurely or to act peremptorily.

"Carillon, and its garrison, will still be there whenever we arrive to besiege it. I have every intention of meeting it with adequate force and proper supplies and accomplish my task with deliberation, instead of failing it with unnecessary haste as my predecessor clearly did. That was the command of my king, and I will fulfill it . . . unless ordered otherwise."

There was a long pause, and Amherst focused his attention on the royal prince seated before him. When he finished speaking, Edward was looking intently at the map of the Hudson Valley; but as the room remained quiet, he looked up at Amherst, meeting him gaze for gaze.

"I think it would be improper to change those orders at this time, General," the prince said at last.

Yet he does not abdicate the authority to do so in the future, Amherst thought. *Interesting.*

"What is the situation of the troops at Albany, General?" Wolfe asked.

"I only know what my dispatches tell me," Amherst answered. "Perhaps you might wish to inspect their disposition yourself."

"Are you proposing to send me to Albany, sir?"

"It is within my authority, sir," Amherst snapped back. "But as you may in some way be obliged to His Highness, I would be more inclined to make it a request. I am sure we would both benefit from the direct observation of a trained military man."

Wolfe appeared to be ready with a response, but Prince Edward held up his hand.

"I beg your pardon," he said slowly and deliberately, not taking his eyes from Amherst. "As your expected deployment date is several weeks hence, General, I would assume that it would be possible to travel to Albany and back in the interim and obtain first-person intelligence. Am I correct? I do not have more than a very . . . superficial knowledge of this country's geography. Every stretch of land seems unutterably vast."

"It is a week's journey by boat up the river, now that spring has come," Amherst said. "Perhaps five days' ride, though that might be strenuous. A hundred and fifty miles."

"I assume one man on horseback could make better time than that," Wolfe said.

"Two men," the prince said, placing his hand on his breast.

"*More* than two men," Amherst said, before Wolfe had a chance to reply. "If His Highness is determined to go by horse or riverboat to Albany, he will be accompanied by a troop of soldiers."

"That will slow the trip down considerably," Wolfe said. "General—"

"I brook no disagreement. A prince of the House of Hanover traveling with only one companion through the wilds of the Colony of New York? Preposterous."

"The . . . 'wilds of the Colony of New York,' General? This land was settled more than a century ago. Surely—"

"It does not matter, Wolfe. We are at war; the wild part of the colony commences as soon as you pass beyond the Haarlem village. Your Highness says he does not understand the vastness of America? Well, here it is—on display, not a half-hour's ride from where we sit.

"So, *surely not*, Wolfe. No royal person will be traveling anywhere, including within the boundaries of this city, unless he is escorted in a manner that befits his station. Am I understood?"

In the end, it was only two dozen men from the 40th, which had in part accompanied the prince to New York, who were detailed to ride with him and General Wolfe to Albany. It was less than Amherst wanted to send; he knew that Wolfe was impetuous, and eager to be in action—but he recognized the need for the group to move quickly and conceded.

Still, as they rode away from New York the following morning, a fifer playing "God Save the King," Amherst felt a palpable dread.

Chapter 19

It is no place to go

Albany

To most residents of the colony of New York, "Albany" meant "the rest of the colony"—everything upriver from Manhattan, the great wilderness where trappers caught beavers and savage Indians lurked with their scalping-knives. The troopers of the 40th were on edge during the entire journey upcountry, but Prince Edward was welcomed by gentleman farmers—*patroons*, in the half-Dutch half-English parlance that prevailed out in the country—and met no trappers (or knife-wielding Indians) during the entire journey.

Still, it was clear that rumor of his travels ran ahead of him at unheard-of speed, so that by the time they came upon Albany town—a compact settlement on the left bank of the Hudson River—his arrival was expected. On the south boundary of the town, near the gates of a spacious plantation that spanned a wide, well-maintained bridge, there was a banner bearing the royal coat-of-arms. A delegation of city fathers led by a substantial man of middle years was waiting for the dignitary and his entourage when they approached.

Wolfe was strongly in favor of nodding and riding on, but Prince Edward was having none of that; he raised his hand and the troop halted. The portly man stepped forward an offered what to Wolfe seemed to be an insufficient bow, and then spoke before the prince did—both of which made Wolfe want to swat him with the flat of his sword.

"Your Highness," the man said in accented English, "permit me to present myself. I am Jacob Van Schaick, the sheriff of this county. We are honored and pleased to welcome you to Albany city."

The young prince did not respond in a way that suggested that the provincial insulted him; instead, he was extremely cordial.

"You honor me with your welcome, *Mynheer* Von Schaick." The Dutch title made the portly man smile, making Wolfe want to swat him a second time. "I am not sure what role the sheriff fills here in America, but I am sure that you must be a person of some stature to be chosen to lead those sent out to meet me. Is the entire—city—in your charge?"

"Oh, no, no indeed," the man answered. "Within Albany itself I am an alderman—a subordinate in charge of one of the city's wards—"

"I know what an alderman is, *Mynheer*. Pray continue."

"Ah. Yes. Of course, your Highness does." He gathered himself and continued. "But I assure you that, while a subordinate, I am fully qualified to serve as an emissary of the proper station to receive Your Highness and his . . . servants."

As Wolfe bristled but remained silent, Prince Edward turned slightly toward him and said, "This is General James Wolfe, *Mynheer* Von Schaick. His heroic action at Louisbourg last summer helped secure that fortress for our King. He will be inspecting the troops here; I am sure that you will show him all of the courtesies—and *respect*"—his voice acquired a serious, hard edge that the alderman clearly noticed—"that his rank and station deserves."

"Of course, Your Highness." Without another word, Von Schaick bowed as he retreated, then mounted his own horse. He and the others who had accompanied him—and who remained unintroduced—led Prince Edward and General Wolfe into Albany.

Though bigger than Halifax, Albany did not impress Wolfe as anything more than a frontier settlement. It was a trifle less grimy than he would have expected, as a place where fur traders and trappers met to do business; perhaps that was due to the nominally Dutch nature of the place. The streets were clean, and the houses were neat. Troops were deployed on the bluffs to the west of the town, along one of the creeks that flowed into it. After paying their respects to Von Schaick's household—his wife Catharina and his four young children, as well as his older brother Sybrant (another alderman), Sybrant's wife, and six other young ones—and a handful of cousins and "family members" who clearly wanted a glance at a royal prince—they were able to make their way to the encampment.

Prince Edward and General Wolfe were escorted at once to the tent of the commanding officer, Brigadier-General John Prideaux. He welcomed them politely but cordially, showing little of the awe that the alderman of Albany had possessed. He was a tall, plain man, about the same age as Amherst, who seemed comfortable in his uniform—a true veteran soldier.

Edward noted that, like Amherst, Prideaux was acquainted with Wolfe.

"Dettingen," Prideaux explained, when the three men were seated, and the prince remarked upon it. "Young Wolfe here and I were both on the battlefield with His Royal Highness that day. And, I think, we both acquitted ourselves with honor."

"I agree," Wolfe said. "Though General Prideaux was of a somewhat higher rank and, therefore, with greater responsibility."

"I was an adjutant, nothing more. But we'll have greater things ahead of us, I hope," Prideaux noted. "Though . . . I am somewhat disturbed by reports I have had from our rangers."

"What sort of reports?"

"I think it would be better that you have that directly," Prideaux answered. "I've taken the liberty of sending for—" he stopped and looked up at a figure who had appeared in the doorway of his field tent. "Ah, and here he is. Tell me, Major Rogers, did the sentry admit you, or did you just sneak past him?"

"I am responding to your orders, General," the man answered. His broad drawl made him out to be an American, though Wolfe could not place him. Rogers was a tall, spare figure, dressed in something that only approximated a uniform; it was clothing better suited to wilderness travel than a parade ground, and it showed signs of frequent, and hard, use. He gave a salute to Prideaux and then to Wolfe and sketched a bow to the prince.

"I have chosen to forbear discussion of your report, Major Rogers," Prideaux said. "I thought it would be more informative coming directly from you."

Rogers smiled slightly; the expression furrowed his forehead, making obvious a scar that creased it. At a gesture from Prideaux he took a seat on an upright crate.

"Your Highness will accept my apology for the mode of presentation," Rogers began. "I am unaccustomed to . . . a royal audience."

"I am sure it will be informative, Major. Please do proceed."

"As your Highness may be aware," he began, "my command has been given the responsibility for scouting and investigating for His Majesty's forces here in the country. We undertake such missions as might be needed—intelligence and sabotage, whatever the situation requires. We are the army's eyes and ears—and, occasionally, hands.

"Three weeks ago, at the orders of General Prideaux, I took a company of rangers north along Lake George to scout the situation at Fort Carillon, the French fortress that General Abercromby tried, and failed, to take last summer. He informed me that he was particularly interested in the disposition of French troops, and the status of the artillery.

"I would not trouble Your Highness with the particulars of our journey, or of the precautions and procedures we employ in the wilderness. Suffice it to say that, as in the past, we were able to approach very closely."

"A few winters ago," Prideaux said, "I hear that rangers tossed grenades by hand over the walls of Carillon and set their storehouses afire."

"Aye, we managed that," Rogers said, and the grin came back for a moment. "These days we have somewhat more dangerous opponents in the field. But that is neither here nor there; we still have, as we say in New Hampshire, a few tricks up our sleeve. With a small troop we were able to cross Lake George, hide our boats and make our way through the woods to a favorable vantage that overlooked the French fortress—and we beheld a remarkable sight."

"Don't keep us waiting, man," Wolfe said. "What did you see?"

"The fort was completely abandoned, General. Even the flag had been taken down."

"The French have retreated?"

"It seems so. But there's more, sir. Among the abandoned works—and below on the shore—figures were moving about. Not Frenchmen . . . but rather Scotsmen. I spied their distinctive costume and I heard the occasional skirl of their bagpipes."

"Scotsmen? What were they doing there?"

"It was hard to tell. You see, General, they were not living beings, but rather shades—phantasms. They were transparent, and either ignorant of, or indifferent to, our presence."

Prideaux looked from Prince Edward to General Wolfe. "I realize, gentlemen, that this report is somewhat hard to believe or accept—"

"You might be surprised what we might believe," the prince said. "We have seen some extraordinary things in the last several weeks. The idea that ghosts might have gathered around Fort Carillon certainly ranks with them. But I am moved to ask—if there are ghosts, why Scotsmen?"

Prideaux' face darkened. "That is due to the results of the battle fought over the fortress a year ago. Our forces were led by General James Abercromby, since recalled by our king to England. He chose to send infantry in a direct frontal assault against the abatis, where more than five hundred died and nearly three times that number were wounded.

"Our Indian allies suggest that the Highlanders, unlike English soldiers, have some attachment to the ground where they were slain; that their . . . souls are unquiet, and will not rest until they revenge themselves for the loss of life."

The men sat quietly for some time, until at last Wolfe said, "Rubbish."

"I beg your pardon?" Prideaux said. "What do you mean, sir?"

"It seems to me that if this is true—and I only give it the most nominal credence—that these Scottish ghosts, if such they be, have done a signal service to their king. They have scared off the French. I think it only remains to us to march up and occupy the fort."

"I am loath to disagree with you, General," Rogers said. "But that is no place to be. I am not certain that anyone should go there."

"Nonsense. It is a military strongpoint, and a key place to secure in our movement north. We can't leave it to the French."

"According to native scouts," Rogers said, "the French sent an expedition there some days ago and did not reoccupy the place. I don't think it belongs to them anymore."

"Then to whom does it belong?"

"It belongs to the ghosts of the Highlanders," Rogers said. "And only to them."

✣ ✣ ✣

When Rogers had departed, Prince Edward was silent for a time and then said, "I think our course is clear."

"Obviously General Amherst will have to be informed," Wolfe said.

"Yes, of course. But first I have to speak with these Highlanders."

Prideaux and Wolfe reacted almost at once, both objecting vehemently. Prideaux yielded to Wolfe, who finally said, "Highness, that's out of the question. There is no question that it is far too dangerous."

"I agree," Prideaux said. "Rogers stated it succinctly: that is no place to go."

"I will not be gainsaid," Edward said. "I am not subject to your orders, General Wolfe, nor to yours, General Prideaux."

"But you are the only person of royal blood on this continent," Wolfe answered. "Your safety is my concern, General Amherst made that abundantly clear. He did not wish to have you journey as far as Albany, and I am sure would forbid any interaction with—"

"With *ghosts*," Edward said. "Ghosts of loyal men who died serving crown and country. Tell me, General Wolfe; why are they there at all?"

"The comet, I suppose."

"The comet. Of course. But why are *they* there? Because they are unquiet. They feel that their lives were given needlessly, and they are unsatisfied."

"As opposed to merely being dead," Prideaux said. "This is beyond my ken, Highness, and I would think it is beyond yours as well. I understand the desire, perhaps even the need, to address these . . . ghosts . . . but I think General Wolfe is correct. If it must be done, then go when the army is with you, when General Amherst advances up the valley. There is no reason to do it now."

"I would think time is of the essence," Edward replied.

"I must disagree with Your Highness there," Prideaux said. "If they are indeed unquiet spirits, they are the shades of men who died—tragically—*a year ago*. A few months along, they will still be there, and still unquiet. In the meanwhile, they appear to have frightened the French away. This is intelligence best suited for General Amherst's ears.

"Until then, it is my advice that you simply let them be."

Chapter 20

We are at war

Jamaica

Namur had a sounding chart of Kingston harbor, courtesy of—*well,* Boscawen thought as he examined it, *with the grudging generosity of*—Governor Pinfold. It was scarcely adequate, more landsman's decorative cartography than a sailor's chart, but it at least gave some notations for soundings and the shoals near the entrance.

Kingston itself was protected from the open sea by a long finger of land called the "Palisadoes," at the end of which lay the ruins of Port Royal—a notorious pirate haven that had been destroyed by an earthquake more than half a century earlier. According to the chart there were emplacements and forts that protected the narrow strait leading into the harbor proper. When the topman first sighted the rocky peaks on the west side of the island, Boscawen ordered the display of the royal standard and his admiral's pennon. In wartime, there was no reason to risk any sort of misunderstanding.

He expected to find the island on guard, prepared for its part in the war. What he did not expect was that war, of a sort, had already come.

At minimum sail, *Namur* slowly made its way toward the port side of the entrance, keeping distance from the sandy shoals around the ruins of Port Royal. With his glass, Boscawen could make out the guns on the high ground (labeled "Twelve Apostles" on his map); but to his surprise, instead of being positioned toward open ocean and a potential attacker, they had been oriented to overlook the inner harbor. His attention to the view was sufficient that he did not notice someone beside him until there was a tug on his sleeve—which surprised him and almost caused him to drop his glass.

He was ready to deliver a few choice angry words, but found himself face to face with Mademoiselle LaGèndiere, who had intruded on his quarterdeck. Several feet away he saw a red-faced sentry, who no doubt had made some attempt to prevent her but with little effect.

Boscawen gathered himself, setting his anger aside, and offered a slight bow and inclined his head. "Mademoiselle. What brings you to my quarterdeck?" He gave her the slightest of smiles, and then communicated with the sentry with a glare that was intended to make a young man quake in his boots.

"What land are we approaching, Monsieur Admiral?"

"We are in sight of the island of Jamaica, Mademoiselle."

"Which is . . . an English colony, yes?"

"For a century or so, Mademoiselle. If there is nothing further—" he began to turn away, but she plucked at his sleeve, and he turned again to her.

She gazed at him with an intensity he could not imagine that a woman of her tender years could possess. Then; from an inner pocket of her apron, she drew the unusual instrument that she and Messier had brought aboard—the device that, for some reason, had pointed its contents steadily at *him*. Except now it did not incline that way: it was pointed forward, toward *Namur's* bow end—whether it now targeted some other person or thing he was unable to tell.

"I thought you should see this," she said. "The instrument's orientation has changed."

"It no longer finds me of interest?" Boscawen asked, not sure quite what to say.

"It now points toward our destination," Mademoiselle LaGèndiere said. "It seems as if this place is of particular esoteric interest."

"I confess," Boscawen said, "I do not know quite what that means. Does it portend danger, like a—a *kraken*—or some such?"

"I do not know, Admiral."

"Then I do not know what use it is to me. I thank you for conveying this information to me, Mademoiselle; but I must ask your pardon, for I have many things to do."

This time he did turn away, and she did not pluck at his sleeve. He walked toward the aft end of the quarterdeck, raised his glass again toward the Twelve Apostles, and left her standing alone, the alchemetical compass in her hands. After some moments of silence, she turned and walked away.

While it was still making its slow headway into Kingston harbor, a boat rowed out to meet *Namur*. It carried a dozen soldiers, turned out in what might be called uniforms, as well as a familiar figure, wearing something that resembled a Royal Navy captain's coat and tricorn. At Boscawen's orders, *Namur* hove to and waited for it to come alongside.

"Captain Fayerweather," Boscawen said from the main deck. "How may we be of service?"

"Welcome to Jamaica, Admiral," Jack Fayerweather said. "Tell me, sir, did you heed my advice?"

Boscawen looked up at the sky. It was bright and blue and cloudless—clearly not Fayerweather's doing. "Forgive me for not recalling."

"The blackbird," he said. "Did you put him over the side?"

"I did not, nor do I plan to do so."

"Then I am afraid, sir, that you cannot be permitted to come into Kingston harbor. The governor has imposed . . . shall we say . . . a *quarantine*, and I'm here to enforce it."

"A quarantine? Of what sort?"

"Against negroes. We are at *war*, Admiral."

"With the French, certainly."

"Besides that," Fayerweather said, putting his hands on his hips as he stood up in the boat. "Were you to come to the dock you could hear them, the blacks in the hills, beating their voodoo-drums day and night. They mean us ill, Admiral. *All* of them. Not excluding your boy there—and as long as he is on board your ship, you will not be permitted to come ashore."

Boscawen crossed his arms over his chest. "And who will stop me?"

Fayerweather looked up at Twelve Apostles, where the cannons were clearly in sight, and gestured past *Namur* at the former town of Port Royal. "I suspect those lads will have something to say about it." He spat in the ocean. "Sir."

Boscawen considered replying, but instead said, "Perhaps you should come aboard so that we may discuss this like gentlemen." He gestured, and a rope-ladder was thrown down to the boat.

Fayerweather looked at his troops. "That sounds fine to me, sir. Come on, lads, prepare—"

"Not them," Boscawen said. "Just you."

"They go where I go, Admiral. Governor's orders."

"I'm not interested in having them aboard my ship. Come aboard, Captain, or go to perdition."

Fayerweather considered this for a moment, spat again, and shrugged. "All right then." He climbed nimbly up and after a few moments stood on the deck of *Namur*, looking about him as if he were measuring the place.

"Let us speak plainly," Boscawen said quietly. "What do you propose?"

"It's not a matter of *proposing*, if the Admiral pleases," Fayerweather said. "Governor Haldane has placed a strict prohibition on any negroes freely setting foot on the island of Jamaica until the current matter is resolved. Now, if you'd turn your boy over to us for, shall we say, *safekeeping*, I'm sure that the governor, and Admiral Cotes, would welcome you with all due honors." He smiled and looked about again—this time as if he was looking for a place to spit.

"Turning him over to the man who suggested that I pitch him into the ocean? No, sir. I think not. And as for your cannons opening fire on my ship—on a ship in His Majesty's Navy—there does not seem to be any need to show the poor marksmanship of the troops manning them."

"What makes you think they couldn't hit a target as big as this one?" Fayerweather snapped back.

"Given the quality of your own . . . *lads*, your escort, I'd say all the competent soldiers on Jamaica are busy with actual important tasks. And for Governor Haldane to employ *you* suggests that he is desperate indeed." Before Fayerweather could reply, Boscawen continued, "You will not have Gustavus, but you *will* take letters from me to Governor Haldane and Admiral Cotes. I personally know both, and they will not have expected me to arrive here. They may be assured that I, and my ship, stand ready to help with their current difficulty."

"And in the meanwhile . . ."

"In the meanwhile, we will remain here. But do not try my patience. I expect a reply at once. And then we will see whether *Namur* is permitted to come to harbor."

"I'm not sure—"

"I did not ask for your opinion, Captain, and if you were truly in the service you would know better than to talk back to a superior. I will have letters ready for you within the hour; in the meanwhile, get off my ship."

Fayerweather appeared to consider a reply, but instead offered a sloppy salute and turned away to the rope-ladder. Before he slung his leg over the rail, he spat once more, and then disappeared. Lieutenant Pascal, who was standing nearby, took one step forward, but Boscawen raised his hand slightly.

Instead Pascal waved to a seaman. "Get a mop," he said. "I don't want any trace of that filth to remain."

The Honorable George Haldane was a man whom Edward Boscawen had first met when they served in Parliament a dozen years earlier. He was, by any account, a prodigy: an ensign in the Scots Guards at eighteen, he fought at Dettingen and Fontenoy with his regiment and then stood for Stirling at twenty-five. His father had favored the late Prince of Wales, and that had hampered both his own and his son's political career, but the redemption had been the appointment as governor of Jamaica only the previous year. Boscawen had assumed that their paths would thereafter diverge. Only circumstance, and the event that placed *Namur* on this present course, had changed that.

"Truth to tell," he told Boscawen as he settled into an armchair opposite the one where the admiral sat, "I am more angry than mortified." His Scotch burr and flashing blue eyes made his statement even more earnest. "It would never be my intention to prevent one of His Majesty's ships from entering Kingston Harbor. Captain Fayerweather shall have a piece of my mind."

"He seems a rum sort of fellow," Boscawen said. "We are previously acquainted."

"Truly?"

"We met on the high seas some days ago."

"Truly. You would think he might have mentioned meeting someone as important as yourself."

"I assume he has his reasons. Tell me, Haldane, what is this difficulty you are having here in Jamaica?"

"I wish I could explain it." Haldane gripped the arms of his chair.

"Some weeks ago, there was a slave uprising upcountry. This sort of thing happens from time to time. I'm not unwilling to admit that it's often due to the mistreatment of the negroes—sugar growing and refining is a hard business, especially on the poor sods who have to do the hand work.

"This occasion was worse than most—the slaves have a leader they call Tacky. He was a king in his village back in Africa, they say—a commanding presence, with a definite plan. They seized a storehouse of arms, and they gathered the so-called *obeah*-men to them and proclaimed their intention to drive every white man from the island."

"Fayerweather spoke of this. What do you make of this— superstition?"

"In normal times," Haldane answered, "I would put no stock in such primitive nonsense. The *obeah*-men claimed to have concocted a powder that prevents firearms from harming the rebels, and it appears to have some efficacy. They claim that now that the broom-star is not in the sky—"

"The comet."

"Yes, yes—the comet. Now that it is gone from the heavens, *their* star is in the ascendant. Naturally I cannot allow this to stand, but I find myself short of might to suppress it. You can understand, My Lord, why I am pleased to see you arrive here."

"What would you have me do? I carry only a small complement of troops. Good lads, but not accustomed to fighting in the tropics."

"I would not ask your Lordship to place his ship's crew at my disposal. Instead, I think *Namur* could serve in two ways: first, to transport my own soldiers to coastal locations where the rebels have lodged; and second, to take advantage of its firepower against such places where they prove obstinate."

"I would be happy to assist in that way. I . . . we have no definitive orders at present, so this seems a good use of our resources. However, I fear we are in need of provisioning, and I have no voucher with your local agent."

"I'm sure we can make suitable arrangements," Haldane answered. "And as for Fayerweather . . . I suspect he did not know whom he was dealing with. But ignorance is no excuse."

"I am gratified," Boscawen said. "So. When shall we begin?"

Chapter 21

This was without doubt a war zone

Jamaica

Before they raised anchor at Kingston, Admiral Thomas Cotes paid a call to *Namur*. The visit of the admiral on station gave Boscawen the opportunity to order a thorough deck-to-hold cleaning of his vessel, turning out the crew and officers in their best uniforms, and attending to rigging and fittings to make certain that *Namur* was seaworthy. As with Haldane, Boscawen knew Cotes, though again not well; still, they shared their joint service in the Royal Navy.

Captain Fayerweather was nowhere to be seen as Cotes' barge was rowed across to the shallow part of the roadstead where *Namur* was anchored, and Boscawen had a full complement of sideboys when Cotes was piped aboard.

"Admiral Cotes," Boscawen said. "A pleasure, sir." He introduced his senior officers, as well as his French passengers. The portly Admiral of the Blue raised an eyebrow but did not make any remark in front of Messier and the young lady, but as soon as the inspection was done and the admiral's cabin door was closed, Cotes fixed Boscawen with a frown.

"I assume you have an explanation."

"For Messier and Mademoiselle LaGèndiere? They were shipwrecked on Barbados."

"For your presence here as well. Admiralty dispatches said you were en route to the Mediterranean, My Lord. What brings you to the Caribbean instead?"

"The same thing that brought Messier here. A storm, the likes of which I have never seen."

"Which pushed you thousands of miles off course."

"It is no tall tale, Admiral. That is exactly what happened. What's more, I have reason to believe that there is no way to return."

"What does that mean?"

"There is a barrier between this part of the world and Europe. I cannot explain how, or why, but we are isolated. All of us—in Barbados, here in Jamaica . . . I don't really know how far it extends."

"That's absolutely preposterous, my Lord. What could have caused such an unbelievable circumstance?"

"The same thing that has caused the slaves to revolt up-country. I understand your skepticism, sir. I am by nature rational. But I have already seen things that make me doubt that rationality."

"And the timing of these events . . ."

"Coincides with the passage of the comet." Boscawen reached to a shelf and brought down the Halley book. "What's worse, there is some indication that this was predicted long ago." He handed the volume to Cotes. "Though, I must say, not in detail."

"And what does Messier have to do with this? You called him an astronomer when you introduced him. How do you know he is not just a spy?"

"In truth, Admiral, I do not." Boscawen was about to explain about the mysterious alchemetical compass, but hesitated. Cotes was a good man, a capable sailor, but clearly skeptical about such things. Slave revolts were simply that, the uprising of poor devils in bondage—brigands and rebels, nothing more, not some evidence of a great mystical change in the world.

I was equally skeptical, Boscawen thought. *Until recently.*

For some reason he could not adequately explain, he refrained from mentioning it.

"I exercised my judgment and chose to be sympathetic to their plight. There may be an opportunity to put them ashore at some French establishment: Martinique or Guadeloupe, perhaps."

"With an intimate knowledge of the workings of a British man-of-war? That seems unusually reckless, if Your Lordship pleases."

"They know very little of the *workings*, as you put it, Admiral," Boscawen answered. "All they have seen is changes in rigging and sail; and I am fairly certain the French go through such exercises in the same way we do. Still, if it troubles you so much, I can remand them to your custody."

"Jamaica is no place for two French civilians, sir. Especially now."

"And a man-o'-war is no place for them either. But given your reaction, they will remain aboard until a better alternative presents itself."

Boscawen was relieved to have *Namur* out at sea, even as it hugged the shore of Jamaica island en route to Port Maria on the north side—where, Cotes suggested, the ship's guns might do some good. He did not intend to remain at Jamaica. They had agreed that since his was a detached vessel with a flag officer aboard, it would be helpful if he took *Namur* north to Charleston, in hopes of determining what the state of supply vessels might be in this new environment. Cotes had not completely accepted the notion that Europe was beyond some impenetrable barrier; and furthermore, though he had shown respect for his old acquaintance, Boscawen was sure that he was more than willing to have him out of his hair and away from his command.

What Haldane and the admiral had told him regarding the campaign thus far were not encouraging. Several weeks earlier, the rebels led by the slave Tacky had seized control of two plantations in Saint Mary Parish. There had been violence—and, based on the reports of Bayly and Cruikshank, two plantation overseers who had escaped with their lives and stumbled, exhausted, into Kingston—there had been worse things.

The *obeah*-men, so the two men said, had not only assisted the murderous slaves in killing men, women and children on the plantation, but they had caused those dead to walk again, adding to their forces as they marched north. Within a few days Haldane had dispatched five dozen men from the 74th Regiment of Foot, following the road over Archer's Ridge; a week later another detachment was sent after them. There had been no word received from either.

We will not go ashore, Boscawen told Cotes before leaving Kingston. *My men are not infantrymen.* And as for the *obeah*-men, whatever they had the power to do, he hoped they could not do it at a distance.

It took almost three days for *Namur* to cross through the Windward Passage and make her way westward along the north side of Jamaica. The ship's chart room was becoming crowded with information on Caribbean soundings; it had originally been outfitted for Mediterranean sailing, and Boscawen wondered if he would ever have use for those charts again.

The shoals and rocks of Jamaica were not as much an issue as the weather. This was the time of year where vessels in the Americas usually made their way north; the winter hazards were mostly gone, while spring and summer presented the threat of storms and wind— and shipworms. It was not in the admiral's personal experience, but the Navy possessed considerable knowledge of and experience with the destructive creatures. The nearest shipyard was Charleston. If *Namur* became sufficiently unseaworthy to make it there, his status as vice-admiral and Admiralty lord would be worth even less than it had already become. Accordingly, he kept the men busy examining the lower hull looking for any sign that the creatures had attached themselves. It was unpleasant, dirty work, but he was willing to have crew members curse his name down in the dark, damp recesses of the hold than to be forced to scuttle the ship and become a reluctant landsman.

Even before the ship passed the promontory marked on his chart as "Blooming Point," Boscawen could see the fires from inland. The destruction along the coast was apparent even without use of a glass: wrecked buildings and toppled windmills were visible, and there was not another vessel in sight. He had seen this before on the coasts of Acadia, where Britain and France—and its Indian allies—had waged a destructive campaign, sinking ships and burning villages. This was without doubt a war zone.

Port Maria was a small town, nestled in a cove that faced east, and was slightly sheltered from the open ocean. It had no ships in port— perhaps they had cleared out in advance of the rebels. *Namur* came in as close as was prudent—within cannon range—and Admiral Boscawen ordered the guns run out, though he did not know what the target might be. While he was considering his options, he saw a small boat rowing out from the shore with a white pennon flying from a post at the bow.

The boat did not approach too closely. It bore a black man

standing upright wearing something approximating an officer's uniform, while two ragged men rowed in a somewhat mechanical fashion. Through his glass, Boscawen could see that the two rowers had been badly injured in some fashion . . . and when the boat came as near as it seemed willing to go, he found himself looking into two pairs of dead eyes.

"Commander," the uniformed man said. He seemed to speak the word in a normal tone of voice, but it carried well, resonating across the water. "May I inquire regarding your intentions?"

"I might ask with whom I am speaking," Boscawen said.

"My name is *Takyi*, which you whites pronounce as 'Tacky.' I command here."

"By whose authority?"

The black man laughed derisively, as if it was the most ridiculous question. "Why, by my own, of course! Among the Fante people I was a king, before cowardly men sold me with many others to labor here. But we are free now, free!"

"That is not your decision to make," Boscawen answered. "I may have something to say about that."

"I doubt that," he said. "*Obeah* makes us powerful. Your bullets cannot harm us."

As Boscawen considered his reply, Pascal came beside him. "Would you like me to test that assertion, My Lord? He's giving us a pretty clear shot."

"No," Boscawen said quietly. "It accomplishes nothing; if you shoot him down for nothing but insolence, it might well inflame his followers. If indeed he cannot be harmed by rifle fire, it will disquiet the men."

"But that insolence deserves a reply, sir."

"I intend to reply, Pascal. Hold your fire." Boscawen took a deep breath and said, "I am sure you believe that, Tacky, or whatever name you give yourself. What I know is that you have committed murder and other crimes, and you may save the lives of your followers if you surrender to me. I am not beholden to the governor of this island and will show more mercy than he is likely to do."

"Mercy, is it?" Tacky said. "You speak of mercy—to people who have been dragged from their native land to labor here against their will, to suffer the lash and torture, to die from injury and disease so that whites can put sugar on their tables and rum in their bellies. What mercy derives from *slavery*, Commander?"

"I cannot judge your situation. I only seek to enforce justice."

"I spit on your justice." He reached inside his uniform coat and touched something; the two dead-eyed rowers began to turn the boat about. "I advise you to leave Port Maria, Commander. In fact, you would be best served to leave Jamaica entirely. My—servants—" he smiled, and the expression disturbed Boscawen—"will otherwise take your fine ship away from you."

"I doubt that," Boscawen said. "Get out of my sight, before we test your theory of invulnerability."

Tacky laughed again, as the boat slowly began to retreat toward the shore. "I have given you fair warning," he said.

Boscawen felt, rather than saw, Pascal come to attention.

"My Lord, I ask leave to take a boat and teach that boy a lesson he won't soon forget."

"Refused."

"Sir—"

"*Refused*, Lieutenant, unless you are contemplating mutiny against my authority." He angrily turned to Pascal. "This is an unknown situation, with unforeseeable perils. This Tacky will be dealt with in due course, and not by a hotheaded junior officer and some restless marines. Do you understand, sir?"

"Yes, sir. Of course, sir."

Boscawen turned away again and gazed through the eyepiece of his spyglass at the shore, where Tacky's boat was approaching. As he watched, he could see figures begin to walk out of the little town onto the dock.

Silently, he cursed himself for losing his temper, even modestly. The lieutenant had every right to feel offended at the way in which his commanding officer had been addressed—and by a black slave at that!—but he repeated silently what he had told Admiral Cotes: *My men are not infantrymen.*

Tacky's boat came up alongside the long dock that projected into the water; but instead of disembarking, he remained on board, cupping his hands and shouting something toward the half-ruined town.

There was a long, disturbingly quiet pause that gave Boscawen a chill despite the heat and humidity. Then, as he watched, the people on the dock—moving with a strange, jerky shuffle—began to walk forward and drop into the water. As they bobbed to the surface they began to move slowly out to sea, heading for *Namur*: first a half dozen, and then a dozen more, and a dozen more after that—men and women, young and old, with vacant, unseeing eyes.

My servants will take your fine ship away from you.

"Orders, Admiral?"

Pascal had looked across the water at the people coming slowly toward the ship; he looked anxious and perhaps afraid, but ready for orders.

"Where is Gustavus, Lieutenant?"

"Below decks, My Lord, helping with the guns."

"Fetch him, if you please, and pass the word to our passengers to come above decks as well."

"During a—" Pascal began, then saluted. "Yes, My Lord," he said, and dashed down the steps onto the main deck. Boscawen could hear him calling for Gustavus as he went.

The dead-eyed men and women continued to drop into the water. They had ten, or perhaps as much as fifteen minutes . . . and if, indeed, they were somehow unaffected by musket fire . . .

A broadside would tear a few of them apart—but even with chain shot loaded it would not be very effective with small targets near the waterline. And there seemed to be more and more of them coming.

To take my fine ship, Boscawen thought. *They are coming to take the ship.*

He saw Messier escorting Mademoiselle LaGèndiere up the steps on to the quarterdeck. She looked remarkably composed and held the alchemetical compass in her hands, as if she was expecting to make use of it.

"I do not wish to disturb you, my lady," he said to her, "but I think that we are about to come under attack by . . . "

"Revenants," she said. "Walking dead." She held up the compass, and he could see the liquid within tilted in the direction of the land. As she walked, however, it seemed to change direction very slightly, as if it was focusing on one particular place. As always, the young woman seemed completely composed. She had shown little emotion of any kind since coming aboard *Namur* and appeared completely unfazed by the idea of animated corpses crossing the water.

Gustavus appeared at the top of the steps. He looked fearful as he glanced from Boscawen to the water and back.

"Come here, lad," Boscawen said. "Tell me what you can of this business."

"It's . . . it's *obeah*-magic, My Lord," Gustavus said. "Those are dead people. Some *obeah*-man, or perhaps more than one, have animated them. They will feel no pain and will move as long as they are controlled."

"These *obeah*-men. They would be close by?"

"Close enough to see their work, yes, My Lord. And for such a working they would be together, sharing their power."

Boscawen looked about him and located a piece of marking-chalk. He took it and drew a rough circle five paces across, then gestured to Mademoiselle LaGèndiere to stand within it.

"Now turn, my lady, if you please. Clockwise. Very slowly."

She did as she was asked, and Boscawen watched as the liquid inclined itself higher in the glass—and then began to decline once more.

"Stop!" he said. "Turn back. Again, slowly."

It reached its highest point, and Boscawen held up his hand. He bent down and drew a line perpendicular to the bow and stern, and then another line from the center of the circle through the place where the young lady was standing, and out to its edge.

"Mr. Pascal," he said, "if you please, turn us about . . . two points to starboard. And prepare to fire."

The order was passed. "When we raise sail, My Lord, they'll think we're running away."

"Let them think as they like. Two points, no more. Fire on my order."

The sails began to fill with wind, and the ship slowly began to turn. Boscawen watched carefully as the ship moved . . .

"Fire! Now!" he shouted. "Come one point to port, and fire again when ready!"

The roar of more than thirty cannon erupted, hurling chain shot—intended to take down rigging, and crew, from an enemy vessel—directly upward and toward the shore, where it crashed into the partly-destroyed buildings at the edge of the town. When the smoke cleared and the echo of the blast began to dissipate, he could hear the sounds of gun crews hauling the cannon back and preparing them for the next volley.

For several seconds more, the revenants—or walking dead, or whatever they could be called—continued to make their way toward the ship . . . and then, of a sudden, like puppets whose strings had been cut, they stopped moving and subsided, some sinking, some floating on the water, so that the calm water between *Namur* and Port Maria was suddenly littered with the dead.

Chapter 22

I saw nothing but mist and darkness

Fort Johnson, Colony of New York

"Joseph."

Joseph Brant had been dozing in a window-seat on the second floor of Sir William Johnson's handsome stone house. The sun streaming in through the glass panes had pulled him into quiet dreams—but he could not quite remember them, as the pain in his hands returned to his notice while the dream-threads slipped away.

He sat up to see Sir William Johnson standing before him, a roll of parchment in his hands, obviously intent on showing him something. He was leaning over in order to do so, and Joseph could see his sister Molly behind Johnson looking over his shoulder. She had a concerned look on her face, although that wouldn't have been evident to people who didn't know her as well as her brother did.

Joseph sat up, shaking off sleep.

"You did not hear me call, I see. Well, no matter. Sleep is no doubt good for you." Johnson looked at Joseph's bandaged hands, then back at his face. "How are you feeling?"

"It hurts less than it did."

"I told the *Tadodaho* you would receive better care here in my house than beside the Council Fire, and so you have. You will be using that bow of yours in no time."

"You are very generous, Elder Brother," Joseph said. "You said . . . you were calling me?"

"Yes. I wanted to ask you a few questions about your vision."

Joseph knew very well which vision: it was the one he had had just after the *Konearaunehneh* had appeared and he had tugged away the cord that held it to the earth. Unlike most dreams before or since, that had not left him . . . the world, a great oval, spread out before him as clearly as a view from a high mountain peak.

Johnson beckoned to him and he rose and followed to a great table in the hall, a single slab of wood cut from some mighty tree, smoothed and polished so that it shone with reflected light from the windows. His sister followed behind them. Johnson unrolled the parchment to show a large and highly detailed map of the continents, stretching from the sketched-in lands of the far north to the unknown places of the south, marked with dozens of annotations in Johnson's own hand. He weighted the parchment down at the corners with Molly's help and then stood upright, looking over the document.

"Where did the land end, Joseph?"

"There was a range of high mountains at the edge of the sea," Joseph said, pointing to the Atlantic Ocean. He clumsily drew a line with a finger while trying not to rub his bandaged hand across the map. He started east of the lands of the Abenaki (where the map showed schools of fish) and passed southward as far as the great bulge on the east side of the southern continent. "And another on the other side."

He was more vague about that, as he knew nothing of the actual geography on the west side of the continent. No one did, so far as Joseph knew, among either the Haudenosaunee or any their neighboring tribes. But he moved his finger from north to south out in the ocean, as he remembered what he saw there in his vision.

Johnson peered closely at the map as Joseph pointed. "Are you sure about this, Joseph? It's very important."

"I am not totally sure, Sir William. It was a dream and it was . . . "

"Yes. Of course. It appears as if Acadia is on this side of these mountains, and so is Jamaica, and the Leeward Islands . . . this chain of islands, Joseph: did you see them in your dream?"

"I think so. The mountains were further out to sea. But I can't be sure."

Johnson continued to stare at the map, his brow furrowed in concentration.

"Sir William, why is that important? One little group of islands—"

"Because, young brave," Johnson said, straightening up and arranging his vest, "that *little group of islands*—Jamaica, and even more especially Guadeloupe, Martinique, and Barbados—are the richest pieces of land in the world because they are covered with sugar plantations. That is the backbone of the economy of the French, as well as the British, Empire. Who holds them holds the purse-strings of the world."

"So is it better that they are in the part of the world we can see, or worse because your land-across-the-water can no longer reach them?"

"That," Johnson answered, "is a very interesting question. Which is more important, that we have sugar for our tea, or that London does not?"

"If there even *is* a London anymore," said Molly, sounding skeptical.

Her husband frowned at her. "If there is . . . what do you mean? Beyond the mountains—"

"Beyond the mountains, Sir William," interjected Joseph, "I saw nothing but mist and darkness. I saw no London, I saw no Africa where the black slaves come from—or Cathay on the other side, for that matter. All I saw was what lay between the mountains. The entire world."

"It was a dream only," Johnson managed by way of reply.

"Of course," Joseph said. "But if it was no more than a dream, why does it trouble you so much, Sir William? Why is it so important that I am sure what I saw—if it was just a dream?"

A decade and a half before, Sir William Johnson had built his great house on the land that King Hendrick had given him—and, to hear the Iroquois tell it, the story of how it came to him proved that Johnson put great store in dreams—and also why they held him in such high esteem.

Hendrick Theyanoguin, the old Mohawk chief and diplomat, had visited Johnson at his much more modest home in Warrenburgh years ago; and while there, he had seen a beautiful scarlet coat that he very much admired. In the morning, he told Johnson that he had dreamed that he possessed the coat and did not hesitate to tell his host of the fact.

"Ah," Johnson was said to have replied. "Do not dreams come

from the Great Spirit?" Hendrick readily agreed, and received the gift of the coat, which made him very happy, and it was much admired by his people.

Sometime later, Johnson visited the old sagamore in Caughnawaga, the richest part of the Mohawk lands. In the morning, after he had slept in Hendrick's home, he told the Mohawk chief that he had had a dream in which he possessed nearly all of that land. Hendrick was surprised by this declaration, but Johnson retorted: "Do not dreams come from the Great Spirit?"

It was said that Hendrick pondered for some time, looking for a way to escape the snare that his avarice had set for him—but in the end he had to admit that Johnson was right, and was no simple white man to be gullied. At last he said, "Yes, brother, the land is yours—but you must have no more such dreams!"

The one dream had been enough, and Johnson had built his great stone house high on a hill, with a sawmill and other outbuildings nearby. When the war began a few years earlier, he had built a palisade around it, giving it more the appearance that the title suggested—Fort Johnson. It had come to be the gathering place for war councils for those natives who supported the British crown.

Skenadoa had helped escort Joseph from Onondaga to Fort Johnson as soon as he was recovered enough to walk. To the young native, every sense seemed enhanced, every perception sharpened as he traveled across the land toward Johnson's home. Birdsong, tree signs, and even the way in which the sun filtered through the forest canopy seemed to hold new and special significance. When they reached Fort Johnson, the older man had remained for a time and then took his leave of the great house, traveling west to see what he could learn.

Joseph had always been skilled at tracking and following trail-sign; among his tribe and clan he was highly regarded. But this was new and different—something had happened when he had confronted the *Konearaunehneh*. Perhaps he had been chosen by the Great Spirit and would now be a shaman rather than a warrior—a prospect he dreaded. Shamans did not run along trails or hunt in the woods. Prophesying and visions were for old men.

Except . . . he had *experienced* a vision. And nothing ordinary, like the coming of rain or the quality of the hunt—it was a vision of the whole world and its boundaries, with only mist and darkness beyond.

"This is healing up nicely," Molly Brant said, carefully wrapping a clean bandage around Joseph's right hand. When her brother didn't answer, she said, "Are you listening to me?"

Joseph had been daydreaming, seeing the vision again in his mind, and watching motes of dust drift through a strand of sunlight coming in through the window.

"Of course I'm listening to you."

"It didn't seem that way." Molly smiled, and Joseph, as always, was put in mind of how beautiful his sister was. She spoke and dressed like a European but had the features of an Iroquois—and that was important, especially now, since she carried Sir William's child. She was just starting to show, but it clearly did not keep her from the many household tasks that she performed and oversaw for him. "You were lost in your dreams."

"I keep thinking of my vision. Sir William questioned me about the edges of the land . . . I'd never thought that the land *had* edges—that the Great Water went on and on until it reached the white man's home."

"The land, and the water, is on a great globe. You know that. If you travel beyond the lands of Europe and across—I don't know, Russia or Cathay, you come to another great water, and then around to where you started. The English have done that, sailing their great ships all around."

"That's not what I saw."

"You had a fever, something to do with the attack of the . . . " she placed her hand on her belly and lowered her voice. "*Konearaunehneh,*" she said, as if she were trying to make sure that her unborn child did not hear the word. "Who is to say what your mind may have imagined?"

"So you don't think it's a true vision. Is that what you're saying?"

"I don't know," she said, tying the bandage in place. "I don't know quite what to say about it. It is all beyond me, matters for men of science or shamans or some such thing. Who believes that the world can change from the way the Great Spirit made it? Do you?"

"I don't know either. I only know what I saw," Joseph said, standing up. He placed his hands gently on his sister's shoulders. "And I believe it came from the Great Spirit, and it is the way that the world really looks now. Sir William thinks it is a true seeing also."

"He does not believe in the Great Spirit, Joseph, no matter what he says to the sachems of the Haudenosaunee. Why would he think this now?" She gently shrugged off Joseph's hands and picked up a cloth, wiping her own. "Get well and rest, then go home. The world hasn't changed."

"The *Konearaunehneh*—"

"Have always been there, in the darkness, waiting to invade the world of men. This is a time of war, Joseph—it must have smelled blood."

When Skenadoa returned to Fort Johnson, he was not alone. Joseph and Molly Brant and Sir William Johnson watched as two dozen Indians—men, women and children—walked between the stone gateposts into the front yard of the house. They were burdened with possessions and accompanied by animals—they had come to Fort Johnson to stay, at least for a while.

They were not the first such refugees. By now, somewhere on the order of two hundred people had gathered in the shelter provided by Fort Johnson. Most of them were crowded into the compound itself, but others clustered against its wooden palisade. The majority were Mohawks, but not all. There were Onondagas, Oneidas and Tuscaroras there too, and even one small group of Hurons.

The Hurons—or Wyandot, as they were also called—spoke an Iroquoian language but were traditionally hostile to the Six Nations. Something very frightening must have happened to drive them to seek refuge in Mohawk lands.

Skenadoa gestured to the others and walked forward. Sir William stepped off the porch and into the yard, where the two men consulted quietly for a short time.

Johnson turned and called into the house; three servants appeared, and he gave orders to assist the natives in settling onto the grounds. Then, without a word to Joseph or Molly, he walked into the house.

Skenadoa stood alone in the yard, gazing up at the sky as if there were answers to questions hidden there. Joseph walked up to him, and the older man looked down.

"What is happening?"

"There are more of them," Skenadoa said. "Out there." He gestured westward, the direction from which he had come. "Flying Heads, and worse. They have heard the call, and they answer."

"Heard the call? What do you mean?"

"When the world changed, young brave," Skenadoa answered, "things awoke from their sleep. Many things. They had no goal other than to darken the sky and frighten . . . but a strong man could harness those things to his purpose.

"Sir William has an enemy toward the sunset," he added. "A runner came to their village—" he gestured toward the people in the yard who had recently arrived—"and told them that since they had taken up the calumet with Warraghiyagey, they no longer belonged to the land."

"So they came here," Joseph said. "For protection from . . . "

"The strong man."

"Does the strong man have a name?"

Skenadoa spat, a deliberate gesture. "I will not speak it here, but yes, it is a name that Warraghiyagey—'Chief Big Business'—knows well."

"One of our people?"

"A Seneca." The westernmost people of the Confederation—the "guardians of the Western Door"—had long been inclined toward the French rather than the English. They were fierce and independent.

"Does he speak for all of the Seneca people?"

"No one opposes him, at least now. Whether all will come when he calls—it depends on what he offers or if they fear him. With Flying Heads at his command, they might fear him a great deal. But there is one thing that is certain, young brave."

"What is that?"

"The Covenant Chain is broken. Now let us go in and see what 'Chief Big Business' has to say."

Chapter 23

It is always about true and false

Fort Johnson, Colony of New York

"What does he want?" Johnson asked. "What does he *say* he wants?"

Skenadoa looked around the drawing room. A half-dozen warriors stood around the room, watching and listening. Johnson sat in an armchair, his hands pyramided.

"He *says* he wants all white people to leave the lands of the Longhouse," Skenadoa said at last.

"He's looking to drive us out of our homes?"

"Huh." Skenadoa walked to the window and looked out across the yard, where the refugees had pitched their tents. "*Your* homes. The Six Tribes called these lands *their* homes long before you."

"There are treaties," Johnson said. "Those of my people who have settled here have bought their land and live on it legally."

"Tell me again of the treaties and the purchases, Warraghiyagey. Tell me of the Walking Purchase and the treaty made at Easton in Pennsylvania. Tell me how the people of Plymouth and Massachusetts-Bay treated Metacom after he . . . asserted his right to revenge for the murder of his brother.

"Tell me, Warraghiyagey. Tell me why Guyasuta is *wrong* to want what he believes is his."

"You are in my house, Skenadoa," Johnson said. "Do you believe that this Seneca chief is right? Do you make common cause with him? Because if you do, then you and your people can take your leave now."

Johnson's anger was in his eyes, but his voice was level. Skenadoa did not change his expression either.

"I accept the world as it is, Warraghiyagey," Skenadoa said. "My people are in it; your people are in it. But you must understand what Guyasuta believes if you seek to oppose him. He believes that the treaties are false, that the land belongs to no one. Instead, we belong to the land. Your people believe otherwise."

"And now Guyasuta has suddenly decided to change things, to upset the balance? Why now?"

"You already know the answer, Warraghiyagey. It is because of the coming of the broom-star, the change in the world. Guyasuta senses an opportunity unlike any that has ever come before."

Johnson waited several moments before replying. "Tell me about Guyasuta."

"He is a Seneca chief who came to the Ohio valley when he was young. He is now, I would say, about three dozen summers old, and is highly regarded among his people for his bravery and initiative."

"Are his sympathies with the French?"

"Once, he was considered a friend of the English. He guided the Tall Hunter—a young officer named Washington, from Virginia, when he was sent as an envoy to the French at Presque-Isle. But the Seneca are not of one mind with regard to their loyalties—English, French or Iroquois.

"I think you are asking whether he acts on behalf of the French. I would say no. He serves another purpose and is his own master. He wants the French gone as well."

"He is a warrior?"

"Yes, assuredly."

"Then—how is it that he 'senses' this opportunity? Is he a shaman as well as a warrior?"

Skenadoa did not answer.

"He has someone in his retinue," Johnson continued. "Someone has told him this—incited him to this. Guyasuta does not speak for all Iroquois, and he likely does not speak for all Senecas. He has decided to undertake this because he is an opportunist."

"What do you mean by that, Warraghiyagey? Do you say that he is false?"

"This is not about true and false, Skenadoa."

"It is always about *true and false*, Warraghiyagey. Chiefs of tribes from the Longhouse take up the hatchet and go to war because they feel a *true* need for action, or because they feel that they have been *truthfully* hurt, or because they have received a *true* vision from the Great Spirit. So I ask again: do you say that Guyasuta is false?"

The tension in the room had gone up suddenly, though neither Skenadoa nor Johnson had changed facial expressions. Johnson did not answer at once. He rose from his seat and walked to the fireplace. He took down a long, thin clay pipe and held it before him.

"I was adopted by the People of the Longhouse, friend Skenadoa, and given a name so that I might sit among them. The *Tadodaho* smoked this calumet with me as a sign of the bond we made, and I asked him if I might keep it as a reminder that it had been done, so I would never forget."

"I remember. I was there, Warraghiyagey."

"Then you know I call no brother false, because I know what it would mean to say those words, to take up that hatchet. It would make this—" he held out the pipe before him—"a meaningless token. So let me say that I have formed my words in a way that you did not understand, and that is my fault; or that I have failed to see what you meant by your words, and that is my fault as well.

"So, unless you no longer feel that you can call me brother, we should find other words to speak. Or I can simply break this pipe and grind the pieces beneath my feet. I leave it to you, my brother."

Skenadoa showed neither fear nor anger and did not respond. After some time, Johnson placed the pipe carefully back on the mantelpiece.

"We must find out who has moved this chief Guyasuta to threaten us," Johnson said. "Those of you who will ride with me make ready; at first light we will ride west and get answers."

"Warraghiyagey—" Skenadoa began, but let the sentence falter, as if he could not see which path it would take.

"You can ride with us if you choose, Skenadoa. But I will have answers."

As it happened, answers came to him.

On the morning of the second day after the gathering in Johnson's study, a lone rider approached the gate of Fort Johnson. He was a

Seneca, attired and painted for war, but showed no hostile intent. He was escorted into the yard and remained on his horse; Johnson came out on the porch of the house.

It was no one he knew. The Indian carried a bundle in his hands wrapped in a deerskin. With a grunt, he unwrapped it and tossed it on the ground in front of him: six arrows bound together and snapped in the middle. The bound arrows—like the *fasces* of Ancient Rome—were a symbol of the Covenant Chain, the league of tribes that comprised the Iroquois Confederacy.

"My chief sends word to you, Chief Warraghiyagey," the native said, without greeting or initial courtesy. "The . . . *arrangements* . . . between your people and ours have ceased. You should prepare to leave the lands of the Longhouse or face the wrath of the people."

"Which people?" Johnson spread his hands, gesturing toward the people camped in the yard, many of whom had emerged to watch the scene. "*These* people that you have driven from their houses and hunting grounds?"

"My chief has seen a vision," the messenger replied.

"Guyasuta is no seer," Johnson answered. "I have looked into his eyes. They are clear, a warrior's eyes."

"*My* chief is Sganyodaiyo," the man said. "The son of Gahonneh, of the Turtle Clan. The Great Spirit descended from the sky-kingdom and granted him a vision. He has a warrior's eyes as well, and has given the word of his vision to Guyasuta." He gestured toward the bundle of broken arrows. "Those of the Haudenosaunee who serve and consort with the white people have broken the trust of the rest. It is they who have destroyed the League. We will carry their scalps back and make them trophies."

"Will you take a message back with you?"

"What words could you speak that would have any value?"

Johnson's face darkened. "Then you had best leave my land, warrior, before you are killed for sport. I will deliver words personally to your chiefs—after I kill their braves and burn their longhouses."

The Seneca did not respond but turned his horse and rode slowly out of the yard, as if he had not the slightest fear that anyone there would harm him.

In the morning twenty grim mounted men—six Englishmen and

the rest natives—rode slowly out of the compound. A light drizzle accompanied them, further sombering the occasion. Molly Brant watched them go; her facial expression was impassive, but something in the tight set of her shoulders indicated her disapproval of her husband's mission. She'd tried to talk Johnson out of it the night before—they'd argued long into the night. Unusually—but he'd stubbornly insisted it had to be done.

Joseph was not among them. He had asked Johnson to accompany the troop as a scout, but the white man had turned him down: as valuable as his scouting skills might be, Johnson wanted him to continue to recover from his injuries.

"Also," Johnson said, "I want you to protect and defend your sister. I . . . fear for her. For all of us." It was very much about *true* and *false.*

Chapter 24

The situation has changed

Montréal, New France

On a large, flat table in the Arsenal, pitted and scarred from years of serving as a work-table and an idle carving surface for bored artillerymen, Lévis had carefully laid out the Bourbon banner he had recovered from Fort Carillon.

Truly, Lévis had no idea what the marquis might say about his tale; it was no bold or brave account, but rather the evidence of surrender, as if it was one more defeat in the series of defeats that the *patrie* had suffered in the last year and a half. Nominally, losing Carillon meant that the English could put Montréal, and thus all of New France, in their sights—except that they had not lost Carillon to the English.

"I am surprised that you accept my report, Monsieur," Lévis said when he finished. He had provided a written letter with the details of his expedition; Montcalm had asked him to describe it in more detail.

"Why would that be?"

"It is . . . somewhat hard to believe."

Montcalm ran his finger along the edge of the banner without looking up. "You might be surprised what I would be prepared to believe. After what I have seen in the last few weeks, and what intelligence has recently come to me, I would be willing to accept it just as you describe."

"Ghost Highlanders, Monsieur? I was in no position to gainsay them when they told me I must depart. But a concerted force—"

"No." The Marquis de Montcalm looked up. "That is not an option. We will not undertake such an expedition against Carillon—it clearly is not in the hands of the English. It is in enemy hands, but not English hands."

"I don't understand."

"Bring that map here," Montcalm said. He carefully folded up the banner and set it on one corner of the table.

Lévis picked up a rolled map and spread it out, weighing down each corner with a cartridge-box. Montcalm took out his jack-knife and pointed to Montréal.

"Here we are, at the center of our pitiful domain of New France. Below us on the Saint-Laurent is Québec, our isolated but—for the moment—well-defended capital. The coast is lost to us, as of last summer. Beauséjour and Louisbourg, all of Acadia." He gestured toward the east, and then along the Atlantic coast. "Here are the English, from Annapolis-Royal to Charleston, and beyond into the West Indies. We have New Orleans and the great river, forts in the interior, and footholds wherever our *couriers de bois* and *bateaux* can travel. We were heading toward a great confrontation this coming year, one which we most certainly would have lost."

"Monsieur!" Lévis said. "We—"

"We are outnumbered ten to one in America," Montcalm said, sighing. "As a patriotic Frenchman, and servant of his Most Christian Majesty, I would never venture such an opinion. But when the English king, damn his black heart, decided to take the matter seriously, our efforts seemed ultimately doomed to failure. It might have taken some time, but they would find their way to victory."

"I have never heard you speak thus." Lévis seemed so genuinely shocked that he even forgot to end the sentence with an honorific.

"I have refrained from doing so and would not do so now . . . except that the situation has changed." He pointed to the Maritimes again. "From what I have learned, the expected armada that Britain was sending to invade New France was destroyed at sea. They will not be coming to reinforce our enemy. They say there is some manner of barrier out in the ocean—as hard as it is to believe, it is the truth.

"But we have our own problems. Not too far upriver from here, some . . . thing has declared a limit to our hegemony. It is powerful in ways I do not understand—and while it has designated a boundary between their dominion and ours, I have no confidence that they will keep to that bargain."

"This is why you received my report with favor," Lévis said. "This is why you were willing to accept what I told you."

"And it is why the situation is changed, my friend. We are isolated here—but *so are they.*"

Lévis did not answer; he knew Montcalm was coming to a point.

"For decades we have considered them the enemy—but I believe that our enemy is now the things that create barriers in the oceans, or assert their power to our west, or haunt fortresses to our south. This is the enemy of the British here as well. In order for either of us to survive, we must reach an accord."

"That is surely up to monarchs to decide."

"No," Montcalm answered. "It is not. They are not *here*. They cannot be here. We cannot ask them. Have you not heard what I said? We are all isolated here, perhaps permanently, opposed by forces we scarcely understand. There are no kings to make those decisions."

Lévis looked from the marquis to the Bourbon banner, carefully folded on the corner of the table.

"You have a plan, Monsieur."

"I do. And it begins with Monsieur Bigot."

It took two days for *Soleil* to travel downriver to the capital. Québec was even more crowded with refugees from the western villages; normally, the arrival of someone as consequential as the Marquis de Montcalm would have been met with reverence and deference—but under the circumstances, it was no more than an inconvenience.

Montcalm, with Lévis and the young Lieutenant D'Egremont in tow, made his way to the intendant's palace in the low town. Despite the crowding in the city, the street outside the palace was clear; two soldiers in Bigot's service were standing on the steps. The three men walked past without stopping, and past the obsequious servant waiting to take their hats and cloaks. Montcalm led his companions up the stairs and into the audience hall, which they found disturbingly empty, a stark contrast to the crowded streets of the town.

A great table was burdened with books and papers, the records of the colony and the intendant's office. Montcalm pointed to the table.

"Do not let a single document be taken away," he said, just as Bigot came through an arched doorway, speaking over his shoulder.

"Domitien," he was saying, "be sure you set aside the—"

He stopped abruptly when he saw the three men in the room. His disdainful expression disappeared, and even his posture changed.

"My lord Marquis," he said, offering a slight bow. "I did not know you had returned."

Montcalm could smell the *ozène* from where he stood; as always, it made him dislike the man all the more. "Just a short while ago, Monsieur *Intendant*. It is time we had a discussion."

"Oh? On what subject?"

Montcalm picked up one of the record-books from the table. Bigot took a single step forward, then froze as he saw the expression on Montcalm's face.

"I have been looking into your . . . activities over the past few years," Montcalm said. "The colony receives considerable supplies from the mother country, and yet we always seem short of something, this or that, which you are miraculously able to procure . . . at considerable cost to the colonial authority."

"Governor Vaudreuil considers it to be the greatest of my talents, Monsieur. He has complete confidence in me." He reached into the sleeve of his coat and drew out a lavender-scented handkerchief and dabbed his nose.

"He has had little choice."

"His Most Christian Majesty has full confidence in me as well," he added with what Montcalm could only describe as a smirk.

"That opinion is no longer of any consequence."

"I cannot divine your meaning, Monsieur."

"We are no longer in contact with the mother country, Bigot. We will be receiving no further supplies from France. We are on our own, which means that the considerable wealth of goods you have *stolen* from the people of New France will have to be made available for our continued survival."

The smirk vanished. Bigot lowered his hands to his sides, though he continued to clutch the handkerchief.

"I object to being characterized as a thief," he said. "We will see what the governor has to say about this."

"He will say nothing about it," Montcalm said. "Except after the fact. D'Egremont, take hold of the Intendant, if you please. We're going to go for a little walk."

The young lieutenant crossed the room and took hold of Bigot by the arm; the intendant sought to shake him off, but the young man's grasp was firm.

"Unhand me," he said, looking from D'Egremont to Montcalm. "This is an outrage! I will—"

Montcalm folded his arms in front of him. "Yes, Monsieur *Intendant*? What will you do? Particularly when the details of your activities become public knowledge. I don't think there will be anyone who will leap to your defense."

"The king—"

"Is not here," Montcalm interrupted. He gestured toward the door. D'Egremont pulled Bigot along.

Against his will and with considerable protest—which his guards seemed to studiously ignore—Montcalm and his companions took Bigot through the crowded streets of Québec to the Upper Town. Montcalm's presence had been largely met by indifference, but Bigot, apparently unused to walking through the streets of Québec, seemed to be roundly disliked. When the intendant demanded to know where they were going, Montcalm ignored him.

D'Egremont never let go of Bigot's arm; if anything, he held it more tightly. As they went up into the Upper Town, Bigot appeared to give up struggling, though he did mutter about reporting this to Governor Vaudreuil and writing an angry letter to the king.

Montcalm said nothing, leading the group to the parapets at the Sailors' Battery, which overlooked the swift-flowing river below.

"I assume you have some explanation for this unseemly behavior, Montcalm."

"I am not accustomed to having a base commoner address me by my name only, Bigot. You should show some respect, given your circumstances."

"And what exactly are my *circumstances*, Monsieur?"

"*Régarde*," Montcalm said, gesturing at the parapet. "With the smallest gesture, I could command the young lieutenant beside you to hurl you over the edge into the river. It would rid me of your onerous presence once and for all."

"You would not dare."

"Do not trifle with me regarding what I might or might not dare, Bigot. For as long as I have been on this post in New France, I have witnessed your venality and your base behavior. I wonder if even Governor Vaudreuil would shed a tear for your loss."

"He—"

"Yes?"

"He would . . . miss my counsel."

"I very much doubt it."

Bigot looked from face to face. Lévis looked mildly surprised at the turn of events; D'Egremont was eager to please his superior officer. Montcalm, for his part, was adamant and stern.

"If it was your intent to kill me," Bigot said at last, sniffing, "you would surely have done so by now. There is something you want, Monsieur." He shrugged his arm loose from the grasp of the young lieutenant. "Tell me what it is, and I shall see if I can oblige."

Montcalm waited long enough to answer that Bigot took his lavender-scented handkerchief and dabbed at his nose. The intendant was clearly uncomfortable with the silence.

"All of the goods that you have stolen—"

"Monsieur—"

"Ah, *now* you choose politeness? *Non*, Monsieur Intendant. *Stolen*. All that you have *stolen* from His Highness' supplies must be stored somewhere. You will apprise me of that information."

"Or—or what? You will toss me off the parapets into the river?"

"Perhaps," Montcalm said. "You're right. I would have to conduct a most tiresome search if you do not tell me what I want. So instead of doing so, I might permit one of our Indian friends to test your bravery. I am sure that the spectacle will be most amusing."

"You wouldn't dare," Bigot repeated, dabbing again at his *ozène*, but this time he seemed far less sure of Montcalm's intentions. The marquis did not answer.

"What guarantee," Bigot said at last, "for my safety, if I tell you what you want to know?"

"None."

"Not even your word as a gentleman?"

"I do not owe you any such assurance, Bigot, and you are presumptuous for even suggesting such a thing. But we are in uncharted territory here: and there may be a time when even someone such as you are useful. So you have my word—as a *gentleman*—that your person is safe if you tell me what I want to know."

"I have nothing to fear from His Majesty," Vaudreuil said. "Bigot may tell him what he likes. I daresay after your actions, Monsieur, he will have more to say about *you* than about *me*." Vaudreuil poured wine into two glasses and offered one to Montcalm with a little bow.

"Bigot will not be saying anything to anyone," Montcalm said. "Or, more specifically, there is no one to hear him. We may never speak with the home country again, if what I have heard is true."

"How would you know?"

"You read the reports of Fort Carillon, and our visit upriver, and what seems to be happening in the New England colonies. We are facing an unknown threat, Governor, and we are on our own. Except . . . "

"Except?"

"For the English."

Vaudreuil frowned, as if the wine he had just drank had gone sour. "What about the English?"

"They are on their own as well, and face the same enemy. We have more in common with them than we have with these . . . forces, and our chances of survival are greater if we make common cause."

"*Survival?*" Vaudreuil made the same face. "When did this become a discussion of survival? And let me remind you, Monsieur, that we are *at war* with the English and have been so for some time."

"Ask Father Récher if he thinks this is a struggle for survival, Monsieur Governor. He saw what I saw—and when combined with the knowledge, the *sure* knowledge that we are cut off from our homeland—perhaps forever—suggests that we are not at war with the English any longer.

"I don't know what we are fighting, Governor. But only a fool goes to battle with an enemy at his rear."

"This is based on an entire cavalcade of assumptions, suspicions and fears, Monsieur. To go against the Crown—to end the war—based on that, seems irresponsible." He set his glass down at the edge of a table and looked at it for a moment, as if it might not obey his wishes and remain there. "You truly have no idea if we are cut off from the mother country."

"I am not certain, no. I am not certain about anything—except that this in unknown ground. The situation has changed forever."

"Enough so that you're willing to threaten Bigot's life."

"You object?"

"He has powerful friends at Court. That is consequential, unless, as you suggest, that is no longer of consequence. Past that, you can send him to a knacker for all that I care."

"A tempting suggestion."

Vaudreuil picked up his wineglass and raised it, catching the candlelight and breaking it into a thousand colored fragments.

"Remind me not to anger you," the governor said at last.

Any further, Montcalm thought. He raised his glass and drank appreciatively. *I will keep that in mind.*

Chapter 25

The trees themselves were not consulted

New France

The Marquis de Montcalm had ordered more extensive patrols of the area, particularly between Québec and Montréal. All of the staff officers were assigned turns at leading patrols, and Olivier D'Egremont was no exception.

It was always an invigorating experience to leave the safety and quiet of the habitations and travel out into the wilderness, like a *courier de bois*—but better armed, and with a limited and particular mission—to make sure there were no infiltrations. For most of the officers, *infiltrations* meant British soldiers, or irregular cadres like the infamous Rogers' Rangers; but following his own experiences, he was aware of other possibilities that might be lurking in the woods.

The patrol—two *bateaux*, twelve men including himself—left the St. Lawrence at the Chaudière, the swift-flowing river replaced with a lazy, muddy stream. Out of the sight of the great river, the vegetation was thicker, the trees hung heavy and closer to the ground; sunlight was occluded and sound was muffled.

"Let's put in over there." D'Egremont gestured toward a small cove, where there was an obvious trail leading from the water's edge into the woods. His second nodded from the other boat, and the men poled the flat-bottomed *bateaux* against the current until they bumped up against the shore. The men disembarked, shouldering their small field packs and weapons, and formed up along the trail, making room for D'Egremont to come to the head of the line.

"*Allez*," he said. "And no chatter. I expect silence—and attention." He glanced back at his second, a scarred veteran of the Austrian Succession whom the younger men admired, and the older ones feared; from the rear of the column he nodded and scowled at the men ahead of him.

They set off at a brisk pace. Though the French soldier of the line was no Indian scout, under the watchful gaze of authority and the presence of the dark, primeval forest, each man appeared to be on alert, tramping as quietly as possible along the path.

D'Egremont could see, though, that the men were nervous. He was, too: the path was narrow, the underbrush uneven, the vegetation thick and entangling. Five hundred feet along the trail, they had lost sight of the boats and the sun was almost completely invisible through the tree canopy.

Then, suddenly, the cloying quiet was interrupted by the sound of a voice—a man somewhere ahead, speaking aloud—in English. D'Egremont held up his hand; if there was room, he would have immediately deployed his troop in a skirmish line, but there was no space. He turned, gestured to the sergeant, then drew his saber and began to move forward.

There was a clearing fifty feet further along, a remarkable circle of trees in the midst of an overgrown dense forest. At the far edge, an older man was on one knee, plucking at a plant at the base of a tree.

"Perfect," the man was saying. "I would say . . . *Agastache nepetoides*." He took the plant and tucked it into a cloth bag hanging by a strap over his shoulder. He rose to his feet and turned, noticing D'Egremont for the first time.

"Hello. Or should I say *bonjour*?"

The man was tall and middle-aged, wearing a modestly-cut suit somewhat out of fashion. Over it he wore a sort of smock with a wealth of pockets, some of which appeared to have tools and other items stuffed into them. A pair of wire spectacles lay low upon his nose, and he peered through them at the Frenchman.

"Who are you, and what are you doing here?" D'Egremont asked in English. "And we can speak in your language if you prefer."

"That would be my choice," the man answered. "My French is somewhat rusty."

"I asked you a question, Monsieur."

"Did you?"

"I did." D'Egremont waved, and the others came forward, forming a line at the edge of the clearing. "I asked you who you are."

"Bartram," he said, removing his hat and offering a slight bow. "John Bartram, at your service."

"John Bartram, you are an Englishman in the territory of New France and are therefore trespassing."

"Truly."

"Yes, *truly*," D'Egremont said, somewhat aggravated. "I am still waiting to hear what your business is here."

"Well, *here*," Bartram said, "*Agastache nepetoides*. The yellow hyssop. An extraordinary plant, and very important for the pollination of insects. I found a remarkable sample at the base of—" he turned around. "*This* tree. No, wait—I think rather it was *this* one," he said, gesturing at where he had been kneeling. "Really a remarkable—"

"I do not care about the flower—"

"The hyssop. You don't care? Regrettable," Bartram said. "I've hardly found any, though I assume I will find more closer to the river."

"Monsieur Bartram, you should not be here."

"In this forest?"

"In New France."

"Brother," Bartram said, "I assure you that the trees make no distinction as to which country they happen to occupy. Indeed, there is no boundary line that I can see."

"The boundary line," D'Egremont answered, "is the one on which your king and my king agreed."

"An arbitrary mark made on some map thousands of miles from here? I assure you, sir, that the trees themselves were not consulted at all in the matter. Therefore, I do not see how it matters to *us*."

D'Egremont was not at all sure how to respond to the comment; instead he gestured at two of the troopers. "Take Monsieur Bartram in charge—"

He stopped and looked beyond his line of soldiers and noticed that the path they had taken from the river seemed to be obscured by trees and foliage.

"Ah," Bartram said. "I suspect you have no idea just how angry these trees are with you."

"I'm not sure I understand."

"No, of course you do not, Lieutenant—is that the correct title? One must be punctilious in these matters. You see, the trees have not been consulted in all of this mapmaking and boundary-marking. And that is not to mention the clear cutting and lumbering, the slashing and burning . . . they are angry, Lieutenant. Very angry indeed."

The two soldiers whom D'Egremont had ordered stopped in arm's-reach of John Bartram and looked to their commander for direction.

"I am not sure I completely understand," D'Egremont said.

"For the best part of three decades I have traveled through this wilderness," Bartram said, seemingly unaffected by two heavily armed soldiers close by. "Between Peter Kalm and myself, we have constructed a catalog of nearly every species of plant in this part of the continent. This land is familiar to me, and of late I have begun to realize that I can *feel* it as well."

"Of late . . . "

"Since the comet," Bartram said. "The forest is beginning to awaken, Lieutenant. The beings that comprise it know their friends . . . and their foes as well."

If D'Egremont had not traveled to Carillon with the Chevalier de Lévis and seen the shades of Highlanders—if he had not heard the report of *Soleil*'s voyage upriver—he might have scorned the curious Englishman's assertion. But this was one more incomprehensible thing in a world that suddenly seemed full of them.

He turned, saber in hand, looking around the clearing. Somehow the trees looked closer, their boughs had dipped lower, and the canopy of foliage obscured the sun even more thoroughly.

"I take it that they call you friend, Monsieur."

"I flatter myself to think that they do."

"And what do they think of *us*? Or have they not imparted any intelligence regarding that subject?"

"They are not especially fond of white men, Lieutenant. Nationality is a matter on which they are utterly indifferent, though I daresay the French have been slightly more respectful of the wilderness than my own countrymen. They do not seem to be loyal to the red man either—but the natives understand that the natural world has its own jealous privilege."

D'Egremont was once again left with no idea how to respond. Here was an Englishman who might or might not be a spy; the correct thing would be to take him into custody and convey him to Québec . . . perhaps the Marquis would know what to do with him.

"Will you come with us voluntarily, Monsieur Bartram? I will personally guarantee your good treatment."

"As a prisoner?"

"As our guest."

"I have no interest in being anyone's *guest*, Lieutenant. And I assure you I am much more comfortable in this environment than in some *habitation* in New France. So I regret to say the answer is no." He held up a hand. "And before you order these stout young men in front of me to do violence to my person, I will remind you of what I said about friends and foes."

D'Egremont looked around him, the open area now dim from the overhanging foliage. It was as if the bright spring day had been transformed into grim autumn. There was no path at all. The clearing was a very small island surrounded by impenetrable forest.

"You place me in a difficult situation," he managed at last.

"It is not difficult at all. Go and report my presence if you must," Bartram responded. "But I will be on my way, and you will permit it or face the consequences."

"From you?"

"From *them*," Bartram said, gesturing to the trees that surrounded the clearing. Then he looked away toward the tree he had been examining and held out his hand. As D'Egremont and the soldiers watched wide-eyed, a path opened up. Bartram offered a slight bow and began to walk away. The two men nearest him made to follow, but D'Egremont shook his head.

Behind the Frenchmen a similar path appeared, and D'Egremont gestured toward it.

Go and report my presence if you must, he thought.

He wondered what the marquis would make of it.

Part IV: Orientation

June, 1759

Ye monsters of the bubbling deep,
Your Maker's praises spout;
Up from the sands ye codlings
peep,
And wag your tails about.
                —Cotton Mather, *Hymn*

Chapter 26

The broom star has made old things new

The Ohio Country

Spring had not quite come to the land; the days were lengthening as normal, but the nights were cold, and the wind was stiff. It should already be planting season, but the ground was hard and unyielding; the sun seemed distant and the shadows it cast seemed dull and stark. Guyasuta did not know whether this was some sign from the Great Spirit, and Sganyodaiyo gave no insight except to say, *Brother, these are the strangest of days.*

That was nothing he did not already know. He walked through Logstown without giving away his unease: he had made his choice, and the people who looked to him as their chief did not need to have doubts. Sganyodaiyo remained in his house, neither walking among the people nor speaking to anyone other than Guyasuta himself— and to the Great Spirit, of course.

On the cold afternoon when the messenger returned from his mission to Warraghiyagey, Guyasuta sat in front of his own house, watching people pass by, offering nods and greetings. He had stopped to pack and light his pipe when a shadow passed in between him and the sun; he looked up to see someone standing before him, arms crossed in front of him.

"Friend Shingas," he said, beckoning to a seat beside him. It was courtesy only: the Delaware chief was not one he would necessarily call a friend, but since the tribe had been driven from Pennsylvania into the Ohio country, more and more of them had settled in Logstown—including their young, headstrong chief.

"There are rumors," Shingas said.

"There are always rumors. What now?"

"Flying Heads," Shingas said. "And Maneto, in the great river. I had thought those things to be nothing more than legend, to frighten young children. But these stories do not come from children."

"Of course not." Guyasuta took a long draw on his pipe, and after a moment offered it to the Delaware, who did the same. "Because they are not legend."

"Should I be joyful or fearful?"

"When it comes to such things, Friend, one should always be fearful. They do not make distinction between the tribes and the whites—Flying Heads attacked the Council Fire of the Haudenosaunee. The Great Spirit is angry with the People of the Longhouse for becoming too close with the English and French. The whites are intruders on our land—"

"I do not need to be told that," Shingas interrupted.

Guyasuta was a young man by any measure, and only the separation of the tribes in the Ohio country from their Haudenosaunee overlords had elevated him to a high position among a less numerous people. But Shingas was younger still and burned with hot anger at the injustices done to the Delawares, particularly over the last few years. To Shingas there were only enemies and rivals—no real friends.

"The Haudenosaunee must renounce their alliances and turn their back on the whites," Guyasuta said. "All of the things that come to them as gifts and trade goods are things they must do without."

"Yet the whites will still have them. Ships come across the sea and bring more every season."

"No longer."

Shingas was about to reply but stopped, his face a mask of surprise. "What do you mean?"

"The ships will not come any longer. Sganyodaiyo has seen that the world is changed since the coming of the broom star."

"I don't understand."

"You will in time."

Shingas frowned. "What am I to tell my warriors, Friend Guyasuta? That the broom star has made old things new, that the sky and the earth have traded places, and all because one Seneca brave, who cannot bear the light of the sun, says so?"

Guyasuta took us his pipe again. "Yes."

"The Delawares are not prepared to accept that. Not from you, not from anyone."

"Why? I know it is not because you are afraid, or that the Delawares are afraid." Guyasuta smiled as Shingas frowned even more. "It is because you do not understand."

"I said that."

"You did. And I am prepared to make it clear to you—or, rather, Sganyodaiyo will make it clear. He will explain to you what has happened, and what is going to happen next."

"When will this happen then?"

"Soon. I am expecting a messenger. When he comes, I will find you, and we will go to Sganyodaiyo—and he will tell you of the sky and earth and old and new and all will be clear."

The messenger came to him as he stood before Sganyodaiyo's house. The man had ridden hard without sleep for two days but showed no sign of weariness.

"Tell me what Chief Big Business told you."

"He was not happy with the message you sent him, Chief," the man said. "He knew what the broken arrows meant."

"Did he also know of the Flying Heads?"

"Yes. The young Mohawk was at his stone house, recovering from injury."

"Young Mohawk?"

"The one called Joseph. He found a way to destroy a Flying Head, but it burned his hands."

"I did not know there was a way to defeat them without a shaman's medicine. That is . . . interesting. What did the white chief answer to the message?"

"He spoke these words: 'I will deliver words personally to your chiefs—after I kill their braves and burn their longhouses.'"

"Those words exactly?"

"Yes, Chief. After he told me I should leave before I was hunted for sport. I thought reporting to you more important than my personal honor, but I will unsheathe my tomahawk and blacken my face to avenge it when you walk to war."

Guyasuta placed his hand on the young brave's shoulder. "Of course you will, my friend, and I will welcome you by my side."

At a nod, the messenger departed for some much-needed rest, and Guyasuta went into the house of Logstown's shaman and fellow chief.

Though the sun was grim and wan, it was very bright compared to the dim interior of the simple house. The ground floor was divided into two rooms, one each to the left and right of the front entrance. There was a rough stair at the far end of the short hallway that led to the sleeping chambers above.

A young man, younger than the messenger, stepped out of the left-hand room, with the air of someone looking to repel intruders; when he saw it was Guyasuta he relaxed.

"Kaintwakon," Guyasuta said, and extended his hand. They grasped forearms. "How is he today?"

"Awake, at least," the young man said. "My brother is too often lost in dreams. He does not like to be interrupted when he sleeps."

"It is bad medicine to interrupt a shaman's dreams," Guyasuta said. "But I have need of his counsel."

"I can see—"

"I will go in myself, Kaintwakon. If he does not wish to be disturbed, he can be angry with me and not with both of us."

Sganyodaiyo's younger brother looked relieved and stepped aside so that Guyasuta could enter the left-hand room. It was spare and neat, with only a few things—a sleeping pallet, a small table—visible in the dimness. A thin blanket separated the far part of the room, and through it Guyasuta could see the shadow of a seated man, rocking slowly back and forth.

He stepped forward and pulled aside the curtain. Sganyodaiyo looked up as he stepped into the sectioned-off chamber, which was stuffy and close, warmed by a fire in the fireplace. The shaman was seated cross-legged on a somewhat thicker blanket that covered the floor; there were a number of small items—carved wood, bone, three feathers, a few pieces of colored stone—spread out before him in some pattern that Guyasuta could not discern.

"Brother—"

"Shhh," Sganyodaiyo said, and passed his hands, first the left and then the right, over the objects. When he was done, it seemed as if several of them had shifted position, though Guyasuta could not be sure.

Guyasuta waited patiently. At last Sganyodaiyo looked directly at him, as if noticing for the first time that he was there.

"The whites are stirred to anger," he said, slowly gathering up the objects and depositing them one by one into a leather pouch by his side.

"They are coming to try and punish us, Brother, like little children who defy their father."

"It is how they view it," Sganyodaiyo said. "The Great White Father is displeased, and will not spare the rod, as they say."

"They are afraid."

Sganyodaiyo stared at Guyasuta, the fire reflecting eerily in his eyes. "There is reason for them to be afraid, Brother. They have only seen the beginning of our power."

"The Great Spirit has shown this to you?"

Sganyodaiyo did not answer. He reached into the bag and drew out a small circle of pale cloth, three small stones which had been roughly carved into human figures, and a small piece of dried snakeskin.

"The Great Spirit," Sganyodaiyo said, "has given me the power to bring forth his servants. He does not show me what He has done—I call on them myself." He extended his hand over the snakeskin and said, "*Maneto*." He then touched the circle of cloth and said, "*Dagwanoeient*." Finally, he pointed to the three carvings and said, "*Genonskwa*."

When he looked up again at Guyasuta, his eyes were dark, reflecting none of the firelight.

Guyasuta was a warrior. He had fought both with other Senecas and with his brethren in the Ohio country, more and more independent of the Haudenosaunee. He had charged at other natives and at whites, he had used axe and arrow and musket. He would have said, and would have fought any who disagreed, that he feared nothing.

But looking down at the seated shaman with eyes filled with darkness, he felt something near panic. The stone figures began to shake and then slowly struggled to their feet. They turned in unison to face Sganyodaiyo and stiffly bowed.

"*Genonskwa*," Sganyodaiyo said. "Stone Coats. Each one will summon two more until there is an army of them." Sganyodaiyo stared at Guyasuta. "They will march to the English fort at the Forks of the Ohio and they will tear it apart stone by stone."

"And then?"

"And then, Brother, they will advance on even more important targets . . . until there are none left."

Chapter 27

On terms favorable to the Crown of Great Britain

Colony of New York

Major Rogers and a half-dozen of his picked men led the way, following trails they knew better than anyone—or, at least, better than any white man. It was a hundred miles from Albany through the wild country north of the town, along the west side of Lake George, to the place where the French had planted their flag: four days' easy ride, if there were no obstacles or mishaps.

The Rangers were used to traveling by foot or *bateau*, but the chosen men were all skilled riders; they set a brisk pace. Prince Edward, General Wolfe and the men of the 40th had no intention of being shown up as unprepared or soft, and made no complaint as the party picked its way into the wilderness.

They made cold camp as they went. At the first sign of grumbling from the soldiers, Wolfe spoke quietly and sternly to the subaltern in charge of the troop and the grumbling ceased. The prince refused to be treated differently than anyone else on the march: and not only for the sake of morale, but because he realized—and Rogers assured him—that the group was surely being watched. No one passed this way without the knowledge of the tribes.

"General," Prince Edward said, as they prepared to sleep on the second night of their trip, "You would not think it absurd if I told you I felt we were being closely watched?"

"The major has told us we should expect that, Your Highness. The Indians—"

"No. Not by the Indians." Edward took Wolfe's sleeve and pulled him close so he could say quietly, "By the trees."

"The trees."

"Yes. I . . . don't know quite how to describe it. I cannot be certain, but it feels as if our clearing has gotten *smaller* since we set up camp. It . . . may be just my imagination playing a trick on me. Or it could be some other manifestation that we do not understand. I cannot control it in either case."

"Have you spoken to Major Rogers about this?"

"Of course not."

"We are already undertaking an expedition to converse with shades of Scotsmen killed almost a year ago. Why would this . . . feeling . . . be any harder to accept? I can convey your respects myself, and—"

"No. Let it be."

The next morning was overcast, with a hint of rain in the air; progress was slow, and the trail seemed almost invisible. The travelers had dismounted and were leading their horses through underbrush, with the tree canopy thick with early-spring leaves that obscured the sky.

If it had been up to him, the prince felt that he would have given up the course and declared himself insolubly lost. Rogers, however, seemed undaunted, and in the early afternoon they broke free of the woods and ascended a hill that overlooked the river valley. In the far distance, with the aid of a spyglass, they could make out the southernmost point of Lake George.

Laid out before them, the land was not hostile or threatening. It was beautiful and wild, largely untouched by plow or woodsman's axe, stretching off into the west. Some distance away they could see smoke rising from an Indian village located on the opposite shore, but otherwise it was unsettled land, of the sort that scarcely could be found in England.

"This is the whole world, isn't it?" Edward said to Wolfe as they stood together.

"I'm not sure I understand, Your Highness."

"There is no England or Scotland anymore. We're not going home—this is home now. Instead of the Midlands we have New York; instead of London, Boston."

"That's what we've been told," Wolfe said, his angular face and pointed nose in profile. "At least for now we seem to be on our own and making the most of it."

"When we're finished at Carillon, General, I intend to travel to Montréal to treat with the French."

"I don't think General Amherst—"

"I am certain that he would counsel against it. I am certain that you are opposed to that course as well, and Major Rogers will resist my orders in this matter. But it is something we must do."

"As much as I do not want to disagree with a royal prince—who might well soon be my sovereign—it is *not* something we must do, Your Highness." Wolfe faced Prince Edward, his face solemn. "Not now, and certainly not without due consideration and preparation. I will go to Montréal, my prince, with an *army*. I do not desire to enter New France in any other way."

"You're not listening, General Wolfe. I want to—"

"I am listening very carefully, Your Highness. And as your general, and as your subject, I strongly advise you not to consider this course. Major Rogers would agree. If it comes to it, I suspect that he—like I—would be forced to prevent you."

"*Prevent* me?"

Wolfe held the prince's eyes, wanting to look away but not doing so.

"Yes."

Prince Edward looked away, across the river. "It will have to be done, Wolfe. Eventually it will need to be done, because the French are not our enemies. Not anymore. We have discussed this."

"If this is all the world," Wolfe said, "and we must reach an accommodation with the French, then I suggest . . . I *insist* . . . that we do so on terms favorable to the crown of Great Britain."

"At the head of an army."

"If necessary. It might not be the only choice, but in my opinion, it is the *best* choice. Your Highness."

Prince Edward did not answer. He turned away and walked down the hill to where Major Rogers and the others were waiting, leaving Wolfe alone.

At the southern point of Lake George, the party crossed the river and made its way along the west side of the lake. Rogers provided a narrative, describing how His Majesty's forces had landed at the top of the lake and followed a road around the southern French outpost, making their attack from the west toward the fort.

As they made their approach, Wolfe noticed that Prince Edward became increasingly ill at ease, as if the descriptions by the colonial major were being depicted in his mind's eye. Wolfe had studied the battle, which had been an utter disaster, badly managed and a desperate waste of manpower, particularly by the 42nd—the Scots Highlanders who died charging the abatis. But while he had no trouble imagining the movement of forces on the ground they were now traversing, it was merely an academic exercise.

For the prince, it seemed to be something else entirely.

As they reached the abandoned sawmill near the river, Edward sat upright on his mount, his eyes focused directly forward, his gloved hands tight on the reins.

"Listen," he said.

"Listen to—"

"*Listen*," he repeated. "Tell the men to be quiet."

Wolfe raised his hand; the troopers and rangers fell quiet. For a moment there was nothing to be heard but the noises of birds and insects and the soft rushing of water in the nearby river; then Wolfe heard it: a distant, discordant skirling of bagpipes. He recognized it at once: "Scotland the Brave," the piping the Highlanders played as they charged into battle.

Edward did not move. Rogers looked grim; he had been present and in command of troops on that fateful day, months ago, when the British forces had been repulsed here.

"They're here," Edward said quietly, and cantered his horse forward. Wolfe thought about reaching a hand to grasp the prince's reins but discarded the idea and followed closely behind.

The day, which had been bright, now appeared foggy as they approached the former battle lines. They could make out figures. At first, they were dim shadows, but they gradually became more and more distinct. A small group, led by a man dressed in Highland regimentals, bearing a bullet-wound in his right temple and a limp right arm that ended at the elbow, stood directly in the path of Prince Edward's horse, which snorted and tried to shy.

"I am Major Duncan Campbell. What is your business here?" he asked in clear English with a decided Scots burr.

"I am Edward Augustus, Prince of the House of Hanover, Commander in His Majesty's Navy. If the barrier that separates us from the mother country is permanent, then . . . I shall claim the right to be called your sovereign."

"You call yourself our king."

Without hesitation, Edward answered, "Yes, I do."

"We were told that Abercromby has left America," the shade said. "Returned to England—and thus out of our reach. We wish to be avenged for our deaths. Will our sovereign help us with that?"

"You have a right to be angry—"

"We have a right," the shade interrupted, "to be *avenged* for our deaths. We have a right to go to our rest, and not walk unquiet on the earth where our blood was spilled."

"It was nearly a year past," Edward said. "The dead—even the unquiet dead—rarely remain present, and in such numbers. Tell me, Major Campbell. How is it that you and your countrymen are *still here*?"

"I do not understand the question."

"*Your Highness*," Wolfe said, moving his mount forward.

"I do not understand the question," Campbell repeated, frowning, jutting his chin out.

"There are a fair number of you here, Major Campbell, roaming about the battlefield—*unquiet*, as you say. In the many accounts and histories of our wars, when has that situation ever prevailed? Are there ghosts flitting about at Hastings, or Marston Moor, or—bless me—Prestonpans or Culloden? There are not. But still, you are here. Why is that?"

Campbell the Scotsman bore an expression that, in Wolfe's view, constituted no less than malice. But after a moment, the shade replied, "I do not know."

"I do." Prince Edward reached down and patted his horse, which was once again upset by its surroundings. "It is the work of the event that separates us from the homeland. I don't think we completely understand it yet, but it has made it possible for such things as unquiet dead to appear. I think it is a matter of belief; stolid, rational Englishmen—or Frenchmen—do not take readily to supernatural beliefs, while you Scotsmen proclaim blood oaths that prevail beyond the grave."

"Aye," Campbell said, with a tone that suggested that he understood exactly what the prince was saying.

"And the Indians—" Edward swept his hand across the wooded land to the west of the battlefield—"believe even more strongly in such things. The manifestation of their beliefs, Major Campbell, may be the greatest threat of all. Against that menace, I ask your help."

"'Ask'?"

"Unless you permit it, Major, I cannot command you to serve. You have given the last full measure of your loyal service in battle with His Majesty's enemies. But in order to requite your passions, I offer you the opportunity to serve once more."

"What reward awaits us?"

"Not revenge," Edward said. "But perhaps . . . rest."

Wolfe was not sure how the shade would react—nor did he know what, if anything, the figure could do.

But as he watched, more of the shades joined Major Campbell, arranging themselves in ranks beside and behind him.

"General," the prince said, without looking away from Duncan Campbell. "*There* is your army."

Chapter 28

We might as well take our ships apart

Off Virginia

Neptune was nine days out from New York when the topman sighted the other ship, off in the mist, making difficult headway toward the mainland. It was a big one, a ship of the line, enough for Admiral Saunders to call the men to quarters and run out the guns.

Sir Charles Saunders considered himself a fair tactician, and though he would not praise them aloud too highly, he was proud of the crew of *Neptune*. But the ship that was sighted was clearly bigger and better armed than his own: 80 guns, or perhaps 90. He had no desire to be brought down or pinned on a lee shore, especially on the rocky shoals of Virginia's Outer Banks; but he was damned if he was going to let a Frenchman cruise with impunity off the outer coasts of His Majesty's Atlantic plantations.

There were two saving graces to the situation. First, it did not seem as if the big ship had sighted *Neptune* just yet. And second, it seemed clear that it was making insufficient headway for a landfall anywhere on the Virginia or Maryland coasts—it was almost as if it didn't know where it was. That was an opportunity—some careful sailing might give *Neptune* the weather gauge, and that might give Saunders' crew a chance to show the other side what British seamanship was really about.

Then, as *Neptune* made its careful way upwind, the top called down with a remarkable report: the ship was flying His Majesty's colors, along with a familiar blue pennon—one that Saunders had not expected to see ever again. As the ship made its way out of the fog, it was clear that it was indeed a Royal Navy vessel: *Namur*, the flagship of Admiral Boscawen.

"You are most welcome aboard, Sir Charles," Boscawen said. The quarterdeck was vacant except for the two admirals. Saunders had brought his sailing master aboard, and he was consulting with his opposite number aboard *Namur*.

"Thank you, my Lord. I have to say that I am surprised to see you here."

"No more than I. There are stories I could tell that you would not believe."

"Actually, sir," Saunders said, "you might be surprised what I am disposed to believe. It is certain that some great change has taken place, and we are now essentially on our own."

"I know."

"You do? How did you—I mean to say, sir, not to be disrespectful in any way; but how do you come to be off the Virginia coast?"

Boscawen looked at Saunders for several moments, as if he was unsure what was meant by the question. At last he answered, "I did not expect to be off Virginia, Admiral. It was my intention to try and reach Charles Town in the Carolinas. But I have very few charts for the Atlantic Coast. I did not realize that we had been drawn so far north."

"I see."

"That was not the precise nature of your questions, was it?"

"No, sir. Not exactly. I . . . there were two squadrons bound for Halifax to assist in the investment of New France. As a result of the—event—only a few of the ships and a fraction of the troops reached North America. I had not known that your Lordship had also been designated to this command."

"The Lords of Admiralty hadn't done, Saunders," Admiral Boscawen said. "We were underway to the Mediterranean, and somehow found ourselves transported near Barbados. I am reliably informed that there is some sort of barrier that will not permit us to return. Any of us."

"A barrier, sir?"

"A mountain range in the ocean. I have seen it, east of the Leeward Islands . . . I am not sure how far north it extends."

"The world has become strange," Saunders said, looking away from Boscawen, toward the mist from which *Namur* had emerged. To Boscawen it seemed that the younger admiral was apprehensive.

"We are still at war," Boscawen replied.

"The French have the same problem as we do, my Lord. If we cannot return home, or receive help from there, they cannot either. We had planned to take six thousand soldiers up the St. Lawrence to take Québec and Montréal. Most of them . . . are not with us.

"We may be at war with something more dangerous than the soldiers of His Christian Majesty, My Lord. I don't know what you have seen—"

"Let us be honest with each other," Boscawen said, stepping closer to the rail. "Sir Charles. The navy's lifeline runs from England and Ireland. Without ship's stores, without powder and shot, without water and provisions, we might as well take our ships apart and use them for firewood.

"I had hoped to reprovision at Charles Town, or—I suppose—at Williamsburg, now that we have been driven this far north. But any help they can offer will be only temporary; the Atlantic plantations are not well-equipped to supply the Royal Navy. This is our greatest advantage, and if we cannot deploy at sea, it vanishes—no matter who the enemy might be."

"The Royal Navy is not equipped for—"

"For what?"

"Sea monsters," Saunders said. His face was stony, matter of fact. "Whatever you might choose to call them. None of us are equipped in any way to handle them. As for the French, My Lord, they cannot do so either; but we have more in common with them than with any . . . supernatural forces we face. We must make peace with them, and we must do it soon."

"Neither you nor I are entitled to make peace with anyone," Boscawen said. "To do so without the express orders of our king is tantamount to treason."

Saunders took a moment to reply, and then said, "If Europe is inaccessible to us, my Lord, then *our king* is my executive officer, Prince Edward. And you, as the ranking naval officer in this changed world, are First Lord of the Admiralty. If you wish to call that treason and place me in irons, I humbly suggest that you do so now—but there are not enough ships and not enough admirals as it is. I think, sir, you are far more pragmatic and sensible than that."

"First Lord of the Admiralty?"

"*Pro tempore*, if it please your Lordship. But yes."

New York

Though he had not intended to end up in the West Indies, Admiral Boscawen had been taking *Namur* on station; accordingly, he was reasonably well equipped for most contingencies, including the opportunity to meet a royal prince. The dress uniform, including gloves and sash and his very best cocked hat, had been carefully packed aboard, and he was wearing it as he came down the gangplank onto the grimy dock of the city of New York. Jeffrey Amherst and an honor guard were there to receive him—but no royal prince.

The explanation for Prince Edward's absence was a surprise to Sir Charles Saunders, but it was a shock for Boscawen.

"Let me be completely clear," he said to Amherst, forcefully enough to convince the general that he was carefully leashing his anger—but quietly enough not to embarrass the man before his own subordinates. "You let the prince—who, by what Saunders tells me, might as good as be our king—travel into the *interior*? On an inspection tour?"

"I could scarcely refuse."

"You were under no obligation to permit it, sir."

"It was tantamount to a royal command. I imposed a suitable escort on the young man and sent Wolfe with him. Much to that . . . worthy's . . . consternation."

"I can well imagine." Boscawen and Wolfe had taken Louisbourg together, after all, and the admiral had experience with Wolfe's supercilious and arrogant nature. "But the prince . . . "

"Our king, God save him," Amherst answered, "led troops at Dettingen less than twenty years ago as a sitting monarch. The prince himself has been a naval officer aboard Sir Charles Saunders' flagship for some time. You know, and I know, that at any time during that period, a single musket ball or a stray shot from a broadside could have killed him. I know," he continued, holding up his hand as Boscawen continued, "that he is the only prince we have. But we can only shelter him so much. He is due to return shortly, and his firsthand observations will be valuable."

"I do not like it, sir. I do not like it at all."

"Your opinion is duly noted, my Lord. And you are more than welcome to express it personally to him when he returns to New York."

The evening of *Neptune* and *Namur*'s arrival, the matter was resolved by the appearance of a messenger at Fort George. Amherst and his staff had brought out a wealth of records and ledgers, tracking the logistical requirements of His Majesty's forces in North America. Whatever Boscawen had privately concluded regarding Amherst's judgment in permitting the prince to be exposed to danger, he was impressed by the man's exceptional attention to detail.

If this was the whole world, it was clear that Amherst had a good deal of it counted and sorted, which wholly appealed to Boscawen.

The messenger was not dressed at all like a soldier. Boscawen took him at first to be a *courier de bois*, one of the French trader/explorers who roamed the backwoods of New France; he supposed the man to be, perhaps, a captured prisoner. But he offered something resembling a salute to Amherst, who received it with diffidence.

"My Lord," Amherst said, "this is one of Major Rogers' men. We have at our command a small contingent of highly skilled . . . irregular soldiers. They are quartered at Albany, His Royal Highness' destination."

"I see."

"Well, man. Let's have your report."

"I was directed to come with all speed to report to you, General," the man said. "Prince Edward and General Wolfe do not intend to directly return to New York. They have other business among the Iroquois. His Highness has been . . . reinforced."

"By what?"

"By . . . the Highland Brigade, if the General pleases."

"They were decimated at Carillon last summer! How could they . . . "

Amherst stopped suddenly, surprise crossing his face. He looked from the ranger to Admiral Boscawen, then back to the ranger.

"You mean to say," he said quietly, "that the Scotsmen have somehow . . . manifested?"

"They have been there since the battle, General Amherst. They seem to have materialized—and they now follow Prince Edward's command."

"And what has he ordered?"

"The Iroquois report that some force they do not understand has extinguished the Onondaga Council Fire. There was some indication that the Highlanders wished to seek out the cause of that event."

"Are the Iroquois now our enemies?" Boscawen asked.

"I cannot say, My Lord," the ranger answered. "We once counted the Iroquois as our friends, but the war with the French has divided them. Some of the western tribes threw in their lot with the enemy, but the Fire was considered to be neutral territory, where hatchets could be buried, and graves could be covered. The French are not behind this event, so Major Rogers says."

"Is he a reliable source?" Boscawen asked Amherst.

"Without question."

"Then who is the enemy?"

"If I were to answer simply, my Lord, I would have to say that our enemy might well be the future."

Chapter 29

We are in a world where there are stone demons .

Pennsylvania Colony

Even by the time he was able to convey the story in his biography, years later, Edward was still not completely certain of the details. The rangers had begun to be accustomed to the unusual . . . the *supernatural*, he supposed. The men of the 40th left their apprehensions behind within the firm structure of their military training, following orders rather than trying to make sense of what was happening before their eyes.

General Wolfe scribbled it all in his personal journal, a leather-bound commonplace book he carried with him. Edward was not sure what he wrote, and never later found out.

Duncan Campbell, the ethereal leader of his company of Highlanders, informed him that they—as beings from the Beyond, he presumed—could feel the presence of other such intruders, and felt it an affront to His Majesty's person; accordingly they would convey him to the site with all dispatch. Sir William Johnson could wait: the enemy, whatever or whoever it was, came first. The land seemed to slip beneath them as they walked and rode—in short order it became necessary to cover the horses' eyes so that they were not unnerved by the mode of travel, which was like a dream.

If it had been the Scotsmen's choice, there would have been no rest and certainly no sleep—but the living members of the troop, both human and equine, required both. Thus, in the dark woods they made camp, the sleepless Highlanders keeping watch, and nothing troubled them—at least until the moon was high.

There was a disturbance at the outskirts of the camp of which the prince was only apprised when the subaltern of the 40th appeared at the entrance to his tent, touching his hand to his cap and imploring the royal pardon.

"There is a soldier who wishes to convey his respects to Your Highness," the subaltern said.

"A soldier?"

"He claims to have escaped . . . Your Highness, I think it best that he tell you himself."

"Present him then, and ask General Wolfe to attend me."

The man touched his cap and departed. Presently another man, clearly somewhat worse for wear, appeared, and gave a perfect salute. He had no hat or wig, and his uniform showed evidence of rough travel. His face was impassive, but Edward could see fear in his eyes.

"At your ease," he said. "I understand you have a report to make."

"If . . . if it please Your Highness," the man said. "Private Kenneth MacArran, recently posted to Fort Pitt at the forks of the Ohio."

"'Recently'?"

"The fort . . . Highness, the fort has been overthrown. I escaped with my life, along with a few others."

"Are you a deserter, MacArran?"

"If I were, Highness, I would not seek to report to you. I did not desert my post. There is no post to desert. It was destroyed by . . . "

At this, MacArran reached up and touched his hand to his forehead, covering his face.

Before he could continue, General Wolfe came in behind him, saluted, and took up a position behind the young soldier, who removed his hand from his face and looked from Wolfe to the prince, not sure what to do next.

"Tell your story from the beginning, MacArran," Edward said. "Omit no detail. Do your best, young man."

"Three nights ago," he began after a moment, "everything was as it had been for some months—very quiet, since we took the place from the French. A fine fortress it is, Your Highness . . . or was. The watch reported movement in the wood, and then—they began to come. Great tall soldiers, taller than a man, and like . . . like nothing I had ever seen.

"I was not on the watch, so I only saw them when they forced their way through the gate. Musket fire was useless against them, only chipping bits off their sides, like flint. They were not men—they were made of stone, and yet they walked and fought as men."

"Stone men?" Wolfe said, as if refusing to believe.

"They were made of stone, sir, I swear it!" The young man looked anguished, as if his story was not believed—and under normal circumstances it would have been dismissed. "We have—we had—a few Seneca at the fort, Your Highness," he continued, speaking to the prince. "They called them *Genonskwa*. Stone Coats. The Indians fled as fast as they could manage and told us to do the same.

"They did more than just slay the soldiers, Your Highness. They tore apart the fort, stone from stone. And they spoke a chant. I can still hear it." He covered his ears with his hands. "I can hear it—and the screams—"

This time, heedless of the presence of a prince of the blood and a general in His Majesty's army, the man broke down, hands over his face.

Prince Edward stood and took hold of the man's elbow and steered him to sit beside him, a gesture that was completely divorced from royal hauteur. Wolfe's expression showed what he thought of it, but Edward ignored him. The young man had lost any semblance of military dignity, and it took a few minutes for him to gain control of himself.

"So," Wolfe said, after Edward had beckoned him to another seat, "Fort Pitt has fallen to stone demons."

"So it seems. I should like to ask," Edward said, "now that we are in a world where there *are* stone demons—do they come of their own accord, or did someone send them?"

"The French would want Fort Pitt destroyed, just as we wanted Fort Duquesne destroyed before it. Tell me, Private MacArran," he said to the young man who sat uncomfortably at the right of Prince Edward, "when these stone demons attacked, were there any Frenchmen with them?"

"No, sir," the man said. "Only Indians."

"What sort of Indians?"

"I am no expert at telling the bastards apart, begging Your Highness' pardon," he said, "but they weren't the same sorts that were within the walls. They say that the Indians in the Ohio Country are their own tribe now. They call themselves *Mingo*, and they pay no heed to the Covenant Indians."

"Covenant—" Edward began, but Wolfe said, "the Iroquois, Your Highness."

"Ah. So Fort Pitt was destroyed by demons sent by renegade Indians from the Ohio country. That is an additional complexity, I suppose. Though not for our Highlanders."

"Is this the threat they seem to perceive?"

"I suspect so, General. And when we have rested, I expect that we will be going to meet them."

By the time dawn had arrived the next morning they were traveling as before, the world passing by as if projected by a magic lantern; Campbell had warned them not to step too far away from the rough circle of Highlanders for fear of being left behind.

Sometimes the Scotsmen sang. It was somewhat discordant, harsh soldiers' songs of battle and lost loves and missed opportunities, made even more difficult by the certainty that their battle was lost, their love was a thing of the past, and the only opportunity that presented itself was the chance to serve and—perhaps—redeem themselves on behalf of the prince who had promised them rest. The situation was so tense and surreal that those among the troop who still drew breath had little to say to each other.

Late in the day, when the irregular, rough hills had begun to cast long shadows, the strange mode of travel halted. They found themselves in a wide clearing—what appeared to be a cleared hard-packed dirt road, stretching east to west.

Duncan Campbell presented himself before Prince Edward.

"They are coming," he said. "Ye can feel it in the earth."

Edward glanced at Wolfe, who nodded. Beneath them, they could feel a small, regular shuddering in the ground, enough to make the horses snort and neigh. Wolfe called the men to order, but Campbell held up his hand.

"This is our fight, General," he said. "Should we prevail, there is nothing for you to do. Should we fail, you should be ready to leave as quickly as possible."

"We are no cowards, Major Campbell."

"I did not say you were, sir," Campbell replied. "But this is beyond your ken. Musket and sword will not harm these. Yon lad—" he gestured toward MacArran, who was standing with the men of the 40th—"can tell you the truth of it. We will turn the tide of the enemy in the king's name, or you will have to make other plans."

Wolfe appeared ready to make a sharp reply, but the prince nodded to Campbell, and he thought better of it.

And suddenly, the ghostly figures of the Highlanders faded away, leaving the rest of the travelers alone in the dusk.

Moments later, they began to see large human-shaped figures coming down the road. They moved slowly and deliberately, walking in step four abreast, looking like tall Indian braves. Instead of showing any sign of war decoration, their skins bore scales, like great stone snakes. The faces were fierce and devoid of expression.

"Form skirmish line," Wolfe said, not taking his eyes off the advancing forces. He exchanged a glance with Prince Edward, wondering if he was thinking the same thing: *where the hell are the Scotsmen?*

The regulars and rangers formed a line abreast; each had his musket shouldered and aimed. The stone Indians continued to advance, four by four, coming closer and closer—

And just as the Highlander ghosts had vanished, they materialized once again in the path of the oncoming enemy. There was a far-off skirl of bagpipes and a banshee chorus as the ethereal Scotsmen collided with the stone demons. The Scots had been almost transparent, like wisps of dull fog, but in the impact they transformed, glowing brighter than day, more like sheets of flame, white and blue. Had they been men and not spirits, the stone figures might have overwhelmed them, but it was clear to the prince and the general that the fight was taking place in some way, in some realm that they could not see.

The men stood, transfixed and silent, watching the battle take place a hundred yards ahead of them where the stone Indians had stopped and now seemed to be crumbling and melting as the shades of the Scotsmen passed through them in unstoppable waves.

It only took a few minutes. When the light of the battle faded, there was still light in the western sky beyond the hills. No sign of either stone figures or ghostly soldiers remained.

"I think we have given them the battle they desired," Prince Edward said at last. "I pray that means that they can rest."

"I cannot disagree, Your Highness. Now we must attend to ourselves," Wolfe said. "I am not sure exactly where we are, but I suspect this is the colony of Pennsylvania. If Fort Pitt is to the west—" he gestured toward the direction from which the stone Indians had come—"then we should travel east and north, toward Fort Johnson."

"Is that not some considerable distance away?"

"Yes, it is."

"And . . . no one knows that we are here. I imagine our arrival is likely to cause some surprise—as is our disappearance."

"After what we have seen—here and elsewhere—nothing should surprise anyone," Wolfe said. "What I fear is that if these stone demons were summoned by someone inimical to our Crown, other, similar things could also be summoned. Our brave Highlanders are gone. What happens when the next enemies march down that road?"

In the gathering dusk, Prince Edward had no answer.

Chapter 30

We were already enemies

Fort Johnson, Colony of New York

From the time she awoke in the pre-dawn she was reminded of where she was, and why she was there.

The little life growing inside Molly Brant was what she had of William. There had been no word on her husband—which he *was*, whether some acknowledged it or not—and the men who had followed him out of the fort in pursuit of the leaders of the Indians that threatened them. Joseph, his hands almost healed now, chafed every day to go out in search of their trail, but Molly had told him, asked him, begged him not to do so.

He had his place, and she had hers.

She was mistress of Fort Johnson now, directing the staff to aid the refugees who arrived daily from the west. The first ones were encamped near the low stone wall that surrounded the estate, with later arrivals finding spots on the hill; they had come close enough that now from the porch of the Hall she could smell their cookfires when she emerged in the morning. There might come a time when they would be in the building itself, though Skenadoa had advised against it.

"They cannot all be trusted, Sister," he had said to her. "We should not let just anyone through the gate."

He warned her not to walk through the camps alone; but she ignored him in this, today as on every other day. Anyone who came to the gate, from whatever tribe and clan, was admitted and given a place—and she went among them daily to see what their needs might be.

This morning she walked along a narrow lane formed by a group of makeshift tents more than halfway up the hill. A group of elder squaws had brought—or found—a large cookpot and were working at preparing a morning meal for those with them. They were chattering in some dialect—Cayuga, she thought—but greeted her in English as she approached.

"How is the little one?" the oldest one said, setting aside her work to approach. The others seemed to draw back, as if deferent to their senior sister.

Molly placed her hand on her stomach; as if in response, she felt movement—a slight kick.

"He will be strong, I think."

"You know it is a boy?"

"No," Molly said. "Only the Great Spirit knows. But I hope it will be a boy. But it will be loved, boy or girl." There were some tribes, she knew, where girl children were uncared for.

The crone stepped forward and reached an old, gnarled hand; Molly let her come close and touch her belly. There was another kick in response.

"Strong, eh," the old one said. "A boy." She smiled at Molly and drew off a small bracelet from among the many that hung loosely on her right wrist. "Take this."

"You are kind."

"I am *old*," the woman said. "My chief husband gave that to me fifty summers ago. He is with the Great Spirit now—he would want to be remembered."

"So do we all."

"Many will not," she said. "But you, Degonwadonti, you will be."

"You know who I am."

The old woman chuckled. "All know who you are, wife of Chief Big Business. We heard that you were taking in those who lost their homes, and we came to you."

"Sir William has always been generous—"

"*You*," she interrupted. "We came to you."

Molly wasn't sure how to respond to this, so instead asked, "Where have you come from, Elder Sister?"

"Our village was Ichsua, by the river. We traveled half a moon to reach here. The messenger came and told us to leave and seek shelter—or to stay and die."

"Messenger?"

"You have not heard the tale?"

When Molly shook her head, the crone grasped her by the elbow and took her over near the cookpot, settling into a seat on a blanket. She made room for Molly, who sat beside her.

Others stopped their work and gathered; even if they knew the story, they appeared to be interested in hearing it told.

"Ichsua," the old woman began, "was a fine place by the river." She extended one stick arm and drew a jagged line in the dirt in front of the blanket, then placed a few sticks beside it. "Here were our houses, and here we planted maize and beans and squash. The river gave us fish, and the men brought back game. The Great Spirit smiled on us . . . until the messenger came."

"Tell me about the messenger."

"He smiled too much," the old woman said. "He came alone, not a warrior, but he was unafraid of our braves. None challenged him when he crossed the bridge into Ichsua."

"He had a bandaged hand," one of the other crones said; and another hissed something under her breath: Molly heard the word *baby*, but nothing else.

"He had a bandaged hand," the storyteller acknowledged. "With his right he held a walking-stick, but he kept the other close by him and covered." She wrinkled her nose. "It had an odd smell."

"What did the messenger say?" Molly asked.

"He told us that Guyasuta, the Mingo chief, was two walking days from Ichsua. He would spare no one who remained. He did not offer parley, or any terms. Stay and die, leave and live."

"We had heard that Guyasuta was gathering allies from the western tribes."

"Not from Ichsua. We trade . . . we traded . . . with the English. We were already enemies."

"Why did your braves not kill this messenger? Surely, he insulted their honor, Elder Sister. Were they afraid of him?"

The crone looked at the assembled audience, which had become much larger now. She took her time to reply, as if she did not want the words to pass her mouth.

"Yes," she said. "They were afraid."

"The hand," one of the other old women said. "They were afraid of the hand."

"The bandaged hand?"

"He was something out of the ordinary," the crone added. "His hand was a—"

"Not in front of the baby," someone said—the one who had whispered before. Molly placed her hand protectively on her belly.

"Tell me," she said. "What was the hand?"

"Among the Cayuga there is a legend," the old woman continued. "Maybe it is not known to the Mohawks, or the other eastern tribes among the Haudenosaunee. There is a spirit hand called an *Oniate*, a dry hand, or arm, that comes from the corpse of a dread warrior. Shamans who serve the gods below instead of the Great Spirit above sometimes replace their own hand with the *Oniate*, giving them power; and sometimes they wield the *Oniate* like a weapon."

"What does this *Oniate* do?"

"Those it touches are struck down by disease or killed," the woman answered matter-of-factly. "Our braves were afraid of the *Oniate*. The messenger knew our fear. He smelled it, and he smiled."

She reached out with her hand and rubbed out the river and scattered the sticks and stones. "Ichsua," she said, "is no more."

Skenadoa caught up with Molly down near the Fort Johnson gate, where she was speaking with a pair of elderly sachems. His long stride took him directly to her side, and the older natives stepped away silently.

"This is dangerous, Younger Sister," he said. "Particularly for one bearing the chief's child."

"I am not afraid of them," Molly said, hands on hips. "And I was trying to learn something before you scared them away."

"Learn something? About what?"

She lowered her voice and said, very quietly, "*Oniate*."

"That's a tale told by old squaws to frighten children."

"The refugees from Ichsua say differently."

"Do they. Did they *see* one? Was it floating through the air, a dry hand grasping for them—" He reached his hand out, mock-serious, snapping his thumb to the tips of his fingers menacingly.

She steered Skenadoa away from the group and toward the broad path leading up to the Hall. "In this time of great change, Elder Brother, why would you have any trouble imagining that such a thing as a Dry Hand might actually exist? *No*, they only suspected they saw a shaman who had replaced his hand with one. But it seemed to have the ring of truth to me."

Skenadoa thought about this for a moment. "Who knows of this?"

"There were a number of people who heard the tale." She gestured uphill, toward where the recently arrived Cayugas had camped. "I don't know how far it's traveled."

"This is *dangerous*, Little Sister," Skenadoa said. "Fear is like wildfire—it spreads easily, and even if you stamp it out in one place it will spring up in another. These people already believe the worst, and now they have to hear of this."

Molly crossed her arms across her chest. She felt another slight kick from her belly, but ignored it. "I will not lie to these people, Skenadoa. They already feel unsafe. They have come here because we offer them some security. If there are *Oniate* out there somewhere, it is better that they know—and know that they are not here."

"Are you sure?"

"Am I sure of what? That no one has come within the gates who might have let his own arm be severed so he could be joined to a Dry-Hand? Or is carrying one?"

Skenadoa did not answer the question, but turned slowly around, making a complete circle, taking in the view of all the refugees who had gathered on the grounds of Fort Johnson.

Before she could answer her own question, Molly Brant began to have the strangest sensation. It was as if the world had become flat, like a painting, all around her; dimly lit, with only occasional sparks of brightness. Beyond the gates of Fort Johnson's acreage, in the not-too-distant forest, those sparks were etched in ebony, painful to look at, like vicious gouges in the landscape. Yet the bright spots within the enclosure, the sparks—which seemed to correspond with older individuals, including the two sachems who stood at a respectful distance from herself and Skenadoa—were gentle light, like the warm, inviting glow of a fine beeswax candle viewed at a distance.

This is your place, she heard in her mind. *The evil spirits cannot enter here.*

"No," she said. "No . . . one has come here. No one can come here."

No, she thought. *I will not permit it.*

The lights winked out, and the painting faded away, leaving only an empty, gray sky.

"Molly?"

She found her eyes had closed. She opened them and found herself lying in her bed. A concerned Joseph stood beside it, holding her hand; Skenadoa stood at the window, looking out. There were long shadows outside.

"What—" she began and tried to sit up, but Joseph placed his other hand on her arm and she relented, lying back. "What happened?"

"You spoke a few words I did not understand," Skenadoa said, turning away from the window to face her. "Then you collapsed. I brought you back here."

"There are people waiting to hear that you are all right," Joseph said. "Are you all right, sister?"

"I feel just fine. The baby—" It made its presence known, and she placed her hand on her belly, not letting go of her brother. "It seems to be all right as well. I may have to be a little more careful."

"A lot more careful," Skenadoa said. "And many people know about *Oniate*. But . . . there is something strange about it."

"What is that?" Molly asked.

"Everyone who knows told me more or less the same thing. 'We are not afraid,' they said. '*She* will protect us.'"

"She, being—"

"You, Younger Sister," Skenadoa said. "I do not know what you said to them, but everyone seems convinced that you—personally—have the power to keep them safe."

The evil spirits cannot enter here.

She had heard that in her mind. It was unclear where it had come from, except possibly from the Great Spirit, but in her heart she believed it.

This is my place, she thought. *I will—I must—keep these people safe.*

"They are right to believe this," Molly said. "This is their sanctuary. I shall do what they believe I will."

"How?"

"The Great Spirit," she answered, and hoped it was enough.

Chapter 31

We can't see the future

Pennsylvania Colony

During their journey with the Highlanders, it had been largely unnecessary to post guards when they camped; the shades did not sleep, and mortal dangers such as wild animals sensed their presence and stayed away. What might have happened if they had encountered a French or Indian patrol was another matter. Prince Edward suspected that it would not have gone well for them.

Another feature of sleepless, spectral guards was that it had rarely been completely quiet, even in deep forest. It was deathly silent during the night following the surreal battle between the Highlanders and the stone demons. Edward managed to sleep—his experience in the Royal Navy taught him well to sleep whenever time allowed; but his sleep was full of strange images, mixing fear and reality in equal measure. When one of Rogers' men woke him it was still dark, but it came as a relief to return to the world.

As he sat on a stump outside his tent, pulling on his boots, he watched General Wolfe consulting with the ranger, after which the general came and stood before him.

"What is our status?" he asked.

"We have done some scouting in the area, Highness. This isn't really the rangers' regular territory, but we do have some idea where we are."

"And?"

"Our best guess is that we are in northwest Pennsylvania, as we suspected. There is a ridge line to the southeast, with higher hills beyond. We found a river not far to the east that we think is the headwaters of the Allegheny. The trail signs are hard to read, but we are either in the hunting lands of the Delaware or the Erie tribes—"

"And not the Iroquois, or the Ohio."

"No, Your Highness. The Six Nations are to the north, and the Ohio tribes are . . . well, their territories are undefined. We are some distance from the Ohio Country."

"How far, do you think?"

"It is further away than Fort Pitt, and we think we are some days' ride from there. When we begin to travel, we will be moving yet further away."

"Are we in danger?"

"I'm not sure I quite understand Your Highness' question," Wolfe said, with his usual air of half-diffidence and half-annoyance.

"I mean to say, are there any more stone demons out there?"

"They didn't find any overnight, Your Highness."

"Then it should be a simple matter to retrace our path," the prince said, standing and straightening his tunic. "Without any supernatural obstacles—"

"I beg Your Highness' pardon," Wolfe interrupted. "I did not say that there were no *supernatural obstacles*. I said that we did not find any stone demons during our scouting. There is no telling what might lie between us and civilization."

"I have absolute confidence in the skill of the men."

"I'm sure that's appreciated, Your Highness, but there's no way to know whether anyone has the skill to deal with what we might encounter."

In daylight, the prince could see how the rangers navigated through the deep woods. There were trail signs—not terribly obvious, but visible when pointed out—and marked paths that the local natives used to traverse the otherwise trackless wilderness, and to avoid hazards such as bogs and swamps. The path they took—moving carefully, so that the horses did not lose their footing—skirted the edge of a large, ill-defined lowland at the base of the ridge of hills to the south and east, and seemed to twist and wind to deliberately avoid more areas that might have been more hazardous.

Just past midday they crossed a wider, more clearly marked road that ran roughly north and south. The party halted to rest and consult on direction.

"I would think that we should go north," Edward said, gesturing up the road. "It would be easier for the horses than continuing through these woods."

"We are still near Cayuga lands, Highness," Wolfe answered. "It's not clear where their loyalties lie—with the king or against him."

"I would think we are well enough armed to make them unwilling to confront us."

"If it were a simple matter of a handful of savages with bows and arrows, or even muskets, I would agree. But they can muster other forces. We are severely lacking in ghostly Highlanders to oppose them."

The prince thought about the general's answer for a moment, then said, "I understand. But if that is our response whenever we are confronted with natives, we will grow afraid of them—and eventually we'll be afraid of our own shadows."

"Your Highness, I—"

"No. I'm as scared of stone demons as you are, sir. But we are soldiers of the Crown, part of the greatest empire the world has ever known. If we begin to falter on small things, we will ultimately falter on big things as well. If there are hostile natives up the road, we will confront them and do our duty."

"I admire your bravery, my prince," Wolfe said. "But if I may be so bold as to say: there is a very small difference between being brave and being foolhardy. We only have one of you."

"We only have one of each one of us, General Wolfe." Edward stroked the mane of his horse, looking away from Wolfe and toward the north, the gentle early-summer breeze ruffling his hair. "We can't see the future and we can't see what will happen to us. Giving in to every fear is no way for honorable men to live."

Wolfe began to reply, thought better of it, began to reply again, thought better of it again, and fell silent.

"Where do the rangers say this road leads?" the prince said, gesturing northward.

"Some Indian village."

"Extremely descriptive, General. Anything further?"

Wolfe sighed, as if there it was a matter of no importance. "There is an Indian village at a bend in the Allegheny. They believe it is either a Cayuga or Seneca village, and there are several smaller camps nearby. They may be friendly, or hostile—there is no way to know."

It took until the next day for the troop to reach the village, but they knew of its fate long before it came into view. A pall of smoke was visible from some distance; when they first caught sight of it at the crest of a hill, they pulled up for a view.

"It doesn't matter which tribe they are, I suppose," the prince said. "Not now."

The village—or what was left of it—was alongside a sluggish stretch of the Allegheny River, either in Pennsylvania or New York Colony. There were thirty or so huts arranged along the bank, plank walls and thatch roofs, with gardens planted in between. The huts had been methodically fired, and the plots torn up, as if someone not only sought to do violence, but wanted to send a message. Even the seines in the river had been torn apart.

The rangers walked through the settlement, muskets held loosely in their hands, looking back and forth at the devastation. Wolfe and the prince stayed near the wooden bridge at the head of the village.

"There aren't any victims," one of the men said, from within the cluster of burned-out huts. "And no survivors either. There's no one—"

The sentence wasn't completed. From beyond the second-to-last row there were sounds of a scuffle, and one of the rangers emerged holding on to another man—not a native, but a European: a middle-aged man wearing an apron or overcoat. Some sort of tool fell out onto the ground, and he shrugged off the ranger's grasp, bent down, and picked it up. He adjusted his hat and walked toward the prince and general.

"I confess to be surprised," the prince said. "We did not expect to find anyone here—at least anyone alive."

"Things grow everywhere," the man said. "Why would I not be here?"

"I do not know your name, sir."

"I do not know yours either," he answered. "But as a gentleman, I shall oblige. My name is John Bartram. At your service."

"Bartram? As in 'Bartram's Boxes'?"

"The same, sir. Though, I am afraid, no more of them will make their way to the Royal Society, now that it—like all of our mother country—is beyond our reach. But I am honored to be known. And you, sir?"

"Edward Augustus of Hanover. Prince of Great Britain."

Bartram had seemed confident and dispassionate, but when the prince introduced himself it was as if a mask dropped. He fell to one knee and bowed his head. "Your Highness," he said. "An honor."

Edward glanced at Wolfe, then back at the man kneeling before him. "Rise, Mr. Bartram. Be at ease, and tell me what you can about what has happened here."

"And why you are here," Wolfe added.

"That would be helpful, yes," the prince added.

Bartram rose to his feet; another tool fell to the ground, but he left it where it lay. He adjusted his hat once more.

"I have been traveling," Bartram said, "continuing my work, and visiting friends."

"You had friends in this village, Mr. Bartram?"

"No, not precisely. I have friends nearby." He gestured toward the river, toward the woods. As he did, a breeze started up, riffling through the branches of the trees.

"What happened here?" Wolfe asked.

Bartram sighed. "There are some among the Indians who have decided, due to recent events, that white men no longer have a place in the New World. I don't agree, Highness, but I concede that they have a point. We have given them—by which I mean the Indians—a wealth of reasons for their anger. And they're not alone."

"Meaning?"

"I walk through the forests here. Comet or no comet, the work goes on. But the things I hear worry me, Your Highness. They are angry."

"Who, exactly, is angry?" Wolfe asked, his nose arching in the air.

"The trees."

"I confess that I do not understand," Wolfe said. "Are you suggesting that there are . . . *angry trees* all around us?"

"Yes," Bartram said. "That's exactly what I'm saying. I do not know why you would find this any harder to believe than . . . anything else you may have seen or heard since the world changed."

"The trees are angry," Edward said. The rangers had assembled behind Bartram and were waiting for orders. "Very well, sir. Perhaps, if you are informed of their mind, you can apprise us of the cause of their anger, and what might reasonably be expected of us."

"Of *you*, Your Highness."

"Of me, then. What might reasonably be expected of me."

"They wish to be consulted. In all of the mapmaking and all of the working of the land, Highness, they have been left to suffer the consequences of decisions made beyond their control."

"Surely both red men and white men have made use of trees—to build houses and canoes and other things. Men are men; trees are trees."

"They understand that, Your Highness. But white men clear indiscriminately. They have changed the land in a way that red men have not. Now that the world has undergone a transformation, they demand to be heard, just as the Indians who seek redress demand to be heard."

"I cannot hear them, Mr. Bartram."

"But I *can*, Highness." He drew his hat off, examined it as if it contained some defect, and then placed it back on his head. "Since the change swept across the land it is in my ears, almost constantly."

Edward nodded, as if considering the idea. "What has happened to the villagers who lived here?"

"They abandoned this place. They—and many others, from various villages in this part of the Six Nations—have become refugees. They have gone to Fort Johnson, to seek the counsel of Sir William Johnson."

"Then we should go there as well."

"Perhaps," Wolfe said, "Mr. Bartram might consent to guide us there. I am sure he knows these lands better than we do."

"Surely Your Highness is familiar with them," Bartram said. "Otherwise how could you have come here?"

"You would be surprised," Edward said. "Or perhaps not. In any case, we would be glad of your help."

"And counsel," Wolfe added.

"And counsel," Edward agreed. "Please see fit to accompany us, Mr. Bartram. We will discuss the matter of the trees as we travel."

Bartram thought about it for a moment, then bent down to pick up the tool he had dropped. He tipped his hat and offered a slight bow.

"I would be honored," he said.

Chapter 32

The Great Spirit demands it

New York

They followed a well-marked, narrow path that John Bartram identified as the Great Central Trail—a route that crossed all of the six nations of the Haudenosaunee along the southern boundary between New York and Pennsylvania. The Trail passed through a number of Indian villages that had the appearance of having suffered the same fate as Ichsua. Where crops had been planted, the fields looked uncared for; longhouses and other structures had been broken or burned.

And, of course, there was no one to be found in the villages. But five days into their march, they came into a clearing and encountered two bodies: Iroquois warriors, lying on their backs with their arms extended, each still holding a tomahawk. In the shadowed light passing through the thick forest cover, the expressions on their faces were of indescribable horror.

One of the rangers dismounted and moved to investigate while others kept their weapons ready—there had been more than enough strangeness recently to keep them on their guard.

He knelt to examine one of the warriors, whose vest looked as if it had been torn aside. On his chest there was a burn mark in the shape of a splayed hand, with irregular lines extending outward from the extremities of the fingers.

"There's no sign he's even been touched by predators," the ranger said. "You find a body in the woods and it's usually food for wolves. They stayed away from this one."

"How long has he been dead?" the prince asked.

"Not long, Your Highness," the man answered. "Two or three days. But it's hard to say what killed him. There's no blood on the axe, no real sign of a struggle."

"No Indian warrior stands in place and lets himself be slain," Wolfe said. "How did anyone—"

"What is the nature of the wound?" Bartram asked. He had dismounted, but did not approach. This was somewhat beyond botany.

"It looks like a handprint," the ranger said, reaching out to touch it; but Wolfe said, "No!" and he withdrew.

"We don't know what we're facing, young man," Wolfe continued. "Best we let the dead lie."

"Should we bury the two unfortunates?" Prince Edward asked. "It might be the decent thing to do."

"It might," Wolfe agreed. "I would say, to keep them away from the wolves; but it seems the wolves have no taste for men killed this way. But after a few more days they will start to stink."

The rangers dug a shallow grave in the clearing, and carefully lowered the bodies into it, taking care not to touch the places where the handprints marred the chest. They closed the eyes of the warriors, wondering what it was they must have seen just before they met their deaths.

As they continued to travel northward and eastward, they were troubled by the idea of what had killed armed braves at close range. A few days after finding the corpses, they had their answer.

The troop generally traveled single or double file along the well-marked Indian trails, with two rangers in front scouting the path. There was no particular discipline on the march; Prince Edward would often ride near John Bartram, who was a bottomless source of anecdotes and information about the plant and animal life in the deep Iroquois forests. On a humid, rainy afternoon he was in the middle of a complicated account of the feeding habits of *mustelidae*—weasels—when there was a whistle from up ahead that stopped it.

One of the lead rangers loped back to the prince. "Someone is up ahead," he said, making a hand gesture to indicate the need for quiet.

The troop dismounted and began to approach as quietly as

possible. From his vantage, several yards away through the overhang of moss-coated branches, Edward could see movement, and hear a voice speaking in some Indian tongue he could not understand.

He crept closer and saw a single Indian brave facing three other natives, draped in some sort of ceremonial attire. One of them held a wand or a staff, at the end of which was attached something that looked very much like a withered human hand. The single native appeared transfixed, his tomahawk held loosely in his right hand, his eyes staring straight forward at the wand-holder.

As Edward watched, he thought he saw the fingers on the grotesque hand begin to *writhe*.

Somewhere off to his right, someone—probably not a ranger—stepped on a loose branch which broke with a loud *snap*, making all three of the menacing natives turn. In that moment, the single brave seemed to snap out of his lethargy; and with a sweeping motion, he lifted his tomahawk, his muscles bulging and straining as if it suddenly weighed a hundred pounds, and brought it down with a sickening crack on the head of the wand-holder, who cried out and fell to the forest floor. The other two, still looking for the errant sound, saw their leader fall, and without any hesitation broke and ran—directly toward where the lead ranger scouts were concealed. One of the men moved his hands in some sort of gesture, and one of the rangers rose from his position, took aim and fired point-blank into his chest. The other native began to run, but another shot brought him down.

The armed brave came running toward the troop, but when he saw armed men extended his arms outward and stopped in place.

"Peace, friend, we mean you no harm," Prince Edward said, stepping out from concealment. "What is happening here?"

The brave scowled, as if unsure how to respond; after a moment he lowered his tomahawk, still coated in gore from the man he had slain.

"You come from the west," he said, gesturing toward the direction from which the troop had come. "Do you keep peace with the betrayer?"

Wolfe came up beside Edward. "Which betrayer would that be?" he asked.

"Guyasuta," the man answered. "Betrayer of the Haudenosaunee, breaker of the Covenant Chain. He has called upon Stone Coats and *Oniate* and other evil things to drive white men from the land, as well as red men who keep peace with them. If you share a pipe with him, you are my enemy."

"Our . . . allies fought the Stone Coats," Edward said, "and destroyed them—or drove them away at least. Guyasuta is no friend of ours."

The man's expression did not change, but he visibly relaxed, as if he had been prepared to fight—and die—on the spot.

"Can you tell me," the prince continued, "what it is we witnessed? Who were those men, and what was the—wand—that one of them held?"

"*Oniate*," the man answered. "A dry hand. It is an evil medicine, taught to Guyasuta and Sganyodaiyo by *Ciinkwia*, the spirit of thunder and storm. When a powerful shaman dies they cut off his hand and do their work on it. The *bravest* shamans—" he seemed to spit out the word *bravest*, as if he meant the exact opposite—"make the *Oniate* a part of them, putting the dry-hand in place of their own hand. The evil medicine spreads into their bodies then and makes them powerful."

"This shaman did not do that," Wolfe said, "but he seemed powerful enough."

The man did not respond, but seemed angry, as if unwilling to admit the truth.

"We are heading toward Fort Johnson," Edward said, with a glance at Wolfe. "You are welcome to travel with us."

"We were traveling there also," the man said. "My brothers and cousins were slain by *Oniate*. I am the only one who remains to cover their graves."

"We will bring word of this," Edward said. "This Guyasuta has more and more to answer for."

Chapter 33

Now is not the time for weakness

Fort Johnson, Colony of New York

Since she had fainted while visiting the recent arrivals, the older mothers had decided among themselves to take turns visiting the main house and "checking in" on Molly. She refused their attentions at first, but they proved persistent and would not be deterred or prevented. Skenadoa was suspicious but soon dismissed it as a women's matter, offering no more than polite grunts when one or another woman made her way up the long path to the house and found her way to Molly's rooms.

One of the most frequent visitors was an Onondaga crone named Fourth Sparrow. She was among the first of the mothers to visit and seemed to come more regularly than the others. The usual procedure was to come up the hill in late morning—*the mother needs her sleep*—and to never remain into the evening for much the same reason.

It was thus a surprise to Molly when she felt the bony hands of Fourth Sparrow gently shaking her shoulder. She opened her eyes and looked through the open windows; it was deep night, and the moon, which should have been near full, was invisible beneath low clouds that had brought drizzle and rain all day and evening.

"Please, Degonwadonti. You must awaken. I am sorry to disturb you."

"No," she said. "No." She felt her belly instinctively; Fourth Sparrow's eyes flicked from Molly's face to her midsection and back. "What's wrong?"

"Something near the gate, Degonwadonti. The braves are gathering, but it is nothing they can fight."

"What . . . " she lowered her feet to the floor and pulled on her moccasins. Fourth Sparrow bent down and helped her tie them. Molly was a trifle embarrassed at the attention but realized how much it helped given the baby. She pulled a light shawl across her shoulders and, when Fourth Sparrow was done, she stood and followed the old woman out of the room toward the stairs.

Joseph came out of his room, his bow slung across his back. "What's wrong?"

"Something near the gate. Maybe—"

Fourth Sparrow hissed, as if there was no need—and no desire—to speak of what might be waiting down below.

"There are warriors down there," she continued. "But my Elder Sister says that there is something there they cannot fight. Perhaps you should stay—"

"No," he said.

"Your hands—"

"My hands are fine, Sister," Joseph said. "But you want my eyes."

Molly considered protesting but decided that there was no point.

Fourth Sparrow walked at a slow, deliberate pace, but Molly was unwilling to leave her behind. Joseph had no such restraint; once outside the Hall, he loped away, headed for the lower gate. The rain kept most people inside their tents and makeshift houses, but there were many warriors out and watching. As Molly passed down the hill, they went from squatting near the banked fires to walking down with her—so that within a few minutes she was accompanied by a few dozen young braves, all armed, their faces shadowed by the flickering fires and the gray light from above.

"Who knows of this, Elder Sister?"

Fourth Sparrow looked at her as they walked, her hand clutching Molly's elbow for support. "Those who could deeply feel it knew it first, Degonwadonti. But now everyone knows. And they know you will protect us."

"What do the enemies think? Have they tried to come into the compound?"

"They cannot," Fourth Sparrow said. "At least for now."

"What are they, then?"

"It is best not to say, Degonwadonti." She gestured toward Molly's belly. "For the sake of the child."

"The child will awaken to a world full of these things," Molly answered. "Do not hold your tongue, Elder Sister. What seeks to gain entrance to Fort Johnson?"

"*Oniate*," she hissed. "You heard the tale of Ichsua."

"Yes. The women of that village believe that one of them came to that village and told them to run. They ran here."

"*That* one," Fourth Sparrow said. She turned aside and spat. "That one is here. He is *Oniate*—the dry-hand is his hand. You can almost smell it from here."

A hundred feet away, near the foot of the hill, Molly could see a small group of men just outside the low stone wall that surrounded the Fort Johnson estate. A portion of her heightened perceptions showed her the same ebony sparks she had seen before. For a moment she felt faint, but she shrugged it off as if she was taking off her shawl.

Now is not the time for weakness, she thought, and she was reinforced by seeing Joseph among the warriors at the gate. From the light of torches held by those nearby, she saw that he was tensed, as if he was ready to spring forward to attack the men outside.

Leaving Fourth Sparrow in the care of one of the warriors, she sped up her gait and walked directly to the gate.

One of the men just outside stood forward from the others. He appeared to be completely at his ease. He was dressed as a traditional shaman of the Seneca, properly decorated and painted. He face bore a disturbing smile; he kept his left hand concealed within a draped beaver cloak.

"Who are you," Molly said, standing among the warriors at the gate, "and what do you want?"

"Ah," the man said. "This must be the famed Degonwadonti, the widow of the Chief they called Big Business."

"Widow," Molly said levelly. "Tell me, shaman: do you know something I do not?"

"Little Sister, I know *many* things you do not. I know, for instance, that the man you lay with to make that mongrel that grows in your belly did not die well. He cried and wept like a woman."

Molly's hands formed into fists, but she did not let her expression change.

"Liar."

"Words," the shaman said. "Just words. You chose the white man, sweet little sister, to your shame. Now the ancient gods demand blood, and as they awaken, they will place their shoulders more and more to the matter of scouring the whites from the land. The Great Spirit demands it. *Demands* it."

"The Great Spirit told you that, did he?"

The disturbing smile fell away for just a moment. The man withdrew his left arm from beneath his cloak to reveal his hand: a long-fingered, withered thing that he extended and flexed, nearly forming a fist and then raising it, palm out. Even in the light of the torches, the palm seemed utterly black.

Below the wrist was a crisscross of red veins like cat-gut strings, bound through the webbing between each of the bony fingers and wrapped tightly to the shaman's forearm.

Behind her, she heard murmuring, and a sharp intake of breath— *Joseph*, she thought. She wondered what he saw.

"Look at it, Degonwadonti," the shaman said. "Look into it deeply."

"You do not frighten me," she said. "And you shall not pass here."

"Oh, I will," the man answered. "As soon as *Oniate* consumes you." He stepped forward—and a dozen arrows were nocked in a dozen bows.

"Not another step," Molly heard Joseph say.

"Really, Little Brother," the shaman said. "You do not give orders here. Come, Degonwadonti," he continued. "Come and look into *Oniate*."

Molly stepped forward, near to the stone wall. A hand touched her arm, but she shrugged it off.

"Sister—" Joseph said.

"Come, come," the shaman cooed. "Surrender to the power of the Great Spirit."

Molly took another step forward. There was a rustling in the woods nearby, but no one was taking notice.

Molly and the shaman stood on opposite sides of the wall, scarcely at arm's length. He extended his skeletal hand—and when it reached the stone boundary it went no further forward. The shaman's smile slipped once again. He seemed to be pushing against an invisible boundary, but it came no closer.

"Come to me," the shaman said. "Some foolish medicine keeps me from coming to you. One step, Little Sister, and feel *Oniate*'s embrace."

For just a moment Molly looked as if she was going to do just that—to step forward through the gate, transfixed by the darkness within the *Oniate*. Then, shattering the tension of the scene, a shot rang out from the woods.

It struck the shaman's hand, shattering the extended fingers. The severed parts flew outward, struck the invisible barrier, and fell to the ground; but that incomprehensible moment was quickly replaced by something even more strange.

From within the palm a swirl of utter black erupted, quickly covering the remains of the hand, and then crawling up the shaman's arm and onto his chest.

"*Ciinkawe!*" he shrieked. "Aid me, oh gods of storm and thunder! Come to me—"

Whatever else he intended to say was cut off as the blackness chased itself up over his head, cutting off a hideous scream. He collapsed to the ground, crumbling into a pile of dust the size of a bundled cloak, and then swirling away leaving nothing behind.

The other shamans did not manage three steps before falling to a rain of arrows shot by Joseph and the warriors around him. A moment later, a white man in a rather fancy British uniform stepped forward, handing his weapon to one of the other white men with him. From their clothing and gear, Molly thought they were colonial rangers.

Bows were ready and trained on him; but Joseph lowered his weapon and gestured to the others to do likewise.

"Allow me to present myself," the young white man said, stepping into the firelight, with a glance at the spot where the *Oniate*-bearing shaman had stood a few moments before. "My name is Edward Augustus of Hanover, Prince of Great Britain. I thought it appropriate to intervene when you seemed to be in danger."

He offered a courtly bow that appeared completely out of place in the circumstances, but Molly smiled and politely inclined her head.

"Thank you, Highness," she said. "The shaman threatened, but he could not pass. Welcome to Fort Johnson."

"I regret that I did not know your name, madame, except that the shaman called you Degonwadonti, and the widow of Sir William Johnson. I apologize for speaking of it, but is the gentleman dead?"

"There is no proof," Molly answered. "But he rode west from here some weeks ago and has not returned. I still have hope, but it declines each day."

Joseph touched Molly's arm. "He is who he claims to be," he said quietly. "I can see the aura of kingship around him."

Molly nodded. "I do not know what has brought you to us, Prince Edward, but allow me to welcome you into our house . . . into my house. I am sure you have much news."

The rain continued into the morning, but it brought a cooler breeze into the great house. Molly Brant presided at the breakfast-table, her brother at her side, and Prince Edward was impressed with the young woman's gravity and presence. Indeed, he had never met a native quite like her.

"I was told," Edward said, "that those shamans devoted to the idea actually replaced their own hand with this . . . dry hand. I did not believe it until I saw it."

"I found it disturbing as well," Molly said. "I hope there are not too many others who have done so."

"Most of these men have made wands with the dry hand on them. We have gathered several of them."

"You have *Oniate* wands?" Joseph asked.

"Yes. I'm not sure just what we should do with them."

"Destroy them with fire," Skenadoa said from the other end of the table. He looked as uncomfortable as Molly looked at ease. "Along with the bodies of the others who transgressed the Great Spirit with these abominations."

"Don't you think we should examine them first?"

Skenadoa did not answer, but Molly fixed the older man with her gaze. He returned a blank expression, but she grew angry. "You have already done this."

"It was the only thing to do, Younger Sister. I will not deny it, for you already can read me as readily as this young chief's son—" he gestured toward Joseph—"can read trail sign."

Molly placed her hands flat on the table in front of her, one to either side of her breakfast-plate. "That was not your decision to make. You should have consulted others. You should have consulted *me*."

"When a warrior has his prey in his sights, he does not *consult* before loosing his arrow." Skenadoa stood, pushing his chair back, scraping it along the floor. "If you do not like the choices I make, Little Sister, do not give me authority." Without another word he turned and walked away. Molly rose in her seat, as if she was going to follow him, but remained standing, silent, her hands by her sides balled into fists.

Against General Wolfe's advice, Prince Edward walked out among the refugees later that morning, accompanied only by Joseph Brant. Two of the rangers followed at Wolfe's direction, keeping at a distance; Edward ignored them and made his way down the hill from the Hall. There were two bonfires burning steadily just beyond the gates, raising a noxious stink when the wind blew the smoke their way.

"You seem distracted, Prince Edward," Joseph said as they walked toward the main gate.

"I suppose you could say that," Edward said. "These . . . things. The *Oniate*. This is only the latest horror that this Guyasuta has sent at us. The Stone Coats, the Dry Hands, the Floating Heads of which I have heard . . . I don't know what we are going to do. There seems no end to the monsters he can call forth."

"Are you afraid of him?"

"Of Guyasuta? If you had asked me six months ago if I was afraid of any man, would say certainly not: I am a civilized subject of my grandfather the king of Great Britain, and an officer in his Royal Navy. I feared nothing and no one. But now, facing these—powers— I feel powerless. Sooner or later, it seems, there will be some monster we cannot fight."

"You are not powerless, Prince," Joseph said. "And we are safe within the boundaries of Fort Johnson."

"We cannot cower here forever, like—like—"

"Like refugees?"

"If I were a more sensitive man, or a more haughty one, I might call that insolence, Joseph."

"Then you are neither, I presume."

Edward sighed. "No. I am neither. But while I appreciate that I am safe here, and that Molly has some protective power, sooner or later I must leave Fort Johnson and return, probably to New York. I cannot remain here."

"I understand."

"And while we have overcome many things, I worry that there is something else waiting out there. Waiting for me."

"It is true that your aura might attract enemies, but—"

"My what, now?"

"Your aura, Highness. Your royal aura."

"I do not take your meaning, Joseph. My . . . aura?"

Joseph put his hands on his hips and squinted at Prince Edward, moving his head slightly from side to side and up and down. "You have the aura of a king."

"I am no king. I am not even the ranking prince."

"In this world you are," Joseph answered. "And from what I see, you are a king in waiting. There is an aura that I can see—that perhaps you cannot. It is my gift, my *power*, you might say, to see things. It has been especially present since the broom-star passed, and the world changed. I am certain of it: you will be a king in this world."

"But my grandfather is king."

"Before the world changed that might have been true. But now he is gone, just as your world across the sea is gone. I have seen all the world that there is in a vision, and in that seeing there was no Britain, no Europe, no grandfather king.

"And because of that, you carry the aura of a king."

Chapter 34

In short, they are Americans

New York

Navigating past the shallows off Sandy Hook was usually the most challenging part of the trip from Williamsburg to New York, but the captain of *Wolf* found the task calm and mundane after his recent journey.

Seas could be choppy or stormy. Any sailing man knew that and expected it: the weather in the Atlantic in late spring and early summer had its own dangers, not to mention ever-present rocks and tides and coastal shallows. But it was now clear that there were things out in the ocean that he'd never seen before, and *Wolf*'s captain nearly turned and headed for port a half dozen times. However, his passenger prevailed upon him to continue on each occasion, with a dignity and gravity that belied his years.

I have an urgent message for General Amherst, the young officer told him. *The conduct of the war depends on it.*

If *Wolf* were a ship in His Majesty's Navy, the requests could well have been orders, with consequences for refusal. But it was a merchantman, making a regular trip from Virginia to New York, bearing hogsheads of tobacco and bales of cotton, and one young militia colonel with his urgent message that the captain believed was that important.

It took only a few minutes for the young colonel to walk from the dock on the East River to Fort George. It might have been appropriate to hire a carriage; but New York was full of people going in every direction, speaking very loudly and rapidly, and though he stood a head taller than most of them he felt himself lost in the crowd. The wasted time in arranging a carriage was more important than any potential increase in dignity derived from arriving in one.

Thus, he came to Fort George on foot, and presented himself to the sentinel. While he waited for admittance, four messengers rushed by, two in each direction, paying him no mind. At last he was admitted and conveyed to a large building that overlooked the courtyard.

A clerk led him to a broad room where two distinguished-looking officers were bent over a map. One was tall and slender; the other, more heavy-set, his head bent at a slight angle. They both looked up when the clerk said, "Colonel Richard Washington from Virginia."

Washington stepped forward, tucked his uniform cap under his arm and offered a salute. There seemed to be little point in correcting the clerk regarding his name.

"Colonel," the man with the crooked neck said, standing upright. "What brings you here?"

Washington stepped forward and offered a sealed envelope. The man nodded to the other, so Washington presented it to him. He took up a letter-opener, slit the edge of the envelope, and drew out the contents.

After looking briefly at it, he looked up. "This introduces a Colonel George Washington. I thought my clerk called you Richard."

"George is my Christian name, sir," Washington answered. "I thought it impolite to correct him directly."

"Hmm." The man—obviously Sir Jeffrey Amherst—set the letter on the table. "Colonel, may I introduce Admiral Edward Boscawen. Your letter indicates that you were sent here by Governor Dinwiddie. *Acting* Governor, I should say."

"He thought you should be apprised of conditions in Virginia, General—my Lord," Washington said, offering a respectful nod to Boscawen. "He felt that a personal report would carry more . . ."

"Credibility," Boscawen said. "Because he didn't think we'd believe him."

"Just so, my Lord. I have been fully informed on everything that has happened during the last few months. I regret to say that we have no explanation for any of it."

"We begin with information," Amherst answered. "Before we search for causes, we must know what we face."

"If I am not being too forward to ask," Washington said, "what *do* we face?"

"We are at war, Colonel. Not just against the French, but against another enemy—something harder to identify and understand. But your effort, your bravery and your loyalty are required no less."

"Of course, my Lord," Washington answered. "Governor Dinwiddie directed me to remain at your service as long as you needed me."

"It may be needed. We will call upon you when we are ready to receive your report." Amherst waved at the door. "Consult with my clerk for a billet. Did you bring staff with you?"

"Only a servant, General."

"Speak with my clerk." Amherst looked down at the map, an indication that the interview was over. Washington saluted once more and departed, with Amherst ignoring him and Boscawen watching him go.

"Richard Washington," Boscawen said when the young Virginian had departed. "That name—"

"*George* Washington."

"I seem to recall that name from somewhere."

"You should," Amherst said. "He's the man who started the war with the French."

Boscawen nodded. "That's right. Some battle in the wilds of—was it Pennsylvania? Almost five years ago, before things got hot on the continent."

"Just so. But he also marched with Braddock and showed bravery at the Monongahela. I don't think I'd put him in charge of an army, but he's a good man, and may prove useful."

On Queen Street above Hanover Square, there was a vacant townhouse that was already being called Admiralty House. It was a far cry from the facilities used by His Majesty's Navy in London, but at present it was what the New World had to offer.

Boscawen spent most of his days there. His pennant flew just below the Union Jack; he'd officially transferred it ashore, leaving the command of *Namur* to Pascal, brevetted to commander for the interim—there were no boards of review established, no seniority lists, really no sense of order at all.

It irked Boscawen, now the *soi-disant* First Lord of the Admiralty. Frances would have smiled at it all, especially his use of a French adjective to designate it.

The problems facing Boscawen were more than a matter of precedence or protocol. His navy—he had begun to think of it as *his* navy—relied on a web of logistics that the separation from Europe had torn asunder.

The Royal Navy's ability to go to sea, and stay there, depended on the provision of vital materials: food, weapons, and ship's stores. Men in a ship's company consumed a certain amount of food and drink every day, regardless of duty, whether the ship was in port being careened or sailing in open sea. There was simply no getting around it. Similarly, ships had to have powder and shot for their guns, and for the muskets carried by ship's troops. These could be rationed; the captain of a ship at sea rarely wasted them, knowing that he would be accountable for every measure and every ball. And stores—rigging, sail, caulking, wood, lamp-oil, everything that kept a ship afloat—could be carefully husbanded, but were ultimately consumed and had to be replaced.

Over the course of the last hundred years, the Navy had established contracts with civilian companies to provide everything its ships (and naval emplacements) required. These were scattered throughout the Empire, in the home islands, across the Atlantic plantations and the West Indies, in Africa and India and Asia—wherever Britannia's flag was carried. Contract-holders provided goods and services and their profits, and the Navy's expenditures, were calculated to the last farthing. The Admiralty did not particularly like the system, but liking it was not the point—the Navy was not in the business of ropemaking, porksalting, or powdermixing. There were businessmen across the British Empire who were much more efficient at it, and they were called upon to do so at a rate that at least minimally satisfied both parties.

But now the interconnections between those suppliers and the Navy, and between each other, was broken—possibly forever. Suppliers in Ireland, in England, in India could not contribute to the flow of goods that the navy—Boscawen's navy—needed to consume *every day* in order to function.

And colonial suppliers, only peripherally linked to this web of logistics, were in a position to extract concessions that the Lords of the Admiralty would have never accepted.

"Thirty days," Boscawen said to Edward Hughes, who—like him— was reluctantly ashore and drafted as Boscawen's assistant. He tossed a bundle of reports on the desk between them, which was otherwise uncluttered. "We have thirty days before our funds are exhausted."

Captain Hughes shifted in his seat, which creaked in response. Boscawen had witnessed this for the past few days and expected at any moment for the chair to admit defeat and collapse, dropping the heavy-set Hughes to the floor.

This was not the moment, apparently. "They refuse to take a note of hand? From your Lordship?"

"What's that worth? The Bank of England is beyond our reach. These men—" he tapped on the bundle—"want to be paid in good hard money, and I just don't have it."

"They seem ungrateful for the Navy's protection."

"It doesn't feed their families. If the situation were not so dire, I might sympathize. But based on what we continue to learn about the latest dangers, I don't have that luxury. There are apparently sea-monsters in the Chesapeake, according to Colonel Washington."

Hughes didn't respond. He'd heard enough about sea-monsters to believe they could be in shallow water as well as out in the Atlantic.

"They are neither altruistic nor patriotic, at least when such sentiments conflict with their profit motive. In short, Hughes, they are *Americans*. A rougher, simpler, and less deferential species than His Majesty's subjects in Dublin or Southampton, I daresay."

"I have an interview with the gentleman from the Exchange this afternoon," Hughes said. "We are to meet at Merchants' Coffee House. I expect that it will be less private than I would like—more like a public scrum. But it was his choice of venue."

"Do you think he is trying to intimidate you, Hughes?"

"I do not intimidate easily, My Lord." He shifted in his chair again, and Boscawen awaited the inevitable once more.

"I am gratified to hear it. Was there anything else?"

"Not at the moment, Admiral. If I may have leave to go?" He stood and saluted, giving the chair one more chance for surrender.

"Dismissed," Boscawen said, returning his attention to the bundle on his desk.

Chapter 35

But magic has power over rationality

New York

Edward Boscawen was no stranger to social life, but the last few months had given him precious little opportunity to enjoy it. The invitation from the colonial governor came as something of a surprise; he told Amherst, who shrugged in response.

"I should be careful when you shake hands with De Lancey," Amherst told him. "He has his own agenda."

"I appreciate the advice," Boscawen answered. "But I have served in Parliament."

Amherst's brow furrowed, but then he seemed to realize that Boscawen was joking, and he gave him a smile. "So you did, My Lord. So—will you take Hughes with you?"

"I hadn't thought about it. I wasn't—"

"You must take an adjutant, Admiral. It wouldn't do to appear at the mansion of the Acting Governor alone."

"If I were visiting Sir Charles Hardy, I would go with nothing more than a bottle of Madeira. I scarcely think that I should take a visit to his subordinate more seriously."

"Except that Sir Charles is beyond the edge of the world now, and James De Lancey is for all intents and purposes the Governor of the Colony of New York. He may be a trumped-up colonial, but he has a fine mansion out on the Albany Road, and is connected with every family in the colony. He is a *patroon*, if you please."

"And why did this *patroon* not invite you to his fine mansion, General?"

"He did," Amherst said. "I told him I had a military campaign to plan."

Upon reflection, bringing Hughes with him did not seem to be the right choice. Instead he requested the services of the young Virginian; and Amherst did not hesitate to release him.

Leaving New York on an early summer afternoon, Boscawen took the time to examine the countryside. New York, for all its pretensions to the status of a great city, was really not very large—the houses ran out beyond the commons and were replaced by plowed fields watched over by windmills. It reminded him very much of Holland, the country that had originally settled this land a century before, though off to the north he could see steep hills that might one day mark the boundary of the city.

Beside him in the carriage, Colonel Washington sat stiffly upright, looking neither right nor left. He seemed extremely uncomfortable in his present position, though he had expressed his pleasure at being asked; it was as if he was on duty, rather than in any way at his ease.

"Have you ever met Governor De Lancey, Colonel?"

"No, my Lord," Washington said. "I know only a little about him— he has served for many years as a judge here in New York."

"He has a very nice mansion, I am told. They must remunerate their judges very well."

"I daresay," Washington said. "But I suspect that the mansion is more representative of his family wealth than his civic engagements."

"Just so. He is the descendant of rich settlers of this part of the New World. His roots go back to the Dutch. That still counts for a great deal here."

"The old families in Virginia are important as well. My new wife Martha is from the Custis family, which is prominent there."

"New wife?"

"Just in January, my Lord."

"Congratulations, young man," Boscawen said. "Marriage is a blessed condition. I wish you the greatest happiness."

Washington turned slightly to look at the admiral. "Thank you very much, my Lord. Are you . . . married, sir?"

"Yes." Boscawen took a deep breath. "But Frances is . . . in England. It is becoming increasingly apparent that we will never be together again."

Washington had maintained an emotionless facial expression, but he looked genuinely crestfallen. "I'm . . . so sorry, my Lord. I can't imagine."

"I can't imagine any of this. Monsters in the ocean—ghosts of Highlanders—and a universe of other things that make no sense except now they are part of our world. I wish Frances could see all this. But perhaps she has some wonder to view on her side of the barrier."

Washington did not answer.

"But that is not our concern at this moment," Boscawen said at last. "Obviously, Governor De Lancey has some reason for entertaining us this afternoon. I have brought you along, sir, because you understand how to conduct yourself in polite society. I need you to keep your eyes and ears open, and report to me what you see and hear."

"I will do my best, my Lord."

De Lancey's mansion was set back from the high road, with a broad circular driveway in front. Boscawen's carriage halted at the portico, and the admiral and his young adjutant disembarked with the assistance of liveried footmen. Washington clearly looked impressed by the elegance of the place; but Boscawen saw nothing which would approach a gentleman's estate in England.

Once inside, Boscawen permitted himself to be separated from Washington, who was immediately engaged in conversation with an earnest young man wearing a militia officer's uniform. The gathering was twenty or so people, including Governor De Lancey's wife Anne. She was a sturdy, middle-aged matron; at his arrival he was politely introduced, but her attention was quickly drawn away by some other arriving guest.

A servant poured him a cup of punch, and as he stood by the French doors overlooking a spacious garden, a man approached and cleared his throat.

"Admiral Lord Boscawen?"

"Your servant, sir."

"James Alexander." The man's voice had the slightest Scotch burr, worn smooth it seemed from interaction with the sharp New York accent. "If I may have a word."

There was something unusual about Alexander that Boscawen

could not quite identify—a sort of feverish intensity that made him slightly uneasy. But in the Royal Navy one met all sorts, so he thought nothing much of it at the time.

"How may I help you?"

"My Lord, I understand that you were accompanied to New York by certain guests—Dr. Messier and a Mademoiselle LaGèndiere."

"You are well-informed, Mr. Alexander. I am sure that there are very few in New York—indeed, anywhere in the Atlantic plantations—who are aware of that fact."

"I thank you for not dissembling, sir."

"Would it do any good to have done so? Please, sir, your point. My guests are under my protection, and if you intend—"

Alexander held his hands up. "Please, My Lord, you misapprehend me. I mean no harm to them, none whatsoever. Indeed, their presence is, I think, a great asset to the natural philosophers' community here in New York City."

"Of which you are a member, I take it."

"I am the president of the American Philosophical Society, Admiral. We are eager for the opportunity to meet with these worthies to discuss their research on the alchemetical compass."

Boscawen set his punch on a side-table, untouched. "The alchemetical compass, you say. What can you tell me about this device?"

"Device—bless me, My Lord, are you suggesting that they actually *have* a compass in their possession? From all that we have heard, there is presently no contact with Europe, and I assumed that any such device would have to be built from scratch." Alexander seemed quite animated at the idea.

"If I may pose a question, Mr. Alexander. What exactly does this compass *do*?"

Alexander's face went from excited to curious. "You don't know?"

"Enlighten me."

"Your Lordship is familiar with the principles of the mundane compass," Alexander said. "The globe has a magnetic field, a north and south magnetic pole, and a compass aligns itself to indicate those cardinal directions. The alchemetical compass responds to the presence of lines of force that crisscross the world in various directions, and points particularly to nodes where such force is concentrated."

"What sort of 'force'?"

"Well, sir, different scholars have given it different names—all of the writing on the matter is relatively new. Newton wrote about it first, but others—"

Boscawen held up a hand. "What did Sir Isaac call it?"

"Æther," Alexander said. "He said that there were 'ætheric nodes' scattered across the world. They had always been present, but after the cometary transit in 1682 they began to appear more and more frequently."

"I see," Boscawen answered. "What do others call it?"

"I'm not sure . . . "

"What do *you* call it, sir?"

"I am a man of science, My Lord, but I am also a Scotsman by birth. There are some things that even a man of science can give no other name than . . . magic."

"Magic."

Alexander nodded. "Aye. That is what I would call it. Dr. Messier wrote a monograph based on a reading of a portion of Newton's Waste Book; he used the term *mágie* to describe the phenomenon."

"And the alchemetical compass can locate these nodes of . . . magic, wherever they might lie."

"Essentially, yes. They might be places or things or . . . people."

"People?"

"I think that Dr. Messier has been less forthcoming with you than he might have been, my Lord," Alexander said. "Given the situation, I should think that a conversation with him would be most productive. And the opportunity to see the compass is extremely exciting." Alexander seemed to want to terminate the conversation he had initiated and began to withdraw.

"Wait," Boscawen said. "What 'situation'?"

Alexander halted, having half turned away. "If there is one place where the ætheric nodes are predominant, it is here in the Americas. In Europe, the advance of science and rationality have—shall we say—denatured them. But in places where those principles are rare or unknown, they can flourish. Where they do, magic flourishes as well."

"Are you suggesting that rationality has no power over 'magic'?"

"Quite the opposite, my Lord. But magic also has power over

rationality. The virtue of our position is that we can understand both and react accordingly."

With a polite bow, Alexander stepped away without further word, leaving Admiral Boscawen standing alone, caught between confusion and affront.

Discomfited by the conversation, Boscawen left the house and undertook a stroll through De Lancey's carefully tended gardens. It reminded him—faintly—of a proper English garden. He assumed that the governor had imported someone from the home island to take care of it, a pretension to gentility that amused him.

Alexander's remarks were disturbing, particularly at the end— that these so-called "ætheric nodes" could not only be places, but things or even people; and that whatever power they possessed, they were most potent where rationality was weak. What did that mean?

The alchemetical compass, when he had first seen it, had inclined itself toward *him*. What did *that* mean? If anyone was rational—and dear Frances, were she here, would certainly confirm it—it was Edward Boscawen. Magic wasn't real; of course, neither were 'Places of Bone,' or sea-monsters, or *obeah*, or ghost Highlanders . . . rationality, William of Occam's famous razor, suggested that his eyes and other perceptions did not deceive him and indeed those things *did* exist. And if they did . . .

As he examined an exquisitely trimmed piece of topiary, he saw the acting Governor of the Colony of New York, James De Lancey, approaching. The man clearly had some sense of how to act as a courtier, and he walked very slowly, giving Boscawen a moment to gather himself.

"Governor."

"My Lord," De Lancey said. "I trust you have not found the company incommodious."

"I wanted a breath of air."

"After a conversation with Jamie Alexander, I can certainly understand it."

"I beg your pardon?"

"He's an interesting fellow, Admiral." De Lancey came up to stand beside him. He reached out and pulled a few stray leaves from the topiary as if the shape was somehow improper, and let his hands fall to his sides. "A recovering Jacobite, if you please. Though if my sources are accurate, that distinction no longer matters. We are all Whigs, we are all Tories now that we cannot return to England."

"Your sources are good ones, Governor," Boscawen said. "I agree; those distinctions no longer matter."

"Which makes it more important that we work together, sir."

"Of course."

"Apropos of that . . . I don't know if you are aware, Admiral, of the impact of the event on the economy of our colony, particularly our trade. Without putting too fine a point on it, New York is in . . . perilous circumstances particularly due to the lack of specie. We are goods-rich, but cash-poor. And gold makes the world go around."

"An interesting turn of phrase," Boscawen said. "What would you have me do, Governor?"

"If I am correct, My Lord," De Lancey said, "your original destination was the Mediterranean, to take charge of British naval forces there. I suspect that it would not be too much of an exaggeration to assume that you were provided with some funds to pay them."

"And if that conjecture is true?"

"Perhaps you might be willing to make some of those funds available."

"What exactly do you mean by . . . 'make available'?"

"I thought perhaps in the form of a quiet loan," De Lancey said, absently pulling at another leaf in the topiary. "As you noted, it is important that we all work together."

"A loan. From His Majesty's Government to the Colony of New York."

"Properly signed and approved," De Lancey answered. "With terms for payback. New York is—at least on paper—a wealthy colony, My Lord. We are just in a rather uncomfortable passage."

The rapidity with which the New Yorker had come around to the subject took Boscawen aback, but he wasn't about to show it. A moment's thought suggested that this encounter—this conversation—might have been the proximate reason for De Lancey to have invited him out to the estate: not a matter of courtesy, but a matter of pounds sterling.

If De Lancey had any sort of leverage—and since Boscawen's

naval forces certainly needed to be supplied, he might arguably have it in this situation—this might even be viewed as a species of extortion.

A less experienced or less diplomatic officer might have reacted with anger, with revulsion, or with icy hauteur. But Edward Boscawen had sat in Parliament, and he knew as well as anyone how accurate William Hogarth's engravings truly were. The world was full of James De Lanceys—even this world, even as it was now.

This was about money. Not banding together against the unknown perils created by the cometary transit; not the prosperity or well-being of His Majesty's plantations in America.

"I shall have to consider the matter," Boscawen said. He could see De Lancey's eyes light up, but fortunately the New Yorker made no response, other than to offer him a polite bow. It saved Boscawen from the temptation, however slight, to administer a good beating.

On the carriage ride back to the city, Colonel Washington was again silent, sitting upright and looking straight ahead.

"Did you enjoy your afternoon, Colonel?"

"Very much, My Lord," Washington answered. "Governor De Lancey's estate is extremely handsome, and he showed gentlemanly hospitality."

"Tell me what you heard."

"Heard, Admiral?"

"What did people talk about? How are they feeling?"

"People seemed . . . nervous, sir. They are concerned about the future—about the French and particularly about the Indians. No one knows what is to come."

"Are they concerned about finances?"

"Of course, sir. *I* am concerned about finances; every merchant, every farmer, every shipowner worries about such things every day." He turned to look directly at Boscawen with an expression that seemed to say, *this is the way of the world, my Lord, for just about everyone. Perhaps you did not know that.*

"I understand."

Washington's expression did not change, but he said, "Certainly, my Lord."

Chapter 36

Burn bright in the air

New York

The idea had seemed absurd at first: it came to Boscawen as he lay upon his bed in Admiralty House, trying to sort out all of the things that burdened him. He had always accounted himself a rational man—but perhaps the changes he saw in the world were now being reflected upon him personally, stripping away that rationality that had been a source of pride and confidence. Otherwise he never would have considered the concept that bore in on him in the quiet, cloying darkness.

Perhaps gold can be created. By alchemy.

No one needed to know that such gold, "lent" to James De Lancey by the Admiralty, was not guineas from His Majesty's mint—except that making any such alchemetical substance would have to be somehow made to look like them. And did "created" gold retain its form and identity, or did it dissipate or disappear?

He would have discarded the idea right then, on the spot, except that it nagged at him. In a world of irrational, impossible wonders, why not transmutation? There were no Crown officers ready to pounce and put him in irons for falsely creating currency. There were no rules, and there was no guide to the country he was now in.

In the morning he sent a messenger to the house where Dr. Messier and Mademoiselle LaGèndiere were staying, asking them to call upon him at their convenience. He turned his attention to reports and logistical matters, dismissing all alchemy from his mind.

Just after the clock struck eleven, an aide interrupted to inform him that the two civilians had presented themselves.

He pulled on his uniform coat, adjusted his cravat and descended to the ground floor, where the townhouse's modest morning-room had been converted for the purpose of receiving guests. He found them there, standing nervously, as if expecting a reproof.

"Good morning," he said, entering the room. "Thank you for responding so quickly to my invitation."

"We took it as a summons, Monsieur Admiral," Messier said. "Is there something wrong?"

"No, nothing at all." He gestured to a divan and armchairs. "Won't you sit? I need to consult with you on a matter well beyond my expertise, but well within yours."

The young lady took her seat, perching on one of the armchairs; Messier and Boscawen followed.

"We are pleased to offer whatever help we can," she said.

"I had an interesting conversation yesterday with a Mr. Alexander, the head of a group that titles itself the 'American Philosophical Society.' He seemed extremely excited to hear that you two were in New York—and that you possessed an alchemetical compass. He would very much like to examine the device."

"Of course," Messier said, exchanging a glance with the young woman. "We would be happy to show it to him."

"Capital," Boscawen said. "Now . . . I wish to discuss something with you that must remain in complete confidence. I had a conversation with Governor De Lancey regarding the financial condition of the colony. He asked me for a loan."

"Monsieur Admiral . . . ?"

"He believes that I am able to provide him with money originally intended for my Mediterranean command. If I had it, I might be inclined to make the loan—but I don't have it."

"We don't have it either," Messier said.

"No," Boscawen answered. "But is it possible that you might be able to . . . *create* it."

"*Create?*" Messier said. "Do you mean—"

"He means transmutation," Catherine LaGèndiere said. "He is suggesting that we convert some base metal into gold." She looked at Boscawen. "Alchemy."

"Yes," the admiral said. "I don't know anything about how it works—or even if it can be done at all. But if it can, it is a way for the colony to survive, and possibly for my fleet to be supplied and equipped. So I must ask: is it possible?"

Messier looked thoughtful. "Prior to the 1682 transit, alchemy was no more than speculation; there are numerous texts, mostly unreliable of course—Paracelsus, Trismegistus. After the comet passed, things that had been fantastic were made rational."

"And possible."

"And possible," Messier agreed. "And with the alchemetical compass, we could more easily measure and control the process." He exchanged a glance with Catherine, then looked back at Boscawen. "We would need some equipment, of course."

"I think there is someone to whom you should be introduced."

The headquarters of the American Philosophical Society was located at the corner of Broad Way and King Street, in a pair of stout brick buildings connected by a second-story bridge. Though Messier would have preferred a carriage—if only for Catherine's sake—there were none to be found, leaving them to walk the distance from their lodgings.

Presently they were admitted into a sitting-room filled with a collection of mismatched furniture and unusual objects—things of glass and metal, some clearly from a laboratory or workshop, others with no apparent purpose, like projects half-finished left on a shelf to catch the light. Catherine was examining one of them—a collection of glass tubes connected to an irregularly-shaped wooden box—when James Alexander entered the room.

Messier had long relied on his assistant's intuition and perceptions and took note of her immediate and focused attention on the new arrival. She seemed . . . if not afraid, then at least on edge. She clutched the bag with the alchemetical compass more tightly.

Whatever it was about the New Yorker that troubled her, Messier felt it too—there was something *different* about the man, a sort of heightened, feverish air, like eyes opened too wide. Still, this was the man they had come to see, and this was the place for them to be—it was obvious, at least from the objects they could identify, that the Society took an interest in the arts and sciences.

"The famous Dr. Messier," Alexander said, his New York accent wrapped in a Scotch lilt. "And this must be Mademoiselle LaGèndiere, of whom I have heard." He made a leg. "An honor and pleasure to have you here with us."

"Thank you for receiving us," Messier answered. "Admiral Boscawen said that he spoke with you at Governor De Lancey's reception. He thought perhaps that we might have some commonality of interest."

"Indeed." Alexander's glance went from Messier to Catherine— or, more particularly, the bag she carried. "I understand . . . that you possess a remarkable device."

"The compass."

"Yes," Alexander said. Messier's senses were even more affected by the man as he said it. "Perhaps we could retire to one of the workshops and I could examine it."

Messier looked at Catherine, who had done her best to compose herself. She nodded and offered a smile.

"Of course."

Alexander led them onto a short hallway that led to a narrow stair, at the top of which they turned and walked along the bridge they had seen from outside. There was a long, thick window that gave a view of Trinity Church and the river beyond; someone had made notations on the glass, tracing the outline of the church-spire and marking a series of lines with a column of figures beside it.

At the end of the bridge they went down two steps and then turned left into a wide workroom that smelled of sawdust and carbolic acid. A large, sturdy table held a large array of glass and metal objects; this was clearly a laboratory in active use, though there was no one present to use it. At the far end of the room was a conical furnace, its fire carefully banked but open to the room and hot enough that its radiance could be felt even from the doorway, even in the summer heat.

"You are well-equipped," Catherine said, casting her eyes across the array of devices.

"This is one of the finest alchemetical laboratories in the New World," Alexander said. "I'm quite proud of it, actually."

"You are an alchemist?"

"I am both a practitioner and a beneficiary," he answered.

"Indeed, I am pleased to say that alchemy saved my life. Considering that the practical art was hardly even possible a century ago, that is saying something."

"In what way are you a beneficiary, sir?" Messier asked.

"Three years ago," he said, "I had traveled to our colony's capital, Albany, to confer with colleagues regarding a political matter. Like many of my colleagues, I suffer—suffered—from the gout." He lifted one foot and waved it slightly, indicating the afflicted member. "When I returned to New York, my health was a shambles. I believe I might have died, but for this." He stepped to a cabinet, used a key on his watch-chain to open it, and drew out one of several small glass vials containing a red liquid.

Messier's face registered surprise. "Is that—"

"*Aurum potabile,*" Alexander said, nodding. "The drinkable gold. The Red Lion."

Messier did not answer, but Catherine responded by placing her bag on the table. She reached in and withdrew the wooden box containing the alchemetical compass.

Alexander walked slowly toward her, but Messier took a step forward and held up his hand. For a moment, Messier thought that the other man might try to push past, but instead he simply extended his hand with the vial. Messier took it and held it up to the light streaming through the windows, casting a strange shadow on the table below. Inside the bottle, the liquid seemed to move of its own volition, like an aquatic creature trying to work its way out.

As he examined the bottle, he looked sidelong at Alexander, whose face held a vaguely hungry look that disturbed him.

Catherine had opened the box and placed the alchemetical compass on the table. It was already detecting Alexander's presence, the fluid inside climbing the side of the internal glass in the direction of the New Yorker.

"Extraordinary," Alexander said softly. He took a step, and after a moment Messier stepped aside to let him pass, though he remained close. Catherine watched warily as the two men approached.

"A question," Catherine said. "Monsieur Alexander, how long have you been drinking the Red Lion?"

He smiled. "Almost three years, Mademoiselle. I have never felt better."

The liquid in the compass had climbed almost to the top of the glass; if it had not been sealed, it might have spilled out of the container on to the table. Alexander reached out to touch it, but Catherine interposed her hand, then drew it back as if it had been burned. Alexander stepped back, colliding with Messier just behind.

"Are you hurt?" Messier asked in French, and the young woman shook her head, rubbing the hand Alexander had touched on the cloth of her bodice.

"I think it is wise," Messier said in English to Alexander, "that you not touch the instrument."

"Very well," Alexander said. He reached for the bottle with the alchemetical mixture; Messier handed it to him. He placed it back on its position on the shelf and locked the cabinet. He turned to face his visitors again; for just a moment Messier saw a flash of reddish light in Alexander's eyes, which made him want to cross himself—but he refrained, not wishing to alarm Catherine LaGèndiere.

She seemed already alarmed and said, "Monsieur Alexander, the potable gold is consuming you from within."

"Possibly," Alexander agreed. "But it has saved my life. I would prefer to burn bright in the air than decompose in the cold ground."

The words hung in the air for several moments. At last Messier said, "I would not wish to tell a man how to spend his days; the number of them is after all for God to decide."

"Aye," Alexander said. "Now what can I do for you?"

"Did Admiral Boscawen explain the reason for our visit?"

"He indicated that you wanted to pursue an alchemetical experiment, and in my note to him I responded that we were well equipped. We have whatever you might need."

"Including a spagyric matrix, Monsieur?"

"Why do you need a philosopher's stone? You have the ultimate measuring device there," Alexander said, gesturing toward the compass. "It will tell you when to begin coagulation, or dealbation, or calcination."

"So you do not have one?"

"I didn't say that," Alexander answered, smiling. "It just seems superfluous."

"It might be," Catherine said. "Nonetheless, it might be helpful for our purposes."

"Which are?"

Catherine rubbed her hands again, as if there was still some discomfort left over from the brief interaction with Alexander. "We wish to attempt a transmutation."

"What sort?"

"Base metal to noble metal," she said. "Preferably gold."

"You want to make gold."

"Can it be done?" Messier asked. "Or is there some objection—"

"No, no," Alexander said, holding up his hands. "No objection at all. I see no reason to invoke some sort of Puritan *morality* in this case, Monsieur Messier. You are in New York, not Boston."

"So?"

"So. Such a process is by no means easy, and it *is* time-consuming. Fortunately, we are not merely equipped to carry it out, we have been undertaking it since the comet's passage—when it became much easier."

"That was an interesting response," Boscawen said. "What did you tell him, sir?"

"Only that I was pleased to hear that we might not need to start, as you might say, from scratch," Messier answered. They were walking along the parapet of Fort George, overlooking the bay south of Manhattan Island. The sun had gone behind the clouds, but the day remained sultry, scarcely affected by what little breeze came off the water.

Admiral Boscawen, as always, looked completely at ease, despite his full uniform. Messier wondered how he managed it.

"I must admit that I am surprised," the admiral said. "Even though I began this line of inquiry, I wasn't sure if it was a completely absurd notion. But tell me more of your impression of Alexander. You say that Mademoiselle LaGèndiere was troubled by him?"

"She scarcely spoke of it after we departed, but yes, I could see that he disturbed her. *He is being consumed*, she repeated to me, as if the man's life was somehow unnatural."

"As it might be—and what is this substance that he showed you?"

"It is an alchemetical decoction commonly called Red Lion, or the 'potable gold.' It is said to be the essence of fire distilled in air, a true *aqua vitae*. It is made—well, it is a long and arduous process, described by the ancient practitioners. I have never heard of anyone who consumed it in any quantity."

"How much has he consumed?"

"I do not know how regularly he drinks it, Monsieur Admiral. But over the course of three years he must have ingested quite a bit."

Boscawen stopped walking and turned to face Messier, tilting his head sideways slightly, his face stern.

"What does Mademoiselle LaGèndiere believe will happen when this—substance—overwhelms him?"

"The Red Lion is derived from elemental fire," Messier answered. "I would imagine . . . there would be some combustion. If it happened in a place full of volatile, or even merely flammable, materials . . . "

Messier let the sentence trail off and said nothing further. The words seemed to echo for Boscawen, drifting beyond the parapet to be drowned by the crashing of the waves on the rocks below.

Chapter 37

Those kings are now beyond the edge of the world

Northern New York

Montcalm had always kept an important lesson in mind when dealing with the people. If they were idle, he knew, there would be trouble; this was especially important if they were also frightened.

The refugees from Upper Canada, though few in number, had transmitted their fear to the civilians on the river; rumors—and evidence—of the hostility of the unknown forces upriver had made everyone scared. Fortunately, recent events had offered a solution. One of Bigot's many storehouses yielded a few hundred stands of arms; many residents of New France had been soldiers, and were eager to take an active role, rather than just waiting for some new horror to arrive.

It wasn't much. Truthfully, it wasn't enough—perhaps five hundred new recruits to supplement the roughly three hundred professional soldiers under Montcalm's command that Vaudreuil was willing to let him take out of the province. Montcalm was not willing to engage in a battle of wills with the governor, at least until he was able—figuratively or literally—to throw Bigot over a cliff. So, the *troupes de la marine* and most of the regulars stayed behind to defend against the English, the Indians, or whatever was lurking to the west in the inchoate, mysterious world that had come into existence with the comet's transit.

Overall, what he was given was a good enough force to take a native "castle," or undertake a punitive raid—but not sufficient to march on Albany or Boston or to retake Fort Duquesne (though there was a well-confirmed rumor that scarcely any of the new British works remained, some new unearthly force having reduced them).

It was, however, enough for a demonstration.

In the late afternoon sunlight, the lake was placid and beautiful, the long, flat-bottomed *bateaux* moved with an easy grace through the water, each carrying a number of French soldiers—regular or recruited—and a Seneca guide. It reminded Montcalm of the campaign two years ago, when he had led an expedition that originally led to the siege of Fort William Henry. That had been memorable in a way that the viscount would prefer to forget. After his subordinate, Bourlamanque, had obtained the surrender of the garrison and arranged terms under which they were to withdraw further south, their Indian allies had carried out a terrible massacre that he had not been able to prevent.

As he watched the tree-lined shore pass slowly by, Montcalm wondered if there were ghosts of those men—and women, for there had been civilians and camp-followers murdered as well—lurking in those woods, summoned by the world's change.

If they were there, he could not see them.

There was no Fort William Henry to besiege, and Carillon was abandoned—and, if it was to be believed, occupied by the ghosts of Abercromby's Highlanders. Montcalm disembarked his force on the west bank of Lac du Saint-Sacrement, ordering his subordinate commanders to establish a fortified camp. By sunset it had been laid out, and Montcalm—whose tent had been placed at the brow of a hill overlooking the deployment—was ready to meet with his officers. D'Egremont, whom he had chosen as his aide, leaving Lévis behind in Québec, was waiting for him as he reached his accommodations.

"The army looks to have sorted itself properly, Monsieur."

Montcalm snorted. "To call this group an army stretches the definition to say the least. Most are not soldiers, and there is no rival army they could possibly oppose. But . . . yes, the camp is properly laid out."

D'Egremont looked at the sky, which was slowly darkening following a brilliant summer sunset. "Do you plan to move toward Carillon?"

"I see no point, based on your report, D'Egremont. I am primarily interested in the natives—" Montcalm allowed his eyes to drift upward as well. "And possibly where the English are."

"You want to fight the English? With . . . " he gestured toward the camp. "With them?"

"Fight? No. I don't think that's in order. Most of the English forces were in or near New York, unless they've undertaken a summer campaign. If so, it would be good to know."

"Thus—a demonstration, Monsieur."

"Just so."

If any among Montcalm's expedition were expecting to march the following day, they were disappointed. The *habitants* who had joined the military of New France were subjected to drill and inspection— marching and manual of arms, sweating in the bright sun at lake's edge.

The army—such as it was—exercised for two days, which was— in Montcalm's expert view—in no way sufficient to make these citizens into soldiers. On the third morning after their arrival, a runner arrived at Montcalm's tent to report a visitor.

"What sort of visitors?"

"A group of Indians, Monsieur," the young officer said. He sounded either disdainful or wary—he was a regular soldier from the *corps de marine*, only recently arrived in New France.

"How many?"

"Five," the man answered.

"That seems well short of an invading force. I will receive them."

"They are armed, Monsieur."

"I am not surprised. If that troubles you, Lieutenant, order a guard to escort them to my presence."

The young officer seemed reassured by the idea; he nodded and withdrew. A few minutes later, two natives were admitted into Montcalm's tent: a very tall older man, clearly an elder of some sort, and a younger brave who stood next to him, showing no particular deference to his elder. The other three presumably remained outside.

"Be welcome, Brothers," Montcalm said. "How may I help you today?"

"We are surprised to find you here, servant of the *Onontio*," the older Indian said. "What is your purpose?"

"This is land my king claims," Montcalm answered. "With respect, I do not wish to explain myself to you. But I do not mean you or your tribe any harm."

"Which is why you come so well-armed."

Montcalm ignored the sharp retort and said, "To whom do I have the honor of speaking?"

"I am Skenadoa, a chief of the Oneida. This is Joseph of the Wolf clan of the Mohawk."

"Then I might ask, Chief Skenadoa: what is *your* purpose?"

"You were seen," Skenadoa said. He glanced at Joseph, who had fixed his attention on Montcalm—rather disturbingly, the French commander thought. The young native had a steady, piercing gaze.

"We made no attempt to conceal ourselves."

"There is no army of the king of England to fight," Skenadoa said. "And you say you do not threaten *us*. Are you looking for *Maneto* in the *Andia-ta-roc-te*?" he gestured in the direction of the lake. "He is not there, at least not yet."

"We know where *Maneto* is, or rather where he was," Montcalm answered levelly. "We do not fear him."

"White men have much to fear," Skenadoa said. "For all the wrongs done to our people, the spirits of the land will not be moved to protect them."

"Yes," Montcalm said, waving his hand. "And we are told that the trees are angry as well. Tell me, Chief: are your people looking to fight mine, either on your own or in the employ of the king of England? The People of the Longhouse—any of them—were not always enemies of my king."

"The two white kings each held a hatchet in their hands; but those kings are now beyond the edge of the world. Are you still carrying war in your heart, servant of the *Onontio*? That is what I am here to learn."

"And report."

"Yes, that as well," Skenadoa said.

"To whom? To General Amherst?"

"We do not serve that general," Skenadoa said. "We will tell your answer to our people and our friends."

"Our enemies are things like *Maneto*," the younger native said, the first words he had spoken. It earned him a sharp look from Chief Skenadoa, but the older native made no move to contradict him.

"And not the French."

"And not the French," Joseph said. "And not the English either. The things being sent are evil to both our people and yours, red and white. They want to destroy you utterly. But these things have evil designs for us as well. Make no mistake."

"Interesting," Montcalm said. He folded his hands in his lap. "There are some among your people who consider white men a great evil. They would not weep if we were destroyed utterly. But for every wrong committed by whites, there are massacres and outrages committed by natives. Finding trust between us is a difficult thing."

"You speak truly," Skenadoa said. "Few whites have such wisdom."

"Thank you for the compliment," Montcalm said. "Few natives are so forthright."

"We are always straight in speech. Your ears are often crooked."

It sounded like less of a compliment, but Montcalm was not prepared to take it as an insult.

"Let me be straight in speech," Montcalm said after a moment. "If we agree that the enemies of both my king and the king of England are these—creatures—what would you have of me? I will not submit to any other authority."

"I cannot speak for the prince," Skenadoa said.

"What prince?"

"Prince Edward, who shall be King Edward," the native answered. "Since this is all the world now."

Montcalm had been laconic up to this point, even given the native man's insolence. But this made him sit forward. "Edward. The grandson of King George of England? The younger son?"

"Yes."

"He's here in North America?—Of course, he must have been in the British fleet. Does that mean they survived after all?" *Then why have I not heard of this before now?*

"Only a few of the great ships. He was aboard one of them, so it is said."

"And you are sure this is a prince of the blood."

"Yes," Joseph said.

Skenadoa looked aside at him for several moments, then returned his attention to Montcalm. "Yes. We are sure."

"Will you be returning to him?"

"I will," Skenadoa said. "Joseph will be traveling elsewhere."

"I will write a letter," Montcalm said. "One of my officers will carry it to your prince—"

"*The* prince," Skenadoa interrupted.

"He will carry it to the prince," Montcalm said. He wasn't sure why the distinction was being made but was content to follow the native's lead. "Is this acceptable?"

"If he is ready to leave very soon."

Montcalm stood. "I shall see to it."

Chapter 38

When the world has changed, you need to change with it

Logstown

Kaintwakon knew that he disturbed Guyasuta at his own peril. The Seneca slept lightly, like a true warrior, with hatchet and dagger in close reach. The younger brave might be dead in a moment if the other man reacted too quickly, or because the world of dreams had not quite let go.

Still, there was no other choice, and he entered Guyasuta's sleeping chamber, intending to touch Guyasuta's shoulder and then, if necessary, jump back.

He was saved the need. Guyasuta was awake already, hatchet in hand, his pale eyes visible in the morning light coming past the tent-flap. Whatever woman had been sleeping beside him had already departed to her morning duties.

Guyasuta looked annoyed and was not hiding it.

"Brother," Kaintwakon said, "you must come."

"What is it?"

"Sganyodaiyo."

"What is wrong?"

"He is raving. Shouting and flailing about. He may hurt himself."

Guyasuta stood, not letting go of his hatchet. "I cannot prevent him from hurting himself, Brother. Does he call for me?"

"He does."

"Huh." Guyasuta gestured, and Kaintwakon preceded him out of the tent. For just a moment the younger man had an uneasy feeling

251

about turning his back on a man with a hatchet, but shrugged it off, and the two stepped into the morning heat.

"When did this start?"

Kaintwakon pointed at the sky, a little lower than where the sun stood. "He was shouting about the *Oniate*. One of the older braves wanted to bind him and stop up his mouth."

"Did he—"

"No. Others kept him from it."

Sganyodaiyo's house was as dimly lit as always, and even from the doorway they could hear moaning and muttering. They found their way to his sleeping-room and came face to face with Sganyodaiyo. Even in the dim firelight, Guyasuta could see that Sganyodaiyo's eyes reflected nothing.

"What has happened?"

"Brother," he said. "You are here."

Guyasuta did not answer. He glanced over his shoulder at Kaintwakon, who was immobilized by the scene.

"What has happened, Brother Sganyodaiyo?"

"Do you remember," he answered, "when I showed you the power of the Great Spirit?" He bent down and picked up a drawstring bag and held it next to his face.

"Yes. Yes, of course."

Sganyodaiyo emptied the bag at his feet. Three rough stone figures and a dried snakeskin fell to the floor; a circle of cloth drifted slowly after.

"Someone, or something, killed *Maneto*. I cannot believe that the servants of the *Onontio* are that powerful, but it has happened.

"*Dagwanoeient*. One of the Flying Heads was separated from the earth as it attacked the Longhouse at the Council Fire. The legends say that there is nothing mortal that can harm such a creature.

"And then there are the *Genonskwa*." Sganyodaiyo bent down and gently set the stone figures upright. "They destroyed the fort at the Forks, oh yes, they did!" He laughed, throwing his head back—and then stopped, squatting on his haunches, lowering his head to face the floor. "Something tore them apart and they returned to the earth. Even the *Oniate* were consumed by the darkness, at the gate of the enemy."

He covered his face with his hands. Guyasuta could not tell whether Sganyodaiyo was weeping.

"What does the Great Spirit want us to do, my Brother?"

"I don't know," Sganyodaiyo said, without looking up or removing his hands from his face. "I don't know."

"No," Guyasuta said, seizing Sganyodaiyo's shoulder—

And a burst of energy, a sheet of unburning flame, erupted from Sganyodaiyo, hurling Guyasuta back against Kaintwakon, almost knocking him off his feet. Sganyodaiyo himself was on his feet, his arms wide, his face twisted in anger and, possibly, ecstasy.

"The Great Spirit is mighty," Sganyodaiyo said. "He does not suffer his servant to be touched. He does not know you. He does not see you."

"He—"

"You must come before him, Brother," Sganyodaiyo said, cutting across Guyasuta. "It is time to set aside the Great Spirit's second-hand tools and become one yourself."

"They are better armed than we are."

"They have never been weaker," Sganyodaiyo replied. "The two nations of white men hate each other, and neither will ever again receive help from its home country, beyond the sundering barrier. You must strike now."

His voice had taken on a different timber, as if he was not speaking for himself, but rather someone—or some*thing*—was speaking for him.

"Unless you are *afraid*."

Guyasuta looked from Kaintwakon to Sganyodaiyo. The younger brave had an expression of shock or even horror.

"I am not afraid," Guyasuta said. "You are walking a dangerous path, Sganyodaiyo."

"It has been dangerous for quite a long time, Brother," he said, in the same disturbing voice. "If you find the need to strike me down, then I am ready. But it would be better for you to take your weapon in hand against the real enemy."

Sganyodaiyo turned his back and stretched his arms wide. He leaned his head forward, away from Guyasuta, as if anticipating a blow.

Land of the Five Nations

D'Egremont had not expected to be moving through the primeval forest of America on foot with a middle-aged, inscrutable native; but he knew how to follow orders, and General Montcalm had dispatched him with a letter to an English prince. It would not surprise him if this was a trap—though he could not determine what value he might have as a hostage, or, indeed, a corpse.

Skenadoa did not, in any case, intend him immediate harm, else the man would have attacked him as soon as they were out of sight of the French camp. The native was taciturn, just short of hostile, and spoke little as they followed a trail that D'Egremont could hardly discern.

Skenadoa was of an indeterminate age, but D'Egremont would have guessed that he was in his late forties or early fifties, a mature middle-aged man by European standards. What constituted middle-aged for an Iroquois was beyond his own experience; for all he knew, Skenadoa was old enough to have appeared before the English Queen Anne half a century earlier. Still, though he was no longer young, he was possessed of an unflagging stamina as they traveled westward, neither summer heat nor rough terrain slowing them down.

At sunset the native halted, finding a place for the two of them to camp. D'Egremont had spent considerable time in the wild during the past several months; his pack and even his choice of clothing reflected experience with overland travel. If Skenadoa was in any way disdainful of the Frenchman, he did not show it; and presently they had rigged a rough shelter and settled down with a simple meal.

"What can you tell me about your prince?" D'Egremont asked after they had eaten.

"He is not my prince," Skenadoa answered. "Your chief Montcalm called him that as well." He grunted. "Do I look like an Englishman to you?"

"You do not call our king your lord," D'Egremont answered. "I meant no offense, but I assumed—"

"You assumed."

"Yes."

"Your people are as quick to assume as the English. My people are the People of the Longhouse; my nation is Oneida, though I was born among the Susquehannocks. We have no princes nor kings, and we bow neither to the English king nor the *Onontio* of the French.

"But none of that matters, Frenchman. You have no king."

"I don't believe that."

"Not believing changes nothing." Skenadoa reached into his pack and withdrew a thin clay pipe and a small, battered leather pouch. He packed the pipe and lit it from the fire, then took a long draw and handed it to D'Egremont. As he let the smoke slowly drift out, he continued, "The world of your nation is gone, Frenchman. Who is your king now that your king is gone? Is it Montcalm?"

"The marquis is not a king."

"Well then." Skenadoa extended his hand for the pipe. D'Egremont looked at it, shrugged and pulled in some smoke, then handed it back. "You are in need of a new king then."

"But I have one."

"No," Skenadoa said, smoking again. "No. You do not. This is the world you live in now. Here you live, here you will die. What do you not understand? Even your marquis understands."

"I have not come to terms with it."

"I thought you were a warrior."

"I beg your pardon?"

"A warrior does not pretend that the things are different than they actually are. When the world has changed, you need to change with it." He handed D'Egremont the pipe again. "The Great Spirit has cracked the world and your land is gone."

"Perhaps not forever."

"Forever is a deep, dark forest that has no exit. Don't think about *forever*, Frenchman. Concentrate on today and tomorrow. Yesterday is gone; forever is unknown. You need a king. Who shall it be?"

"I . . . I'm not sure how to answer that. I want to say, *Louis, the fifteenth of the name*, but if I accept what you say, then I do not know."

Skenadoa nodded solemnly. "You begin to see."

D'Egremont and Skenadoa talked at length as they walked along the trail, drawing closer and closer to Johnson Hall. For his part, the tall native became more forthcoming after what seemed to be hostility; it was as if he had discharged his responsibility to be severe, and now that he had evaluated the worth of his traveling companion, it was no longer necessary.

"This is a beautiful land," D'Egremont said as they crested a hill.

"It is," the native agreed. "Do you find it more so than the land of your birth?"

"I grew up in the north part of France," D'Egremont answered. "Every place—every valley, every hill, every river—has been walked upon or navigated or cultivated for hundreds of years. This place seems virginal, like no foot has trod upon it."

"Many feet have walked here, since the Great Spirit created it," Skenadoa said. "Our land is as old as your former one. We simply have not tried to bend it to our will."

"I see that. Many Europeans think that is good and sufficient reason to take it away from you."

"They like to call us savages and primitives as well. It is not how brothers should treat each other."

"It is a misunderstanding."

Skenadoa turned aside and spat. "No, it is not. In my great-great-grandfather's time it was a misunderstanding. Now it is ignorance and hatred. The white people want all of this, but they must learn that they cannot have it. I understand why Guyasuta and his friends do what they do: it comes from anger."

"It doesn't make it less evil."

"Who is to say?"

"You are. And I am, and the marquis, and this English prince. There is good and there is evil. Do you think your Great Spirit approves of all these things we have seen?"

Skenadoa shrugged but did not answer.

"What do you want?" D'Egremont asked after several moments of silence. "What do your people want?"

"It depends on who you ask."

"I'm asking you."

"I want the world to be the way it was, summer and winter. But it cannot ever again be thus. What I want instead is to live in peace—all of us, every tribe, every nation. The world is big enough for that."

"What of this Guyasuta?"

"He wants something else."

By the time the two men reached Johnson Hall, D'Egremont had been informed of recent events: Sir William Johnson's disappearance, the fight between the Stone Coats and the Highlanders, and the confrontation with the *Oniate* at the gate.

None of it, and nothing else Skenadoa could have described, prepared him for Molly Brant.

At first, he felt wrong-footed at being received by a woman—and a native woman at that. He assumed, and the Marquis had assumed, that Johnson Hall was in the custody and control of Sir William Johnson, Britain's ambassador extraordinary. But Skenadoa had informed him en route that the man had left Johnson Hall with an expedition to the west and never returned.

The Iroquois were matriarchal after a fashion, he knew, but this was for all intents and purposes a war, and he expected a war chief to be in charge . . . perhaps someone like Skenadoa. Yet in the moment neither he, nor any other Indian at Johnson Hall, seemed to claim pride of place over the young woman. He sensed something about her, an aura—a presence—that struck him at once.

"Lieutenant D'Egremont," she said, offering him a polite nod. She had a group of Indian braves around her, who seemed significantly less polite, but said nothing. As for Skenadoa, he stood beside his traveling companion of the past few days with his arms crossed, saying nothing.

Another test, D'Egremont thought.

"Mademoiselle," he answered. "It is my honor to be received by you. I bear a letter for someone I am told is your guest."

"Who would that be?"

"Prince Edward of Great Britain."

"I see. May I ask the nature of this letter? You come here in the company of our elder brother Skenadoa, and presumably under the flag of truce; but you are a representative of a foreign power with which he—and we—are at war."

"Mademoiselle, I—"

"I have not finished, Lieutenant. Your country has been an ally of the western Iroquois, including the Cayuga and the Seneca, and has given warm support to the tribes in the Ohio Country. I have no way to know that France is not an ally of Guyasuta himself—and therefore our enemy."

D'Egremont did not immediately answer; he wanted to gather his thoughts and to be assured that Molly Brant had truly finished speaking.

"You have a right to be suspicious," he said at last. "You also are within your rights to ask what message I bear. Yet you must understand that the communication between his Lordship the Marquis de Montcalm and his Highness the Prince is a private letter—" he almost continued the sentence with the words *between gentlemen*, but somehow restrained himself—"and it would be inappropriate for either of us to read it."

"So you do not know what it says?"

"I have my own guess, but no, I have not seen it and the marquis did not confide in me. He merely asked me to present it to the prince in person."

"I could simply have it taken from you." She lifted her chin, as if suggesting that she planned to order just that.

"Mademoiselle," D'Egremont said, "I would prefer that you not do so. I am an emissary from a civilized nation. I have no expectation that I would be received in other than a civilized manner." *In other words*, he thought, *I trust you are not a savage.* "I cannot imagine that *Monsieur le Prince* would keep the message from his allies; but it would be most appropriate for him to see it first."

For several moments D'Egremont was not sure how she would respond: anger, violence, or merely hauteur; instead, she nodded slowly.

"Very well, Lieutenant. Let us escort you to Prince Edward. Perhaps we will all learn something."

Chapter 39

Something on the wind

New York

Gustavus sensed rather than saw the tension in the town of New York as he made his way on errand for his master. Everyone seemed to be on edge; he felt as if he was being watched as he made his way through the narrow, cobbled streets. He was even followed, on two separate occasions, by men he did not wish to be stopped by. Fortunately, he was familiar with towns with narrow streets and was able to evade them.

Lieutenant Pascal had given him a small amount of silver to obtain stores for *Namur*. It was a risk—there wasn't a lot of hard currency floating around the town, especially in the possession of a young black man, *especially* a slave—but it showed good faith, an offer to pay instead of simply presenting a promise from Admiral Boscawen. The admiral's desire to make friends in New York was something Gustavus wanted to help with, if only in a small way.

Chandlers and shipfitters kept their businesses on the wharves and docks along the East River; *Namur* was anchored near the tip of the island, just south of Broad Street, and his destination—a shipfitter's shop belonging to a man named Dunn—was nearly at the northernmost place. Gustavus found his way there after some trial and error; as he stepped into the shop, a middle-aged heavy-set black man emerged from the back room. When he saw Gustavus he closed his eyes for a moment and then focused, frowning, directly on the young man. There was another black man in the shop with broad shoulders; his back was turned to Gustavus, but even so the young man felt a sense of menace from him.

"I do not know you."

"No," Gustavus agreed. "I am from the ship of Admiral Boscawen. My name is—they call me—Gustavus."

"Ah."

"Is there some problem, brother?"

"No," the other man said. "But I am very careful who I call brother. People listen. *White* people especially. So tell me, Gustavus— are you a free man, or a slave?"

"I am a slave," Gustavus said. "But I hope to be free."

"So do all slaves. Let me tell you, Brother, there is merit in being a freedman, but most men do not call you their equal."

"Perhaps that will change."

The other smiled, showing white teeth. "Things have already changed, Gustavus. Or did you not know?"

"I know better than you might think—" Gustavus wanted to say *brother* again, but hesitated, not sure how to complete his sentence.

The large man turned and walked past Gustavus and out of the shop, passing so close that they almost touched. Gustavus felt for a moment that the other might thrust him out of the way and braced for a shove or a slap—but nothing happened, and after a moment he was gone.

"Absalom. Absalom Blackburn. A freedman of New York Colony, if you please. And don't you worry none about Jupiter. He's all scowl."

"I thought he was going to strike me."

"He might have done, but you weren't directly in his way. Best you keep it that way."

Gustavus nodded. "You are a freedman, Absalom?"

"Yes. I'm not bonded, but employed by Master Elijah Dunn, shipfitter and dry-goods dealer." He gestured toward the back room from which he had emerged. "And, no doubt, enjoying a fine afternoon in some public house, lamenting his losses."

"I see," Gustavus said. "I was sent to obtain some supplies." He reached into his wallet and drew out a slip of paper; as he did so, two copper pennies came out with it, rolling along the floor to land at the feet of Absalom Blackburn. Gustavus took a step forward, but Absalom had already bent down to pick up the coins.

"Fine coins, boy. How did you come by them?"

"My master sent them with me as payment." Gustavus extended the paper and Absalom took it, and ran his finger down the written list, his lips moving slowly as he read.

"All of this is going to cost more than two pennies."

"I have more."

"And how do you know . . . " Absalom set the paper down on a large barrel, and carefully laid the pennies on top of it. "How do you know, Gustavus, that I would not just slit your throat—" he made a gesture with his thumb across his bare neck—"and take it from you, no one the wiser?"

"I don't." Gustavus drew himself upright and took a step back. "But you might lose an eye while trying. Might be that it wouldn't be worth your trouble."

"And you'd be missed from your ship, I'd wager."

"I would be missed," Gustavus agreed. "It might be easier if you just gave me what I asked for and took my money than to make this more difficult." He said it levelly but was ready for anything the other man might try.

After a tense moment, Absalom laughed—not heartily, but in a sad, wistful way. "I suppose you're right, boy. You know," he added, picking up the pennies and the paper, "you remind me of a friend of mine. She always says things like that—'Absalom,' she says, 'it would be easier if . . . ' and 'Absalom, why don't you just . . . ' " He tucked the pennies into a pocket and took down a large box from a shelf and opened it. "And she says to me, 'Absalom, you get better custom with an open hand than a clenched fist.'"

"She sounds like a wise woman," Gustavus said.

"Oh, she is that," Absalom answered. "Even more so now."

"Why?"

"Because of the comet, boy. Haven't you felt it? Something on the wind. Something in the ground. It won't be like before, when the white folks were taken by the madness."

"I don't know what you mean."

"Madness," Absalom said. He took things out of the box and laid them on the counter. "A few loose fears, a few lies—and good men are burned to death. But that won't be happening again."

✛ ✛ ✛

"I know what he meant." Pascal held the needle up close and carefully threaded it. "He was talking about the slave revolt—well, the conspiracy."

"Master?"

"Conspiracy. A sort of—" he slowly pulled the thread through, and then took up the trousers in need of mending. "Well. Almost twenty years ago, Gustavus, there was a story that a group of slaves and free blacks cooked up a plan—a conspiracy—to set fires in Manhattan. An Irish girl gave evidence in court, and there were these terrible trials. Officials here were so fearful that they killed many Negroes." He set the trousers aside and looked up at his slave. "Some of them were burned at the stake . . . and from what I read of it all, the girl may have made all of it up to save herself."

"God would not smile on such things, Master," Gustavus said. "Surely."

"I wonder what great plan the Lord has for us, Gustavus," Pascal said. "So many things are unsure. When the city officials thought that Negroes—especially slaves—were ready to burn down the town, the tensions between Negroes and poor whites were at their height. But those tensions may not have ever gone away. Now that no more people are coming from Europe, or from Africa for that matter, they are going to have to learn to live with each other."

The lieutenant rubbed his eyes as if to clear away a vision and let in another. "What did you make of this Absalom?"

Gustavus thought for a moment. "I'm . . . not sure, Master. He was very serious in some ways, but I wasn't sure what he might do next. He was . . . "

"Unpredictable."

Gustavus nodded. "And he talked about change, 'something on the wind.' Is that like the Place of Bone? Did he mean that kind of change?"

"I don't know. It sounds as if he didn't say everything he knew, as if he was hiding something."

"He talked about his friend, a wise woman."

"She sounds like someone worth getting to know. Do you think he might introduce you?"

"I—I hadn't thought about it, Master. He might, or he might be suspicious."

"Of what?"

"Of *Namur*, Master. He . . . when I first went in Master Dunn's shop, Absalom's first words to me were that he didn't know me. It's like he knew everyone in New York, and I was someone he didn't recognize."

"Or he knew every Negro in New York. It reminds me of that Captain Fayerweather we met down south, who wanted us to put you overboard because all Negroes talked to all others."

"I remember," Gustavus said. "I remember very well."

"I know you do." Pascal smiled. "You know that there was never any danger I would allow that to happen to you."

Gustavus didn't answer; his master was a good and caring man, more so than some he had served—but any slave knew that any master at any time could make any decision.

"You're back, boy," Absalom said. "So you're not afraid of me."

"I'm plenty afraid of you. But my master sent me back for other things. Was Master Dunn pleased with our money?"

"It's as good as anyone else's." Gustavus handed Absalom the slip of paper, and he ran his thumb along it again. "Sure enough he'll like more of it."

"You were telling me before about your friend."

"I was?"

"You said you had a friend who told you that an open hand was better than a closed fist. I'd surely like to meet her."

Absalom frowned. "Oh, and why is that?"

"Because you're afraid of her. Anyone you're afraid of I'd surely like to meet."

Absalom reached his hand out as if he wanted to cuff Gustavus, but the younger man was skillful at dodging out of the way of blows, and the hand never reached its target.

"Not afraid of her, no," Absalom said. "Respect isn't the same as fear, boy."

"Can I meet her then?"

"You want to meet her, or your *master* wants to meet her? You a spy for him?"

"Why are you always so suspicious, Absalom? You think I mean you harm? I'm just a—"

Absalom reached his hand out again, much faster this time, and grabbed Gustavus by the shirt-front and brought him close. Gustavus was immediately afraid, but the other man didn't hurt him. Instead he whispered, "You're not 'just' anything. You're never 'just' anything, boy. That's what the white folks want us to believe—that's how they keep us down, make us think we're less than we are.

"That's why there are white men who own black men. Because they decided that we were 'just' something to own. But deep down . . . " Absalom let go of him, but continued, quietly, "deep down, they are afraid of *us* and what we might do if we ever realized it was wrong and evil. Comet comes and changes the world and makes them afraid. Maybe that's not a bad thing."

In a boardinghouse near the ropewalk on Bowery Lane, Absalom and Gustavus climbed a set of narrow stairs to an outside door. Absalom knocked on the door; there was no answer. He looked back at Gustavus, then reached his hand to knock again. But before he could do so, the door opened and a young girl smiled up at the visitors.

Gustavus took a breath: she was strikingly beautiful, and he must have been staring—Absalom nudged him, not entirely gently.

"Welcome," she said. "Absalom. And . . . " she looked at Gustavus. "A newcomer."

"Gustavus."

"My name is Coffey. Please," the girl said, gesturing. "Minerva will be glad to see you."

The rooms were sunlit and remarkably comfortable despite the warmth of the day. Gustavus smelled flowers and fresh-baked bread, and there was a gentle breeze within. Coffey gestured them to a well-worn settle near the fireplace, which had its fire banked low.

"She's not for you," Absalom said quietly. "She's given her heart to a young buck named York. He works with Jupiter, and he'd personally beat the tar out of you if he thought you'd looked at Coffey sidewise. And if that wasn't enough, Jupiter might join in the fun."

An older woman emerged through the opposite door. She was modestly dressed, with a carefully tied chignon according to the Caribbean style; her smile seemed to light up the whole room.

"Thank you, Coffey," she said to the girl. "Absalom. A delight."

Her voice had a Caribbean lilt to it, matching her kerchief. "And who is this?"

"My name is Gustavus."

"Surely not. *Gustavus* is the name some white man gave you." She took his chin in her hand; he felt warmth rise from it—then she let go and stood up straight.

"My mother named me Oladuah, Mistress."

"Oh, la, never! Not *Mistress*, Oladuah. Never that. I am . . . Minerva. A white man's name, but I was born a free black woman here in New York, and that's what is done." She gestured to the settle and took her seat in an armchair opposite. She placed her hand on her breast. "Minerva Mercer. Mercy, they call me here. Absalom said you wanted to meet me."

"He spoke well of you, Mis—Minerva," Gustavus said. "He said that you taught him kindness."

Absalom looked sideways at Gustavus, but Minerva just smiled. "He doesn't like being seen through, that one. But young Oladuah, that is not truly why you are here. What do you want of me?"

"What can you offer?"

"Mind your tongue, boy," Absalom said.

"No, it's all right, Absalom. He is very protective of Mercy, he is. Do you know, many people come to me, and they don't know why. But they all come to me for one reason: they have pain and they want to be healed."

"I'm not in pain."

"Oh, la, yes you are," Minerva said. "New York is not your home; and that British ship is not your home either. You are far from where you came from."

"I will never see it again," Gustavus said, and his heart sank as he thought of it. The land of the Igbo, his home until he was eleven; like so many, he found himself taken away into captivity.

"Pain," Minerva said. "We are all in pain. I can take that away."

"How?"

"I cannot say," Minerva said. "It may come from within, or from above; but since the coming of the comet it has come more easily." She stood and reached her hand out again, touching Gustavus on the forehead. Once more he felt warmth come forth.

He was with his sister again, in the family compound. Mami and

Papi and uncles and aunts were away, working in the fields and the forests, when the men came and took them away. He never saw his sister again . . . he came to Barbados, that hell-place where men's lives were cheaper than a few pounds of sugar, but did not stay, thanks be to God: and then he was transported to Virginia. But Lieutenant Michael Pascal bought him and gave him the name of a great white king. He brought the newly made Gustavus to the true Faith and taught him his letters.

Then the comet fell, and the world split apart.

He felt the tears coursing down his face: for his sister, for the Igbo, for all that was lost.

"What have you done? What are you doing?" He looked through tears and saw someone else standing over him: a radiant figure, glowing bright as the room darkened as if day had turned to night.

"She told you," he heard Absalom say as if from a distance. "Mercy takes away your pain."

Sometime later he came to himself again. He was lying full-length on the settle, a cushion under his head. The sun was low, streaming through the open window. He sat up in alarm and the room swam on him for a moment, then settled.

"I am overdue," he said. "They will think I have run away."

Minerva sat opposite, a cup in her hand. She extended it to him: fragrant tea, a scent from somewhere far away. He sipped it, cupping his hands around it, finding himself cold despite the heat of the late afternoon.

"No, young Oladuah. Absalom has gone to your great ship to find the man who calls himself your master. We will go along to join him when you have found your feet again."

Gustavus thought a moment. Other than the worry that he had been gone a long time and had somehow fallen into sleep in a stranger's house, he felt well. No, he felt *fine*: free of worry, free of fear.

"What has happened?"

Minerva took the cup back from him. "Mercy, my dear one. Mercy."

Chapter 40

We have to learn to live together

New York

"Yes," Boscawen said. "There are a number of people who are quite unhappy that I'm talking to you at all."

Minerva folded her hands in her lap and leaned back on the bench. It had become slightly cooler after sundown. The oppressive heat of a June day in New York had made everyone irritable. Boscawen had taken that into account all day, refraining from punishment of those who committed minor infractions. Now, in the gathering dark, they sat on *Namur's* quarterdeck.

"I am not surprised," Minerva said. She looked at Absalom, and then back at Boscawen. "Many New Yorkers are afraid of Negroes."

"Why would they be afraid?"

Gustavus put his hand up, glancing at Pascal, who nodded.

"What is it, boy?"

"Memories last a long time, Admiral, sir. Eighteen years ago there was a terrible event in New York. Lies, and fear, and hatred led to the killing of many Negroes. I felt people watching me wherever I went, sir."

"People are always suspicious of outsiders," Boscawen said. "Is this any different?"

"People are afraid of dark skin," Absalom said. "Every time they see one of us, they see someone who might burn down their house or slit their throat while they sleep. I was a young man when they burned some people at the stake and hung others. We haven't forgotten either."

267

"Do you think there will be some reprisal?"

"Reprisal?"

"Will they attack us for talking to you?"

Absalom closed his eyes, and then opened them. "No. They might consider it, but they are more afraid of you than us."

"Well, that's good to hear," Boscawen said. "All right, Miss Minerva; tell me what you can do."

"I can take pain away," she said. "Once it was only a small thing—the slight relief of a fever, or head pain, or a toothache. It was a knack; now it is a talent." She looked from Boscawen to Absalom. "Many of us have talents."

Boscawen raised an eyebrow. "Do *you* have a talent, young man?"

Absalom crossed his arms and frowned. "After a fashion."

"Tell me more."

"Do you have a coin, Admiral?"

Boscawen reached into his waistcoat and withdrew a shilling. He extended his hand toward Absalom; but the other man did not reach for it.

"Flip the coin," he said. "Do not show it to me."

Boscawen flipped the coin in the air and caught it, covering it with his hand.

"Heads," Absalom said. Boscawen uncovered the coin to show the profile of King George II.

"Again," Boscawen said; he flipped the coin, and when he had it beneath his hand, Absalom correctly said, "Heads."

The experiment was conducted three more times, and each time Absalom correctly stated the outcome.

"So," Boscawen said, "you are able to accurately predict the flip of a coin. Impressive, but I fail to—"

"A moment," Absalom said. "Admiral, if you would, take your coin, choose a side, and place it under your hand."

Boscawen took the coin he was about to put away, and placed it tails-side-up. He covered it with his hand, showing it for a moment to Minerva. "Will you now tell me what side the coin is on?"

Absalom closed his eyes and frowned. A single bead of sweat escaped his scalp and trickled slowly, unobstructed, down the right side of his face and into his closely trimmed beard.

He opened his eyes and said, "Heads."

"You are sure," Boscawen said.

"Yes."

"Well, young man, I think this charade is at an end, because—" he removed his hand, and resting on the flat of his other hand was a shilling, showing the profile face of the King of England.

He looked at the coin in disbelief.

"You were about to say, sir?" Absalom said, smiling.

"I placed that coin on the other side."

"I know," Absalom said. "I changed it."

"I do not understand."

"I can see choices," Absalom said. "When there are different choices for an event, I can see what they might be, and—nudge—the event toward the one I wish. You had two choices for the coin; I made it become heads."

"But I placed the coin on the other side."

"And it was equally likely you would have placed it on the other side, Admiral. I made you choose the other way."

"But I had already decided and shown your friend. I had already made the choice."

"It doesn't matter. It's easier when it hasn't happened yet, but with small things, like the side of a coin, it can have just taken place. I make it happen how I choose."

"Few people in New York will gamble with Absalom," Minerva said.

"No," Absalom answered. "But they love to go hunting with me."

Boscawen tucked away the shilling. "Imagine changing the path of a musket-ball. Making it strike its target—or miss." He looked at Absalom. "How well does this talent work?"

"You mean, does it always work? Since the comet, Admiral, yes it does. But I can only do it a few times without tiring out. And I don't use it to gamble, Mercy. If God has given me this gift, I would not waste it that way."

"You are a freedman, are you, Absalom?"

"I am, Admiral. And Minerva is a free woman."

"I could impress you into service even so. But I need whatever help I can manage. We are at war, not just with the French—indeed, perhaps no longer with the French—and also with the land itself, and its natives. What I have seen, and heard of, tell me that we must try to fight on their terms."

"You are looking for us to fight for you?" Minerva said.

"Not as a soldier," Boscawen said. "As . . . civilian assistants."

"What would we assist with?" Absalom said.

"Well, Absalom here might use his talent at critical moments; and you might be able to assist with your healing talents."

"What about the others?"

"Others? What others?"

"Mercy—" Absalom said, his eyes flashing angrily.

She held up her hand. "No, Absalom, there is no sense in keeping it secret. I sense that Admiral Boscawen is a good man; his cause is just, and he will remember us when the war is over."

"As Judge Horsmanden remembered us eighteen years ago, Mercy? When half of the Negroes in New York were put in prison, and innocent men and women—black and white!—were hung by the neck or burned to death, based on lies? He promised justice and he—"

Absalom turned away, walking to the railing and looking out across the harbor.

"Madam, I—" Boscawen spread his hands.

"We have learned not to trust anyone," Minerva said. "Our people cannot give testimony in royal court; a Negro can be fined, or imprisoned, or beaten for the smallest slight to a white man. But still we hope for a better day. Meanwhile, many of us have knacks and skills . . . we do not talk about them, because people would fear us."

"They *should* fear us," Absalom said, without turning around. "There are some . . . who they should truly fear."

"It is no way to live," Minerva said, without commenting on Absalom's last remark. "We have to learn to live together. Admiral, I am prepared to help you—but on a condition. You are not a New Yorker; you were not here eighteen years ago when such terrible wrongs were done. I ask your promise that you will take up our cause."

"Meaning—"

"We wish to be treated the same as anyone else—in society, in law. We will need your help in that."

"Every person is a child of God," Boscawen said. "I believe that; but people have beliefs and biases that have existed for centuries. I cannot change everyone's mind—not overnight, perhaps not ever. I cannot promise to do what cannot be done. If that is your condition, there is no way I can meet it."

"I ask only to change *your* mind, Admiral," Minerva said. She smiled, and it seemed that, even in the dim illumination of lanterns hung over the quarterdeck, the whole scene was filled with light.

Part V: Ascent

July, 1759

The universe is change;
Our life is what our thoughts make it.
—Marcus Aurelius

Chapter 41

We have a choice

Albany

Jeffrey Amherst was accustomed to waiting; it was part of the military experience. He was also accustomed to being uncomfortable. Full dress uniform in the sweltering heat of mid-morning in July qualified as the latter, as much for him as for the honor guard that stood at stiff attention—but it was not often that he, or they, were present to receive a member of the Royal Family.

The only member of the Royal Family, he reminded himself. What existed of the House of Hanover was disembarking from a carriage bearing a hastily painted coat of arms, but lacking the customary gilt and ornamentation of one that might roll down a promenade in London.

It will have to do.

Prince Edward did not seem inconvenienced by the lack of decoration, or any other shocking breach of protocol that would have scandalized any equerry at Westminster. He was turned out in a dress uniform with little additional ornamentation, and only a collar of some sort to denote his rank. It had all the trappings of a badly-equipped stage play rather than the presentation of the commanding general of British forces to his—acting—sovereign.

Well, he thought; *that's America for you.*

Edward, accompanied by General James Wolfe—his sharp nose pointed in the air, as always—advanced to where Amherst stood stiffly at attention. At a barked command, the honor guard saluted, and Amherst did as well and then made a leg.

"Rise, General," Edward said. "I think that's about as much formality as we need."

Amherst stood straight. "It is a pleasure to see Your Highness safe and sound."

"It wasn't a guaranteed thing; I'll tell you that." Edward glanced over his shoulder at Wolfe, who said nothing. "But we've seen some wondrous things."

"We all have, Highness. But I am eager to hear of your adventures."

"Have you arranged for proper quartering of your men?"

"Yes. And the—civilians."

"Marquis de Montcalm will be arriving with his escort this afternoon. Will all be in order for him?"

"I trust so, Highness."

If he had been told a year earlier that he would sit opposite Louis-Joseph de Montcalm-Gozon, the Marquis de Veran, commonly referred to as the Marquis de Montcalm, Amherst would have laughed. Commanding an army with Montcalm on the other side of the battlefield, certainly; having him at a peace negotiation possibly, but it would be someone else representing His Majesty.

For his entire life, with a few pauses for peace, his nation had been at war with France. It was the great enemy, the global rival, that stood for everything that Great Britain opposed. Yet here he was, and here was Montcalm. Beside him was a young adjutant and another officer; beside Amherst was General James Wolfe and Prince Edward Augustus, the purest-blooded royal on the North American continent. He wanted to feel as if he was in a dominant position in the conversation; but instead he merely felt uncomfortable.

"Monsieur Marquis—"

Montcalm held up his hand. "Monsieur General Amherst. Perhaps we can merely address each other as 'General,' rather than twisting ourselves around to observe verbal protocol." Montcalm's English was excellent, though his accent was definitively French. "Of course, proper deference should be paid to His Highness the Prince."

Edward might have allowed some informality, but instead he simply nodded.

"Agreed," said Amherst. "General Montcalm, I confess that I am not sure how to approach this conversation. It seems clear that my forces are no longer in a confrontational pose toward yours. It is more than a truce, less than some sort of treaty—which I do not feel that I am in any position to negotiate."

"I confess the same, General Amherst. But here we are. Your sovereign and my sovereign are not here, are not accessible, and are unlikely to ever weigh in on any decisions we might make. We can make a truce, certainly. But we must go beyond that if we are to share a battlefield as allies."

"Allies?"

"Yes. Our enemy is this vicious Seneca, Guyasuta, and the—unearthly—things that his campaign has brought forth."

"I thought it was the comet that brought forth these things. From what Lord Boscawen has told me, there are unearthly events and beings coming into the world far from where Guyasuta is based."

"I think this is a matter of definitions, General, no more."

"I think," Amherst said, "this is a matter of *perception*. You might say that it doesn't matter when it comes to defeating Guyasuta—and you are correct, sir. If our decision is to make this native our principal enemy, and we bend our efforts to defeating him, then we will, I trust, ultimately prevail. But that does not make us safer in our beds. Where Guyasuta stood, another—most likely many others—will take his place."

"And?"

"If this is a war, General, and we are presumed to be on one side and the unnatural is on the other, then it is *that* we must prepare to fight—not just in New France or in New York, but everywhere in the world. Otherwise . . . "

Montcalm ran a finger along the edge of his uniform, smoothing down an unruly thread. "Otherwise, General, our arrangement would be a completely temporary one, and soon we would return to a situation which we would both find more amenable: trying to kill each other."

"You are very direct, General Montcalm. You do not mince words."

"Would you prefer that I did?"

"No, by no means. I prize honesty and despise sophistry. It is a characteristic which is very—"

"French."

Amherst smiled. "I do not impugn you personally, General. It is more the habit of diplomats and ministers than military leaders; *your* forthrightness does not surprise me. Still, your point is well taken. For me to consider your nation to be something other than the enemy is a Rubicon I have difficulty crossing."

"I would agree, except that my nation may now be New France and the rest of French North America. *Your* nation may now be the Atlantic plantations and the Caribbean possessions."

"My king—"

"And *my* king are in a different world. If there is any sovereign prince in our world, it is the man who sits before us."

"You flatter me, General Montcalm," Prince Edward said, the first words he had spoken during the entire conversation.

"I merely state facts."

"What are the facts?" Edward said. "If I am . . . the only sovereign prince, sir, what does that mean for you and your nation?"

"I'm not sure I take your meaning."

"Who is your king, General?"

"Louis, the fifteenth of his name."

"Reigning from another world, as you put it. If you never hear another word from him, who will be your king? Perhaps your 'nation' will choose *you* to be king?"

"Absurd."

"Someone else, then."

"I regret to say that there is no one else."

"Except me."

Montcalm was silent. He appeared to be ready to say something but held back. For the first time during the entire interview, Montcalm looked uncomfortable.

"Another Rubicon, I suppose," Amherst said.

"General," Prince Edward said, "*Alea iacta est.* The die is cast. We are not going home, and we are not simply extensions of our homelands. As much as I might prefer otherwise, it will be necessary for me to choose either to take on a crown or walk away from it forever."

"I understand, Highness," Montcalm said, inclining his head. "It is a felicitous matter that British subjects here in North America have the possibility of this choice. Regrettably, French subjects do not."

"Except me."

"You state the obvious, Highness. Do you think I do not know this? Do you think I have not reached this self-same conclusion? I trust that you are not suggesting that I am dull-witted."

"No, of course not. I—"

"Of course not," Montcalm interrupted, very slightly agitated—enough to commit the unpardonable breach of protocol. "Of course not. But France and England have been rivals and enemies for *seven hundred years*. You ask me to turn away from it in a moment. And—Mother of God!—even if I can come to terms with such an idea, I should have to convince my countrymen that they must do the same.

"Do you know what some of them will say, Highness? *Our ancient enemy gives up nothing; we give up ourselves. Why would we do this?* And I beg you, do not tell me we have no choice. As long as there is powder and ball, as long as there are churches of the True Faith, as long as we have our own language, we have a choice."

"You would wage war on us? I beg your pardon, General Montcalm," Amherst said. "In the end that is a losing proposition. Surely you must see that, and if you do not, there is nothing more we can discuss."

Montcalm closed his eyes and pinched his nose.

"Well?" Prince Edward said.

"*Merde*," Montcalm said. "I beg your pardon," he added, without opening his eyes. "I am not suggesting that we are looking to prolong the war. I am not suggesting anything except that it is not—what is the English phrase?—*cut and dried*."

"Did I suggest that it was?"

Montcalm opened his eyes and let his hand drop to his lap. "In not so many words, yes. It is impossible to erase all distinctions with a wave of the royal hand. It will take time."

"While we wait, General, Guyasuta is preparing his next assault. He sent Flying Heads against the Iroquois, and summoned Stone Coats to destroy Fort Duquesne, and Dry-Hands to overwhelm Johnson Hall. God only knows what will come next.

"He is your enemy as well. He is far more your enemy than I am—than General Amherst is. You must believe me, General Montcalm—my Lord Marquis. France has always been the enemy. It has fought my country, given succor to traitors to my realm, joined in alliances in support of a religion that undermines the laws of England. If things were different, seeking alliance with France would be the last thing I would choose. But things are what they are. I appreciate your difficulty. Please appreciate mine."

"Are we going to have the help of the French, do you think?" Prince Edward asked, after Montcalm and his colleagues had taken their leave.

"No," Wolfe said, before Amherst could answer. He earned an angry glance, but continued, "I'm sorry, Highness. But the Frenchman is stubborn and does not see the truth in front of his face." He sniffed. "I am unsurprised."

"You jump to conclusions, Wolfe."

"I state the obvious, General Amherst."

It was silent for several moments, and at last Prince Edward said, "Who has the right of it? Will the French go their own way and continue the war against the crown—against me? Or will we reach terms with them?"

"They will go their own way," Wolfe said.

"No," Amherst said. "Montcalm is more rational than that."

"He is a Frenchman."

"What does that mean?" Amherst said.

Wolfe sniffed again, but did not add anything to his statement.

"Don't be a fool," Amherst continued. "I assume you're suggesting that because Montcalm is French that he can't come to any rational conclusion. What an obviously stupid insinuation." Wolfe bristled, but he went on. "What is it that Montcalm said? France and England have fought each other on and off for seven centuries. If we're so bloody smart and they're so bloody irrational, why haven't we beaten them in this war? Is it sheer luck that they have survived?"

"What would you have me do? Scale the heights of Québec and attack the walls? Really, General. If it had not been for the comet, this war might be over by now."

"You cannot know that for sure. And it doesn't matter. We've had the comet and are dealing with the consequences. We *will* make friends with the French, and we *will* defeat the savage who seeks to destroy both of us. And you will play a part in it."

"And what might that be?"

"For a start, you are going to make friends with the marquis. Find out what might be needed to bring him back to the table."

"Me?"

"Yes. You, General Wolfe. Because if *you* can reach an understanding with him, *anyone* can."

New York

"I hope the admiral is not making a mistake," said Gustavus, as he and Lieutenant Pascal watched *Neptune* sailing toward the Narrows and the Atlantic Ocean beyond. In the man-o-war's wake came a small fleet. Some of them were warships but most were civilian craft hired to transport British troops.

Pascal pursed his lips. He shared his slave's apprehensions, but didn't feel entitled to express them aloud. Most—almost all, except for some marines—of the ground forces available to Boscawen were aboard those transports, now under the command of Admiral Saunders. If the unrest that Gustavus told him was simmering among New York's black population started coming to a boil, Boscawen would be unable to maintain control of the city without calling on Governor De Lancey to mobilize the militias. And if that were to happen, the outcome was unpredictable—in the lieutenant's opinion, at any rate.

New York's militias were poorly disciplined and prone to committing outrages, but in times past they could be counted upon to suppress slave rebellions. That, for the simple reason that the militias were fairly well-armed, and the slaves generally had nothing at their disposal save tools and kitchen implements.

But Gustavus had told him that there were some among the city's black folk who had gained magical powers; significant magical powers, in some cases. If he was right, and given the changed circumstances produced by what people were coming to call the Sundering, the balance of power might have significantly shifted.

Pascal understood the logic of the admiral's decision. Boscawen had become convinced that peace had to be made with the French in order to deal with the greater peril emerging from the western hinterlands. "Making peace," however, had many aspects, some of them contradictory to each other. Extending an olive branch with one hand was usually reinforced by making threatening gestures with the other. So, he would send Saunders and his fleet, along with most of the soldiers at his disposal, to the recently captured fortress at Louisbourg. From that station, close to the entrance to the St. Lawrence seaway, they could threaten the French at Quebec and Montreal.

Sound logic, on its own terms—but would those terms remain in place?

There was no way to know yet. They could only hope for the best.

Chapter 42

We are fighting forces of nature

Western New York

When the war band of Guyasuta reached the village, the braves and their war-chief were already armed and waiting. Among the Seneca and the Cayuga, it was a matter of posture: even if no one else was watching, the Great Spirit was watching—and the meeting, which might be a confrontation, was about protecting the village on the one hand, and establishing dominance on the other.

The war-chief did not know who had come to his village, but he recognized the emblems of Seneca men, as well as those of the "new tribes" beyond the Ohio. He had heard about them, and about their chief, who now stood before him: Guyasuta, a Seneca, who had turned his back on the Longhouse and—it was said—sought its destruction. But for the war-chief, it was a simple matter: foreigners, even men of his own extended tribe, had come to his village, heavily armed.

Guyasuta did not even speak for himself.

"Hail, great warriors," a shaman said, stepping forward in front of the newcomers. The war-chief immediately was on edge, feeling almost a revulsion: the man kept one of his hands concealed beneath his ceremonial cloak, and his smile was disturbing.

Without lowering his tomahawk, the war-chief took a step forward, remaining otherwise very still. His eyes flicked from the shaman's face to his concealed hand and back.

"Who are you, and what do you want?"

"We look for a pledge, Brother," the shaman answered.

"Oh? Who seeks our loyalty?"

"The great war leader Guyasuta."

"Guyasuta turned his back to the Seneca," the war-chief said. "He sought his fortune in the Ohio Country. Why would we choose to follow him now?"

"Brother." The shaman affected a world-weary voice, as if he was lecturing a young brave. "You must see that the world has changed. It truly would be far easier if you pledged your loyalty."

"My clan and my village make no pledge lightly. Not to Guyasuta, not to anyone."

"Of course not," the shaman answered. "It would be a great disappointment if you *did*. But that being said, Brother, it is important that you understand the stakes."

"I understand the stakes."

"No," the shaman said. "I don't think you do." He withdrew his arm from within his cloak, and the war-chief's eyes were at once focused on the spectacle: a shriveled, blackened hand that had been bound by cords to the stump of his left wrist.

"*Oniate*," the war-chief whispered, and the shaman's smile became broader.

"Brother," the shaman said, "I mean to ask you if you understood what the stakes were for *you*."

"I am the war-chief."

"Brother, if you do not choose to offer the fealty of your village, it will be reduced to dust. You become no more than an *obstacle*."

"If you seek to use that profane thing on me," the war-chief said after a moment, "you will never have the loyalty of my braves or my village. And you will pay for it, *personally*, with your life."

"You're threatening *me*?" The shaman laughed, then spat at the feet of the war-chief.

If he had been a more patient man, the war-chief might have been willing to let the insult pass. But patience was not a part of a war-chief's skill set. Without a moment's hesitation he leapt forward with a vicious swipe of his axe. But the blade did not strike bone or flesh. The shaman was far faster, dodging aside and placing his withered hand on the war-chief's neck.

A yellow-green light exploded from the place he touched, and the warrior cried out and crumpled to the ground. Several braves jumped forward as he fell, but the shaman turned aside from his victim and held up his hand.

"Be very sure, Brothers," he said. "Who will be next?"

Albany

Amherst looked up from the map he was studying to see a young lieutenant waiting to be acknowledged. He appeared to be out of breath as if he had run a long way.

"Well," Amherst said. "What is it?"

"A troop of soldiers is approaching, General."

"What sort of troops?"

"Colonials, sir," he said. "General Wolfe has already ridden out to meet them."

"Wolfe?" Amherst tossed the dividers he was holding down onto the map. "He has no use for colonials. Have my horse prepared." He swept out of the tent before the lieutenant could answer.

From across the meadow he could see Wolfe, his angular chin lifted in the air, his hand stretched out, pointing away from the camp. A colonial officer stood before him, clearly angry.

As Amherst approached, Wolfe lowered his arm and turned to face him. Amherst did not speak until he had dismounted, tossing the reins to a subaltern.

"General," Amherst said.

"General."

"Please be so good as to introduce me."

Wolfe did not seem particularly interested in doing so, but he cleared his throat and said, "General Amherst, I present Colonel—" he tinged the word with distaste. "Richard Gridley of Massachusetts Bay Colony. He appears to have some—men—in his company."

"Colonel," Amherst said, nodding to the colonial.

"General Amherst." Gridley offered a salute. "It is my honor to inform you that I have some six hundred soldiers from our colony that I wish to place at your service."

"Soldiers," Wolfe said, which earned a glare from Gridley.

Amherst ignored him. "You have a commission from your governor, sir?"

"I do, sir. In view of the—events—our governor felt that we would be of use here."

"You are most welcome," Amherst said. "You may find that things have changed somewhat."

"They have changed for us as well, sir. Captain Revere and I have seen a great deal and are eager to provide you with what intelligence we can. The French—"

"Yes," Wolfe said. "The French."

"Has something changed with the French, sir?"

"Oh, yes," Amherst said. "Yes, indeed."

Before sitting in conference with the colonials, Wolfe asked a moment of Amherst's time.

"General," Wolfe said almost as soon as he arrived. "I do not see the point of receiving, much less *encouraging*, these—"

Amherst stood patiently, waiting for Wolfe to finish his sentence.

"—men," Wolfe finally said.

"You don't think much of these colonials, do you, Wolfe?"

"Regrettably, sir, I do not. They are unreliable, badly trained and of dubious loyalty, General Amherst. Given the threat we face—"

"Given the threat we face, Wolfe, we need every man we can manage. I don't think the colonials are any less reliable in the face of that than our regular troops."

"I disagree, obviously."

"And you are *wrong*, obviously. You have seen even more than I have, Wolfe. Haven't you become convinced yet that we are facing something that is no more susceptible to well-drilled fighting men than the efforts of these fellows from Massachusetts? What do you think is going to happen here?"

"We are fighting *Indians*, sir."

"We are fighting forces of *nature*, sir."

"And if we kill the savage chief—which, General, I assume will in all likelihood be accomplished by a trained marksman wearing a regular soldier's uniform—these *forces of nature* will return to nature as they are intended."

"You think that's all that will be required?"

"Yes, sir. I think that is *exactly* all that is required. In truth, General, I am not even convinced that we need the *French*."

"The Marquis de Montcalm has done nothing to convince you otherwise."

"Monsieur le Marquis is of similar mind, General Amherst, though I will say that he has proved more—reasonable—than I would have expected."

"For a Frenchman."

"Just so, sir."

Amherst wanted to reach out and slap Wolfe, but refrained. "You are dismissed, sir."

"General—"

"You are *dismissed*, Wolfe."

The colonials were assigned a place to camp. When Amherst sought out their commander later in the day, he was directed to the encampment of one of the regular regiments; Gridley and one of his officers were inspecting a fieldpiece, engaging in an animated discussion with an artilleryman. Coats had been set aside, and the three men were squatting down, looking at the barrel. As Amherst approached, the regular came directly to attention; the two colonials followed suit, not quite as smartly.

"Be at your ease, gentlemen," Amherst said. "You have some interest in artillery, Colonel?"

"It is somewhat an area of expertise, General. For my adjutant Captain Revere as well."

"I see. Revere, is it? You are from Massachusetts-Bay, sir?"

"Yes, General."

"Are you a professional soldier?"

"No, sir. I am a silversmith by trade. I owe my soldier's education to Colonel Gridley; we were at Crown Point together three years ago. When he gathered forces from the colony, I volunteered to join him again."

"And what do you expect to do here, Captain?"

"I had thought we might join in the fight with the French, General, but Colonel Gridley has informed me that we are—we have a somewhat different attitude toward them now."

"I'm not convinced they're the enemy any longer, though my opinion is not universally held. We have had some strange times in the last few months."

"Yes, sir, we most assuredly have. I daresay we have never seen the like."

Revere was a colonial, and a young man in—by Amherst's estimation—his early twenties; so he was already more forward than Amherst expected or desired. His eyes met Amherst's, a token, perhaps, of perceived equality.

"I trust you are not mocking me, Captain Revere."

Revere's expression didn't change. "I cannot imagine any reason why I might do so, General. Massachusetts is free of predation from French coastal raiders, but we have wild Indians in the western part of the colony and utter madness in one of our largest towns. The great Creator Himself only knows what will happen, or why."

"It is the comet, I am told."

"So it is said, General. I would not venture to speculate."

Leaving Revere and the artillery officer, Amherst walked a short distance away with Gridley.

"Your adjutant is very . . . straightforward."

"Paul Revere is young, sir, but he is very bright. I have every confidence in him. If you feel he owes you some sort of apology—"

"No, no." Amherst glanced back at the two junior men. "I think we beat our officers into submission, and while it assures discipline, it stultifies initiative. But that is not my principal concern. You are probably aware of this, but let me make it explicit: there are some who feel your help is not needed and not wanted."

"General Wolfe, for one."

"He holds His Majesty's soldiers to a high standard, Colonel. I am inclined to consider that sentiment a virtue, not a vice."

"General Wolfe was content to serve with colonial troops when he was showing such bravery at Louisbourg a year ago, General Amherst. If what we have heard is true, he will have to become accustomed to doing so."

"A point well taken," Amherst agreed. "But in the meanwhile, I need him, and regardless of his opinion, I welcome your Massachusetts men. If it comes to pass, are they willing to fight alongside French soldiers?"

Gridley chuckled. "In our colony there are ministers of the Gospel who have spent their career preaching that the fight against the French held the character of a crusade against the infidel. For my part, I am prepared to be more . . . ecumenical."

"I am pleased to hear that. What about young Revere?"

"His family is Huguenot and fled France for America. But that was his father's time; I think Paul has a different perception of the world. As for the rest of them . . . they may not be regimental regulars, sir, but they will handle themselves with honor."

"I wish that was all that was needed." Amherst looked back at Revere and the regular artilleryman, who were continuing to examine the small cannon. He wondered whether he, or Revere, or any of them might be able to stand against forces of nature.

Chapter 43

A temporary alliance, perhaps

New York

Boscawen set the glass aside and sat up straight. He looked across the table at Messier, picking up one of the coins and turning it with his fingers. As he did so, the Frenchman sat quietly, waiting for the admiral's response.

"It looks and feels like a guinea," Boscawen said. "If I did not know otherwise, sir, I might think you simply took the coin from your purse."

"Monsieur Alexander is very skilled," Messier answered, "as is Mademoiselle LaGèndiere. Their work is exceptionally precise."

"And the gold—"

"The process is faultless. It is indeed the precious metal, Admiral. It is indistinguishable from that which might be refined from ore."

Boscawen reached into his vest and drew out a guinea coin, one that he had carried for several years as a sort of charm; Frances had given it to him as part of a birthday present. On its front it bore the left-facing profile of the monarch with the inscription *Georgius II Dei Gratia*; on the other face the royal arms, surmounted by the crown, with a series of letters circling it— *M•B•F•E•T•H•REX•F•D•B•ET•L•D•S•R•I•A•T•ET•E*. If he gave the matter some thought he could have decoded the letters, but couldn't be bothered.

He placed his coin next to the one Messier had placed before him, examining first the head- and then the crest-side. The two were not precisely identical, but two coins were rarely so. Indeed, Messier's alchemetical product even looked slightly worn, as if it had been passed from hand to hand or placed in neat stacks in some London counting-house.

"Remarkable, Dr. Messier. How many such coins do you have?"

"Somewhat over two hundred, Admiral."

Boscawen looked up sharply. "You have manufactured *two hundred guineas*?"

"Why, yes, *mas oui*, Admiral," Messier said, surprised. "Monsieur Alexander had already begun the transmutation process, and with the aid of the compass, we were able to speed it up. In a month or so we should easily have two hundred more."

"The engraving on your coins is remarkably faithful, I must say."

"Ah." Messier smiled. "I can see where you might say so, but that is not engraving *per se*. Mademoiselle LaGèndiere is using an alchemetical process to reproduce the designs on the coin—it is a sort of mimicking, much more faithful than the work of a mere forging. I daresay that if she had continued access to the whole world, she could have considerable impact on the currency of the British Empire."

"As for your particular device—it is not in the hands of Alexander?"

"No indeed. It is still in the possession of Mademoiselle LaGèndiere. She employs it in aid of the project you have requested." Although he clearly tried to conceal it, Boscawen could see that something about the matter was troubling him.

"Is something amiss, Dr. Messier?"

"I do not know what you mean."

"Dr. Messier, I know that you have a custodial responsibility toward the young lady, and I applaud your assiduity in this regard. If there is some affront to your charge, I insist that you inform me."

"No, no," Messier said, holding his hands up. "Nothing of the sort has taken place. It is just . . . Mademoiselle LaGèndiere is uncomfortable in the presence of Monsieur Alexander."

"But he has made no untoward advances toward her."

"No, not in the least. He is in that respect completely honorable; indeed, he is a married man, with grown children. He has been the soul of courtesy. Still . . . he is, well, *different*."

"How so?"

"It is hard to describe. He is . . . he has transformed himself. He has extended his life using alchemy, and as a result my young friend is disturbed by his physical presence."

"I confess that I do not understand what that means. Is it something forbidden to alchemists? And why would this disturb the young lady?"

"It is difficult to describe. But as I say, there is no inappropriate interaction between the man and the young lady."

"You are sure?"

"Yes. As long as the use of the compass is required to make your coins—" he tapped the table—"some interaction is necessary. We will need to be careful and observant."

"I leave that to you. In the meanwhile, I shall have an audience with Governor De Lancey."

After Messier took his leave, Boscawen spent a few minutes examining the coins. They varied in several ways—worn on different edges, bearing a variety of dates. It was a remarkable collection—one might almost think they were genuine.

Except they *were* real. By any reasonable definition, they were the coin of the realm. Whatever realm they now belonged to.

Albany

Prince Edward turned from examining the harness and tack on his mount to see one of the colonial officers approaching. Major Rogers took a step toward him, but Edward raised his hand.

"Captain . . . "

"Revere, Your Highness." He was a young officer, but one who seemed to hold his head high, even in the presence of a royal heir.

"Captain Revere. Of course. What can I do for you this morning?"

Revere inclined his head. "Colonel Gridley imposed upon General Amherst and asked that I accompany you, if you would permit it."

Edward glanced at Rogers, who remained noncommittal. "I admit that I have only limited understanding, Captain Revere, but is there not some amount of . . . bad blood between the New Englanders and the French?"

"Yes, Your Highness. We have a long history, and there are some strong opinions about them. I have my own opinions."

"Is that why you were chosen?"

"If it please Your Highness," Revere said—and he did not cast his eyes downward as he spoke—"you are going to make a personal appeal to General Montcalm to assist in this fight with the natives. Gaining their help may be crucial to the outcome; I understand that. But if we win this battle, if we drive off this threat, we will have to come to terms with the French. Your Highness' plantations—"

"My grandfather's plantations."

"As Your Highness says," Revere said. "If we win this battle, we have an important stake in how we come to terms with our long-time enemy. New York has a stake, but so has New Hampshire and Massachusetts-Bay. Colonel Gridley felt that a provincial should be present, and General Amherst agreed. And here I am."

"Here you are, Captain," the prince agreed. "Very well, I shall be glad to have you accompany us. However, please understand that while I accept—and appreciate—your counsel, it is I who speak for us. Is that clear?"

"Of course, Highness. I would not think otherwise."

It wasn't clear that the prince was expecting another answer, but he seemed satisfied.

"Very well, Captain Revere. Welcome to my entourage."

Prince Edward found Captain Revere an interesting traveling companion. He was five years older, the second son of a Huguenot émigré to Boston. He was a silversmith by profession, apprenticed at an early age, who had entered military service early in the current war; having been at Crown Point when it was first occupied. Recent events had brought him—and Gridley—back into service.

He would have thought that such a man would provide little conversational diversion, but he was surprised. Revere was not only intelligent, but quite insightful. He knew about the political situation in Massachusetts-Bay, but also seemed well informed about the overall picture.

"Why do the people of your colony hate the French so much?"

"Opinions vary about the French, Your Highness," Revere said. "But we are two fundamentally different peoples. Our colonies are primarily Protestant, and while we're more numerous, we don't all agree."

"About the French?"

"About *anything*, Highness," Revere answered. "About religious beliefs . . . land claims . . . anything. Colonists from New Jersey would not lift a finger to help their fellow Britons in New Hampshire, and vice versa. As for the Carolinas—no one outside of the Carolinas gives a damn about them." Revere looked down at his horse's mane and ruffled it with his hand. "Begging Your Highness' pardon.

"As for the French—in America, at least—there are far fewer of them, but they all have the same faith and serve the same king. We have many sides, they have just one."

"I cannot speak for 'many sides,' Captain. I speak only on behalf of our king."

"Our king is at war with the king of France," Revere answered. "And it is more and more clear that we will not communicate with either of them, ever again. Your Highness needs to decide if *he* is at war with the governor of New France. It is the only reality in question."

They rode in silence for a short time; the prince seemed ill at ease. Revere showed no expression: he exchanged a glance with Major Rogers, who said nothing.

"You are very bold," Prince Edward said. "Is that how you are taught in Massachusetts-Bay to speak to a prince of the blood?"

"Highness," Revere answered after a moment, "in all of my life, I have never had the opportunity to speak to a prince of the blood. Indeed, no one who has ever been born and brought up to manhood in the American plantations has ever spoken with one, unless he had the good fortune to travel abroad like Dr. Franklin of Philadelphia. Needless to say, no royal foot has ever before trod this continent."

"You make that sound like an accusation."

"I did not mean it that way, Highness. I meant only to say that . . . speaking to princes was not part of my education. I think you will find that is true of almost every American you meet. We have been largely neglected by our betters—and whenever they have chosen to take note of us, it has not always been to our benefit."

"I trust you have an example to illustrate your point."

"If it please Your Highness, I do. Fifteen years ago, men from the colonies of New England—Massachusetts-Bay, Connecticut, Rhode Island and New Hampshire—undertook an expedition against Louisbourg, the great French fortress. With our only formal help the ships of Admiral Warren's squadron to transport them, the New Englanders were able to seize the fort and capture it. It was an act they thought would greatly help the war effort and reflect honorably on them as patriotic men of Great Britain.

"Yet instead of accolades, they were met with confusion and anger—and instead of reinforcing their conquest, His Majesty's Government saw fit to *give it back to the French* as a part of the peace accord in 1748. It was this very fortress that General Wolfe and his men had to recapture last summer, delaying their advance up the Saint Lawrence.

"Had the fort remained in British hands, Highness, the rest of New France might have been taken a year ago. And we would not now be seeking to engage in polite words with General Montcalm—he would be somewhere on the other side of the edge of the world we now inhabit."

While the troop moved at a gentle pace, Major Rogers and the other soldiers remained on alert. War still existed between France and Britain, and though word had been sent to the Marquis de Montcalm that the prince and his entourage were coming, Rogers was deeply suspicious of the intentions both of French and native forces. It would only take the actions of one well-armed French squadron or one warband roused to violence to capture or kill them all. Prince Edward was either unaware or unconcerned, but the threat of danger hung over most of the rest of his companions like a cloud.

After two days' travel they came to the French encampment near Lake George. A month earlier there had been no French presence this far south. Now, thousands of men were arrayed on the shore of the lake, with a large tent flying the *fleur-de-lys* and the arms of Montcalm on a little hill roughly near the center. Nearest to the lake, they could see tents and structures for the native allies, present in great numbers. Set against the beautiful backdrop of the lake and the surrounding forest, the deep blue sky framing a blazing sun, the scene would have been beautiful to behold—except, of course, that it was a military display of Britain's bitterest enemy.

A troop of horsemen in elaborate uniform, led by a familiar

figure—D'Egremont—approached at a canter. Edward gave a signal to halt as they rode up to meet his delegation.

D'Egremont gave an elaborate bow from the saddle, sweeping his hat from his head, but it was clear that he was angry.

"Your Highness does us honor by visiting," he said. "But your choice of companions sends a message that cannot help but offend."

"I'm not sure what you mean, Lieutenant," Edward answered.

"This man—" he gestured toward Rogers—"is a blackguard, a murderer and a brigand. He should be placed in irons for his many offenses to my sovereign."

Rogers began to respond, but Edward held up his hand. "If I were to answer according to my proper station," he said, "I would declare that you, sir, were in no position to make any comment about who I choose as a part of my entourage. And if I were to answer as a patriot and a soldier, I would feel obliged to point out that French hands are by no means clean as regards atrocities and outrages."

D'Egremont appeared ready to answer, but Edward continued. "But this is not the time for accusations or hauteur; it is the time for us to find common ground against a more dangerous foe. You can either escort me—escort *all of us*—to your commander; or we will return whence we came, and we will deal with the native threat on our own. It is your choice, Lieutenant; be sure it is a wise one."

D'Egremont did not seem happy with the decision; but after a few tense seconds, he decided what most subordinate officers do in situations of great moment—that it was something best left to those of higher authority.

Without another word, he bowed again, and gestured for the British entourage to make its way unmolested into the French camp.

Johnson Hall

From the balcony of the house, Molly could see that warriors were passing Johnson Hall by. Some of them looked up the hill as they passed along the trail to the south of the stone boundary, but most did not. She did not pick out Guyasuta among them. If he was in the company of this war-band—*no,* she thought: *let us call it what it is: an army*—he did not distinguish himself in any way.

She did not know if she was imagining it, or if her changed senses actually perceived it, but there was a sort of aura around the men who streamed eastward along the well-marked trail. It was not the raw anger or bloodlust of the warpath, nor the focus of a brave moving stealthily through the forest. It was, if anything, a sense of despair.

When the stream of braves had nearly completely passed, a runner came up to the house with the news that a messenger was at the gate.

By the time Molly came down the hill, accompanied by more than the usual number of escorts, the messenger had been admitted within the stone fence. She could see that his weapons and possessions had been left outside, with two warriors watching over them.

"What is your message, little brother?" she asked without introduction.

"I speak for the war-chief Guyasuta," he answered. "You are the wife of the chief Warraghiyagey?"

"You are at my longhouse, warrior. Give me your message or leave."

He did not flinch from her gaze.

"My chief commands me to say: you have chosen the whites over your own people, but you have received a gift that permits you to defy him. He does not choose to demand your obedience at this time, but after he destroys the white war-band that gathers against him he will return and demand his due.

"Still, he is not without judgment or mercy. Should you choose to submit to him now, he will reward you richly. But if you do not, he will be most harsh when he returns. He swears this by the gods of earth and sky, and by the Great Spirit, who calls on him to make crooked ways straight and wrong things right."

"Is that all he has to say?"

"It is all I am commanded to speak, sister."

She felt her hands forming into fists, but she slowly, deliberately unclenched them. "Return to your war-chief this message: that I reject his mercy and spurn his judgment. He cannot know what the Great Spirit intends for him, or any of us, red or white. Let him follow whatever path he chooses, but we do not bow to him here, now or ever."

She turned on her heel and began walking slowly up the hill. She felt angry in her mind and awkward in her step, but was determined.

"He will destroy you," the messenger said to her retreating back.

She stopped, and deliberately turned to face the young brave, standing defiantly before a number of men who looked ready to strike him down.

"Did he command you to threaten me?"

"I only tell you—I only tell you what I know, sister. Our war-chief hears the words of the Great Spirit and chooses this moment to drive the whites from our land. He says that it is our last chance, and it will not come again. I believe him."

She wanted to reply. She also knew that with a gesture, the messenger would be slain where he stood. He must have known it as well; his weapons and his gear were out of his reach.

No one would fault her for meeting his affront this way.

"Go," she said at last. "And do not return."

Chapter 44

We could resolve this with a handshake

Prince Edward could not easily conceal his discomfort at being surrounded by French and native troops. The Marquis de Montcalm had been in the British encampment a few days earlier, and had seemed completely at ease; indeed, in conversation with himself and General Amherst, he had been extremely defiant, asserting the identity of the servants of His Most Christian Majesty.

And here he was, placing his hand in the lion's mouth. For every Frenchman in the New World, there were ten Britons—but right here, right now, the only person of royal birth was at the mercy of his nation's sworn enemy. Without question, Montcalm could order him seized and detained, his men possibly tortured or killed and he would be helpless to prevent it.

He thought of what his father would have done. As Prince of Wales, his father had to make his own way in the face of anger and derision from the king and the court; he had gathered his own supporters and had planted his own flag, never wavering as long as he lived.

"I shall be your cupbearer," Montcalm said, bringing him a pewter goblet of wine and offering a bow, before taking his own seat. Captain Revere stood behind him, but Rogers and others remained outside the Marquis' tent. For his part, Montcalm was alone, with neither aides nor servants. Outside, the heat hung heavy, and the interior of his tent was scarcely cooler.

"I could be no better served," Edward said. "I assume you know why I have come."

"You want to achieve where General Wolfe fell short. Forgive me for being less than optimistic, Your Highness. What exactly do we have to talk about?"

"Danger has crept closer," Edward answered. "We understand that Guyasuta's forces have bypassed Johnson Hall and are descending the Mohawk Valley. We need your help."

"We have our own concerns."

"Of course. But if we are destroyed, Monsieur, you will be next. Our mutual opponent does not discriminate. All whites are his enemy."

"You are correct, of course." Montcalm leaned back and sipped wine from his own cup. "We are not making aggressive moves toward your territory because of it."

"Other than encamping here, I suppose."

"I hardly think that is *aggressive*, Highness, and I would beg you to consider your words carefully if you seek my help."

"I beg your pardon, my lord Marquis—except that this *is* the sovereign territory of the Colony of New York, not some untenanted land to the west where our respective kings dispute. So let us not mince words. Still," he hurried on, before Montcalm could interrupt, "I do not seek to anger you—as you observe, I *do* wish your help. Further, I seek something more than a temporary suspension of hostilities. I seek an alliance."

"An alliance? Between Britain and France?"

"No. Between the British plantations and the French colonies. A permanent, lasting arrangement—not just for the present threat, but for the future."

"We are at *war*, Highness. It is not up to us—"

"Yes, it is, my lord. It very much is up to us. You and I. Right here, right now. You must have reached the same conclusion we have: our mother countries, our kings, and our rivalries are all beyond the sundered borders. Despite my . . . youth, I am effectively the sovereign of my country. You are the most prominent leader of yours. We could resolve this with a handshake, two men of gentle birth giving their word and their bond."

Montcalm did not respond at first; he appeared to be taking stock of the young prince who sat before him.

A few months ago, he had been standing on the Heights of

Abraham when a luminous fog drifted past and made him believe, for a few moments, that he was back on the battlefield of Piacenza. It was the effect of the sundering, the comet's transit, that changed the world. He'd heard of many such events from that day.

Our kings are beyond our sundered borders.

"You are suggesting something momentous, Highness. I cannot speak for all of the French colonies in the New World, though I concede that I could reasonably exercise authority over New France and perhaps the Maritimes . . . do you speak for all Britons everywhere? All along the Atlantic seaboard, and throughout the Caribbean?"

"I am their king."

"Uncrowned."

"I daresay that is the least of the obstacles we would both face. A suitable ceremony could be performed."

"Your Archbishop of Canterbury is unavailable."

"So is Westminster Abbey. But it seems to me that you have a clergyman of that title resident in Québec."

Edward heard a sharp intake of breath from Captain Revere, but to his credit, the colonial did not say a word.

"You—" Montcalm set his wine cup on a small folding table beside him. "You would request—you would permit a Catholic archbishop to crown you king of—king of North America? Isn't that a violation of the Test Act, among a number of other statutes and proclamations?"

"It is, but I would dispense with it by a royal decree. What is more, it would be a gesture of goodwill to everyone in New France at least. Catholic or Protestant or Mussulman or Jew, it should no longer matter."

"Your people would be unlikely to accept this—a Catholic archbishop from another realm settling the crown on their new king's head."

"He would not be from 'another realm,' Monsieur. I would hope that he would be the senior Catholic authority in *my* realm. You ask if my people would accept such an arrangement. What about yours?"

"You ask me—all of us—to swear allegiance to *you* as king?"

"Yes."

Montcalm took a moment, gathering himself. "I thought I made my feelings clear on these matters at our last interview, Highness."

"You did, and you reiterated them to General Wolfe privately afterward. I have thought about those feelings and realized that in order to convince you that this course is the best one would require an extraordinary gesture. I am making such a gesture. I do not ask you to give up your language, your religion, or your essential culture. But I dare to dream that in time—perhaps not in your lifetime, perhaps not even in mine—those things might all grow closer. I do not know if Massachusetts-Bay would ever enjoy camaraderie with New France—" he turned and glanced at Revere, who was staring straight ahead, trying to contain some measure of fury—"but the two places might find some commonality of purpose. I believe that we must."

"We would retain our language."

"Of course."

"And the Church."

"Yes, though I imagine you will have to decide what the absence of Pope—and Rome—will mean. Doctrinally, your faith is up to you."

"Your more . . . assertive subjects may have something to say about that," Montcalm said, glancing at Revere.

Prince Edward didn't turn to look behind him, but he nodded. "Of course. It will be difficult for everyone."

"I would like to think, Captain," Prince Edward said as they rode southward, "that you would welcome this overture of peace."

"It is not my place to offer praise or criticism," Revere answered.

"Even if I solicit it?"

"Your Highness gives me a voice of authority that is beyond my station. But if it *is* my place, sir. I would say that this is a reckless course, and in many quarters it would be viewed as an affront."

"Those are strong words."

"Your Highness did command that I speak."

"And speak you did. But is not peace better than war?"

"Honor trumps peace, Your Highness. And so does blasphemy."

"Blasphemy?"

"The Popish faith has been the enemy of the people of God for a hundred and fifty years on this continent. To permit a Catholic to place a crown on your head—" Revere sighed. "It is scarcely to be imagined."

"What do you expect, Revere? If this—all of this—is the world there is, then surely there will have to be a place for French Catholics in it."

"Without a pope, what does Your Highness expect they can do?"

"I imagine they will have to create a pope somehow—I am not intimately familiar with the process by which popes are created. There is some sort of—some sort of council, I believe. Perhaps they will choose the Québecois archbishop—in which case, so to the horror of the New England Puritans, it may be a pope who crowns me."

The messenger stood at attention as Amherst read the message, then tucked it into a sleeve and drew out his spyglass. He scanned the western horizon, then lowered the glass and turned to Wolfe.

"They will be here by sunup," he said. "I see no sign of them, and no indication of fire, but I rely on our scouts." He saluted the messenger and dismissed him.

"Are they greater in number?"

"Overall, yes. But not all of them will arrive tomorrow. Still, Guyasuta has attracted followers—and servants—from many disaffected tribes. I don't know if he will be able to keep them ordered once they are all together, but when they do, his numbers will be far greater than our own."

"If so, some good shot and powder from well-trained troops should be enough to hold them off."

"And whatever unearthly powers he commands—or directs—will give them an advantage. I expect every man to do his best, General, but I fear that it will not be enough."

"And the French will sit idly by, and watch us be overwhelmed," Wolfe said. "Our prince must realize the fruitlessness of seeking an alliance with them."

"He has not given up hope."

"He should," Wolfe said. "Montcalm will not realize until too late that he can no more stand without us than we can without him."

"We can hope that he changes his mind," Amherst answered. "His Highness placed his hand in the lion's mouth—"

"His Highness," Wolfe answered, sniffing, "is young, and untrained, and idealistic. He sees a different future than any practical man can easily embrace."

"Have you spoken those words to the prince?"

"No. Of course not."

"I think he might welcome such plain speaking," Amherst said, scarcely smiling—though his sarcastic tone seemed to go unnoticed by Wolfe.

"In the morning," Wolfe said, "every man will do his duty—even the prince. God will determine the outcome."

"Unless God Himself is on the other side of the barrier and has left us to fend for ourselves."

"General?"

"Nothing, General Wolfe. You're right, I suppose. No soldier can know what will happen when battle is joined."

In the heat of the summer night, Amherst stood on the hill where his command tent was placed and looked over the encamped British forces. In the dark, trained veterans and raw recruits and potentially unreliable colonials all looked the same—groups of shadows gathered around their campfires, taking whatever comfort they could before a battle.

Amherst was reminded of the *Iliad*, in which the poet had described the watchfires of the Greek soldiers as stars. It was easier for a commander to rely on such a metaphor, distancing himself from the actual living men who would fight tomorrow, and many of whom would die. He had ordered men to their deaths before—but who could know who would live and who would die?

If God was watching, He would surely know. But He might indeed be beyond the Sundering.

Chapter 45

New York

Admiral Boscawen straightened up from the table, rubbing his lower back for a moment. He had been bent over studying the diagram for quite some time, and, much as he hated to admit it, he was no longer as limber as he'd been in earlier years.

"You really think you can make this?" he asked, frowning.

Messier made a little expressive shrug, in a very Gallic manner. "Make it? Certainly—even easily."

He tapped the center of the diagram. It was quite large, four feet by three feet, so he had to lean over in order to do it. "It looks complex, and to a degree it is, but no more than an organ or a loom. You could consider it a combination of both, if you will."

Boscawen's lips twisted into a little grimace. *Combination.* To him, the machine depicted in the diagram looked like the bizarre product of a *mating* between an organ and a loom. There was something vaguely disturbing, almost obscene, about the thing.

In the corner of his eye, he caught sight of a quick smile coming and going on the face of Mademoiselle LaGèndiere. She'd deny it, but he was sure that she shared a similar apprehension about the device. Uncertainty, at least; if not outright doubt—even though she'd apparently been the one mainly responsible for designing it. According to Messier, she'd been working on it whenever she could find the time, ever since the encounter with the revenants at Port Maria two months earlier.

By now, it was clear to Boscawen that when it came to practical applications of magic if not theory, the young Frenchwoman was the dominant partner in her relationship with Messier. She was adept at disguising the fact, and the British admiral doubted if Messier realized it himself, but fact it remained, nonetheless.

"The real question," Messier continued, "is whether the device will work at all."

"At least, as intended," qualified LaGèndiere. She leaned over, scrutinizing the drawing. "There's no question that it can and does produce commotion in the elemental forces. We tested a smaller and simpler model just yesterday and . . ."

She made a wry little shake of her head. "The environs got . . . unsettled."

"And those environs were?"

Messier pointed to the side with his thumb. "Not too far from here, but outside the city's limits."

"No one would have noticed anything except us," said LaGèndiere. "But the results of the test could hardly be called correlation."

Messier chuckled. "Hardly that!"

LaGèndiere shook her head again. "Unless we can improve our control, I'm afraid we'll have to call the device an elemental perturbator rather than an elemental concatenator."

There was silence in the room—a small office not far from Boscawen's own—for half a minute or so.

"But you think you can manage that?" the admiral finally asked.

LaGèndiere's nod was firm; Messier's . . . less so, but it was still a gesture of assent.

"It will take a while," said LaGèndiere. She gestured toward the diagram. "Fortunately, while the device is bulky it is not—will not be, I should say—especially heavy."

"Two hundred pounds, at most," added Messier. "We can easily transport it along with all the parts and tools we need on a wagon drawn by two horses. And, of course, the mademoiselle and I will need a carriage for our own transport."

Boscawen frowned. "Do I understand that you propose to finish the design—experiment with it, actually; let us be honest here—on the journey itself?"

"We have no choice," said LaGèndiere. "Not if we wish to bring the elemental concatenator to Amherst's forces in time."

Again, there was silence. Then Boscawen said: "And you are certain that you need this—this—thing. You cannot simply conjure up the magic by . . . by . . . "

The Frenchwoman's smile was so wide it was almost a grin. "By chanting spells and waving wands and suchlike? No, Admiral, we can't." LaGèndiere nodded toward Messier. "He can explain it better than I can, if you want the theoretical technicalities. But the gist of the matter is this: The way that magic is seeping into our new world—pouring in, in some places—is channeled by the existing . . . What should I call them?"

She looked at Messier. "Philosophies, perhaps?"

"Too—ha!—philosophical a term," said Messier. "Call them thought patterns."

"Thought patterns, then. The problem we face, Admiral, is that the thought patterns of Europeans—at least, Europeans of our class—has been heavily shaped over the past few centuries by what we French call the *Lumiéres*."

"The illuminated ones," Boscawen translated, in what was almost a murmur.

"Men such as Spinoza," Messier said. "Copernicus, Montesquieu, Diderot—your own John Locke and Isaac Newton."

"It has been a veritable movement in European thought and letters for at least two centuries now," added LaGèndiere. "The Italians sometimes call it *illuminismo;* the Germans, the *Aufklärung*. I don't believe you English have a specific term for it, but 'enlightenment' would be suitable."

Boscawen looked back down at the diagram. "And whatever value this—ah, thought pattern might have in a world governed solely by natural laws and reason, it does not suit this new world we're in very well at all."

"Let us say rather that it can often get in our way," qualified Messier. He smiled. "It is not *always* a hindrance, Admiral. After all, firearms still work—for the most part, anyway—and the making of such mechanical contrivances is still largely a European monopoly. What is necessary is for us to *adapt* the emerging magic to our own thought patterns. Hence—"

"The elemental concatenator," his French compatriot finished for him. LaGèndiere rapped her knuckles on the table. "We may not be able to use magic in what you might call a *direct* manner, Admiral Boscawen, but we can devise ways to channel its forces using our own technological ways of seeing the world."

"Mechanical magic, you're saying." Boscawen scratched his jaw for a moment. "Thaumaturgical machines that anyone can use."

"Ah . . . " said Messier.

LaGèndiere shook her head. "I am afraid not, Admiral. Just as only a small number of natives and people of African descent can apply the forces of magic—at least, in an effective manner—the same is true of we Europeans."

"There are only a few of us who are really adept at this, even using contrivances like the alchemetical compass or"—Messier pointed to the devise drawn on the diagram—"the elemental concatenator. I comprehend the abstract and theoretical issues rather well, but I am inept at applying that knowledge."

He turned to LaGèndiere and gave her what amounted to a little bow. "Quite unlike Mademoiselle Catherine."

The realization of what Messier and his young French companion truly intended was finally clear to Boscawen.

"You plan to be the operator of this device—in battle!—not simply its designer," he accused LaGèndiere.

The mademoiselle had a distinctly smug expression on her face. "I prefer to think of myself as the gunner."

"Ridiculous!"

LaGèndiere stared at him. In the end, it was the admiral who looked away.

That evening, following a private dinner to which he had invited the two French scholars, Boscawen raised another issue.

"If the two of you insist on haring off into the wilderness in order to test your elemental concatenator in an actual battle, who will maintain the supply of specie here in New York? I don't believe Alexander can do it on his own, especially since you will be taking the alchemetical compass with you." The admiral shook his head. "You will understand that, given the nature of the project, I want as few people as possible to know the origin of the gold and silver I'm using to sustain the navy."

Messier grunted. "Sustain half the economy of New York as well, from what I can see." He drained his wine glass and set it down on the dining table.

"Yes, you're probably right."

"Perhaps you yourself could . . . " LaGèndiere started to say, before her sentence trailed off.

Boscawen shook his head. "As you said yourself, the use of magic—even transmitted through mechanical means—requires a certain aptitude. Which I do not have any more than Monsieur Messier."

She nodded. "The problem you face is that the two people I can think of who would most suit your purpose would be Minerva and her friend Absalom. From what you described of your encounters with them, both have in their different ways an affinity for magic."

Boscawen's grimace was pronounced. "Put the financial fate of . . . well, everyone, in the hands of negroes? That seems most unwise, Mademoiselle LaGèndiere!"

"Not as unwise as placing that fate in the hands of such as Governor De Lancey," LaGèndiere retorted.

"There would actually be some advantages, Admiral," said Messier. "The two negroes you speak of are, like all such, outside the environs of power and influence. They would not be in a position on their own to engage in massive specie manipulation. Some, to be sure—but so what? Whatever gold and silver they embezzled from you—if 'embezzle' is even an applicable term—would be fairly small. Not enough, I think, to have a noticeable effect on New York's commerce. And if that's the case—"

He shrugged. "As the Bible says, thou shalt not muzzle the kine that treads the grain."

Boscawen thought about it for a few seconds, draining his own wine glass in the process. "I see your point. But what would stop them from seeking an alliance with someone in New York who *does* have access to power and influence?"

Before either Messier or LaGèndiere said anything, Boscawen answered his own question. "Not likely, I grant you, since any such person of power in New York would almost certainly have been implicated in the slaughter of innocent black people in the troubles twenty years ago. The navy has a far better reputation with New York's negroes than any other white people in the city."

He set the empty wine glass down. "I will consider the idea further. In the meantime, can you see to it that I have a large supply of specie before you leave?"

"Yes," said LaGèndiere. "Transmutation does not go quickly, but now that we have experience with the process, we should be able to provide you with . . . "

She looked to Messier. "What do you think? Another two hundred guineas?"

"At the very least," replied the Frenchman. "At a guess, more like two hundred and fifty. It's not as if we can charge off all that soon anyway, what with the other preparations we need to make."

Relaxed, now, the admiral settled back in his chair. "More wine?" When both Messier and LaGèndiere nodded, he rang a little bell to summon a servant. After the wine was brought and poured, and the servant had left the room, Boscawen shook his head. The gesture was one of bemusement more than anything else.

"I have to say I'm a little astonished at the readiness with which the city's merchants have been willing to accept our specie as— literally, not figuratively—good coin. Not one of them has so far raised any questions or doubts at all."

"It's not really as surprising as all that, Admiral," said Messier. "Do you recall what Mademoiselle Catherine said about thought patterns?"

"Yes. Quite well."

"You are seeing another manifestation of it here. After the eruption of trade around the world these past few centuries, your average European—at least of the dominant and governing classes— have just as much faith in money as they do in mechanical matters."

"More, I'd say." That came from LaGèndiere. Smiling, she reached for her glass. "It's like that aura of kingship that is said to envelop Prince Edward. Call it the 'aura of Mammon,' if you choose."

Boscawen made a face. "Hardly that! It's all being done in a good cause. No, let us rather think of it as . . . " Grasping for a suitable term, he sipped at his wine.

"Midas' mesmerism?" LaGèndiere suggested.

"Better, certainly. But still not . . . "

"Midas' charisma?" was her next suggestion.

"Splendid!" said Boscawen.

Chapter 46

Every man will do his duty

The British camp had built some defensive works, though there was nothing like a fort—but Amherst was not expecting a siege. Guyasuta was not a European general, nor had he even been trained as a soldier; formation and assault was not how the savages fought. Apart from other considerations, there should have been no question of the outcome.

But, as Amherst well knew, there were *other considerations*.

The troops were roused while it was still dark, while the nearby forest seemed full of encroaching, threatening trees. The pickets were alert, hearing scattered war-cries in the darkness; somewhere out of their sight, native troops were preparing to attack. Their plans, and their intentions, were unclear; but as Amherst emerged from his tent, having had little in the way of sleep, he saw a pair of soldiers approaching, a native held between them.

"General," one of the soldiers said, saluting, as the other grasped the native's arm more tightly.

"What is this?"

"A spy, sir," the soldier answered. "Or a turncoat. He claims to have information for you."

"Indeed." Amherst placed his hat on his head, and looked at the native—a young man, dressed as a scout—trousers and vest, moccasins, and painted face and arms designed to conceal him in foliage and underbrush. The man seemed fearless, meeting Amherst eye-to-eye in the light of flickering torches that pushed back the pre-dawn darkness. "Does he speak English?"

"I do," he answered. "You are the chief of the whites?"

"I am General Amherst. If you have something to say, then say it."

"I am Donehogawa, once of the village of Ichsua. I have walked the paths of the forest in the war-band of Guyasuta, who calls himself Chief of Chiefs, Scourge of the Pale Ones, Beloved of the Gods. I have come to give you warning, Chief Amherst."

"What sort of warning?"

"Guyasuta, Chief of Chiefs, and his brother Sganyodaiyo, have called forth much evil medicine to further their cause against the whites. Though they say this is blessed by the gods, I know that some of it is an abomination. I will no longer serve that cause."

"Why are you serving it in the first place? And, again, what warning do you bring?"

"I had no choice." Donehogawa's shoulders seemed to slump ever so slightly. "Guyasuta sent a Dry-Hand shaman to my village, and those warriors who would not follow the Chief of Chiefs were touched by the Dry-Hand medicine. I chose not to die, Chief Amherst.

"Sganyodaiyo has brought a medicine to the warriors of Guyasuta. Many of them wear what he calls a *ghost shirt*, which he says will ward off the bullets from the whites' guns. I do not know if this is true—but if it is, it places you all in danger. It is well known that you whites cannot fight without your guns, so his warriors can easily overwhelm you."

Amherst began to reply, then realized that the young native might well be trying to make him angry—perhaps to show that he was not cowed by being made a prisoner.

"Do you have such a garment?"

Donehogawa shrugged free of his captor and pulled aside his vest to reveal a plain muslin shirt, off-white and unadorned by decoration.

Amherst stepped forward and took a bit of the cloth between his fingers. "Guyasuta says that *this* can stop bullets?"

"He says that a warrior wearing it cannot be harmed by the white man's guns."

"Do you believe this?"

"Many warriors believe it," the young man said. "They say that medicine's power grows by the strength of belief."

"Shall we see if *you* believe in it? I am sure that there are enough men in this camp who would be eager to find out."

To his credit, the young native did not waver or look away; but he did not respond.

"And what do you want, young man? You have said why you have left Guyasuta. What do you want from me?"

"I want to live, Chief Amherst. I want to live in the new world that the Great Spirit has made. Guyasuta thinks there is no room for whites. But I think there is enough room for all."

"How do I know you can be trusted?"

"You have my oath. And I *want to live*," he repeated. "If I do something not worthy of your trust, you can put me to death. You have the hatchet in your hand, mighty chief."

"I will think about what you have said. Confine him," he said to the soldiers, who took hold of the native's arms again.

"What is my fate?" Donehogawa said, as Amherst began to turn away.

He looked back at the native. "For now," Amherst replied, "you have your wish."

As the first rays of the summer sun peeked over the hills to the east, catching the tips of the bayonets and the brass decorations of the soldiers' uniforms, groups of wildly painted natives began to emerge from the trees. The close ranks of British soldiers held their fire, waiting for the native warriors to come into range of their muskets. Behind them stood their officers, swords drawn, preparing to give the order.

Amherst and Wolfe watched the deployment from the hill behind the British lines. "There are shamans coming behind the warriors," Amherst said. "The ones without axes or rifles. The troops are ordered to target them whenever possible."

"Don't let them get close enough to touch anyone," Wolfe said. "Those are the 'dry-hands' of which I spoke. Nasty."

"They can be killed by bullets, I assume, unless these 'ghost shirts' are truly effective."

"You don't believe what the informant told you?"

"I believe that Guyasuta has given these shirts to his warriors, but I don't believe that they will have any effect. And I see no reason to share this information with the men: they should have no cause to believe that the savages have some . . . supernatural protection. If belief makes truth, there is no reason to engender such belief."

"That is somewhat irrational, if the General pleases. The idea that what people believe changes reality—"

"Truly, General Wolfe, is there anything rational about floating monsters? About ghosts of Highlanders and stone warriors? What about this war—this world—remains rational?"

"There is nothing to be gained by adding to it. Sir."

Amherst's hands tightened on his horse's reins, but he forced himself to relax them. Wolfe's tone was mildly arch and superior, but he had a point. Someone, somewhere, had to decide to put a mark in the ground and decide to exercise reason in the face of . . .

"Soldiers must fight the war that is in front of them, not the one drawn up on a map or written in orders. There are floating monsters, and ghosts, and stone warriors—and there is still the honor of the Crown and the duty to king and country. Every man will do his duty."

"Or die trying."

"Yes," Amherst agreed. "Or that."

Prince Edward stood outside his tent, listening to the shouts of the officers and the war-whoops of the natives as they emerged onto the battlefield. He had remained away from the encounter at the urging of General Amherst.

We have many soldiers, Highness, he had said. *But only one prince.*

His grandfather had been in the van at Dettingen while king. Whatever else could be said of him, George II was a brave man: he had not remained behind in his tent while his troops were exposed to danger. Of course, he had adult sons and young grandsons, so that if he fell Britain would still have a king. But even with that fig leaf— that there were no others with royal blood in the world—it troubled Edward that he was (in his mind) *cowering* while loyal men exposed themselves to danger.

If Amherst's forces prevailed, then it would be remembered that he had been away from danger. If the natives overwhelmed them, he would have to fight for his life nonetheless—or flee—or die in his tent.

In the moment, Edward resolved to do none of those things. He called to his groom to bring his mount.

Paul Revere stood with the men from Massachusetts and Connecticut, their ranks deployed well behind the British regulars.

He saw the warriors advancing across the field and wondered when—or if—the general would order the colonials to advance.

"Why don't they fire?" someone said from the ranks.

"Waste of ammunition," Colonel Gridley said. "They have to come closer. A great deal closer."

"They'll only have one volley," Revere said. "Then it'll be bayonets."

"I agree. But I don't think the regulars will have any problem with that. The natives can do all the shouting they like, but they're no match for cold steel."

"You would think that the general would want us to be helping with that," Revere answered. "We've been fighting natives for a hundred years."

The comment hung in the air for a few moments, then Gridley turned and put a hand on his junior's shoulder and led him aside.

"You know very well why we're standing here rather than over there," Gridley said quietly. "I don't intend to have a policy debate with you in front of the men. General Amherst is relying on his regulars for this fight. We're here because we came here, not because he *wants* us here."

"You'll forgive me for saying so, Colonel, but that's a damn waste of good talent."

"I agree. But this is neither the time nor the place—"

"Truly? Begging your pardon, sir. But when will it be the time or place? This is our land the natives want to take back. The general and his fine troops just got here, to fight a war against the French—and we're not even fighting that war anymore. The men of Massachusetts-Bay and Connecticut and Rhode Island and New York, and all the rest of the colonies, have civilized this land, planted and settled and built, and the savages want to tear that all down. Why shouldn't we want to fight for it?"

Gridley took off his hat and ran a hand through his hair. "How do you expect me to answer that?"

"I'm not sure, Colonel. But if the savages come anywhere near us, orders or not, the men will want to fight for their country—and their king."

"Our king is far away."

"No," Revere said, pointing toward the camp, from which a rider was approaching at a gallop, followed by several others. "Our king is right here."

Gridley turned away and walked over to meet the rider, who stopped and dismounted.

"Your Highness," Gridley said, bowing. "How may I be of service?"

"Colonel—Gridley, is it? And Captain Revere." Edward smiled. "Revere and I are well acquainted. Tell me, Colonel. Are your troops ready to fight?"

"Never more ready, sir. But General Amherst has ordered us to wait in reserve."

"I . . . " Edward looked away. The sounds of musket fire and a cloud of smoke rolled away from where the regulars were deployed, waiting for the leading native warriors to reach them. "When you are called forward, I will go with you."

"Highness, I . . . cannot, I am not sure I can guarantee your safety. General Amherst—"

"I will be responsible for my own safety, Colonel Gridley. Make sure your men are ready to advance." Without another word, he turned on his heel and walked back to his mount.

Gridley looked aside at Revere.

"Well, Captain," he said, "you may get your fight after all."

The regular infantryman in His Majesty's service understood that for musket fire to be effective, he and all his fellows had to fire at once; the volley would assure that some bullets would at least strike their target. They followed the manual of arms: load the ball; pour the powder; ram; take aim, and on command fire all at once. Good infantrymen could manage several volleys a minute; while one rank fired, the other would retire and prepare for its next shot.

The natives charged toward the British line, seemingly heedless of the danger that awaited them. Most of the troops, while regulars, had never faced this sort of attack, but their training held them to the rigid sequence of loading, readying and firing, doing the job that men to their left and right were doing at the same time. The officers had prepared them to see a foregone conclusion: mangled bodies on the ground, felled by the murderous fire . . . but when the smoke cleared, most of the attackers were still coming, unaffected by the first volley. Some of the native warriors had been struck down by the gunfire, but nowhere nearly as many as should have been.

A second volley by the next rank met with similar results.

Officers raised their swords and shouted, "fix bayonets!" There was scarcely time to do so before the first of the attackers reached the British lines. Beyond, the regulars could see elaborately dressed natives beginning to walk, almost casually, toward the line of battle.

From their vantage, astonished, Amherst and Wolfe watched as the natives continued to advance into the vicious melee with the regular troops. More and more were emerging from the trees; soon the British would be outnumbered.

"Wolfe," Amherst said. "Go take charge of the colonials. It appears they will be needed after all."

"Someone has already made that decision," Wolfe said, pointing toward them. The men of the colonies had begun to advance toward the fight, in something only vaguely resembling a formation. Their muskets were slung behind them, but with axes, cutlasses and even cudgels in their hands, they were well prepared for a fight. In the van, the two generals could make out a small group of mounted men, swords drawn, charging forward.

"If Gridley advanced without my orders—"

"No, General," Wolfe said. "I do believe that is the prince."

The fighting was brutal and chaotic. There was little semblance of formation on the part of the colonials, and soon the regulars were fighting in the same manner; each dealing with the man in front of him, and then the next man, and so on, paying no heed to the overall situation. Shots rang out, sometimes felling a Briton or a native, but often simply going awry, an echo above the din of the battle, smoke rising and drifting away.

After several minutes that felt like hours, Revere looked up to see a man a few feet away who was dressed more ornately than the others. He was a sachem, perhaps, or a shaman: he didn't know the distinctions among savage tribesmen, as they rarely walked the streets of Boston. The man had a disturbing smile, and his left hand appeared thin, almost skeletal, with sinew or cord wrapped in between the fingers and around the wrist.

As their eyes met, the sounds of the battle seemed to become dim and distant, as if a shroud of fog had been spread around where Revere stood.

Come here, the shaman said, and beckoned with the malformed hand, curling each finger in turn. Revere stood up straight, his short sword held at his side, unable to look away.

He took one step forward and then another. The sounds and sights of the battle were almost out of reach now.

This is where your story ends, pale one. This is your fate, and the fate of all of your people. The world belongs to us.

Your cities will burn and your farms will be laid waste. Your roads will be covered with underbrush, and in a generation, no one will know you were ever here. The Great Spirit will not even be able to find your bones.

Though he knew he was being compelled, Revere could not resist. He thought of everything that had happened in his life, as if it were a story-book laid out before him: his youth in Boston's North End, his brothers and sisters and extended Hitchborn family; his struggles with his father over his profession and his own faith; his father's death, and his time in the provincial army; his return to Boston to take up the silversmith's trade, and his marriage to Sarah . . . dear Sarah . . . their whole life was ahead of them.

No, the shaman said. *Your whole life is behind you.*

A few steps further, and Revere knew he was almost in reach of the shaman's extended hand. He could see nothing now but the hand: it was a skeletal appendage, bound to the stump of the shaman's wrist, and it shone like brightly polished silver except that the light hurt his eyes. He could make out every curve, every articulation of the hand that reached for him as he stood, transfixed, waiting for its touch—

And then he saw the shaman stagger, blood spouting from his neck and upper chest. The horrible hand fell to the savage's side, and he slumped forward, almost in slow motion, to the ground, landing scarcely a foot from where Revere stood.

And as suddenly the sound and sight and smell of battle returned in a rush that made Revere stagger. He looked up to see the mounted figure of Prince Edward, bloodied sword in hand, silhouetted against the sun, though to Revere's suddenly clearing vision he seemed more like an armored knight, a great and noble figure.

At Revere's feet was the sprawled body of the shaman who had spoken to him.

"Welcome back," the prince said.

No, Revere thought, looking at the corpse. Your *story ends here. And the Great Spirit will search in vain for* your *bones.*

Chapter 47

It cannot be undone

Against the fierce counterattack by the colonials, the natives retreated into the forest. Shouted orders by officers kept the British soldiers, regular and colonial, from pursuing, and with the sun high in the sky the British found themselves masters of the field.

Amherst came into Prince Edward's tent without introduction or leave. He saw Captain Revere being attended to; the colonial stood, shrugging away the man attending to a wound. The prince did not, but looked up at the general.

"You are dismissed," Amherst said to Revere, who saluted. But Edward put a hand on his sleeve.

"No, Captain. Remain, if you would. How may I be of service, General?"

"Prince Edward, you have shown yourself to be reckless and foolhardy. I cannot adequately explain my anger at your behavior." Amherst clenched his fist. "You could have been killed—and for no reason."

"I think Captain Revere would disagree, sir."

Amherst looked from Revere to the prince. "I am sure the captain appreciates your effort, Highness. But he is one among many—as am I. You are the only person of royal birth in the New World. If Revere is slain, if I am slain, there will be men to replace us. If you die, there is no one. Why do you not understand that? Must I have you confined?"

Edward stood to face Amherst. The two men were about the same height, but Edward was younger, a trifle less heavy—he had the lithe grace of youth.

"I defy you to do so, General. We will see who will refuse the order."

Amherst did not reply at once, but instead rubbed his forehead with his right hand.

"I cannot serve in my current capacity if my orders are not obeyed, sir. And you are an officer in His Majesty's armed forces, seconded to my command. By entering this battle in direct violation of my orders, even if you acquitted yourself with exceptional valor, you should be subject to a court-martial. Perhaps you can clarify for me why I should not pursue one."

Edward's expression seemed to convey shock at such a suggestion, but it changed as he met Amherst's eye.

"The colonial troops drove the savages off the field," Edward said. "I ordered them into battle, which—in my opinion—you should have done, rather than leaving them idle . . . nonetheless, upon reflection, you are correct, General Amherst. Regardless of my intentions, I subjected myself to unnecessary personal risk."

"I am glad that Your Highness realizes that."

Revere, who looked very uncomfortable, offered another salute and left the tent. Edward did not prevent him, and Amherst simply ignored the young officer. Once the colonial had left the tent, Amherst said: "I welcome Your Highness' advice on what I am to do in this circumstance. I do not wish to have this particular conversation again."

"I understand, General. But it ill befits me as a sovereign, even a sovereign-in-waiting, to cower within my tent while brave men are fighting and dying. I will not expose myself to unnecessary risk in the future, but I will not remain concealed in camp."

"I do not know how I can protect you."

"So be it. If it is God's will that I die, then . . . I die. But if I am to be king, I must have not only the obedience of my subjects, but also their respect."

"And you will not be deterred from this course, even though you are irreplaceable."

"No, General. I will not. I will be obedient to your orders, but I will not be left behind."

The sachem stood unmoving, looking straight ahead, his

expression neutral. A few feet away, Guyasuta squatted by the fire, looking at the flames flickering in front of him.

"Tell me how many Dry-Hands died today," Guyasuta said, without looking at him.

"Three," the sachem answered.

"Three," Guyasuta repeated. "And tell me, Brother, where the white men's prince lies dead. And where General Amherst's corpse can be found."

"They are not dead, Brother."

"No," Guyasuta said. "They are not." He stood up, taking a branch and placing it in the flames until it caught fire, and lifted it so that it cast flickering shadows across the dark clearing.

He walked to stand in front of the sachem.

"It was not my order that you attack the whites, Brother," Guyasuta said. "Many of our people are still making their way here; we were not ready to attack."

"You say."

"And what do *you* say? What moved you to attack before I ordered it?"

"The whites were weak," the sachem said. "The servants of the *Onontio* did not come to the aid of the others. I saw the chance for glory; I saw no need or reason to wait."

"It was the deed of a fool."

"You say," the sachem repeated.

"*I* say," Guyasuta said, holding the flaming brand high, etching the profile of the shaman in light and dark. "I say, and I lead. I have quenched the fire of the Covenant. I have gathered the tribes to do what must be done—to drive the whites from the lands of the Great Spirit. Your rash act threatens our success. The ghost shirts worked—"

"Some of them worked."

"*Most* of them did just what Sganyodaiyo said they would. We only lost because you launched the assault too early, before we had assembled enough men."

"It is done," the sachem said, still looking straight ahead, impassive in the face of Guyasuta's anger. "It cannot be undone."

"But you can be prevented from making such mistakes again."

"I am not afraid of your anger," the sachem said. "Or your fire. If you take my life, my sons will take yours."

"I will not take your life," Guyasuta answered. "And as for your sons, they may watch as I exact my justice."

He raised his torch in the air, and the sachem heard gasps from those watching, scarcely visible, out of the firelight. He looked at Guyasuta, who was looking in the air over his right shoulder; the shaman's gaze moved there, and he saw something round, bearing the vague features of a human face. It glowed weirdly with an inner light, filling the sachem with a sense of dread.

"Its hunger needs to be met," Guyasuta said. "You will serve admirably."

"My sons—"

"Let them try and seek justice," Guyasuta interrupted. "The mission is greater than you, and greater than them."

Without another word, he walked away, leaving the sachem to deal with the Floating Head. It was only then that the sachem at last moved—but he was already too late.

Revere located Prince Edward in the large medical tents set up near the base of the hill. It was not a scene for the faint of heart: the English had held the field, but at a cost—and those who paid that price, and were not already dead, showed the effects of the battle.

The prince was seated beside one of the young soldiers; his back was turned to Revere as he entered the tent. The patient was being attended by a chirurgeon who—thankfully—looked to be sober.

Revere came close, but remained a few feet away so as not to intrude. After a few seconds, Prince Edward noticed his presence and rose.

Revere made a leg. "I beg your pardon, Highness. I did not mean to interrupt."

"I'm merely taking a moment to visit," Edward said. "The chirurgeons seems to have this well in hand. Were you looking for me?"

"By your leave, Highness, yes I was."

"Let's step outside," Edward said, gesturing toward the tent entrance. They stepped out of the sick tent into the bright late-afternoon sunlight.

Edward removed his hat and wiped sweat from his brow with the sleeve of his shirt. "What can I do for you, Captain?"

"I—I'm not sure how to explain, Your Highness. I wanted to seek you out—I wanted to thank you personally for saving my life. I am not sure how I can adequately express my appreciation. You risked great personal harm to be there, at the very moment when I—"

Edward smiled. "I will not dismiss it or say that it was nothing. My grandfather the king fought on the battlefield of Dettingen many years ago, and saved a few lives and, I'm sure, had his life saved during that battle. Saving a fellow soldier from death is no small thing. But I was just doing my duty."

"Surely you had more important matters—"

"What, than saving your life?" Prince Edward laughed, and reached out and placed his hand on Revere's shoulder. "If General Amherst had his way, I would have remained in the camp, and that duty would have fallen to someone else—or perhaps no one else."

"I don't understand. The general didn't order you to lead us forward?"

"Not a bit. And he threatened me with court-martial."

"I heard him do so, Highness. I would think you might find that a mortal insult."

The prince dropped his hand to his side and shrugged. "Personally, I thought it was rather an affront, Captain. But as a sworn man in His Majesty's Forces, I am obliged to obey the orders of my superior. And I *did* act against orders. But you, and the other colonials, acquitted yourselves with honor and skill. The regulars were not sure what to do when their first volleys had little effect, but you men showed that you knew what to do in close combat with the savages. I think your troops won the battle."

"If you say so, Your Highness. I am in no position to judge."

"In any case, I accepted his rebuke, and will say nothing further about it. As for you—I would not expect you to take the time, sir. I thought I had quite offended you by my suggestion to the Marquis de Montcalm that I might let a Papist place the crown on my head. I believed that I had quite lost favor with you."

"A brush with death lends some perspective, Your Highness."

"I expect it does. Well, I accept your thanks, Revere: there is a life between us now."

"Yes," Revere said. "There is. I spoke with Colonel Gridley about this, and he assured me that he would make no objection if I approached you and . . . offered my personal service to you."

"Personal service? Revere, I am far too junior to warrant an aide of my own."

"You are to be our king."

"I am not yet king," Edward answered. "And in any case, as I say, I have someone in the regiment who polishes my boots and arranges my shaving brush, along with several other officers. I don't really need an equerry, though I suppose someday I shall have to staff a royal household."

"I would like to be a part of that household."

"From what I understand, Captain, you are a businessman and a family man back in your native town. Boston will suffer without your presence, I should think."

"Wherever Your Highness establishes his court, I can serve. I feel it is my personal duty to you."

"I understand your obligation, Revere," the prince said. "But . . . " he was pensive for a few moments. "Very well. I will think about it. The deed is done; it cannot be undone. When this is over, perhaps there will be a place for you. It is only practicality that stays my hand. I think highly of you, Captain, and will continue to do so. Do not doubt my affection."

Revere bowed. "I am greatly obliged to you, Your Highness."

Edward smiled, and Revere felt reassured, though he knew that it was not the answer he had sought. With nothing further to say, he begged leave to go, and walked away across the field to where the New Englanders were encamped. He turned around once to see Prince Edward standing in place, watching him go.

Chapter 48

Best safety lies in fear

New York

"We could stay here," said Mademoiselle LaGèndiere. She gestured at the bizarre contraption atop the wagon she was standing next to. "The elemental concatenator might make a difference if trouble breaks out."

Her tone was not as confident as the words themselves, however. Messier shook his head and put her own doubts into words.

"Not likely, Catherine." His expression was rueful, with a trace of apology. "If unrest does erupt here in New York, I can't think of a weapon more poorly designed for fighting in the streets than the concatenator."

He was right about that, and she knew it herself. The concatenator was a magical device—say better, a mechanical aid for LaGèndiere to focus her own inherent magical skills—for combining and harmonizing the various powers of the four elements: air, earth, fire and water. In the nature of things, those elements were weakest in artificially created urban environs.

"I see no reason for you to remain in New York," said Boscawen, shaking his head. He gave the street they were on a quick glance, north and south, and then pointed with his chin toward the area of the city where the freedmen population was concentrated. "Gustavus told me that while the negroes are restive, he does not think they are on the verge of any sort of upheaval. He says their attitude seems to be one of waiting to see what develops given the new . . . ah, conditions."

LaGèndiere opened her mouth, as if to speak, but then closed it again. She had reservations about the slave Gustavus' assessment of the situation. Although he was a slave himself, most of Gustavus' interactions with New York's black people had been with freedmen like Minerva and Absalom. She thought his reading of their attitude was probably accurate—but did that same attitude extend to the considerably larger population of slaves?

She didn't think so. She'd seen enough of the harsh treatment meted out to most slaves to doubt that what the admiral called "the new conditions" produced in them the same caution it produced in the freedmen. She was rather inclined to suppose they were encouraged to outright rebellion.

But what did she really know about the slaves? Less than the city's freedmen, certainly. Her reservations were simply that, being honest—reservations, not solid opinions. And the point made by Dr. Messier was certainly true. It remained to be seen how effective the elemental concatenator would be in the wilderness. She did not doubt for a moment that it would be largely useless in urban surroundings. Cobblestones, fumes, sewage and stoves were a poor substitute for the earth, air, water and fire the device was designed to affect.

"Very well," she said. "Let's be off, then. We have a long journey ahead of us."

No sooner had Admiral Boscawen gotten back to naval headquarters than he received the news he'd most dreaded.

"Governor De Lancey is calling out the militia," Lt. Pascal informed him. The young officer nodded toward the black man standing next to him. "Gustavus just returned with the news."

"Returned from where?" Boscawen demanded. He was only idly curious as to the answer. Mostly, he'd asked just to gain himself a little time to think.

The scowl on his face must have been ferocious, however. The slave stepped back half a pace, his expression visibly alarmed.

The admiral waved his hand in a reassuring gesture. "I am not angry with you, Gustavus. I simply don't understand how you could have gotten the news before I did." His next handwave indicated the streets outside. "My couriers are quite alert and efficient. They would have brought me word of Governor De Lancey's decision as soon as he informed them of it."

Relaxing, a little smile came to Gustavus' face. "Begging the admiral's pardon, but I'm sure there was at least one slave present in the governor's chamber when De Lancey gave the order to his own adjutants. He—maybe she—would have spread the word as soon as possible. From there . . . "

He shrugged. "There are a lot of slaves in New York, and they have their own communication networks. Which—meaning no offense—are probably the most efficient, at least within the city limits. Fastest, for a surety."

Boscawen took off his hat and ran fingers across his scalp. He thought Gustavus was probably right.

"And you found out from one of the city's slaves," he concluded.

"Two, actually." Gustavus waved his own hand in the direction of the streets outside. "They accosted me almost as soon as I left the headquarters. They are quite frightened, Admiral."

As well they might be, Boscawen reflected grimly. At the best of times, colonial militias were notoriously undisciplined—and New York's were no exception. The mere rumor of slave unrest could bring militiamen to a state of mixed fear and fury that could—that *had*, not more than a generation earlier—produce the most horrible and bestial behavior.

He put his hat back on his head. "What triggered De Lancey's decision? Do you know?"

Gustavus shook his head. "No, sir. None of the slaves knew, either. But it could have been . . . " He shook his head again. "Almost any sort of rumor would do, given the tensions in the city since the Sundering."

He was probably right about that as well, thought Boscawen.

"Well, I don't see where there's much we can do, beyond securing our own headquarters." The admiral was now regretting his decision to send most of his available troops with Saunders' expedition.

But there was no way to recall those troops now, so there was no point dwelling on the matter.

"Have you spoken to Minerva or Absalom?" Boscawen asked Gustavus.

The slave shook his head. "Not in two days, Admiral. Do you want me to seek them out?"

"Yes, do. Perhaps they might have some important tidings."

Not likely, of course. As impressed as Boscawen had been by the two, in the end they were simply freedmen. No more powerful, really, than any slave in the city.

Judging from the dubious look on his face, Gustavus shared the same opinion. But the young slave made no protest. A moment later, he was gone.

The trip to the freedmen's district was a nerve-racking business. As yet, Gustavus could see no signs of the militia's mobilization. But, clearly, word had spread. New York's streets were almost empty of traffic. White people had scurried for cover, not just negroes. He only encountered an old male slave and a middle-aged white woman. The slave shuffled past, ignoring Gustavus completely. From the distance of a block away, the white woman spotted him coming, uttered a small cry of distress, and hurried away.

What did she think he might do? Here, in broad daylight?

She probably had no clear idea herself; no coherence to her terror. She was just following Laertes' advice to his sister Ophelia from Shakespeare's Danish play:

Be wary, then. Best safety lies in fear.

If she'd ever seen the play, which was unlikely. Gustavus was familiar with the bard's work because his master treasured the plays and poems and encouraged his slave to read them. He'd even taken Gustavus to a couple of performances—*Macbeth,* and *Antony and Cleopatra*—although the slave had been required to stand in the pit rather than share his master's box. (Required by custom, not by Pascal himself.)

The problem—what Gustavus feared, in that moment—was not the advice given by a brother to a sister. It was the observation made by Antony's friend Enobarbus, in the second of the plays Gustavus had seen:

To be furious is to be frighted out of fear.

For the moment, fear might reign. But it wouldn't be long before fury took its place—fury, and the savagery that came with it.

✥ ✥ ✥

Happily, Gustavus made it to Minerva's boardinghouse without any trouble. When he was let in by the servant girl Grace, he was not surprised to see that Absalom was already there.

"Yes, we know," Absalom said, before Gustavus could get a word out. "The whites are getting ready to run wild again. I don't suppose your precious Admiral Boscawen can put a stop to it?"

Gustavus shook his head. "He would if he could, but he sent almost all of his soldiers north with Admiral Saunders' fleet."

"Stupid," said Absalom, scowling.

"Be fair," countered Minerva. "He had no way of knowing De Lancey would call out the militia based on nothing more than rumor, and New York is not the only place he's responsible for."

Absalom's scowl didn't lighten a bit. Clearly, he was in a less charitable mood than Minerva was.

"It won't be the same massacre it was last time," he said, his tone cold and harsh. "The slaves have nothing but their bare hands—some kitchen tools, at most—but the freedmen have been arming themselves."

"With what?" Gustavus asked skeptically. "You're not allowed to possess firearms. Nor swords or any sort of real military equipment. How much can you do with axes and shovels?"

"No, Absalom's right," said Minerva. "Things are different now that our ancient magic is returning. If need be, I myself can—" She broke off abruptly, shaking her head. It was not so much a gesture of negation as one of distaste.

"That's an ugly business, that is," she said. "I won't use my powers except as a last resort, but others won't be as hesitant."

"Some won't hesitate at all," said Absalom. "Like that Jupiter. They say he can summon demons, at least those that are afraid of him."

"*Who* says?" asked Gustavus, dubiously. He wasn't very familiar with New York's slaves, but he was a slave himself and knew how prone such people were to believing rumors. Being fair about it, slaves were deliberately kept as ignorant of the world as possible. His own situation as Lieutenant Pascal's slave was highly unusual. Plus, as a sailor, he had seen a great deal more of the world than most of the slaves in the city. With a few exceptions, they saw nothing much beyond their immediate places of labor—cleaning homes, cooking in kitchens, working in small shops, and always restricted to as small a portion of New York as was feasible. It was no wonder most of them were superstitious and prone to believing tall tales.

Still . . .

There *was* magic spreading through the world, Gustavus knew. And he remembered enough of his upbringing to know that the peoples in Africa possessed power over witchcraft. Some of them, at any rate—especially blacksmiths. In the part of western Africa that he came from, there was widespread worship of Ogun, the god of iron and war. His people did not consider Ogun an evil god, but he was certainly a fierce one. Those men who knew how to create and shape iron had a special affinity for Ogun and could summon his aid at times. In the folklore of Gustavus' own people, that aid generally took useful forms. But here, across an ocean and after a great sundering of the world . . . who could say what asking for Ogun's aid might produce?

Land of the Five Nations

They had discussed the matter for two days and nights, with scarcely a break to attend to personal needs. The clan mothers of the Iroquois were nothing if not sturdy.

It was easy enough to say no. The *Tadodaho* was against the idea of relighting the Council Fire. It had been extinguished by medicine, he had said, and it would be medicine to bring it back to life. The Fire was the place where clan chiefs and clan mothers came to settle differences and smoke the pipe of peace, to bury hatchets and cover graves—it had been so for hundreds of seasons, uniting the nations against internal threats and external ones, making big wars into small ones and small ones into peace.

It was difficult to accept a world in which it was gone. But it had been absent since medicine had extinguished it.

"What would be the point?" Neani had asked, when the moon was already down and most of the warriors and other clan-mothers were sleeping. Only she and Osha were awake. Neani was a Cayuga clan-mother, one of the few who had come in the heat of summer at the *Tadodaho*'s request.

"You know what it represents. We have gone over this point, Elder Sister."

"Yes. And the symbol is not enough. The Covenant is broken, and Guyasuta and Sganyodaiyo have broken it."

"The Covenant is not broken."

"Of course it is! Brother is coming to fight brother."

"The war-chiefs have not decided what to do."

"At Fort Johnson—"

"Ah." Osha leaned back on her hands. "Now *that* is a symbol. Degonwadonti would have none of the *Oniate* in her house. Good for her. But the warriors held their tomahawks and did not fire their bows. It has not come to war, not yet."

"What would you call it?"

"Resistance."

"You sound like Chief Big Business himself, playing at words. Speak plainly—it is only the two of us. Tell me, what is the difference between 'resistance' and 'war'? If an *Oniate* or some other fell thing came into the longhouse now, would you not fight it? And what is that if not war?"

"I did not say that there will not be war. There will surely be war. But our warriors have not taken up their weapons nor trod the paths of battle. Not yet. It will be up to us to convince them."

"By relighting the Council Fire? With one nation absent and most of another absent with them? The Mohawk, the Oneida and the Onondaga are not all of the Haudenosaunee. Or do you say now that they are?"

"It was always voluntary. If the Seneca choose their own way, then the Western Door is that much closer. Or do *they* now instruct *us*? No fire is a symbol of despair. We have built so much, and to cast it away dishonors the ancestors.

"I do not wish to meet unquiet ghosts," Osha said, shuddering very slightly. "Not since the broom-star fell. They would be even more present than ever. We owe them this much—to try and repair what is broken."

"Once broken it will never be the same."

"But that is no reason to grind it into dust. We should build what we can and unite."

"Half of the Haudenosaunee against *Oniate*, and Stone Coats, and—"

"Half of the Haudenosaunee," Osha said. "And Chief Big Business' people as well. There are those who can be trusted. Ask Degonwadonti; she walks in two worlds.

"It may be time for a new Covenant—a different one. When our warriors walk to battle, let them do it with a relit Council Fire. Let us honor our ancestors."

Neani did not have an answer to that statement. She was a dozen seasons older than Osha—sometimes she thought the younger clanmother was impetuous and emotional, not seeing the world for what it was, rather than what it should be.

But after a moment she reached out and took Osha's hand. In the firelight the old hand and the young one did not look that different.

"Let us speak to the *Tadodaho* together."

Chapter 49

Fortune was taking a nap

He hadn't been born with the name Jupiter, of course. His family had given him a proper Ashanti name. But he'd been captured and sold into slavery at the age of thirteen, and the man who eventually bought him in New York didn't even think to ask after the boy's birth name. By then, despite his youth, Jupiter's mighty physique was already quite evident. Since his new master was the owner of a blacksmith shop and intended to use the youngster as one of his apprentices, he'd thought naming the boy after the mightiest of the old pagan gods was appropriate.

There was no telling what the owner thought of the name now. His corpse was lying in a corner of the blacksmith shop, along with that of his son and the older of the two black slave apprentices. Jupiter had smashed all of their heads with his hammer, as quickly and easily as a housewife might crush insects she found in her house. *Thud—thud.* That had done for the two white men in the shop. Jupiter had then paused for a moment to see the reaction of the two black youngsters. The older one had seized a hammer for himself, perhaps intending to avenge the death of his owner—who'd been a kind enough man, for a slave master.

He'd had no chance at all against Jupiter. *Thud,* and his skull was another crushed mess of blood, bone splinters and brains, spilling out all over.

York, the younger of the two apprentices, had saved his life by the simple expedient of remaining frozen in place, his eyes wide and his mouth agape, while Jupiter carried out his murderous work. By the time he came to his senses and began moving again, Jupiter was satisfied that he posed no threat.

And, besides, he needed an assistant. Not even a man as powerful as Jupiter thought he could overthrow the city's white authorities by simply using his muscles and his hammer.

No, it was time—finally!—to call upon Ogun. From other Yoruba slaves he'd encountered over the years, Jupiter had filled out what little he remembered from his upbringing. He was a self-confident man—some said an arrogant man, too impressed with his own strength to think clearly.

Whether from self-confidence or arrogance, Jupiter was quite sure he could summon Ogun. Or, at least, one of Ogun's orishas.

"Get me a dog," he commanded York. "The master's dog will do fine. And bring some chains from the dog's pen."

York didn't question Jupiter's intent in giving those orders. He was much too terrified of him. Even before today's slaughter, Jupiter had been a harsh man. Outwardly subservient to his master, he'd always been quick to administer punishments on the two black apprentices he lorded it over.

The unasked questions soon became a moot point. York knew very little about the pagan beliefs and practices of his African folk. He'd been born a slave, right here in New York, not brought over on a slaver ship. But no man, no matter his ignorance, could fail to realize the grim purpose of Jupiter's rituals.

The chains stretched along the walls of the shop, now hung with all sorts of metal implements—knives, axes, hammers, wrenches, tongs, even scissors. That had not been especially frightening, in and of itself. But once York had finished hanging the chains and seen the brutal way Jupiter dragged the dog out of its cage, he'd realized they were part of a larger and bloodier ceremony.

Sure enough. The dog had been sacrificed—and not in any neat and surgical procedure. Jupiter had bludgeoned the poor creature to death with his hammer and chopped the carcass into pieces with one of the axes he'd taken off the chains on the walls.

He'd then formed a circle with the chunks of dog meat and taken a position within it. By now, between the human corpses and the butchery of the dog, the floor of the shop was covered with blood. But Jupiter seemed quite oblivious.

"Bring me a chain and what's hanging on it," he commanded.

York hurried to obey. It took but a few minutes to festoon Jupiter with the chain, wrapped and draped all around and over him. Tools and weapons hung everywhere. Only a man as strong as Jupiter could have sustained the weight for more than a short time.

"Step out of the dog circle," he now commanded. Then, glancing toward the entrance to the blacksmith shop, he pointed to a shelf on the opposite wall. "You'd best get up there, York. And keep quiet, and very still."

The ledge was shallow, barely wide enough for York to lie on it, but it was sturdily built and—best of all—six feet off the ground. As soon as Jupiter began intoning his chant, York was glad of the distance.

He had no idea what the words meant. But after three or four minutes, the chunks of dog meat began to quiver, as if they had a life of their own. Within another minute or so, they began to transform into shapes. Soon they were rising from the floor.

And rising. And rising. York pressed knuckles into his mouth to keep from making any noise. He had enough control over himself that he wouldn't have screamed or shouted, but he was afraid his teeth might start chattering.

The—*things*—into which the dog meat was turning were hideous. Like nothing he'd ever seen. They had the torsos of men, more or less, but nothing below the waist was human. The legs were long and skeletal, ending in huge feet pointing both ways. The distance from the tip of one taloned big toe to that facing the other way was at least two feet, in some cases close to three.

The heads could never be mistaken for those of a man, either. The brows were low and the skulls behind swept back and formed heavy crests. York could see the thick jaw muscles attached to those crests and did not wonder for a moment why they were needed. The teeth of the monsters were at least an inch long and seemed to be made of iron. They were shaped roughly like human teeth, not the sharp teeth of carnivores, but what difference would that make? Anything those jaws clamped down on was as doomed as if they'd been bitten by an alligator.

The eyes below the brows were large, protruding and bloodshot. Blessedly, none of them were looking York's way, perched as he was above them.

At least a foot above them, for which he was profoundly thankful. If there was any one redeeming feature of the creatures, it was that they were not very tall—five feet, at the most.

Squat, though, and obviously very powerful. And, then, as the first of the bat wings began to unfold, York had to press his knuckles still more fiercely into his mouth. The horrid things could *fly*?

Whether they could or couldn't, York would not find out at the moment. As soon as the monsters finished growing and taking final form, Jupiter raised his blacksmith's hammer over his head and shouted something in a language York was not familiar with.

The meaning of the short phrase was clear enough, however,

Follow me! Jupiter lumbered out of the blacksmith's shop, with the chain and implements attached to it, like a gargoyle's version of chain mail armor. He almost took the door off its hinges just brushing against it. By the time the third monster passed through, the door had been ripped off its hinges and was lying on the ground outside.

The creatures all poured out. And out and out, using a peculiar side-to-side crablike motion. York realized there must have been dozens of the things, formed from chunks of dog meat. How had they all fit into the blacksmith's shop? The interior wasn't really very roomy.

He had no idea. He didn't know—and he was pretty sure he would never know.

Which didn't bother him in the least.

Still perched on the shelf, he could hear the screams beginning outside.

Some things were best left unknown.

As it happened, York misinterpreted the screams. Most of them were simply cries of fear. Except for one old white woman who had the misfortune to be walking down a nearby street, all of the people screaming were black themselves, just like Jupiter. He barked commands which allowed those people to be spared by the monsters—but didn't lessen their screams any, when they witnessed the savagery with which the white woman was literally torn to shreds and then eaten—parts of her, anyway, before Jupiter's bellowed commands dragged the monsters from their feast.

Jupiter and his horde moved off down the street, headed for the more central parts of the city. The witnesses of that first brutal murder continued their screaming.

It was the unsettling screams more than her own fear that sent Coffey racing into the blacksmith's shop. Had she realized that shop had been the source of the monsters, she wouldn't have gone near it, of course. But she didn't know, because she hadn't seen them emerge and she hadn't spotted Jupiter—and that shop was where the boy she was interested in worked and lived. Coffey had no family of her own—none left, at least—and in the chaos of the moment, York was the one person she could think of to find shelter with.

She didn't even think to find shelter with her own mistress. York's master was a kindly man; Coffey's was a milliner whose temperament could most charitably be labeled *austere.* Even though Coffey was a freedwoman, not a slave like York, she was treated much more harshly.

She hadn't taken more than three steps into the blacksmith's shop before she spotted the blood splattered all over. She came to an abrupt halt and looked around fearfully.

"York . . . ?" she said in a soft, frightened voice.

She was immensely relieved to hear his voice. "Up here, Coffey."

It took her a moment to spot him, because she didn't think at first to look up at the shelf. When she did, she raced over and leapt for the shelf herself. Coffey was a big girl—big and strong—and she could have pulled herself onto the shelf easily enough. But York seized her by the wrists and hauled her up in an instant. He was a lot bigger than she was, and an awful lot stronger. He didn't have Jupiter's physique—she'd never seen any man who did—but York was a very muscular youngster, as you'd expect from someone apprenticed in the blacksmith's trade.

Not more than two seconds after Coffey joined York on the shelf, she gasped. The height of their perch allowed her to see into the corner of the shop where the three corpses were lying.

"What—?" She calmed her nerves by taking a deep breath. Coffey was a steady girl, especially for someone only seventeen years old. "What happened?"

"Jupiter killed them."

"Why?"

York shrugged heavy shoulders. "Mr. Jamison and his son, because they were white. Cumberland . . . " He shrugged again. "He'd grabbed a hammer, but I don't think he was minded to attack Jupiter. I think he just grabbed it out of fear and excitement. But it didn't matter. As soon as he picked up the hammer, he was a dead man."

His expression was grim. "Coffey, we've got to get out of here." He pointed to the blood-soaked open center of the shop where Jupiter had made his ring of dog meat. The ring itself wasn't evident any longer. Most of the poor animal's parts had been scattered when the monsters surged out of the shop.

"But . . . where will we go?"

"I don't know. Anyplace except here. Sooner or later, I figure Jupiter's bound to come back since this is where he summoned the things he has with him. So let's go."

York didn't exactly hop off the ledge, since it was a little high off the ground for that. But he was on the floor in an instant. Turning, he held up his hands toward Coffey.

"Jump, girl. I'll catch you."

With any other boy, Coffey would have sniffed and gotten down on her own. Quite easily, thank you. But she was taken by York, so she was perfectly happy to have an excuse to end up in his arms.

She thought he took longer than he needed to, before he let her go. That was the first and only pleasant thought she'd had all day.

The day was still young, though. It wasn't noon yet. If God and Fortune smiled on her, she might still have some happy moments this day.

The way things looked, though, God's attention was elsewhere and Fortune was taking a nap. The day was more likely to end in horror.

On their way out, York snatched up one of the hammers in the shop. Coffey was skeptical that the hammer would do them much good, but she supposed it was better than nothing.

Chapter 50

Familiar with the Second Commandment

They encountered the first horror not more than five minutes later. After hurrying down the street a few blocks, just enough to be out of sight of the blacksmith shop, they stopped near a street corner and leaned against the side of a building to catch their breath. The building was three stories tall and there was a grocery in the first-floor corner.

They were no longer in a freedman's area of the city. There would be slaves like York in these buildings, but they'd be mostly servants, not craftsmen. This was a prosperous white section of New York and normally York and Coffey would be apprehensive about being there in the street, unaccompanied by a master or mistress. Today, though, the chances of being accosted simply because of their skin color seemed rather remote.

"Where do we go, York?" Coffey asked.

He shook his head. "I don't know. Wherever it is, we'd best make sure—"

Coffey screamed. Coming from somewhere above—probably one of the building's ledges—a ghastly form dropped onto York's head and shoulders. Coffey couldn't tell what it was at first, until York slammed himself back against the building wall and threw his torso to the side. That almost dislodged the creature and Coffey could now see that it was a giant spider. The central body was six inches across, and the abdomen even larger. The eight legs were moving around too much for her to even estimate their lengths—but, whatever it was, it was completely unnatural. No spider she'd ever heard of was this big; not even close. She'd never seen or heard of a spider so brilliantly colored, either: blue and white stripes on its back and a mottled orange on its underside.

She saw the spider was getting positioned to drive its fangs into the back of York's neck. Still screaming, but now with fury rather than fear, Coffey seized one of the monster's legs, yanked it off the boy and flung it down the street.

She didn't fling it far, though. Making a chittering sound that she'd hear in nightmares for months to come, the spider scrabbled onto its feet and charged at her. It was about a foot tall and had a leg span of three feet or so.

York strode forward and kicked the spider, sending it flying back down the street.

It wasn't about to give up. Scrabbling erect, the spider came charging at them yet again.

But York was ready now. He had the hammer in his hand and once the spider got within a few feet he hurled it down on the hideous creature. The tool was a short-handled sledgehammer, weighing five pounds. With York's strength behind the blow, the spider's trunk was completely smashed. The creature thrashed around for a while thereafter, but its legs were no longer functional. Like all arachnids, and unlike insects, spiders used hydraulic pressure instead of muscles to extend their legs. With its body ruptured, the creature's legs just curled up underneath it. The spider was immobilized and effectively dead the moment the hammer struck.

York and Coffey didn't stick around to watch the monster's final throes. As soon as York snatched back the hammer, they raced away.

They were moving north toward the city's large open area known as the Common, which people also called "the square" even though it was shaped like a triangle. As they drew nearer, they could hear a commotion of some sort ahead of them.

Coffey stopped. "Maybe . . . "

York shook his head and took her by the arm. "We have to find out what's happening, Coffey. Until we do, we're just wandering around with no purpose."

"All right," she said. She wasn't at all sure York's plan wasn't foolish, but she had nothing to offer in its place. "Just be careful."

He smiled and held up his hammer. The spider's blood had now dried on it. "This'll help," he said.

York and Coffey followed a tangle of streets for a few blocks until they reached a side street that led to the Common. Peering along it, the two youngsters saw a mass of militiamen milling about on the square. They weren't looking down the side street; their attention seemed fixated on something on the north side of the Common.

"Keep going," Coffey whispered. York nodded and hurried up the street two more blocks until it reached another side street. There, he and Coffey made a quick dogleg up to Prince Street, which they followed for one block until they reached another side street. They were now past the Common, so he decided it would be safe—safer, at least—to approach the square still two or three blocks away.

When they reached King George Street, the smell of the nearby tanners' yards was powerful enough to be slightly nauseating. As much to get away from that stench as anything else, York moved down King George Street to the southwest. They were not more than a block away from the Common, now. There was nobody in sight anywhere, but they could hear a lot of shouting and some other peculiar noises coming from the square. They still couldn't see the square, though, because of the intervening buildings, most of which were two or three stories tall.

"Look, York!" Coffey hissed. She pointed to one of the buildings, which had an exterior staircase leading up to the roof. The roof was flat, unlike most of them in the area.

The staircase looked to be on the rickety side, but . . .

If they wanted to see what was happening, that rooftop would provide them with a good and relatively safe vantage point from which to observe anything in the Common.

They hurried to the staircase and began climbing. Both of them were young, healthy and in good physical condition. It took but a short time to reach the rooftop; and then a few seconds to make their way across the roof and look down into the Common.

Coffey and York were both devout Christians who attended church regularly and were perfectly familiar with the Second Commandment: *Thou shalt not take the name of the Lord thy God in vain.*

But they couldn't help themselves. "Dear God!" hissed Coffey; "Jesus!" was York's contribution.

The scene in the Common was terrifying. York was amazed that the militiamen, although clearly frightened, hadn't fled yet. He supposed having a gun—he'd never held one, himself, much less fired one—provided a man with a certain degree of fortitude.

"York, get down," said Coffey. She kept her voice low, but her tone was insistent. Looking down, he saw that she was crouched behind the low retaining wall that ran all around the edge of the roof. It wasn't tall—not more than eighteen inches—but it did provide something of a hiding place.

York looked down into the square below. He didn't think any of the monsters would look up at the roof. Their red-eyed, furious attention was entirely on the militiamen. But in the back of the mob of monsters stood a big man he recognized, even at the distance, as Jupiter. If Jupiter spotted York and Coffey up on the roof, there was no telling what he might do.

He crouched down next to Coffey, keeping his head just high enough to peer over the retaining wall.

Not long after he did so, someone in the crowd of militiamen—you could hardly call it a military formation—gave the order to fire. An instant later, the first of the muskets went off. As volleys went, it was about as ragged as you could ask for.

Still, a lot of muskets had been fired. But looking at its effect upon the mob of monsters, York realized that it had been quite ineffective. One of the creatures was down, writhing about, and two or three others were clutching at wounds, howling like proverbial banshees. But none of the other monsters seemed to have been affected in the least.

They had their bat wings wrapped around them, as if they were cloaks. York wondered if those wings provided a defense against musket balls.

Within seconds, the monsters hurled themselves across the square at the militiamen crowded into their southwest corner of the Common. As they came, the monsters unfurled their wings. They weren't using them to fly—York suspected they were too heavy for those wings to bear them up into the air—but did they provide enough lift to enable the hideous things to run swiftly instead of using the side-to-side crab waddle he'd seen earlier when they left the blacksmith shop.

It didn't take the creatures more than a few seconds to get across the square and fall upon the militiamen. A few more guns were fired, but they had no better effect than before.

The first line of militiamen were engulfed by the monsters, who started tearing them with their claws and biting them with those ghoulish iron teeth. Most of the rest turned and fled toward the Broad Way. There were so many of them trying to escape at once, however, that a large number were forced to exit the Common by racing to the east, skirting the buildings on the southern side in hopes of reaching the side streets.

Only a few of them made it. York could hear three or four racing down King George Street, just below him and Coffey. He was worried initially that they might try to climb up onto the roof themselves, but it soon became evident that they had no intention of staying anywhere in the area. The sound of their shoes and boots slamming onto the street below quickly faded.

It was hard to hear them anyway, because by now the monsters were in full feeding frenzy. Between their cries of glee and the screams of militiamen being rent apart and devoured, a man could hardly hear himself think.

"Get *down*, York!" hissed Coffee. She was now below the retaining wall altogether, curled tightly against it, completely out of sight of anyone—any*thing*—in the Common.

York decided it would be wise to join her. But before he could do so, the sound of a man's angry shouting drew his attention back to the scene in the square.

Jupiter, he saw, was furiously trying to get the monsters he'd summoned to leave off their feeding frenzy and pursue the militiamen who'd escaped down Broad Way. He was not simply bellowing at them, he was striking them with his hammer—which seemed to do a lot more damage than the bullets fired by the militia had. One of the monsters was knocked flat, dazed; another had an arm broken; two more were clutching at bruises and screeching.

In purely military terms, Jupiter's actions made sense. It would be foolish to let an enemy escape with no further harm. But Jupiter was not dealing with undisciplined soldiers, here. He was trying to return order to a pack of monsters.

He'd lost control of them by now. That was obvious to York. One, then two, then three of the creatures leapt onto Jupiter, tearing with their claws and biting with their iron teeth.

Jupiter fought them off. The man was incredibly strong and the hammer he wielded did terrible damage. But more and more monsters piled on, until York couldn't see the blacksmith under the pile of wings.

He slid down and joined Coffey at the retaining wall. She grabbed at him and he gladly returned the clutch. In a world gone mad, this pretty girl seemed to be the only thing left that was sane.

Chapter 51

You do not hurry this sort of business

When Admiral Boscawen reached the corner of Cortland and Broad Way, two blocks south of the Common, he and his small party were forced to take shelter in a recessed entryway to one of the buildings. The few militiamen racing south on Broad Way were in a complete panic, and would trample anyone who got in their way. Boscawen had seen soldiers routed on a battlefield, and he was sure that they had thrown away their guns so they could run faster.

What was happening? He found it well-nigh impossible to believe that poorly armed slaves and freedmen could terrify even the most undisciplined militia enough to produce this frantic retreat.

Once the last of the militiamen pounded past the recessed entryway, Boscawen stepped back onto Broad Way and looked to the north. He couldn't see anything, but he could hear some nerve-wracking sounds. Cries or shouts, not screams, but he couldn't discern any words in that uproar.

He looked at the man standing next to him, who was the only other officer in the small group of soldiers he had with him: the Virginian, Washington, who had remained in New York, helping with the organization of the regular troops that remained there.

"Washington, take one soldier and move up to the Common—softly, now, and stealthily. I need to know—"

"*Admiral!*"

That was a women's voice. Turning, Boscawen saw Minerva emerging from Cortland Street on the other side of the Broad Way. She was alone except for the man called . . .

346

Boscawen searched for the name. It was from the Bible, but he couldn't remember what it was.

The memory search ended abruptly, when Washington shouted: "Admiral! Look!" The lieutenant was pointing to something up Broad Way.

Looking in that direction, Boscawen saw a bloodcurdling sight. A gigantic spider—its legs must have spanned three feet—was coming toward them on the sidewalk. Its cephalothorax was lifted up and its chelicerae were raised, ready to attack and inject venom into its prey.

"Form a line!" Washington said, with remarkable composure. He and Boscawen stepped aside, allowing the seven marines in the party to come forward. Four kneeling in front and three standing behind, they formed a line across the sidewalk, muskets at their shoulders and ready to fire.

Washington ordered, "Ready!"

"It's just a J'Ba Fofi, Lieutenant!" called out Minerva. Boscawen saw that she and her male companion—Absalom; that was the name—were already halfway across Broad Way. The black woman stretched out her hand toward the spider and clenched her fist, exactly the way she might have squeezed the juice out of a lemon.

Looking back up the street, Boscawen saw that the monstrous arachnid had come to a halt. It seemed to be frozen in place, with its legs curling underneath its body.

Then Minerva flung her hand aside, as she might discard a lemon, and the spider fled back up Broad Way. It was clearly no longer a menace, at least for the moment.

Minerva was now at his side. "The things are a nuisance—horrible one; you've got to keep them away from children—but they don't pose a mortal threat to a populace prepared to deal with them." Her lips tightened. "Unlike the monsters in the Common, who are quite capable of slaughtering an entire city. Didn't you hear them?"

He shook his head. "I heard shouts, but I couldn't make out the words."

"Words!" barked Absalom. His lips were twisted into a jeering smile.

"Those are not words, Admiral," said Minerva. "Sasabonsam do not speak any language. Those are just cries of glee, as they feed."

"Feed . . . " His voice trailed off for a moment. Then, clearing his throat: "Feed on what?"

"The militiamen, I imagine," she replied. "And whatever civilians had the misfortune to be in the square also."

"The blacksmith named Jupiter summoned them," said Absalom. "We got reports from people who saw him coming out of his shop followed by dozens of the monsters."

"Sasabo—" Boscawen struggled with the unfamiliar term. "What are they?"

Minerva's expression was stern. In that moment, she looked much older—and much, much more ferocious—than she normally did. "You may think of them as West African ogres. Some of them are vampires."

Boscawen looked back up the street. From their vantage point, two blocks from the Common, he could see nothing. But now that he understood the meaning of the cries coming from the north, he had little trouble imagining the horrid scene.

West African ogres. Dozens of them . . .

There was no chance he could suppress the creatures with the small number of marines he had at his disposal—and the militia was completely dispersed by now. Those of them who had survived.

"Is there anything you can do, Minerva?" he asked.

She looked at Absalom. After a moment, he shrugged. "Can't get any worse."

"Yes, it can," Minerva said forcefully. She looked back at Boscawen. "I can summon grootslang, admiral. But I warn you— they are greedy creatures. They will demand payment, and if they do not get it, they will prove to be even worse than the sasabonsam. Much worse."

"Greedy . . . for what?"

For the first time, she smiled. There wasn't much humor in it, but it was definitely a smile. "Oh, gold always suits them. Silver, also. Gems, jewelry—they're much like your European dragons that way. They like to hoard treasure."

Boscawen scratched his jaw. "How much gold?"

"As much as you have, Admiral," was her answer. "The grootslang are . . . peculiar. However they do it, they know how much anyone owns in the way of gold, silver and jewelry—and they will insist on being given all of it. Assuming there's enough to interest them in the first place, of course."

Boscawen pondered the matter, for a few seconds. If he gave these—whatever they were called—all the specie in his vault, how could he replace it? The two people who knew the process were now gone. Alexander remained in New York, but Boscawen doubted the man could do the work on his own.

"Admiral, look!" shouted Gustavus. He was pointing up Broad Way to the Common. Two horrid-looking creatures had debouched onto the street. They looked like . . .

Well . . . Ogres.

By now, the two monsters up the street had spotted them. One of them began coming their way; the other scurried back out of sight, screeching like a banshee. Calling on his—her?—fellows to join the new feast, no doubt.

Boscawen decided he had to deal with one problem at a time. "I can provide the gold. Summon these grood—whatever."

Minerva looked at Absalom. "I will need your help."

"Yes, of course."

Minerva reached into her gown and withdrew something; then, squatted and cast the objects in her hand onto the street. They were beans of some kind. Perhaps a dozen of them.

"What help can you give her?" Washington asked Absalom. "Is there any way the troops could help as well?"

Absalom grinned—quite cheerfully, given the circumstances. "Oh, no, I don't believe you can, sir. These things are from our homelands, not yours."

Now, he too squatted down. Looking up at Washington, he added: "It's always a chancy business, calling on beings from another dominion, especially ones as mighty as grootslang. But chance is what I have some say over, if you recall."

More screeching came from up the street. Looking, Boscawen saw that eight or nine of the ogres were now coming toward them down Broad Way.

"You'd best hurry," he said to Minerva.

She waved her left hand, as if shooing away flies. "Oh, la! You do not hurry this sort of business." As she was speaking, she was also giving the beans an intent scrutiny. Then—for whatever reason;

Boscawen had not an inkling what it might be—she selected three of the beans and popped them into her mouth. She chewed them briefly and spit the remains back onto the street.

Boscawen glanced up the Broad Way again. The monsters—the sasabon—whatever—were now just a block away. Thankfully, although they'd spread their frightful bat wings, they didn't use them to fly. They were approaching in a peculiar scuttling manner, shifting from side to side, which reminded the admiral of crabs more than anything else.

He had to restrain himself from urging Minerva to hurry again. Glancing down at her, he suspected she wouldn't hear him anyway. Her eyes were closed, and she seemed to be in a trance, murmuring words in a language that Boscawen was not familiar with. One of the multitude of African tongues, he imagined.

Suddenly, her eyes opened wide. "*Ulla!*" she barked. "*Ulla battay!*"

Instantly, the three beans she'd chewed upon began to swell. And swell and swell and swell—and as they swelled, began to take on shapes.

Gruesome ones. That was evident long before the things reached their final size. When they did . . .

Boscawen looked up at them. Up and up and up. The creatures were elephant-shaped but stood at least five feet taller at the shoulder than any elephant Boscawen had ever heard of. They towered over Minerva, who had stepped forward, almost into their midst.

The bodies were elephant-shaped, and so was the basic structure of their heads. They had the huge elephant ears, as well.

But nothing else was particularly elephant-like except the tusks—and there were four of them, not two. The tail was thick, powerful, long and armored, very much like a crocodile's—if a crocodile's tail ended in a spiked ball.

The front of the head—call it the face—resembled an octopus more than an elephant. Six tentacle-like appendages surrounded a mouth which had a beak at its center rather than teeth, just like a cephalopod. But these tentacles were thicker than an octopus' would be, even one with this immense size, and had none of the distinctive suckers possessed by octopi and squid.

The eyes . . . Boscawen looked away; not in fear, but in revulsion. The eyes resembled those of no animal he'd ever seen; not a mammal, not a bird—not an octopus, for that matter. They didn't even look like eyes so much as open, pus-oozing wounds.

Minerva spoke, again in that unknown tongue.

One of the creatures responded in a low rumbling voice. That was definitely a language, but Boscawen understood none of it. He didn't think it was the same one Minerva was using, but he wasn't positive because the voices themselves were so different,

It went on for some time. A number of sentences, if the language had any analog with human tongues.

When the thing had finished speaking, Minerva turned her head toward the admiral. "She says you are very rich and if you try to cheat them you will be destroyed." She grimaced for a moment. "Then she spent some time explaining the manner of your destruction, but I see no need to translate that. It was quite disgusting."

Boscawen could well imagine. He glanced up the street and saw, to his relief, that the ogres had ceased their forward progress and were milling around. By now, there were at least two dozen of them. Clearly, the newly-arrived monsters were making them nervous,

"Will they agree to help us?" he asked.

"Yes—if you vow to turn over all your gold afterward."

Not knowing the proper protocol, assuming there even was one, Boscawen peered up at the one in the middle sand said: "Yes. The gold is yours—*if* you get rid of these sasa—sasa—"

He looked to Minerva for assistance "Sasabonsam," she said. Then, made that same hand-waving gesture. "Oh, la, it's a good thing grootslang don't get offended easily."

Absalom chuckled. "*If* they get rid of the sasabonsam. What a jest!"

The huge grootslang suddenly erupted into motion. Within a few seconds, Boscawen realized the absurdity of his qualification. He might as well have asked a pride of lions if they could get rid of some baboons.

"Oh, la," Minerva said. Then she laughed softly.

Chapter 52

His worst fears had materialized

The sounds being made by the monsters in the Common changed suddenly. York started to rise up to see what was happening, but Coffey jerked him back down. "Will you *please* stay hidden?" she whispered.

That was . . . probably a good idea. So York just listened, as intently as he could.

The sounds for the past few minutes had been the grisly noises you'd expect creatures like this to make while they were feasting. Jupiter's shouts of rage had ended quickly once the monsters swarmed him. York was sure the blacksmith was dead by now—dead, and mostly eaten.

For all their appalling nature, those sounds had been reassuring, in a way. Predators at a feast were not predators on a hunt.

Now, though, the noises changed in tone and timber and grew louder. Then, much louder. Within seconds, the monsters were producing a ruckus that matched the one they'd been making when they were facing off against the militia.

"I *have* to see what's happening, Coffey," he whispered, as forcefully as a whisper allowed.

She glanced up at the retaining wall, and then nodded her head. "All right. But be careful."

Slowly, York raised his head high enough to look over the wall and down into the square. Almost at once, he realized he was in little danger of being spotted by the monsters swarming in the Common below. The creatures' attention was entirely focused on whatever they saw down Broad Way. Like all predators considering potential prey, their concentration was intense. They wouldn't be looking anywhere else for the time being.

Now, the monsters began moving onto Broad Way, with more and more of them vanishing from York's sight altogether.

If he couldn't see them, they couldn't see him and Coffey either. This might be the right time to descend the staircase, return to the streets and make their escape.

Escape to where, though? York had no idea what part of New York might be a safe haven from creatures like these. At least up here on the roof he had a chance of defending Coffey and himself against monsters coming up that narrow staircase. One at a time, with his strength and his hammer, he might have a chance of beating off the horrid things. Let them swarm . . . Not a chance. Jupiter had been doomed the moment that happened.

Coffey's head came up alongside his. "What's happening?" she asked.

"They're almost gone from the square." He pointed down. "See?"

She raised her head a little further, giving herself a better view of the Common. "Where did they go? What are they doing?"

York shook his head. "I don't know what they're doing, or why. There's something on Broad Way that drew their attention. Don't know what—or who—it is."

From York and Coffey's vantage point, they were three blocks from the intersection of the Broad Way and the Common and couldn't see anything on the street itself.

They could *hear* the monsters, though. And from the swelling chorus of their cries and shrieks, York was sure the things were about to launch an attack on someone.

Then, suddenly, a new sound arose. A high-pitched squealing blast, like something produced by a demon's trumpet.

The blast was repeated immediately—and then again and again. York realized there had to be more than one source producing them.

The blasts were *loud*. Unbelievably loud. Even several blocks away and shielded by intervening buildings, York was almost deafened; his mind, numb. He could only imagine what those blasts must sound like—*feel* like—at close range.

Suddenly, the bat-winged monsters came pouring back into the

Common. It was their turn to be panicked by something. Coffey and York lowered their heads again, keeping them just high enough to be able to see what was happening below.

A new monster burst onto the common, followed by another and then another.

Coffey hissed, wordlessly. These things were . . . incredible. They made the creatures Jupiter had summoned seem like lap dogs.

To begin with, they were *huge*. York was glad the building on the roof of which he and Coffey were hiding upon was three stories tall. The shoulders of these newly-arrived creatures were as high off the ground as the windows on the second floor of the buildings along the square—the *middle* of the windows, not the ledge. Fifteen feet, at a guess.

The bat-winged beasts tried to rally now, turning back and squaring off against the three behemoths coming into the Common. York was sure the only reason they did so was their innate savagery. Even outnumbering their foes by ten-to-one or more, he didn't think they had any chance at all. It was like watching a mob of kittens squaring off against mastiffs.

The giants spread their tentacles and issued that horrendous high-pitched bellow. Coffey and York clapped their hands over their ears, forgetting the danger of being spotted if they moved. They had no choice, really.

The squealing bellows stunned the batwing creatures. Dozens of them just froze in the square, paralyzed for the moment.

A moment was all the behemoths needed. They plunged into the gargoyle mob, slaughtering as they went.

Some of the creatures that Jupiter had summoned were trampled to death. Others were gored by huge tusks, their blood and entrails sent flying. Some were smashed into pulp by armored tails. Most of them, though, were torn apart by the behemoths' tentacles. A few were also ripped open by the giant beaks, but most of the bat-winged creatures seized by tentacles were simply dismembered and their pieces pounded back onto the cobblestones.

The butchery seemed to go on and on. Afterward, York realized it all had to have happened within a minute or two. Toward the end, perhaps a dozen of Jupiter's beasts managed to shake free from their paralysis and tried to escape.

Not many of them succeeded. The behemoths, those grotesque manticoran combinations of elephant, crocodile and octopus, could only move in a lumber. But their legs were so long that even lumbering they covered a great distance quickly. And whenever Jupiter's brutes began to forge ahead, another squealing blast would cause them to stumble, sometimes fall. The behemoths simply trampled them under as they continued their pursuit.

Most of the bat-winged creatures tried to escape in the direction of the tanners' yards. But some of them, when they reached it, plunged down the side street leading to King George Street.

York rose and ran across the roof toward the staircase, staying in a crouch the whole way. Once he got to the staircase, he peered over cautiously.

His worst fears had materialized. Four of Jupiter's beasts were coming up the staircase, seeking shelter from the behemoths.

Coffey joined him. As soon as she spotted the monsters coming up the stairs, she screeched and looked around the rooftop. Spotting some lumber stacked nearby against the retaining wall, she raced over and came back clutching a board that was about six feet long and four inches in its other dimensions.

York realized instantly that, under these circumstances, the board would make a better weapon than his short-handled hammer. It would be heavy and clumsy, but he was strong enough to use it like a spear.

He held out the hammer. "Switch with me," he said. Coffey didn't argue; she just handed over the board and took the hammer. From the fierce look on her face, York knew that if it came to that she'd use it as a weapon herself. Try to, anyway.

She was quite a girl. Really pretty, too.

But this was no time for such pleasant thoughts. The first of the monsters had gotten past the second-floor landing and was coming up the final stretch of the staircase. By now, it had spotted York standing at the top and was gnashing its iron teeth at him, its bat wings extended outward.

That was for show, York thought. The creatures couldn't really fly. Like squirrels displaying their tails, they used the bat wings to make themselves look much larger and more frightening.

As if they *needed* to look more frightening!

The beast was within striking range. With his right hand cupping the end of the board to provide most of the force and his left providing the guidance, York smashed the end of the board into the monster's neck.

York was very strong. Not as strong as Jupiter had been, but much stronger than most men. The strike had been perfectly aimed, too. The board crushed the beast's windpipe and sent it reeling back down the staircase, clutching its throat.

It didn't go far, though, because the next creature was only a few feet behind. But the tangle when the two of them collided took a few seconds to get sorted out. During the course of those seconds, realizing that she'd do more good to provide York with another board than to brandish the hammer herself, Coffey had raced back to the pile of lumber and was bringing back another board.

Smart girl, too.

By the time Coffey got back with the second board, the next creature was swarming up the stairs. York tried the same spear-thrust, but the monster batted the board-end aside and charged forward. The two of them grappled. The only thing that kept York from having his flesh torn off by those hideous iron teeth was that he'd been able to interpose the board between them. Even so, the beast's claws were tearing into his back and it wouldn't be long before it was able to bite. The thing was *strong*, despite being a foot shorter than York.

Suddenly, a hammer smote the top of the monster's head. Coffey had leaned over the staircase rail and taken a swing at it. The impact knocked the hammer loose from her grip and it sailed down onto the street below. But the blow had stunned the thing long enough for York to break free from the grapple and strike its face with the board held crossways.

The thing stumbled down two steps, giving York enough room to shift his grip on the board. Again, he drove it like a spear and this time the end of the board struck true—smack into the monster's face. The iron teeth didn't break, but the monster's jaw did. It collapsed onto the stairs.

Unfortunately, before it did so the beast managed to seize the end of the board and yank it out of York's grasp. The next monster just clambered over it, coming at York. Frantically, he turned and Coffey handed him the second board. But that took enough time that when the third monster arrived York didn't have enough room for the spear strike. Again, he had to use the board simply as a shield of sorts.

He was starting to despair, now. But he and the beasts on the staircase were stunned, when another of those incredible squealing sound-blasts struck them. Looking down, in a daze, York saw that one of the behemoths was standing at the bottom of the staircase.

There would be no rescue, though, since the huge creature couldn't possibly get up the stairs. But the giant solved the problem by seizing the base of the staircase in its tentacles and just ripping the whole structure off the building. The four iron-toothed horrors came down with it—proving, along the way, that those batwings were useless for flying.

Once they struck the street surface, the behemoth finished the business, stamping all of them into bloody paste.

That done, it looked up at York and Coffey for a moment before lumbering away.

"Now what?" asked Coffey. "How do we get down from here?"

Chapter 53

There will be a new dispensation

The scene Boscawen saw as he came into the Common with Minerva, Absalom and his marine escort reminded him of the carnage on his ship during the First Battle of Cape Finisterre, twelve years earlier. *Namur's* deck had been awash with blood, but what he'd always remembered most were the dismembered bodies and often unidentifiable body parts strewn all over. It had been like something out of the Italian poet Dante's *Inferno*.

Cannon balls and—still more—the huge splinters which they sent flying when they struck a wooden ship had that effect on human bodies. The monsters Minerva had summoned, the ones she called "grootslang," had had the same effect on the sasabonsam. They'd simply ripped the ogres into pieces and flung the pieces everywhere.

After taking not more than a dozen steps into the square, the admiral stopped and turned to Washington. "You'd best get the specie now, man." He reached into his coat pocket and extracted a large set of keys on a ring. Then, selected one of the keys and handed it to the young officer. "My compliments to Lieutenant Pascal; instruct him to offer you all assistance."

"Yes, sir," replied Washington. He hesitated for a moment. "With your permission I shall take Gustavus with me, but I think I may need the help of two of your marines."

Briefly, Boscawen estimated the weight of the specie, and nodded his head. "Yes, I believe you will. And you can find a cart and draft horse in the stables. Tell the hostler you have my permission to use them. He won't argue the point."

Once Washington was gone, Boscawen surveyed the area for a full minute before saying anything further.

Unlike New York's streets, which were generally paved, most of the Common's surface was compacted dirt. That was perhaps a blessing in these circumstances, for the soil had absorbed most of the blood produced by the grootslang slaughter and what remained on the surface was drying out rapidly. It was a hot day, even for July.

The admiral looked up at the buildings fronting the south side of the Common. Most of them were three stories tall, and now he could see a few heads appearing in the windows. Even from the distance, the fear and apprehension on those faces was obvious.

He couldn't be sure until he questioned those people, but he doubted if many of them—quite possibly any of them—had actually witnessed the events that had transpired here. Once the mob of ogres had been led into the Common by Jupiter and had dispersed the militia which had gathered there, most of the residents would have fled also. All the buildings would have doors exiting onto back and side streets.

Some would have stayed, though, too old or too feeble or just too frightened to try to escape. But they would have hidden somewhere in their apartments, not spent the time gawking at mayhem out the windows.

"There's someone up there," said Absalom. He was pointing to one of the buildings on the southeastern corner of the Common. Following his finger, Boscawen saw two negroes atop the roof. One was a man, the other a woman, and they both appeared to be quite young.

"They might have seen something," suggested Minerva.

"Let's hope so," said Boscawen. He started walking toward the building. They were too far away to make themselves understood to the couple on the roof, even if they shouted.

As they drew near to the narrow side street leading to William Street and King George Street, Boscawen turned to the ranking marine in the little group. "Corporal Hammond, take a man with you and inspect the back of the building." He pointed at the entrance to the side street. "You should be able to reach it through there. Let me know if there's a way for these youngsters to get down to the street. Quickly, now. We have no time to waste."

The corporal trotted off, after detailing one of the privates to follow him. Not long thereafter, Boscawen and the rest of his party reached the base of the building.

Cupping his hands around his mouth, he shouted to the two youngsters above: "Did you see what happened here?"

The girl shouted back, "Yes, sir! We saw it all!" She pointed toward Broad Way. "Jupiter brought the bat-things out here from the blacksmith shop and they drove off the militiamen. They started to chase after them but then these other monsters arrived and started killing them. The bat-things, I mean. The new monsters were *huge*."

The young man next to her shouted: "I think they were some kind of elephants, sir!"

Some kind of elephants was as good a description of the grootslang as any Boscawen could think of. Clearly, these two young people had witnessed the events.

"Come down!" he shouted.

The negroes on the roof looked at each other, and then looked behind them.

"We can't, sir!" That came from the girl. "The bat-things tried to get up the stairs—York fought them off for a while—and then one of the elephant monsters arrived and tore down the stairs. There's no way down!"

Boscawen frowned. There had to be some sort of internal staircase in the building. He couldn't imagine anyone designing a three-story structure with no way to get from one floor to another.

Corporal Hammond appeared, trotting up the side street. When he reached the admiral, he said: "There are several bodies of the"— he glanced at Minerva—"sasabon-things lying in the street. Someone—something—probably one of the"—he glanced at Minerva again—"groot-things, must have torn the staircase apart. There's nothing left of it except pieces of wood strewn all about."

Boscawen looked back up at the two people on the roof. Again cupping his hands around his mouth, he shouted: "There must be another staircase that reaches the roof from inside the building! Find it and come down!"

The youngsters disappeared for a minute or two. Then they came back to the edge of the roof.

"There is one!" the boy shouted down. "But the door's locked."

Boscawen was getting impatient. "You look like a strong lad!" he shouted. "Just break it down!"

But the large negro didn't move.

"He's probably a slave, Admiral," said Absalom. "Even if he's a freedman, he's in a part of the city where he'll be viewed with suspicion—downright hostility, more like. He's worried about the trouble he'll get into if he does something like smash up a door in a building like this."

Boscawen started to throw up his hands, but controlled his aggravation. The Absalom fellow was probably right.

He strode toward the entrance of the building—only to discover that it, too, was locked.

But he was a white man and an admiral in the British Navy to boot—and he had the wherewithal to deal with the door, which didn't look all that sturdy to begin with.

He stepped back and pointed at it. "Hammond, smash this door in."

Quite cheerfully, the corporal went about the work, using his musket butt to good effect. It took no more than fifteen seconds to leave the door splintered and hanging off its hinges.

Boscawen strode into the building and looked around. He was in a narrow corridor, perhaps fifty feet long, lined with doors on either side at regular intervals. The entrances to apartments, clearly enough. At the very end of the corridor, he could see the lower portion of a staircase leading upward.

He headed toward it, followed by everyone else in his party. They encountered no one along the way, which didn't surprise the admiral. Whoever might have remained in the building would still be hiding in fear.

It didn't take long to reach the final flight of the stairs, which led up from the third floor to the roof. There was a small landing at the top, barely big enough for two people.

But quite big enough for a solidly-built corporal with a musket. Boscawen stepped aside and motioned Hammond forward. "If you would, Corporal."

Just as cheerily as before, Hammond made short work of that door as well. Once it fell away, Boscawen could see the two young negroes standing there.

"Come along," he said. "I need to question you further."

The two negroes looked at each other. Apprehensively, still.

"What is the problem now?" Boscawen demanded.

The girl looked at him. "Well, sir . . . York here is a slave. I'm a freedwoman—my name's Coffey, sir—but I do have a mistress—she's not a kind lady—and . . . and . . . "

Boscawen was becoming thoroughly exasperated by some of New York's customs.

"Never mind all that!" he said brusquely. "If need be, I'll buy this—what's your name, lad? York?—from his owner. And since you're already freed, Miss Coffey, I'll just hire you away from your employer."

The girl still looked uneasy. "Mrs. Eastgate probably won't like that, sir."

"Ask me if I care!" said Boscawen, almost—not quite—shouting.

He heard a little giggle coming from down the stairs. Turning, he saw that Minerva was grinning up at him. For some reason, those shining teeth lightened his mood greatly.

He chuckled himself. Then, waved at York and Coffey to follow him. "Don't worry about your master and mistress," he said. "If need be, I shall set them straight as to the new dispensation."

And there will *be a new dispensation*, he said to himself as he went down the stairs. *I have had quite enough of New York's so-called authorities.*

By the time he exited the building and came back out onto the Common, he saw that the three grootslang had reappeared. The giants were more horrible-looking than ever, coated as they were with blood—even some body parts, which they hadn't bothered to brush off.

Thankfully, Boscawen could see that Colonel Washington had reappeared in the square also. He and Gustavus were guiding a horse-drawn cart onto the square. The two marines who had gone with them were following, their muskets at the ready.

Those muskets wouldn't do the least bit of good against the monsters that Minerva had summoned. But they'd have been enough to deter any would-be robbers they might have encountered along the way.

There was an exchange between Minerva and the grootslang. As before, Boscawen thought that they were not speaking the same language. But, despite that, the woman seemed able to communicate with them well enough.

One of the grootslang moved toward the cart. Gustavus had already unhitched the horse, and he stepped away from the conveyance in a manner that could be called brisk. Washington and his two soldiers had already done the same.

The monster pulled open the crate resting in the cart, examined the contents, and issued what Boscawen hoped was a hoot of satisfaction.

Apparently so. All three of the grootslang surrounded the cart, obscuring it from view. Then, suddenly, they disappeared, along with the cart. In the place where they had been, three bean shoots were sprouting from the soil of the Common.

"I recommend uprooting and destroying those bean shoots, Admiral," said Minerva. "The beans won't taste good and . . . there could be other problems for anyone who eats them."

That seemed like excellent advice. "Corporal Hammond, see to it. Don't touch them with your bare hands and make sure you burn everything."

He turned back to Minerva. The admiral was eager to question the two youngsters further, but he had an even more pressing matter to attend to first. The reward—more like a ransom—he'd just paid the grootslang had left his coffers bare, and Messier and LaGèndiere were gone from the city for an uncertain duration. Under the circumstances, the suggestion made by Messier and LaGèndiere before they left that Boscawen seek Minerva's help with the creation of more specie was . . .

He thought it might be unwise, still. But he no longer had any choice.

"I have something I need to show you," he said to her. "Back at my headquarters."

Reluctantly, he added: "Absalom should probably come as well."

After he finished his explanation, back in his office, Minerva smiled and shook her head.

"I will give you what help I can, Admiral. But for this—anything that involves money—you really need to have Absalom's . . . well, 'skills' isn't quite the word. Let us say 'aptitudes' instead."

Boscawen looked at the black man, who was grinning outright. As uneasy as he was at asking Minerva for her assistance in the project, the prospect of working with Absalom was considerably more worrisome.

But, again, he could not see where he had any choice. The most he could manage was a feeble statement of uncertainty.

"But—but— I thought his . . . aptitudes, as you call them, simply involve matters of luck and chance."

"And what else is money, Admiral?" said Absalom. The grin never wavered.

Settling the issues involving the two young negroes, after he was done interrogating them, was simple.

As it turned out, since York's owner and his son—who'd been his only close relative, the man being a widower—were both deceased, the admiral had only to negotiate with the blacksmith's cousins. By and large a feckless lot, they were quite willing to sell the young slave to the admiral for a reasonable price.

As for Mrs. Eastgate, once Boscawen forced the obstreperous woman to admit that Coffey was simply one of her employees, not an indentured servant, the issue was settled. Coffey gave notice—two minutes was sufficient enough, the admiral decreed—and was promptly employed by the Royal Navy in whatever capacity might be needed.

Boscawen still had no military force large enough to force his will upon New York—not even the city, much less the colony as a whole—but he wasn't terribly concerned about that problem.

First, because he had a monopoly on the colony's supply of money.

Second, because he had the aid of the city's most powerful sorceress. Even if most of them had stayed in hiding, enough of New York's residents had seen the grootslang deal with the sasabonsam to make sure that tale spread widely.

And as it turned out, there was a third factor at play. While it seemed all the sasabonsam had been dealt with by the grootslang, the same was not true of the giant spiders whom Jupiter had apparently also summoned. By accident, Minerva believed. The blacksmith had possessed a great talent for magic, but he'd grossly overestimated his ability to control that talent.

After the first child was devoured by one of the hideous creatures, Minerva became the most popular inhabitant of the city. She and she alone, it seemed, could deal with the monstrosities easily and simply. The militia should have been able to do so as well—a single musket volley would splatter one of the spiders quite nicely—but their morale could at best be described as shaky.

Other terms were used more often.

Jittery, wobbling, faltering, quivery, tremorous, unsound—there were quite a few. Some were downright unkind, especially the ones spoken in taverns. *Craven, gutless, yellow-bellied, lily-livered.* "Useless as tits on a bull" was heard often as well.

It was noteworthy, however, that none of those who used the terms—not a one of them—volunteered themselves to join the militia.

Part VI: Determination

August, 1759

Natura nihil frustra facit.
(Nature does nothing in vain.)
—Leucippus

Chapter 54

We have all the medicine

The assembled chiefs were wary of Guyasuta. The story of the example he had made of the chief who had attacked early had spread throughout the war bands, to the point that even the bravest walked softly and carefully around him.

But everyone—from the eldest chief to the youngest brave—was *terrified* of Sganyodaiyo.

Unlike most of the warriors, who moved on foot, Sganyodaiyo traveled on a small pony; he was wrapped in a long robe with a hood that covered his head. Only a few spoke to him—Guyasuta, of course, but also Kaintwakon, Sganyodaiyo's younger brother. It was said that his eyes were deep pools and no man could hold his gaze.

It had taken almost five days for all the tribal groups to gather in the wood west of the whites' army camp. Some consisted of fifty or more braves, experienced war bands who had traveled and raised the tomahawk together; others were twos and threes from small villages across the western part of the lands of the Haudenosaunee. Some had taken up the cause voluntarily, following the lead of the red man's new champion, while others had joined to save their village from the threats of the Dry-Hands. Those shamans walked freely through the camps, shunned and avoided like diseased men—which, in a way, they were.

But of the supernatural things that Sganyodaiyo commanded— the Floating Heads and other things—there was no sign. It was as if the creatures were following out of sight, a silent, ominous menace hanging in a dark place just nearby.

✣ ✣ ✣

Sganyodaiyo's tent had been pitched near the top of a hill, away from every other. Only Kaintwakon entered it; all the other braves stayed clear.

Deep in the night of the new moon, with the sky full of stars, Sganyodaiyo emerged from his tent to stand in the dark. Five Dry-Hands had come up the hill to stand in a row before the banked campfire, in answer to the summons that had passed through the camp. Most of the warriors were asleep, resting for the following day, which, it was said, would be the final march to battle with the whites.

The Dry-Hands stood silent, their enchanted hands concealed in the folds of their robes, waiting for direction from the powerful shaman.

"It is time," Sganyodaiyo said without preface, "to perform the Dark Dance and call forth the Jo-Ge-Oh."

"The Little People?" one of the Dry-Hands said. "How can they help us?"

"They are angry," Sganyodaiyo answered, not looking at the questioner. "We will use that anger."

"They will want gifts."

"Oh, yes," Sganyodaiyo answered. "They will want many gifts, and we will offer them what they want."

Sganyodaiyo threw back his hood and shrugged off his outer robe. In the dim light of the fire, his face was not clearly visible, but it looked unearthly, devoid of expression and emotion, like someone who was detached from reality. Haltingly at first, and then with sinuous motions, he began to slowly dance around the fires, chanting in an ancient version of the Seneca tongue. The Dry-Hands followed in turn, copying his motions and, after a short time, his words— repetitive, sonorous, not musical but atonal and difficult to hear.

The dance went on and on, for what seemed like hours but which might have been only a few minutes. Those who dared to watch from beyond the fire light later said that they thought they saw figures in the fire dancing as well, keeping time with Sganyodaiyo and the shamans as they moved.

At a signal from Sganyodaiyo they began to slow and then stop. He gestured toward a stand of trees, where there was movement in the underbrush; a group of four figures, who were each scarcely two feet high, emerged, approaching cautiously.

Sganyodaiyo walked slowly toward them; they took halting steps backward, but Sganyodaiyo stopped approaching and spread his hands wide.

"I am An-De-Le, leader of this band. Who . . . who summons us?"

He spoke his name and his lineage in brief. Had this been a longhouse or a gathering of chiefs or mothers, he might have traced it at length—but the Jo-Ge-Oh would probably not care.

"When the broom-star fell, little Brothers, you felt the change in the world. I call you to join us in our great Work, to drive the unwelcome and offensive whites from the world the Great Spirit made."

"We have no interest in the quarrels of the Big People," An-De-Le said. "Your fight is not our fight." He looked around the clearing, focusing on the Dry-Hands. "And we do not clasp hands with *Oniate*." He said the last word with obvious disgust.

"They are servants of our great Chief," Sganyodaiyo said. "And so am I. But come, little Brother. This is no time to sit quietly by. It is a time of great change—surely you feel that."

"I do," An-De-Le answered. "We all do. We felt the passage and the change. It frightened us."

"It is a frightening thing," Sganyodaiyo said. He squatted down on his haunches, and even then, he was a foot taller than An-De-Le and the others. The little man took another step back, fear in his eyes. "But we will take your fear away."

"What do you offer?"

"A place where you will be safe. A place of your own, where you can hunt and fish, away from the quarrels of the Big People. The whites, who call you demons and evil spirits, will be gone."

"The whites are everywhere," An-De-Le said. "They are even more intrusive than the reds."

"Many of our people have turned from the old ways," Sganyodaiyo answered. "But I can make a promise that this time is over. We will respect the lands of our Brothers."

"Big people only call on us when they need help with the weather, or with their planting. And they only call on us when no one is watching, so that their own gods do not hear them. I do not think you care for our advice on the rain or the planting; and you make no secret of the Dark Dance.

"So what do you want of us?"

Sganyodaiyo smiled, an expression that seemed completely devoid of warmth. "Little Brother, I want you to take up the tomahawk."

"Against who? The whites? They will kill us with their firesticks and with their medicine."

"I can make it so that their firesticks cannot hurt you. And they have no medicine, An-De-Le. *We* have all the medicine."

"I don't believe you." The little warrior placed a hand on the hatchet at his belt, and jutted his chin at Sganyodaiyo. "For sun after sun the white men have advanced into our lands, taking what they wanted, chopping down trees and destroying hunting grounds. They have *plenty* of medicine, and they will destroy the Jo-Ge-Oh. You—you raise up the *Oniate*, and it must be you who has called up the *Maneto* as well. You are not of the Great Spirit if you do these things, and we will not take up the hatchet and follow you."

"You refuse to take my hand."

"We are not like you, shaman. We are afraid of many things, and we are afraid of what you do."

Sganyodaiyo considered this for several moments, then stood up, raising himself to his full height. An-De-Le's eyes held Sganyodaiyo's glance as it rose to high above his head.

"We have performed the Dark Dance to bring you forward, An-De-Le. You must know that, having called you forth, I cannot permit you to return except as my ally."

"Do you seek to frighten me with your threats, Big Brother?"

"You already said you were afraid of everything."

"No," An-De-Le replied. "I did not say I was afraid of *everything*. I am of the people of the Great Spirit, descended from the Sky Woman, a child of the earth. I am afraid of many things."

"But I am not afraid of you."

"You should be," Sganyodaiyo said, absently. "You should be. I can find other Jo-Ge-Oh who will join me, An-De-Le. I do not need you."

"Harm me," An-De-Le said, "and all Jo-Ge-Oh will know that you have done so. Kill me, and the Jo-Ge-Oh will turn away from the Big Brothers forever. Is that what you want, Big Brother? Truly?"

Sganyodaiyo did not answer, but balled his fists in anger.

An-De-Le and his companions began to slowly back away, their hands on the hilts of their tomahawks. A dozen steps and they were gone, absent as if they had never been.

Sganyodaiyo stood stiff and still for several moments more, then turned to the fire and raised his hands. It roared up to a height above his head, and made a terrible noise as if something within it was crying out in agony. Then it flashed once and was gone, cloaking the clearing in darkness.

No one saw Sganyodaiyo walk away, but after a moment he too was gone.

Chapter 55

He is still a man

"I do not know that name," Amherst said, looking at Prince Edward.

"But I do, General," the prince said. "I met him at Johnson Hall. He is highly respected among the Iroquois. Skenadoa is a senior chief, sir."

"Why is he here?"

"Perhaps you should ask me directly."

Skenadoa walked into Amherst's tent. He offered a nod to Amherst, and a slight bow to the prince. And then, to the surprise of both the Englishmen, he reached his arm out to Amherst's camp table and a small man—perhaps two feet in height—climbed down to stand on it.

Amherst got quickly to his feet. The little man assumed a fighting position, his tomahawk in his hand. Prince Edward extended his hand and touched Amherst's arm.

"General Jeffery Amherst," Skenadoa said. "Prince Edward. This is An-De-Le."

"Who—" Amherst began. "Or, rather, what—"

"He is a Jo-Ge-Oh. Some call them Makiawesug. The Little People. He was watching the camp."

"What brings you to our encampment, Brother Skenadoa?" Prince Edward asked.

"I bring word from Degonwadonti, Molly Brant, from Johnson Hall," Skenadoa said. "I will give my report in due course. But in the meanwhile, you should hear what An-De-Le has to say, though it must be through my voice—he does not speak the white man's tongues."

"Do I not?"

All three men turned suddenly to face the little man standing on the camp table. Skenadoa looked surprised, and then covered it with an annoyed expression.

"A spy," Amherst said.

"An observer," An-De-Le countered. "I was watching you. All of you."

"Apparently unnoticed," Amherst said.

"He is very small," Skenadoa said. "I would not have noticed him at all if he was not so bad at spying."

"Observing."

"*Observing*," Skenadoa said. "But he frightens easily. I caught him *observing* your camp and decided to bring him to meet you." He looked down at the little man. "Now put your tomahawk away, Little Brother, and tell the general why you were . . . *observing* the camp."

An-De-Le carefully sheathed his hatchet in his belt, and sat down on the table, stretching his legs out as if he had not a care in the world.

"The Seneca shaman did the Dark Dance and summoned us," he said. "But he smelled bad."

"Guyasuta has a shaman ally," Skenadoa said. "His name is Sganyodaiyo. He is the one who summoned the Stone Coats and the Floating Heads. At his direction, some of his shamans became *Oniate*. There may be other horrors that he has brought forth, out of hatred of whites."

"*Maneto*," An-De-Le added. "And other things."

"What is—"

"A creature of lakes and rivers," Skenadoa said.

"So all of these things that oppose us," Amherst said, "they are all due to this shaman, this Sganyodaiyo? Not the comet?"

"The broom-star is the reason the shaman can do all these things, foolish white man," the Jo-Ge-Oh said. "He could not do them before."

Amherst seemed ready to round on the little man at the phrase *foolish white man*, but again Edward touched his arm. "I'm not sure we knew that, General Amherst."

"That the comet has changed everything—enabled powers and brought out all sorts of monsters? I'm sure we knew *that*, Your Highness."

"But not that the natives who oppose us have a shaman directing their supernatural activities. Not the powers of nature on their own—not because the stars are aligned but because there is someone in charge."

"We knew that there was a shaman accompanying Guyasuta," Amherst said. "An informant told us this. What you are saying is that this shaman controls all the monsters."

Skenadoa crossed his arm. "He is a far more dangerous enemy than Chief Guyasuta. But he is still a man. A single musket shot or arrow can kill him."

"The warriors we fought yesterday wore shirts that *deflected* musket shots," Amherst said.

"Not on their heads," Skenadoa said. "A good marksman could hit him there." He let his arms fall to his sides. "*I* could hit him there."

Amherst looked at the Jo-Ge-Oh. "You can identify this shaman?"

"Of course, white general."

"Then when the time comes, Skenadoa," Amherst said, "you will have your chance."

"That is well," Skenadoa answered. "Now let me inform you of my reason for coming.

"The Council Fire has been relit. Those still loyal to the Covenant, who call the English friends, walk to war. Within a few days a force will be here—Oneida, Onondaga and Mohawks. We stand ready to fight against the betrayer of the Haudenosaunee."

"Indeed," Amherst said. "And how are they armed?"

"Some muskets," Skenadoa said. "Bows as well."

"And tomahawks," An-De-Le said, placing his hand on his own weapon.

"Tomahawks as well."

Amherst glanced at Prince Edward. "I do not know if . . . " he let the sentence drift off.

"You doubt that the People of the Longhouse are brave enough?" An-De-Le said. "They might find that insulting."

"This is not a private quarrel between natives," Amherst said. "We have already had one fight with these beings, and they have fearsome—unworldly—assistance."

"So do you," Skenadoa said, gesturing toward the Jo-Ge-Oh. "We may understand this business better than you do, General."

"Of course, we do," An-De-Le said with a smirk. "The whites walk different paths and listen to other songs. They know nothing of this, and I don't think they want our help."

"I didn't say that—" Amherst began.

"We do not turn away your help," Prince Edward said. "If the General pleases. It would be foolish to reject any ally. There is some need for a plan so we can work together. Are your warriors ready to follow as General Amherst directs?"

"The war-chiefs would want to meet."

"That doesn't answer the question."

"I will not answer for them," Skenadoa said. "But I believe that they will, if they are given an honorable part in the battle."

Amherst appeared ready to give another sharp retort, but Prince Edward said, "Then when they arrive, send them here. I'm sure there will be plenty enough honorable parts to go around."

"You asked for me, General?"

Wolfe took a long look at the colonial standing before him. There was a time—not too long in the past—when he would not have bothered to even speak to a colonial militiaman, much less summon him. All his experience in the colonies had made him disdainful and unwilling to even assign the title of "soldier" to such a man. But things had changed, particularly in the last few days. Whatever their training or discipline, it had been colonial militia who had faced the vanguard of the native army and driven it back. No general worth his salt would be so foolish as to let prejudice interfere with realism.

"I have a question for you, Colonel Gridley. Who among your troops is the best shot? Perhaps Captain Revere?"

"I would have to think about it, sir. Revere is a good man, and a fair shot with a musket, but there are country lads who are better. But to be honest, General, the best shot among colonial troops is probably Major Rogers."

"The—tracker? Woodsman? What does he call himself—a—"

"Ranger, sir. The very one."

"And he's a very good shot?"

"I would venture to call him the best among colonial troops, General." Gridley paused, and then asked, "may I inquire, sir, why you need a crack shot?"

"We have learned that the various—things—that we might face are controlled by a single man. A—a shaman, if you please. It has been decided that if it is possible for us to kill this one individual, these things would no longer be at the command of the natives."

"I see, sir . . . but that begs the question who would then command them."

"Well, no one, I suppose."

"Excuse me for pointing out, sir, that if no one commands them, they might do as they please."

"Or they might go back where they came from."

"It seems like a risky business, begging the General's pardon. Based on what I've heard, there are some fearsome things at this shaman's command, and his control of them makes them dangerous to us—but without that command they might still be here."

"I have my orders, Gridley. And you have given me the information I desire. Dismissed."

Richard Gridley might have wanted to say something more, but he apparently thought better of it. He touched his hand to his cap and left the tent.

✛ ✛ ✛

Joseph ran sure-footed, following trail sign that led him southward toward New York. Molly wanted him to stay at Johnson Hall, but he was restless; he and Skenadoa each had a mission—the older man was bound for the whites' army camp, he for the city, each bearing news of the movement of Guyasuta's army.

He felt much more in harmony with the forest now, recognizing the signs and placing his feet confidently on the paths. He saw other things as well—the movement of woodland creatures and . . . other features that he was sure that no one else could perceive. It was as if he had walked through the world with one eye closed, and suddenly the broom-star had opened it.

Four days after parting from Molly, he was following a hilly trail. He paused at the crest of a rise that overlooked the great river and immediately his heightened senses were drawn toward a boat slowly making its way northward. There was something unusual about it that caught his attention.

He drew out a small spyglass, a gift from Sir William, opened it and put it to his eye—marveling, as always, at how it brought distant things so close. Shortly he managed to find the boat and saw that it was heavily-laden—something large was lashed to the deck. With his opened eyes he knew that was what had attracted him; but he also took notice of two people standing at the rail, watching the river flow by—two whites, an older man and a young, beautiful woman.

And as he watched, the woman's eyes looked away from the river and directly at him—as if she had a spyglass of her own. She tugged at the sleeve of the man beside her and pointed—

Joseph pulled the spyglass away and crouched in the underbrush, the scene vanishing—but he still felt as he was being observed.

He had two choices. One was to turn and run away, to follow a trail southward, away from the river, and avoid the encounter entirely; the other was to run toward the river, and perhaps find out what had attracted his attention in the first place.

He didn't know the people on the boat—but he felt that somehow the woman had noticed, and perhaps even identified, him.

It took him only a moment to decide.

They met at a gentle bend in the river, the flatboat secured at a sandbank. Joseph approached cautiously, noting that there were several men in uniforms near the rail, muskets in hand, watching him carefully. The young woman moved toward the rail, but the older man held her back.

"That's as close as you need to come, boy," one of the soldiers said, raising his musket very slightly. Joseph stopped, his hands spread wide.

"I don't mean any harm," he said.

"You speak the King's English, at least," the soldier replied. "That'll make this easier. We're only stopped here because the lady asked it. State your business and be quick about it."

"What are you carrying?"

"None of your concern, but why do you care?"

"I can—" he began, then thought better of it. "It caught my attention. That box." He gestured toward the cargo. "Whatever it is."

The soldier looked at the woman, who ignored him. She came to the rail, also ignoring the older man, who looked slightly alarmed.

"Lieutenant, I think we should permit this young man to come aboard."

"With respect, ma'am, we don't know what he's about. It's a risk—"

"Which I'm willing to take. Please allow him to join us."

The older man stepped next to her and said something; Joseph was fairly sure it was in French, which surprised him; could this be a French boat, this far below Albany? *No,* he decided: *they talked about the King's English.*

With what seemed to be great reluctance, they extended a stepped ramp from the side of the boat to the sandy shore, and Joseph walked carefully up and onto the boat. The two soldiers held their muskets tightly, as if they were ready at any moment to fire them.

"To whom do I have the pleasure of speaking?" the older man said. "My name is Charles Messier. I am honored to escort Mademoiselle Catherine LaGèndiere." He gestured to the woman.

"My Christian name is Joseph, son of Brant. I am of the Wolf Clan of the Mohawk people. My sister is Molly, called Degonwadonti, the partner of Chief Big Business, Sir William Johnson."

"And why do you take an interest in our cargo, young man?" Catherine said. "Do you . . . "

There seemed little point in keeping it to himself. "I can feel it. It feels—different."

"Then you are very perceptive. Is that a skill you have always had?"

"The Great Spirit has given me wider vision in recent months," Joseph said. "I notice things that others do not."

"What happened to your hands?"

The question, asked without preface, made Joseph's stomach jump. He held his hands before him, palm up; they still bore very slight evidence of where they had been burned by the filament that had connected the Floating Head to the ground.

"They were burned, lady."

"And in an unusual way." She took his left hand in hers and traced a line along his palm. Her finger felt like fire as it followed the scarcely-visible scar from his contact with the Floating Head.

"Yes."

"We are on our way to the British army camp," she said. "What we are bringing—"

"Catherine—" Messier began, but she continued.

". . . is something we hope will make a difference."

"I can feel it."

"Can you indeed?" Catherine turned to Messier. "Monsieur," she said, "I think we should continue our journey with this young warrior as our guest."

Messier looked dubious, but at last he nodded, gesturing toward the pilothouse.

"Lady, I was meaning to go to New York—"

"No," Catherine said. "No, young warrior, you don't want to do that." She had not let go of his hand, and now held it tightly. "Someone has brought things from the earth, terrible things. It is no place to be."

Messier looked alarmed. "What—"

"Come with us," Catherine continued. "I will show you what we are bringing. We will save both our peoples."

Joseph thought for a moment, his gaze captured by the young Frenchwoman.

"As you wish," he said.

Chapter 56

We must cling to what we understand

Prince Edward, often accompanied by Captain Revere, spent part of his day walking through the encampment, making sure he was visible to the assembled troops waiting for the native army to attack. He issued no orders and gave no direction; it was a matter of visiting with wounded men, listening to complaints and answering questions. He did not wear his dress uniform and did not powder his hair—he wanted to meet his fellow soldiers as one of their own, a prince who was willing to fight with them and suffer with them. Most of them had scarcely ever seen, and certainly never met, a scion of royal blood; he could sense that there was something that impressed them beyond his words or his appearance.

The comet has done something to me as well, he thought.

He remembered the eerie fog that had enveloped *Neptune* on the night the comet fell—the event that was beginning to be called 'the Sundering'—and the vision of his father, eight years dead.

Can you see me now, Father? he wondered. *Do I meet your expectations?*

It was no surprise that he received no answer.

The supply train was located in a protected valley south and east of the main camp. On a late summer afternoon a few days after the battle, Edward—with Revere accompanying him—was conversing with two of the sutlers when he noticed the approach of a group of horsemen. He gracefully excused himself and stepped away.

At the head of the troop was a familiar face—the Marquis de Montcalm, turned out in a resplendent dress uniform, from highly polished boots covered with bright white gaiters to an elaborate hat bearing a fleur-de-lys cockade. He was accompanied by a dozen similarly-dressed soldiers—enough to constitute an honor guard, far too few to be an attacking force. There was also a black-cassocked priest among the group, a stark contrast to the brightly arrayed men.

Montcalm saw the prince from some distance; he lifted his hand to stop their progress and dismounted. He turned and nodded to another man whom Edward recognized as D'Egremont. Presently the two Frenchmen began to approach; they stopped a dozen feet away and made a leg.

"Monsieur le Marquis. To what do we owe the pleasure?"

"Your Highness. I am glad to encounter you first. We have reached a decision regarding the matter we previously discussed."

"Your Grace, I am not the person of authority with whom you must treat. I would be honored to escort you to General Amherst—"

Montcalm walked closer, so that the two men were able to speak quietly. "No. It is you with whom I wish to speak."

Edward wanted to demur further, but thought better of it. "Let us walk," he said, and they walked away together.

"I have been thinking about our last conversation," Montcalm said. "What's more, we have had reports of your recent encounter with the savages."

"We acquitted ourselves the best we could."

Montcalm looked over his shoulder at Revere, who appeared uncomfortable waiting with D'Egremont. "I was referring, Highness, to *your* encounter. And your bravery in battle."

"I don't need to tell you, Monsieur, that in combat one does what is necessary. It brings out both bravery and cowardice, and for those who have had only occasional experience it is unclear which will come to the fore."

"It is a matter of character."

"That might be the case, sir. I do not feel qualified to make any judgment. And as was pointed out to me in no uncertain terms, I acted in contravention to orders. That hardly recommends me as an expert. Again, General Amherst—"

"No." Montcalm stopped walking. "This is for you first." Edward stopped as well.

"What is?"

"After consultation, Highness, I have been authorized to place the forces under my command at your disposal. The ultimate decision regarding the government of the lands claimed by His Most Catholic Majesty is still in the future; but in the meanwhile, the army of the savages coming out of the west must be defeated."

"You are exercising your . . . power of choice."

"I daresay."

"I still must insist, Monsieur, that I am not in any position to accept your generous offer. As you say regarding French lands, the ultimate disposition of my grandfather's colonies here in America is still very much an open question. And that is dependent on whether we defeat the hostile natives—and whether I live to be presented with the crown you seem to think is already on my head.

"I am a prince, but . . . to be perfectly honest, sir, I am not king of anything, nor am I general of anything. I can acknowledge your gesture—but unless so directed, I cannot immediately accept it."

"This is not an offer to General Amherst, Highness. This is an offer to *you*."

"Then, with all due respect, Your Grace, I must decline."

"The participation of my command might make the difference between victory and defeat, Highness, and you are deferring to *protocol*?"

"Even in view of the highly unusual circumstances, Monsieur, it is incumbent upon us to fall back upon such things—it is a part of who we are. Regardless of what the future holds for all of us, we must cling to what we understand and find familiar. Otherwise we will be adrift, strangers in unfamiliar country."

Montcalm sighed. He looked to be equal parts angry and exasperated.

"I ask that you present yourself to General Amherst, Monsieur."

"I will not offer my services to General Amherst. Only to you, and you personally."

It was Edward's turn to sigh. He knew that with a word he could accept Montcalm's offer; that Amherst, and Wolfe, and for that matter everyone above him in rank such as Admiral Boscawen, would eventually be compelled to come to terms with the situation. It was looking increasingly more likely that he would have to consider taking on the role of sovereign, and that would erase any shortcoming in his present rank—making it what the French might call a *fait accompli*.

Yet for all that, such a thing was in the future, not now, and if he asserted his royal prerogative now, the other men might bear a grudge later. They needed to accede to this situation in the present.

"He has the right to hear of this, at least. Come, Monsieur. Let us see what General Amherst has to say."

News traveled fast in the camp. Before Prince Edward could send a messenger to Amherst, the general came to find them. Montcalm had sent D'Egremont back to the French camp along with his escort and stood alone to meet the British commander.

"*Mon General*," Montcalm said as Amherst approached.

"I heard that you had favored us with your presence, My Lord," Amherst said. "You have changed your mind?"

"In a manner of speaking. I have come to offer my assistance."

"With conditions," Edward said.

"What sort of conditions?"

"I have come to offer my services, General Amherst. To Prince Edward."

"He does not command here."

"Nevertheless."

Amherst looked from the French commander to Prince Edward and back. "Monsieur Marquis," he said, "You put me in an uncomfortable position. The chain of command—"

"I understand the chain of command, General—"

"The chain of command," Amherst repeated, "will not permit you to serve under the authority of a mere commander in His Majesty's Navy, regardless of his gentle blood."

"I can resign my commission, General Amherst," Edward said. "I am willing to do that at once."

"If there were a court of inquiry, a direct line of communication to the Admiralty—if there were authorities to whom I could appeal, if there was someone who could decide . . . " Amherst sighed. "But there is not. Except for me."

He paused for a moment, thinking. "There is a simple solution, Highness. I am empowered by no one and endowed with no specific authority to do so—but . . . *nevertheless* . . . I hereby commission you as General of His Majesty's Forces in America. In that capacity, you are authorized and enjoined to accept the service of the Marquis de Montcalm and the forces under his command.

"And now, General Prince, you are ordered to report to me at your earliest convenience as to the disposition of those forces and their readiness to face the enemy."

Paul Revere was surprised to receive the summons to come to Prince Edward's tent, since he had been told that there was no opportunity for him to directly serve the man who had saved his life. But there was no refusing such a command, and even if he had considered it, Gridley told him to *move at double time, for Heaven's sake*, and to shine his boots and wear his cleanest cravat. Thus, in shined boots and a clean cravat, he made his way through the colonials' camp to the prince's place, where two regulars from the 40th were standing guard.

"You're Revere," one of them said, more a statement than a question.

"I've been summoned—"

"Yes, yes, of course. Stand straight, Colonial," he interrupted, and reached out to straighten Revere's coat and brush a few specks of dirt from his shoulder. Without as much as a by your leave, he made an adjustment to the neckcloth, tightening and straightening it with military precision. "There now, you're barely presentable, but go in. And take your cover off as you enter. Show some damned respect."

Revere considered a reply but bit it off and drew his hat from his head as he came into the tent, where he was presented with the most unusual sight he could have imagined.

Prince Edward was standing casually before a man fitting him with a coat with general's epaulets. He seemed distracted by a map spread out on a camp table, over which a Frenchman was bent. Standing on the table—literally, *on* the table!—was a native man in miniature, no more than two feet tall. As Revere entered, all three men other than the tailor turned to face him.

"Highness, if you please," the tailor said, straightening the lapels.

Prince Edward smiled wryly. Clearly, he found it somewhat absurd that he was being fitted with a new uniform at such a moment.

"Revere. Good of you to come so quickly. May I present the Chevalier de Lévis, adjutant to his Grace the Marquis de Montcalm. And An-De-Le, a . . . Jo-Ge-Oh. A warrior."

Revere didn't know quite how to respond—to the general's coat, to the presence of a French nobleman, or to a two-foot-tall native, so he saluted and said nothing at all.

"I realize that I was dismissive a few days ago regarding your desire for service with me. Well . . . circumstances have changed. Our French associates have offered to join us in the fight against the army of the enemy, but it appears that they will only serve if I am their commander. Thus—" he extended his arms, and two or three pins holding a sleeve came loose, making the tailor sigh in exasperation.

Edward carefully took the coat off and thrust it at the man. "We'll continue this at another time. You have my leave to go."

The tailor took the garment, looked from Edward to Revere, at whom he levelled a scowl worthy of a Boston merchant, and backed out of the tent, offering Edward the merest of bows.

"'Thus,' Highness?"

"Thus, sir, I am a general. And as of this moment, with the certainty of confirmation by General Amherst, *you,* sir, are my adjutant, with the rank of colonel, as befits your station. It may take a little time for the proper compensation to catch up with the rank, but we'll see what we can do to make sure you have the badges appropriate for it. In the meanwhile, let us take a look at our deployments."

"Of course, Your Highness," Revere said, looking at An-De-Le. "I . . ."

"You don't like me," An-De-Le said to Revere. "I can smell it. Are you afraid of me?"

"Huh. If you were three times your size I might be," Revere answered. "I have young children bigger than you."

"Are they skilled with the hatchet and bow?"

"No, but I am. I've just never seen someone so small who *wasn't* a child."

"We do our best to hide from Big People," An-De-Le said. "Where is your village?"

"My . . . village is the town of Boston in Massachusetts-Bay. It's far off to the east, on the ocean."

"Massachusetts-Bay!" An-De-Le did a little dance on the table, disturbing the map under his feet. "Oh, they don't like *us* there. But there's not much medicine left in the forests of Massachusetts-Bay. The black crows have cast their own spells to dry it all up. They don't like the Big People either."

"You mean natives."

"Yes, yes, that's what I mean. Isn't that what I said? Most Big People don't even know about the Jo-Ge-Oh, no they don't. But we watch them. There are lots of things we can't un-see. You know, don't you."

"I think I do."

"The Jo-Ge-Oh have agreed to serve as scouts," Prince Edward said. "Whatever they think of us—colonials from the Bay Colony included—they like Guyasuta and his shamans even less. I have promised to help protect them if we can win this battle."

"Promised," An-De-Le repeated. "We hear his words and see his—" the little man spoke some word that slipped past Revere's hearing. Instead, he felt it underfoot, like a small shiver.

The Frenchman cleared his throat. "Shall we return to the matter at hand?"

Prince Edward gestured to the map. "I expect that General Amherst will wish to engage his regulars first, but we should be ready to reinforce them. Despite our previous experience, I assume this will be the case. Your troops should expect to do as much melee as musket volleys, Chevalier."

"I'm sure our professionals can handle that, Highness."

Revere scowled at Lévis, who looked back at him, a challenge.

"I'm sure that our troops can do what they have done before, Highness. Though I am mildly concerned that some of our men might find fighting alongside *Frenchmen* uncomfortable."

"I can't imagine why," Lévis said.

"We have decades of grievances against the *hábitants* and their minions," Revere said. "I cannot imagine they will disappear in a single day."

"They must," Edward said, very forcefully. "Chevalier, I suggest that you become accustomed to cooperating with our colonial soldiers. And as for you, Colonel Revere . . . if there are objections to the French, it is your task to overcome them. Whatever you need to do to convince them you will have to do so."

"Highness—"

"It is why you are in my service, Revere. Your alternate choice is to serve as a militia captain. I would be sorry to dismiss you, but if I must, I shall."

The moment stretched out as Revere considered it, but at last he said, "I shall endeavor to do my best."

Chapter 57

Down and up

New York

"This is utterly outrageous!" Governor De Lancey almost sprang out of his chair, as he came to his feet. "Outrageous, I say!"

"Sit *down*," commanded Admiral Boscawen. His failure to use the governor's title was deliberate. Boscawen was fed up with De Lancey—with his stupidity and incompetence even more than his blatant corruption. A capable thief he could have tolerated as the colony's governor, but not this man.

"This is not a negotiation," the admiral continued. "I am simply giving you the courtesy of a private explanation of what I intend to do, whether you like it or not."

De Lancey remained on his feet. Glaring at Boscawen, he said: "We shall see about that. Do I need to remind you that all you have at your disposal are a handful of soldiers, whereas I have the entire militia."

Boscawen couldn't stop himself from laughing. "The *entire* militia? Oh, I think not, Governor. Leaving aside the dozens who were slaughtered by the monsters summoned by the slave Jupiter, most of the rest are either hiding in their homes or drowning their sorrows in the city's taverns."

Since the governor seemed determined to remain standing, in a rather childish effort at dominance, Boscawen pushed back the chair from his desk and rose to his feet.

"This is how it will be. I am hereby declaring martial law in the city of New York, until such time as Prince Edward returns." He waved his hand dismissively. "If you wish to continue passing yourself off as the governor of the province, feel free to do so—but I warn you that if you clash with the Iroquois do not expect to get any help from me. Prince Edward is seeking to make peace with the Mohawks, Oneidas and Onondagas."

"What if *they* attack *us*?"

"I think that highly unlikely, given that they are now allied with us against the menace rising from the west. If I were you, sir, I would let Molly Brant handle the situation in the countryside. She's been doing quite well, by all accounts I've received."

The governor sneered. "She's nothing but William Johnson's squaw. That so-called marriage of theirs is not legally valid. Besides, Johnson's now dead. That's what everyone says."

Boscawen didn't reply for a few seconds, just giving De Lancey a cold stare. "I told you," he said abruptly, "you may do as you wish outside of the city. I expect you'll behave as recklessly as you did here, when you called out the militia in response to nothing more than rumors. But I warn you—when I say I will give you no help if you clash with the natives, that includes financial assistance. Of *any* kind."

That finally seemed to register on the man. Apparently, he'd just recalled that with the collapse of any contact with Britain, De Lancey was now depending on Boscawen to pay his salary as governor. The admiral was still the source of most of the colony's specie.

"Now get out," said Boscawen.

De Lancey drew himself up, as if . . .

To do . . . whatever.

"Get out. *Now*," repeated the admiral.

As he had hoped, Boscawen found Minerva and Absalom in the chamber toward the rear of the American Philosophical Society's building which served James Alexander as both a sitting-room and laboratory. The three of them were intently studying a peculiar iron contrivance perched on a large table toward the middle of the chamber.

To his surprise, the admiral saw that two other negroes were present as well—the two youngsters he'd rescued from their perch on the roof overlooking the Commons, York and Coffey. He had no idea why they were present.

Hearing him enter, Alexander turned his head and looked over his shoulder.

"Admiral Boscawen! You're just in time."

"In time for what?"

Alexander gestured toward the iron . . . whatever it was. The thing was shaped like a huge ornament. Seven iron bars were bent in semicircles, all of them attached at the top to something that looked vaguely like a crown and fixed at their base into a seven-pointed star.

"If all goes as we hope," he said, "this device will substitute for Mademoiselle LaGèndiere's alchemetical compass." Alexander pointed to York. "He constructed it, guided by Minerva and Absalom."

"Oh, la," said Minerva, fluttering one of her hands, "we did not guide the lad so much as we counseled him when he veered astray."

"York has more than a touch of the blacksmith power," added Absalom. "Not so much as Jupiter, though, for which we can all be thankful—especially York himself. It can be a dangerous talent if it's not guided by clear knowledge and understanding."

"So how does it work?" asked Boscawen.

Alexander and Minerva and Absalom all glanced back and forth at each other. After a few seconds, it was Minerva who spoke.

"It doesn't exactly 'work,' Admiral," she said. "You think of it as a machine because that is the way white people think. But we who are from Africa look at what you call 'magic' in a different way."

She pointed to the iron construct. "That is not so much a machine as it is an appeal to Ogun, the great god of iron. An offering, you might say."

Boscawen looked at Alexander, who simply shrugged. "I am mostly here as an observer, Admiral. What I can tell you is that Minerva is quite right that there are many paths to the divine forces which go by the name of 'magic.' I myself could do even less with this"—he pointed to the device on the table—"than I could with Mademoiselle LaGèndiere's alchemetical compass. Like Monsieur Messier, my comprehension of magic is mostly theoretical."

"Then who makes it work?"

"That would be me," said Absalom. The grin that was so often on his face was on full display. "As I will now demonstrate."

He stepped forward and rubbed his hands over the iron bars. Then, drew a pair of dice out of a pocket.

"Oh, la! Oh, la!" exclaimed Minerva. It sounded almost like a chant.

Absalom tossed the dice into the cagelike center of the device. From the very top, crownlike cupola, a dull gray ball appeared. It rolled off the crown and fell into the cage.

"A bullet," Absalom announced. He reached in, picked up the round ball and handed it to Boscawen. "Should you get into a duel, Admiral, I recommend using this ball."

Boscawen studied the ball for a moment. It seemed to be a perfect sphere. Then, juggled it in his hand.

"Lead," he announced, "judging by the weight."

Absalom nodded. "A near miss. Lead and gold are cousins. Again, then."

Boscawen tried to think of any way that gold and lead were related, other than both being heavy. There was none that he could see.

Absalom rolled the dice again. And . . .

This time, a gold coin appeared. It teetered for a moment on the cupola and fell into the cage.

Absalom gestured toward the coin. "I believe this is yours, Admiral."

When Boscawen hesitated, Minerva smiled. "Oh, la. It's quite safe, Admiral. If Ogun was angry with you, something else would have appeared."

"Really?" asked Alexander, keenly curious. "Such as . . . ?"

Absalom shrugged. "It could be anything made of metal. If the great god was just annoyed, it might be a lump of pewter, shaped like a toad or a turd. But if he was in a fierce mood, it could be a brass serpent—mind, one that could strike you and inject you with metallic venom."

Minerva nodded. "Mercury, most like."

A bit gingerly, Boscawen reached in and drew out the coin. Rolling it over in his hand, he saw that it was a Spanish doubloon. He didn't doubt for a moment that it was genuine—as "genuine," at least, as magic could make anything. The weight was right, and so were the various markings and inscriptions.

But . . .

"Why a doubloon?" he wondered. He looked quizzically at Absalom; who, for his part, shrugged.

"I have no idea, myself," said Minerva.

When Alexander spoke, his tone was excited. "It must—well, not 'must,' that's too strong—but it likely means that the Spanish territories came through the Sundering. Some of them, at any rate."

He pointed to the coin in Boscawen's hand. "They were minted in Spain, of course, but also in the viceroyalties of New Spain, Peru, and Nueva Granada."

That was . . . interesting, at the very least. No one had any idea, so far as Boscawen was aware, of the full extent of the New World after the Sundering. Were central and southern America still part of it? If Alexander's surmise was correct, at least some parts of Spanish territory still existed—and with them, presumably, some Spaniards as well.

But that was a problem for later. For the moment, he needed to find out the limits of the . . .

"What shall we call this device?" he asked.

"Don't call it anything," Absalom said hurriedly. "If you choose the wrong term, Ogun might be offended."

That struck Boscawen as a lot of superstitious nonsense. On the other hand . . .

Maybe not. And there was no reason to take a chance.

So he just pointed at York's iron construct. "How many coins can you get from it?"

"Let's find out," said Absalom, juggling the dice again.

Four coins, as it turned out. All gold doubloons except the last one, which was a silver dollar—what was often called a piece of eight, because it was worth eight *reales*.

The silver coin was apparently something in the way of a warning that Ogun was getting peeved at the demands made on his time. The very next item that Absalom's dice drew forth was a lump of tin shaped like a clam.

"Best we stop now, at least for the day," said Minerva, making a waving motion with her hand at York and Coffey. "Let us be off." And with no further ado, she left the chamber with the two youngsters in tow.

Boscawen wondered if he should take offense at her unceremonious departure. But after a moment he decided that would probably be unwise. It was unclear what authority he really had over the woman. True, he had great rank and, once the fleet returned, considerable military force. True also, however, that Minerva could summon giant monsters.

All things considered, that was probably an issue best left unresolved, at least for the time being.

Absalom was looking at him, the admiral realized. The expression on his face had a sly sort of cast.

"Very wise man," the freedman murmured. "Very wise indeed."

When Boscawen emerged from the American Philosophical Society's edifice, he saw to his surprise that the sun was beginning to set. He hadn't thought he'd spent that much time in there.

Washington was waiting for him, with two soldiers.

"My apologies, Colonel," he said. "I'm afraid I lost track of the time."

"No matter, sir," Washington said. He sounded stoic, but Boscawen had gotten to know the colonel well enough to realize that stoicism was second nature to him. A somewhat unusual trait, that, in such a young man.

On their way back to naval headquarters, Washington said: "I trust the day has gone well for you, Admiral."

It was not a question; simply a statement of good wishes. But Boscawen saw no reason not to confide in the colonel, at least to a point. He was coming to have a great deal of confidence in Washington.

"Quite well, I'm thinking. A governor abased and a currency uplifted—all in the same day!"

Chapter 58

It is a question of control

To bring the concatenator from Albany to the encampment, Messier and LaGèndiere used a letter of introduction provided by Admiral Boscawen and countersigned by Governor De Lancey. In the instance, Messier was more than happy to leave his female companion to do most of the talking; her English was much less affected by a French accent, and she had other, more obvious charms that were attractive to Sheriff Jacob Van Schaick. In service to Boscawen and General Amherst, Van Schaick was able to provide a heavy, lumbering cart and a pair of draft horses to pull it.

Messier had been apprehensive about traveling through the wilderness once they left the region of Albany, with only a small number of soldiers as an escort. But they were favored by good fortune—although the men who escorted them were initially so startled and frightened that they almost ran off.

Not more than thirty miles from Albany they encountered a large party of Mohawk warriors who had been sent by someone named Molly Brant—an Iroquois woman herself, apparently, despite the name—to join the forces assembling against the menace emerging in the west. According to the leaders of the Mohawk party, other Mohawk warriors were on their way as well, along with men from the Oneida and Onondaga tribes.

The soldiers who'd been escorting Messier and LaGèndiere reacted to the Mohawk offer of serving as a much larger escort in a manner that LaGèndiere (although not Messier) found rather amusing. So might a small party of mice have reacted to several hundred cats serving them as an escort.

But there was no trouble. The warriors ignored them, but the party of Mohawks was accompanied by about thirty women. LaGèndiere soon became on familiar terms with several of them who spoke either English or French.

All in all, the journey went quite well. Better than Catherine had expected and much better than Messier had feared.

The cart, its cargo and occupants arrived at the army encampment on a hot, humid morning. The Mohawks had parted company with them a few miles earlier. From what the women told Catherine, they wanted to avoid clashing with the English—especially the colonials, between themselves and whom no great love was lost. The Iroquois forces who were joining the fight were assembling a mile or so away from the forces under Amherst's command.

Catherine had slept poorly the previous night at a farmhouse where the letter from Boscawen had provided them with lodging. The farmer and his wife had offered their own bed for her use, while Messier and the soldiers lodged in the barn. While most of the little party slept exhaustedly, Catherine could feel—through the dormant concatenator—the presence of many things not far away that were distinctly unnatural. They troubled her sleep with eerie dreams.

At the boundary of the camp, the cart was halted by a troop of soldiers in irregular uniforms.

The soldier holding the reins to the cart frowned, looking from them to Messier, who sat alongside.

"Colonials," he said.

"You seem unimpressed," Messier said.

"There is no reason to feel otherwise," the soldier said. "Bumpkin amateurs. I don't even know why they're here."

"For the same reason everyone else is," Messier answered. "To fight the enemy."

"They should leave it to the professionals." Still, the soldier composed his expression as the colonials came up to the cart.

With a few colonials in their company, the cart slowly climbed a hill to where the command tents had been pitched. At the summit, Messier and LaGèndiere dismounted from the cart. By the time they had done so, three officers were approaching. If Messier was interpreting the insignias on their uniforms correctly, all of them were generals.

"What is the meaning of this?"

"You are General Amherst," Messier began. "I am—"

"Your pardon, sir," Amherst interrupted. "I do not truly care who you are, or why you have come here. This is no place for civilians."

"I think if you gave us an opportunity to present ourselves," Messier answered, "you might feel differently. I have an introduction from Admiral Lord Boscawen."

"Indeed." He extended his hand, glancing at the other two generals to either side of him.

Messier drew out the letter bearing Boscawen's seal and handed it to Amherst. He examined it, looking over the document at Messier and then back at the writing.

"You are Charles Messier, I take it."

"Your servant, sir."

"And this—" Amherst gestured toward the cart. "This is some sort of device intended to assist the army."

"Yes, Monsieur General," Messier said, his voice becoming enthusiastic. "It is an alchemetical concatenator, a—"

Amherst held his hand up, and Messier stopped. The general gave a polite nod to Catherine, and then returned his attention to Messier.

"Let me make something abundantly clear, Doctor," he said. "We are facing an enemy, an army of savages with magical forces at their disposal. They could come out of the woods again at any moment—next week, tomorrow, this afternoon. It is impossible for me to know if any of the *military* men here have any chance at long-term survival. There is no way for me to protect *civilians*."

"We are not asking for your protection."

Amherst took the letter and began to crumple it, but then seemed to think better of it, and handed it back to Messier. "I . . . don't know what to tell you, Frenchman. Your letter? Commission? Indicates that you are here to aid the effort."

"The concatenator—"

Amherst held up his hand again. "No matter what Boscawen

thinks you're here to do, it is *my* order that you stay out of my way. You can camp here."

Without another word, he turned on his heel and walked away. General Wolfe, who had said not a word during the entire exchange, gave an aristocratic toss of his head and followed Amherst.

The third man, however, remained. He watched Amherst and Wolfe walk away and into the tent, then he stepped forward, smiling.

"You are the savant Dr. Messier? The astronomer?"

"At your service, General—"

The man smiled. "Prince. At least that's what I'm going by at this moment. Edward of Hanover, Monsieur, at your service."

"Edward—" Messier's eyes went wide.

Catherine, who had also remained silent during the conversation, placed a hand on Messier's arm.

"My friend, I believe we are in the presence of Prince Edward, the grandson of His Majesty the King of England. Your Highness," she said, smiling very slightly and offering a perfect curtsy.

"Rise, my lady," Edward said. "We're not standing on ceremony here, at least not court ceremony." He extended his hand and she took it. "May I have the pleasure of making your acquaintance?"

"She is—" Messier began.

"Catherine LaGèndiere," she said, smiling. "General."

Unlike his colleagues, Edward was very interested in the elemental concatenator—what it was intended to do, and how it could be operated. Messier, usually quite loquacious, found himself somewhat tongue-tied in Edward's presence, which troubled him since he had been at ease making presentations at the court of Versailles for much of his professional career. Fortunately, Catherine had the matter quite in hand.

She arranged for the crates carrying the concatenator to be unpacked and set up on top of the cart. The horses were unhitched and allowed to graze, permitting the cart itself to be anchored in place with wooden blocks.

It took the better part of an hour for the device to be assembled. It looked rather like a sort of loom, except that there were stout wires wrapped around the wooden armatures rather than lengths of yarn; and in the place where the weaver might sit there was a keyboard rather like that of an organ, though with fewer keys and no foot-pedals. Mechanisms, scarcely glimpsed, lay in a covered compartment below the loom and in front of the keyboard, and beneath the operator's foot was a treadle that presumably made the entire thing run.

"Mademoiselle," the prince said when she had seated herself at the keyboard, "I consider myself well-educated in the modern sciences, but I cannot fathom what this device is intended to *do.*"

"It is intended to impart perturbations in the æther, High—General," she corrected herself. "It focuses the four primary elements by adjusting the balance of those perturbations."

"Having been told this, I confess that I have learned nothing further from you. What can it actually do?"

"General." Catherine laid her hands upon the keys, then withdrawing them into her lap. "Your opponent—our enemy—has various forces at his disposal, correct?"

"It seems so. His shaman seems to be able to summon forth the forces of nature, according to their own beliefs."

"In order to do so, the shaman must—in some way—adjust the balance of the elements. Creatures of earth, air, fire, water. We are told that there are creatures that float through the air and swim beneath the sea, for example. According to Joseph, who told us many things on his travels with us, there are—or were—creatures of stone who attacked a French fort somewhere to the west. Those are clearly creatures of earth. As for fire, I am not sure, but perhaps these shamans with their poisoned hands call upon that element for their workings.

"I believe that, properly adjusted, this device can act upon each element and possibly counteract any or all of those forces summoned against your army. If that is the case, your regular troops can do what they are best suited to do."

"That is . . . remarkable. If it truly can work."

"It works," Messier said. "It is not a matter of functionality—it is a question of *control.*"

Before the first light of dawn colored the east, the soldiers in the camp came awake to the sound of drums, accompanied by the low, rumbling sounds of distant chanting coming from the Iroquois encampment.

Bugles and drums roused those not already awake, and while

darkness turned into light, the various troops—British regulars, French regulars and colonials—rushed onto the field, following barked orders from officers and subalterns to take up their positions. The Iroquois appeared and took their much less regular formations on the left flank of the white soldiers.

Then, just as the sun began to appear over the trees, both drums and chants suddenly, eerily, stopped. Across the lines of the army, shouts and noises seemed suddenly out of place and discordant.

A fog appeared in the trees on the edge of the encampment, not far from where the colonial troops had assembled. It was completely at odds with the bright sunlight beginning to filter across the field, and the sweltering heat of the summer day. No sooner did it form than there was a deep, heavy thrumming in the ground, as if a hundred cannons were being fired from deep beneath the earth. Something in among the trees caught the morning light—it was slightly above the height of a man, and it was moving. Then the light caught another, and another.

Edward was on horseback, with Gridley by his side and Revere close behind. He lowered a spyglass and looked at the colonial commander beside him.

"Can you see anything?"

"I'm afraid I can, Colonel. I think Guyasuta has obtained the services of some additional Stone Coats."

"Stone Coats, Your Highness?"

Edward took a moment before speaking and then said, "They are warriors made of stone, Colonel Gridley. They are supernatural in origin, and the only time I have seen them defeated was by beings equally supernatural. And we don't have any on hand."

"My boys—"

"Your boys." Edward smiled, very slightly. "Your boys will be powerless against them. They are not human, Colonel Gridley, and if there are enough of them . . . they are a terror weapon, sir."

Gridley squinted toward the woods. Edward handed him the spyglass; Gridley gave a respectful bow of his head, took the instrument and put it to his eye.

After several moments he lowered it. "It looks like a troop of very large savages, encased in peculiar-looking armor of some sort."

"How many can you see?"

"At least two dozen." He handed the spyglass back. "What are your orders?"

"I . . . " He thought for a moment. "Colonel, you must keep your men from engaging these things. But there may be something we can do. Find a few dozen of your strongest men, and gather up coils of rope, as many as you can find. We don't want to fight them—we want to knock them over."

The French troops were arrayed on an area of level terrain, well-trained and perfectly uniformed. As the natives began to charge from the woods, the Chevalier de Lévis took note of a formation above the treetops—five vaguely spherical objects that hovered and drifted forward. As they cleared the forest above the attacking natives, Lévis could see that each of the spheres had a toothy, twisted face, with eyes that glanced from place to place—right and left, out and down.

The chevalier knew what they were: Floating Heads, another abomination summoned from—wherever the native shamans were able to summon them. They were a fear weapon—something intended to frighten those that opposed the native army.

He raised his sword and pointed at the Floating Heads. Then, he gestured to the second ranks of the troops even as the front ranks prepared to receive the natives' charge. With uniform precision, a few hundred musketmen loaded ammunition, rammed it home, raised their muskets, aimed and fired. If their target had been an opposing force of infantry, it would have been expected that some would fall, just as those opponents would mow down some on one's own side.

Whether the Floating Heads were simply too far away, or the volley had simply been ineffective, when the smoke cleared the five spheres were untouched—and now, drawn by the French soldiers' volley, they were beginning to descend toward their position.

Amherst watched the battle develop from the command hill. Montcalm stood beside him, watching as the natives came to grips with his own troops. He had been briefed on the Floating Heads and wasn't surprised that the volley had done nothing to deter them.

"Lévis knew better," Montcalm said. "But he made sure that the men understood."

"Guyasuta is trying to frighten us."

"Clearly. And if we cannot stop these . . . things . . . he will succeed. Admirably."

The two commanders heard a noise behind them and turned. Further back on the hill, out of sight of the crest, the strange machine belonging to the two civilians was in operation. Amherst scowled, and waved to an aide.

"See what is happening with all that racket."

But as he watched, he noticed that a breeze had come up, beginning to dispel the fog that had gathered over the trees. The Floating Heads, which had begun to dive at the French lines, were beginning to twist and toss, as if they had lost their way.

Amherst's aide moved toward the sound, which was coming from some sort of unusual machine at the back of the hill. The young Frenchwoman who had arrived the previous day sat behind it, and the older Frenchman who accompanied her was bent over next to her holding some sort of black stone on a chain.

"The general presents his respects—" the young aide began, but the older man held his off hand up.

He said something in French to the woman, who nodded. Her hands moved across a keyboard spread out before her. Sweat beaded her forehead.

The aide had a strange feeling in the pit of his stomach that he could not identify. He could hear something far off, like the deep echo of a sound that wasn't quite there. He felt a breeze rush by him, though there was none present—the trees on the hill were not moving at all, and the early morning heat lay cloying and heavy.

"What—" he began.

The woman spoke in halting syllables. As he watched, the Frenchman's black stone, which had been swinging back and forth, began to incline forward and stopped, angled upward, pointed directly at him and beyond him downhill toward the battle.

"Tell the general that Mademoiselle LaGèndiere is attending to the problem," the Frenchman said, and gestured in dismissal. Almost involuntarily, the aide turned away to report to the general.

"Look," Skenadoa said to Joseph. "*Konearaunehneh*. They have called forth Floating Heads."

Joseph squinted at the trees; he could see the five horrid things, moving against what looked like a stiff breeze; thin, almost ethereal cords extended up from the earth to their bases.

"We need to cut their cords," Joseph said.

"Huh." Skenadoa scowled. "Not with your bare hands, young chief. But will a tomahawk slice through them, even if a warrior could see to cut them?"

"*I* can see," Joseph answered. "But no, I don't think so. It would need a special sort of tomahawk." He paused, and then he nodded. "Where is An-De-Le?"

"There is no guarantee that the tools of the Little People will work, but . . . they are closer to the Great Spirit. Still, it is a dangerous task."

"It may take some convincing."

"Oh, I know how to convince them, young chief. I will tell them that they are too weak and cowardly to do it."

Clear of the trees, it became apparent that the large figures were made of stone. Edward remembered the ones he had seen in western Pennsylvania colony, weeks earlier. These looked similar—perhaps a little smaller, but about the same number, about two dozen.

And we're simply out of Highlander ghosts, he thought.

But the resourceful colonials had produced a number of coils of stout ropes almost the width of his wrist: the sort of thing that would be found on the deck of a Royal Navy ship. It had taken some time for the Stone Coats to emerge from the trees and line up: perhaps they had not quite awoken from their sleep or were unused to the sunlight.

At his orders, the ropes were uncoiled and held at waist height at each end by several brave, stout colonials, across the most level paths the Stone Coats might take toward the army's position. He had directed them to drop the ropes and run if the creatures veered toward them. He wasn't about to have them give up their lives for no reason.

But they didn't turn; they continued to march—and as they came up against the ropes they strained to move forward, and three in the front rank actually toppled over as Edward had hoped they would. But the others continued in their progress, eventually tearing the ropes out of the hands of the men who held them. The three that had fallen simply got back on their feet and continued to advance.

Looking toward the Mohawk, Onondaga and Oneida warriors, Edward saw that they clearly had no intention of engaging the Stone Coats. He felt like cursing them for a lot of cowards, but his more rational side understood perfectly well that their Iroquois allies were simply better informed than he had been. They knew of no way to stop the monsters any more than he did—except that they'd known that from the start.

The French were ready with bayonets fixed, but the natives opposite seemed to be waiting for the monsters above to descend— they were unwilling to advance until the Floating Heads did so. But the things were not descending; it was as if they were unable to gain control of their movements.

While Lévis waited with his men, two natives came up to him. An older, dignified chief and a young man full of energy and light on his feet. And just behind he saw a group of the small warriors, with their hatchets drawn.

"You command here?" the older native said.

"I am the Chévalier de Lévis," he answered. "I act on behalf of the Marquis de Montcalm."

"We are here to deal with that," the man said, pointing toward the Floating Heads. "I am Skenadoa; this young chief is Joseph."

"The Little People are connected to the earth," Joseph said. "I can see where they are bound, and we are going to cut that connection."

"Surely the natives will not let you simply wander among them for this purpose," Lévis said.

"The connections are in the field in front of us," Joseph said. "But we will need you to protect us while we do this."

"Unless you are afraid of fighting," Skenadoa said, his voice level.

"You gain nothing by insulting my honor," Lévis said. "Unless that is the true reason you are here."

"It is not," Skenadoa said. "Perhaps later. In the meanwhile, Joseph and the Jo-Ge-Oh have work to do."

Without a further word, the young native and the tiny warriors dashed out ahead of the French troops. After scarcely a moment's hesitation, Lévis raised his sword and the French charged forward as well.

✢ ✢ ✢

Joseph remembered the first time he had seen a Floating Head, at Canajoharie when the Council Fire had been extinguished. He could see, when no one else could see, the long, sinuous string that descended from the creature to the ground. He saw them once again—but this time he had no intention of grasping it as he had before. His hands twinged where that action had burned them, and though there had been a great vision as the result of his foolhardy deed, he did not want, or need, to experience it again.

Instead, he drew back his bow and fired into the ground where the string came to earth. The Jo-Ge-Oh ran forward and cut through the air above where the arrow was located, and their tomahawks—no ordinary weapons, but rather what the whites might call *enchanted*—cut through the string, causing bright, scintillating light to stream forth. No one could see it but him—but everyone, the charging French infantry, the native warriors dashing forward to meet them, and the Jo-Ge-Oh moving from one grounded arrow to the next—could hear the hideous screams of pain from the Floating Head as it lost its contact with the earth and sped upward until it was out of sight.

Catherine LaGèndiere slumped over the keyboard of the concatenator for a moment, gasping for breath. Messier was at once by her side, solicitous and concerned.

"My dear girl—"

"No time," she said. "Someone has done something to the Floating Heads. Now . . . " her voice, which seemed to emerge from a parched throat, trailed off into silence.

"I will get you some water. But Catherine—you must conserve your strength."

She did not respond, but instead made some minute adjustments to the knobs above the main keyboard.

Edward watched as the Stone Coats continued to advance. He had heard the story of how they had attacked Fort Duquesne, tearing it apart until there was scarcely one stone lying atop another. He didn't know what would happen when they reached the Colonial lines.

"Perhaps we can knock them over," Gridley said. "Enough blows with axes or hammers—"

"And if they get hold of any of the men, they will tear them apart."

"What do you propose, then? That we retreat?"

"I—I don't know."

"There is no place to run, Your Highness. There are hundreds of us and fewer than twenty of them. If it takes a dozen of us to bring one of those monsters down, then that is a price we must pay."

"I cannot ask you to do that."

"You are not asking," Gridley said.

And then, as they watched, a most curious thing began to happen. As the remaining Stone Coats crossed the ground toward the Colonial lines, they began to slow down. The ground itself was becoming soft and muddy beneath their heavy bodies.

Gridley looked baffled by the sudden change. He squinted at the bright sky, which was completely absent of clouds. The heat of the day was coming on.

The Stone Coats' advance had become much slower, as they were already knee-deep, slogging slowly forward as the ground became more and more soft beneath them.

"I don't understand," Gridley said.

"I think I do," Edward answered, looking toward the hill where Amherst and Montcalm watched—and where, he knew, the Frenchwoman was operating her mysterious alchemetical concatenator. Whatever was happening, it had to be her doing.

In essence, she'd turned the formerly solid soil into quicksand. A normal human could not drown in quicksand; once they sank waist-deep their buoyancy held them up. What killed people so trapped was exposure. But the Stone Coats were much heavier and denser and Edward thought they would sink completely below the surface. He had no idea if that would kill them—were the Stone Coats alive at all?—but it would certainly immobilize them.

The main force of enemy natives began to rush from the tree cover now, charging at the British regulars deployed on the elevated ground below the hill. Another portion of them charged toward the Mohawks, Onondaga and Oneida warriors, who came forth to meet them.

The British troops knew not to waste volleys on them, but instead met them with bayonets and the butt ends of their muskets, fighting in fierce hand-to-hand combat against the fury of the enemy natives.

Occasionally, as the generals watched, one or another soldier would simply collapse, seemingly untouched by an attack—but near an elaborately-dressed native who held one hand outward.

"Those bastards are dangerous," Amherst said to Montcalm. "Wolfe knows what he's dealing with."

"What are they?"

"They call them Dry-Hands. I believe the native word is *Oniate*. Some of them have actually cut their hand off to have a sort of enchanted hand attached. Prince Edward was almost killed by one at the last battle."

"Your troops should shoot for the head."

"You have an elevated opinion of any soldier's ability to hit anything. Massed fire hits the largest targets, as you know. Trying to hit a few individual heads—waste of ordnance."

With the battle swirling around them, Joseph and the Jo-Ge-Oh rushed forward toward the place where further Floating Heads were anchored. The French regulars had been warned about the presence of the Little People, and they worked hard at protecting the little group as it made its way toward the tree line.

As they approached the next of the strings connecting a Floating Head to the ground, Joseph could feel tingling in his hands. It was almost as if he wanted to touch it again—but he tamped down the thought and gestured for the Jo-Ge-Oh to do their work.

As he hoped, the Little People's closer connection to the Great Spirit empowered them to attack the strings, even though they could not see them. But they, along with everyone else, could hear the screams of the monsters as their connection with the earth was severed. Joseph saw an effect that looked like the striking of steel and tinder—making him wonder what those things were made of, if it was any substance that he could understand.

As the French troops and their native allies charged forward, the enemy retreated. Cutting the Floating Heads off from the earth and destroying them frightened the Indian warriors—they may have thought the tide was turning. When the last string was cut, the Jo-Ge-Oh danced in a circle, whooping and shouting.

It may have been the noise they made that masked the sound of a single arrow whistling through the air from the retreating natives.

It caught in the throat of An-De-Le in mid-whoop. He fell onto his back, where he looked up toward the sky with an empty gaze and his hands spread wide.

For Joseph, it was as if time had suddenly stopped. He looked, astonished, along the straight line that the arrow had taken from its origin to the Jo-Ge-Oh chief. It was as if every obstacle along that path had vanished, and he could see a Seneca warrior, whose hand was still on his bow. With speed that he could not have expected, he drew his own bow, nocked an arrow, and shot back at the assailant.

When the arrow struck home, the weird timeless fugue ended as abruptly as it began, and the sounds of the battle returned with a rush. Joseph knelt beside the Jo-Ge-Oh chief whose eyes looked upward toward a sky he could no longer see.

Chapter 59

Words that no white man could understand

As the Stone Coats thrashed in the mud, now sinking rapidly, Edward saw that the natives beyond seemed to have no interest in trying to cross the treacherous ground to reach their colonial enemy. He looked across the battlefield. The French had charged forward toward the woods, while a large contingent of natives was surging toward the hill where Amherst and Montcalm stood.

And, he knew, where Mademoiselle LaGèndiere was operating her alchemetical device—the clear cause of the flat land turning to non-navigable mud.

As Edward watched, however, he saw a grey-brown cloud beginning to form over the advancing natives.

"What's going on?" Gridley asked.

"I don't know, Colonel," Edward answered. "But the battle is there, and we're going to join it." He waved his sword and spurred his horse into motion. His colonials followed after him.

Four *Oniate* remained among the native warriors. As the natives moved forward, the shamans stopped, turned, and began to walk toward each other. In the midst of the chaos of battle, the four men seemed to move, oblivious, as if controlled by some other agency. One of the four, in fact, was suddenly struck down by an errant swing of a native tomahawk; and he fell, lifeless, without even an outcry.

When the three remaining Dry-Hands met, each raised his enchanted hand so that they touched and grasped. From this, a coil of greyish-brown smoke began to rise, pooling sixty or seventy feet above the battle. The cloud began to grow larger and thicker, casting an ominous shadow.

Amherst stepped away from his vantage and walked quickly back toward where the Frenchwoman was operating her device. Messier saw him coming and stepped into his path.

"Something is happening above the battlefield," Amherst said. "Whatever the lady is doing, she should turn her attention to that."

"It occupies her attention already, General," Messier answered. "It is the one thing that concerns her."

"What is it?"

"I cannot say for sure," Messier said. "But it shows that the native shaman is becoming desperate."

"Explain."

"He has brought the three Dry-Hands together, and they are doing some sort of sorcery."

"What *sort* of sorcery?" Amherst asked impatiently.

"I am not sure, General. But it seems to be similar to something we saw previously when we were en route to New York. When Admiral Boscawen's ship was in Jamaica, the negro shamans did a working like this."

"What was its result?"

Messier shuddered. "The shamans . . . animated the dead."

"Preposterous."

"You dismiss things very easily, General. Look at the battlefield: there are summoned creatures drowning in mud; the Floating Heads have been severed from the earth and rendered powerless; and there are Dry-Hand shamans who were striking down your soldiers by simply *touching* them. If the Dry-Hands are being compelled to join their powers together, the native shaman is trying some great working that . . . feels . . . like the one we encountered in Jamaica."

"So they are trying to animate the dead," Amherst said.

"Or something worse."

"I can scarcely conceive of something worse than that."

Messier did not answer.

"What do you propose that we do about this?"

"Mademoiselle LaGèndiere is doing what she can. But in the

meanwhile—those Dry-Hands must be stopped from completing their working."

Edward dismounted before his troops reached the British regulars' position—a man on horseback was altogether too ready a target. Revere and a dozen others gathered around him as the colonials moved forward. He was still well back from the primary melee when he came up next to Wolfe, who was directing the advance of the regulars.

"Highness," Wolfe said. "I am surprised to see you here."

"Hopefully not disappointed."

"No, not at all. Do you know anything about that?" He nodded toward the growing cloud, now beginning to swirl in a disturbing spiral.

"No, but I don't like it."

Wolfe rolled his eyes very slightly, then seemed to think better of it. "The source appears to be over there—" he gestured ahead of him—"where there are three of the Dry-Hand scoundrels gathered together."

"Are they doing some sort of sorcery?"

"That is not my area of particular expertise, sir."

"Yes, I'm aware of that. I believe we should focus on disposing of them above all else."

"That seems prudent, Highness," Wolfe said. "Indeed, it is what the professional soldiers are attempting to do."

"My troops—"

"I think we have it well in hand," Wolfe interrupted. "I'm sure your colonials can find something to do."

Edward was ready to reply angrily, but instead looked aside to Richard Gridley.

"Colonel, pick two dozen of your best men, and take care of those Dry-Hand bastards."

"Yes, sir!" Gridley answered, and as Wolfe reddened, Gridley pointed to several of his men, who grasped their muskets like clubs and moved forward into the fray.

The cloud above the battle had begun to assume human form, with a great protruding head and wide-spread arms. Beams of greyish light sprung from the figure's fingertips, arcing downward toward the battlefield, and each time a beam struck a native warrior, his face went blank and he turned toward the hill, moving forward heedless of obstacles or attacks.

The beams of light struck more and more warriors; first a handful, then a few dozen, then—it seemed—every one of them. They fought with maniacal fury, continuing even after they were horribly wounded. They appeared to feel no pain.

As Gridley's men began to advance, Edward placed his hand on Paul Revere's sleeve.

"Stay here, sir," he said.

"Your Highness, I—"

"No one questions your bravery, Colonel. But your duty is to remain by my side as my aide, and to subdue your passions. You should entertain no doubt that there will be danger right here as well."

The colonials began to confront the blank-faced natives as soon as they advanced. At first it was unnerving; in hand-to-hand combat, pain and injury wasn't enough to drive the enemy back—it took the crushing of a native's skull to bring him down.

Gridley personally killed two natives before he was wounded in his off arm by a giant of a man who slashed him with a tomahawk more than half the length of his own musket. For just a moment Gridley thought he had met his end, but the huge native was felled from behind by his subaltern.

To the end of his days, Richard Gridley remembered the look of triumph on the young man's face—which was still there when another native's axe struck him in the back, dropping him to the ground and out of sight.

The three shamans were in view now, twenty feet away. Their twisted hands were extended in the air, touching at the edges. The stream of dark smoke came from the area in between.

"Cover me, boys," Gridley said, loading his musket. "I'm going to see if I can get a clear shot."

Eight of his remaining nineteen colonials formed a ring around him as he placed the ball, rammed it home, and raised the weapon.

He could feel the slash in his arm and knew he couldn't hold it for long.

He took aim at the three hands held in the air and fired—and as he did, one of the hollow-eyed natives in the intervening space raised his hand and blocked the shot, his own hand taking its full impact, blood and bone spattering.

Gridley cursed, pulled out another shot and rammed it home, and again took aim. Once more, as soon as he fired, one of the natives raised his hand and uncannily intercepted the shot.

"Damn it! First squad, load and fire!" He called to the men close by, who, protected by the men nearest them, performed the manual at arms: loading powder, ramming home a musket-ball, raising their weapons and firing. Of the ten, two were cut down as they prepared to fire, but the other eight managed to get off a shot . . .

Six hands were raised as the muskets fired. Four of them were struck by the shots. One shot went awry, and the eighth jammed in the muzzle. Two other hands narrowly missed the attempt to intercept, and the balls struck: one hit one of the shamans in the back of the shoulder, and the other was dead on target, shattering one of the hideous hands and disappearing into the black pool within.

The three shamans collapsed, the one who was struck first, and the other two atop him. The source of the cloud dissipated, but the column leading up to it withdrew into the sky. The human-shaped figure above bellowed with an unearthly cry, speaking words that no white man could understand.

On the hill, Catherine LaGèndiere screamed as well. Her hands were half-clenched as she continued to work the concatenator, but her eyes were wide, and she was drenched in sweat. Amherst, who had not returned to his viewing position, pushed past Messier to stand before her.

"What—"

"Do not distract her," Messier said, placing his hand on Amherst's shoulder. The general whirled, grabbing hold of the Frenchman's arm.

"You dare to lay a hand on me?"

"Monsieur General. If you wish to give me some sort of—what would you call it?—a *thrashing*, then proceed. But if you interrupt her at this moment, it will mean the destruction of everything."

"*What is she doing?*"

"At this moment," Messier said, shrugging his sleeve loose from Amherst's grasp, "she is trying to dissipate *that*." He pointed to the great human figure hovering above the battle. "It is an elemental spirit of the air—indeed, I think it is *the* elemental spirit of the air. Our only chance to dismiss what the shamans have summoned is for that brave young woman to do what God has placed her on this continent to do."

The hollow-eyed natives fought their way forward, opposed fiercely by both colonials and regulars, and, a bit to the side, the Iroquois allies. The white soldiers had the upper hand in organized discipline, but the natives were relentless, feeling no pain, their eyes unfocused and seemingly blind. Formation and organization had largely vanished—but it wasn't every man for himself; the regulars worked with those to their left and right, while the colonials worked in teams of three and four, like hunters of wild animals. The Mohawks, Oneidas and Onondagas did the same.

The terrible cloud above the battle continued to reach tendrils to the natives that remained on the battlefield. Many had fled after the three *Oniate* were struck down. The natives who had been beyond the quagmire that had swallowed the Stone Coats had retreated, while others were still fighting furiously with the French.

Edward and his bodyguard fought their way to the top of the slope; Wolfe was still somewhere below in the melee.

"Highness," Amherst said, as Edward reached him. "You have proven your valor. You must retire for your own safety."

"Are we out of danger?"

"It does not seem so."

"Then with respect I am obliged by my oath of duty to decline your order."

"We will deal with the matter of insubordination later," Amherst said. "If we live long enough."

"Agreed. How fares Mademoiselle LaGèndiere?"

"She appears to be sorely tried. I do not understand what burden she carries—but I have been told that it is her success or failure that determines our own success or failure. Nothing else matters."

"Keeping these monsters away from her matters."

"Agreed. I ask that you stay close to her. You may yet have a chance to strike a decisive blow."

Edward thought of protesting, but reasoned that if the natives reached the place where Mademoiselle LaGèndiere was doing—whatever it was that she was doing—it would be as dangerous a place as any.

"Sir." He sketched a salute and beckoned to his bodyguard.

Joseph laid the body of An-De-Le gently on a cot within a French tent. He had carried it from out of the melee, with the other Little People around him. In addition to that struggle, there was an even more disorganized fight going on near the base of the command hill, overshadowed by a terrible cloud that he found he could not look at directly.

The remaining Jo-Ge-Oh gathered around the body of their leader, murmuring.

"We will curse the Seneca," one of them said at last. "They will pay for what they have done."

"No," Joseph said. "An-De-Le was slain in battle."

"By an arrow fired by a coward. Why should this matter?"

"An-De-Le knew that our work was dangerous, we all faced that peril and chose it voluntarily. He was killed in battle—whether by a tomahawk or an arrow, it doesn't matter. It would be unfair for the Jo-Ge-Oh to curse the people we face, especially since the one who slew An-De-Le was killed in turn."

"Who will cover the grave of An-De-Le?" The Jo-Ge-Oh was asking a critical question: who, in fact, would compensate the family of the dead. Wars had been fought over this.

"I will," Joseph said. "I take the burden on myself."

"It is not your burden."

"I *make* it my burden," Joseph said. "Take care of your leader, Little Brothers."

He brushed past them and out of the tent.

When he emerged, he looked up at the cloud that had formed over the nearby battlefield. But his sight gave him a different view than anyone else.

Instead of a cloud, Joseph saw the form of a many-handed giant. It was no longer connected to the earth—it was instead tied to the winds, and one of the four was beginning to gather: Ya-o-gah, the North Wind, the spirit of the bear. If that spirit was able to come through and manifest, everything below would be swept away and destroyed. But something was holding it back—something was preventing it from concentrating.

Without hesitation, he ran toward the hill where his enemies were fighting their way up the slope.

Chapter 60

There is no need for challenge

"They cannot see," Messier said. "They do not feel. There is nothing to do but to kill them. But, your Highness, they are not the problem. *That* is."

He pointed to the swirling, twisting cloud above the hill.

"What must I do?"

"Let her continue to operate the machine," Messier said. "It is all that is preventing them from—"

Whatever it was that the Frenchman wanted to say was stopped by a sudden rush of air sweeping toward them, as if the cloud was descending, swirling and squirming like a live thing.

Edward said something under his breath that might have been a prayer or a curse. He raised his musket and aimed it at the center of the cloud, not sure whether it would have any effect—but it was better than just standing there waiting for something to happen.

Is this where I die? he wondered, and then dismissed the thought angrily. He sighted along the line of the musket. Everyone around him was scattering, though to his surprise, Messier remained by his side, unarmed, looking directly at the phenomenon that was growing closer and closer.

Then, when it seemed as if all the sound had suddenly been drawn out of the world, a figure appeared before them. On the slopes of the hills and beyond, everywhere Edward could see except for where Montcalm and Amherst stood and where a young native was scrambling up the hill, everything had stopped; the noise, the movement, the wind.

The figure was a native; a middle-aged man draped in a colorful blanket. His eyes were black and pupilless.

"Red Vest," Montcalm said, walking back toward the native.

"You know this man?" Edward said.

"Yes, Highness. He serves—"

"I serve the *Ciinkwia*," the native said. He gestured over his shoulder at the place where the storm had been. Instead there were two figures hovering in the air—a native man and woman, both very tall. The woman held a staff shaped like a sheaf of wheat; the man had a bow over his shoulder and held a tomahawk.

Montcalm looked at the two figures and crossed himself, his hand shaking as he did so. It was the first time Edward had ever seen the Marquis show the least sign of fear.

"What do you want?" Edward managed to say.

"This is not natural," Red Vest answered. "None of this is a part of the world of the Great Spirit."

"I don't disagree," Edward said. "I am—"

"Your aura says who you are," Red Vest said. "The *Ciinkwia* do not believe that the Great Spirit intended for *Gă-oh* to be summoned at this time, in this place. It is not the place of Sganyodaiyo to do this."

"Yet he has done it."

"What has been done will be undone, although by what hands and what means remains unclear," Red Vest answered. "But you will not be driven from this world, Prince. Not because of what you have done, but because of what you have not done."

"What have I not done?"

"Many of your fellow whites believe that there is no place for the red man in the world, all of the world that there is. It is not what you believe—and they know this is true. But they—" he gestured away, down the hill—"must learn to believe the same."

"You told us that we could only go so far, and no farther," Montcalm said. "The *Ciinkwia* told us that they only became stronger. We broke our word and would break it again in the future. Now they come and speak of peace?"

"You spurn them."

"We do not," Edward said. "We wish to understand them. In every case where the—servants of the Great Spirit—have appeared to us, they have always been hostile. Since the coming of the comet, the powers of this land have awoken and made their presence known. Never have they made any indication that they want peace."

"They were in the service of one who violated the commands of the Great Spirit. The spirit of the winds would destroy all—red and white."

"From what I am told," Edward said, "there are more of the— servants—than the shaman out there has called forth. He did not call forth the *Obeah*-men on San Domingue. He did not make the Place of Bone. He did not drive the men in Massachusetts-Bay to madness from the ghosts of their past. It was not Sganyodaiyo who gathered the spirits of the dead Highlanders around Fort Carillon. There is more to this than the work of one misguided shaman.

"Tell me, Red Vest. Or have the *Ciinkwia* tell me. What will they do to make peace between the red man and the white man, or the black man and the white man, or any race and any other race? They send this *Gă-oh* spirit away, but what next?"

"You are brave to speak thus to gods," Red Vest answered, turning his head slightly to the side as if he was hearing a voice.

"You accord them the title of gods," Edward said. "I respect their power, but my God is different."

"Your cross-god has no power here."

I have nothing to lose, Edward thought. "Ask them if they are completely sure of that."

"You challenge them?"

"We must learn to live together. There is no need for challenge— merely mutual recognition."

"Or—"

"Or this war, or something like it, will *never end*. Graves will be left uncovered, deaths unavenged, the earth itself ravaged by angry men fighting for their lives. Is that what they want, your gods? Is that what the Great Spirit wants? Because it is not what I want. If I am to be king—and it seems that I am—I would want peace. I promise by my God, and by my honor, that those who revere the *Ciinkwia* shall receive justice by my hands, and honor in my dealings. I swear that for myself and my successors."

"Your promises—"

"Are henceforth binding," Edward said. "They can accept that or not. But I have made this promise and I will stand by it."

Red Vest turned away from the prince and looked up at the shining figures of the man and woman. After a moment they each nodded.

"The *Ciinkwia* accept," Red Vest said. "It is done."

As they watched, the two figures—who had completely obscured the cloud—raised their hands as one, and the unseeing, unfeeling natives who had been tied to the phenomenon rose limply in the air, vanishing into the glow that the two deities projected.

"Their essences had been taken by the *Oniate*," Red Vest said. "The *Ciinkwia* cannot restore them to their former state, but can give them new life in the world of the Great Spirit."

Edward nodded, inclining his head.

When all of the natives had been drawn into the light, Red Vest disappeared along with the two great figures. A soft, gentle breeze, fragrant as a summer meadow, wafted across in their wake.

Catherine awoke from a troubled sleep to find herself resting on a comfortable cot. Light was streaming into the tent where she lay, and a native woman sat beside her bed smoking a clay pipe.

"What . . . "

"Calm yourself, white sister," the native said. "The battle is over."

"We must have been victorious."

"You mean—" She took the pipe out of her mouth, looked at it, and tapped it against the side of the stool on which she sat. "You mean did the warriors drive the enemy from the field? No, it ended a different way. But the monsters were defeated, and the betrayer is gone."

Catherine relaxed her shoulders. She wasn't sure what she was being told, but it seemed to be good news.

"How do you feel?"

"Drained."

"You were passed out over your medicine-maker. Whatever you were doing, it hurt the monsters. But it hurt you as well."

"Am I wounded?"

"Not in the body that I can see."

"I—" She sat up, and then immediately thought better of it. Every muscle in her arms, her shoulders, and her chest was sore. She let herself fall back. "Maybe in the body as well. What happened, then?"

"*Ciinkwia* came to the battlefield and stopped the *Oniate* from summoning the spirits of the wind. They called it abomination and would not permit it."

"Who—or what—is *Ciinkwia*?"

"They are the spirits of thunder and storm, in service to the Great Spirit. They came unbidden and took the unseeing warriors who had been bewitched by the *Oniate*."

"I felt the *Oniate*. Those are the Dry-Hands, yes?"

"Yes." The native woman shuddered. "They are no more. They were consumed by their working. But they summoned the winds to tear the land apart, and that was brought to an end."

"By spirits."

"By spirits," the woman agreed. "Do you find this so hard to believe?"

"After what I have already seen, no. I can accept all of it. I . . . Your pardon, Madame. I do not even know your name."

"I am Osha," she said. "Clan-mother. I came with our warriors. When you were taken from the battlefield, I took charge of you and made sure you were cared for. People are waiting for you to awaken."

"Professor Messier?"

"Yes, he waits," Osha said. "But also there is another."

"Another?"

"What you call a prince, I think," she said. "He asked to be told as soon as you woke."

"I—" She looked down at herself, at the thin sheet that covered her. She was unlaced and unpinned, and her hair was loose about her shoulders. In short, she was in no way ready to receive Dr. Messier, much less a prince of any kind. "No, no, that would be . . . "

"He does not care about any of that, white sister. He has talked of nothing but you since you were carried here."

Catherine stared at the native woman, not sure what to say.

"I will bring him," Osha said, rising and walking toward the flap of the tent. Before Catherine could say a word, she was out of sight.

Regardless of soreness, she decided that she would *not* be receiving anyone completely supine. With some effort she maneuvered herself to a sitting position and made an effort to arrange herself as modestly as possible. There was nothing to be done for her hair; she brushed a few stray wisps from her face, but had no cap or pinner to keep it in place.

A few moments later, Osha returned with Prince Edward behind. He had his hat in his hand and looked disheveled—just come from a battle, not from his dressing-table.

"Your Highness," Catherine said. "Forgive me for not rising."

"Mademoiselle," Edward answered. "Please don't trouble yourself. I have been beside myself with worry. All of us have been."

"All . . . I beg your pardon, Monsieur. I do not know what I have done to cause such trouble."

"From what Doctor Messier tells me, it is what you have done that has saved us from the horrors the enemy had in store. You are a heroine, Mademoiselle. There is no doubt of it."

"I do not feel like a heroine. I feel—"

Edward stood, holding his hat in his hands before him. He looked embarrassed, unsure of himself.

"When I saw you at work, Mademoiselle, I . . . felt something. I cannot readily describe it. Protecting you was my duty, but being near you became the most important thing in the world to me. When you collapsed, I was heartsick. I have been waiting outside for word that you had come to yourself."

"Waiting outside—you mean, outside this tent?"

Osha, now standing behind the prince, smiled and nodded.

"I have been waiting since you were brought here." He glanced over his shoulder at the tent-flap; it was obvious that it was late afternoon. "I would have waited all night."

"Surely Your Highness has many other more important things to do."

"Surely I did not. Even General Amherst did not seek to summon me from my post."

"I do not know how to respond to this. I am . . . do you; I mean to say, are you—are you *courting* me?"

"I suppose I am, after a fashion." His expression was startled, as if he had just come to a realization. "Yes . . . " He smiled, then. "Yes. I think I can say that I am."

"This is not seemly, Highness. You are—and I am—"

"Yes?"

"You are a prince of the blood."

"Remarkably," Edward said, "I seem to be the *only* prince of the blood. And there is no court protocol officer; there are no members of Parliament to give or withdraw their assent. There is no one to tell me to whom I may pay court. Well," he added, smiling, "there is one person: you."

Catherine felt herself reddening and looked away. She did not answer.

"I have offended you."

"No, not in the least," she said, looking back at the prince. "I don't know what to think. I want to tell you that your affection is misplaced . . . but your point is well taken. The world has changed and the rules, perhaps, have changed. But there is something else you must know."

"And what is that?"

"It is not for all ears. Please approach."

"I do not wish to offend your modesty—"

She beckoned to him. He came close, and at a gesture he bent close to her, and she whispered in his ear. As she spoke, his eyes grew wide.

He stood up straight.

"Truly?"

"Upon my life, it is true."

"Who knows this?"

"Monsieur Messier, myself—and now you. And I think it would be inappropriate for others to know at this time."

"I . . . agree. I shall hold it in strictest confidence."

Chapter 61

New sensations

The open space where the Stone Coats had been drowned was hard packed dirt now, with no sign of the monstrous creatures summoned by the native shaman. But Joseph, as he walked slowly across it, could see them, frozen, trapped many feet below the surface. They had not moved since the mud had engulfed them. The Stone Coats had not even been able to thrash about much—they appeared almost in formation, below the ground to the height of two men.

Joseph was not sure which disturbed him more—that people were walking across the space where the Stone Coats had been, untroubled, or that he could see them and was.

His fellow natives, especially the Mohawk warriors, kept their distance as he walked slowly around the area. His sight was well known, and he had earned their respect.

The Jo-Ge-Oh, however, had a different notion of propriety. As he stood there in the evening shadows, a group of the Little People approached and stood before him.

"We sit and speak the words for An-De-Le," one of them said. "We want you to sit with us."

"I would not want to intrude."

"When he took his last breath, you were there. You should be there now, to aid his soul in rising to its celestial home."

"I worry that his soul is angry at me for letting him be slain."

"You said it yourself," the Jo-Ge-Oh said. "He knew the risks and accepted them. He lived and died a warrior. You should be there," he repeated.

"I will come."

"I have already sent Major Rogers and a dozen of his best men to scout," Amherst said.

Montcalm attempted to keep his expression passive. Robert Rogers was a French *bête noire*, and Amherst likely knew it; there was no love lost between the ranger leader and the *habitants*. But Rogers was acting in their joint interest now, and there was no doubt of his skill.

"As soon as possible, we should prepare our forces to move west. Controlling this battlefield means nothing."

"Where do you suggest we go?"

"My first thought was Fort Johnson. But better, I think, we should go to the Council Fire."

"Why?"

"We are allies now," Montcalm said. "This battle has ended our war. We have a king in waiting, who has made us a promise: that he will receive his crown from the archbishop of Québec. If the service is performed at a place important to the natives we also call allies, then he binds all three peoples to him."

"Surely the Lord Almighty is everywhere."

"It is a matter of symbolism, *Mon General*, as I am sure you realize. We have only a short time to make this relationship fast."

"What about . . . the young woman? Do you want to wait for her to recover as well, or shall we restrict this to a strictly military operation?"

"What do you think?"

"I want to be skeptical. But after what we saw . . . "

"The Indian spirits? More evidence that the world has changed. That young woman helped defeat the monsters. We need her—she should be ready to move as well."

"You know," Amherst said, "that Prince Edward has taken a great interest in her welfare."

"I'm not surprised. His last duty on the battlefield was defending her and her machine. Like all of us, he saw the native spirits appear and do—what they did—and he carried her off the field. But we shall see if he conducts himself as a prince, or just as a young man."

"I would not blame him in either case."

✣ ✣ ✣

They attended to their dead. The British regulars organized details to search the battlefield to find bodies and bring them back to a central location away from where the fighting had taken place. They made no distinction between British soldiers, Colonials, French or natives; Father Jean-Félix Récher was waiting there to help organize and arrange the fallen. The work was done in relative silence. The British soldiers made no comments about Catholic priests, and Récher was carefully courteous to the Mohawk, Onondaga and Oneida shamans who took charge of the natives.

Putting an army in motion, especially one with many disparate pieces, is no easy task. It is not so much the ability of troops to form up and march; that was perhaps the most trivial part, as soldiers, even militiamen, were accustomed to doing that. It came down to the support systems: how the troops were fed and sheltered, the organization of the supply train, the support and noncombat personnel, the shovels and tent poles and bandages, the bandoliers and anvils and cobblers' tools that went with every army. Picking it all up and moving it, even if there was no opposition, was a significant task.

But the need was great. What remained of the enemy force was somewhere to the west. It might be ready to make a stand, and the men who had just fought it, and its unimaginable monsters, were not interested in giving it any time to regroup. Eighteen hours after the native spirits brought the battle to an end, the army was ready to move.

Johnson Hall

She felt it, of course. But Fourth Sparrow had already come up to the house, as if she had felt it even before it had happened. The little one was early; there might have been another moon, and that might have been better given the uncertainty about Guyasuta and Sganyodaiyo and all they had brought—but the Great Spirit had settled matters and the child was coming.

Molly had never given birth, but at Canajoharie she had helped many times and knew what to expect. Even the pain—it was the spirit of the new child descending into her womb, waking from its comfortable sleep, waiting to emerge into this changed world.

As the contractions began to come, she began to sense her consciousness stretching out to the boundaries of the Hall, to the low stone wall that defended the many people who had found refuge there. What would happen when the birth began? Would she lose her hold on that protection? There was no way to know.

"Concentrate on the child, Degonwadonti, sweet Konwatsi'-tsiaienni," Fourth Sparrow said, as she strained and sweated.

"People are in danger . . . "

"Let others worry about that, little sister."

"But the boundary—"

"*Others*," the old woman interrupted. "Others will worry. You are giving life."

She closed her eyes—

And suddenly, as if she had been thrust from her body, she felt herself hovering in the air, high enough that she could see all the lands around her. From her ethereal body outward she could see a circle of light that bathed the main house, the hill on which it stood, and the circular wall of stone that surrounded it down below. Campfires and tents were scattered around, and within were small glowing patches that she recognized as the many brothers and sisters who had come to Johnson Hall for protection against the darkness that she could sense beyond the edge of the light she projected.

But the darkness had retreated. What had seemed oppressive and frightening—what had terrified her for months, at least since William had ridden away into that darkness and disappeared from her sight— seemed to have suffered a setback, a reduction. Could some great shaman have stopped their advance?

She looked down at her body on the bed. It lay quiet and still, seemingly at peace.

But she could feel the child within her—a son: she was sure of it—a baby boy. Her ethereal form was transparent, and the child was looking up to her, affectionate and anticipating the beginning of his life. Yet this glorious vision, this bodiless existence, was without pain and without constraint. This wonder was something she did not want to let go.

Fourth Sparrow was running her hands over Molly's unmoving physical body below. The delicate cord that connected it to her transparent, hovering form seemed to be fraying. She wanted to remain here forever, all-seeing and painless—

No.

It was a world of pain, a place of normal and mundane sensations . . . but it was life, with all its boundaries and limitations, the existence that the Great Spirit had given to every man and woman. This new world was the same as the old, but there were new sensations and visions.

If this other place, this other existence, was reachable, it could be reached again. With enormous regret, she allowed herself to descend back into her physical body—and with one final push—

Moments passed.

Moments passed, and with a surge of pain, she felt her son emerge from her body and be taken up by Fourth Sparrow and two other women who had come to join her. She looked up through her own eyes and saw the fear in the old woman's eyes retreat. She could hear the first cries from her son, and then her consciousness drifted away.

She woke up to the smells and sounds of an evening meal being prepared outside. She felt as if every muscle in her body had been strained, but now was relaxed; yet she felt more at peace than she had been for months. As soon as she was awake, she saw Fourth Sparrow—who might well have been there for the entire time. The old wise woman picked up her son from his cradle and handed him to her. She reached for him and placed him so he could feed, but before the infant settled to the task he looked directly at Molly and held her gaze for several seconds. It was a disturbingly knowing gaze for a baby only a few hours old, something she would remember for many years to come.

"He will see far, Degonwadonti," Fourth Sparrow said. "And he will be a great chief."

"He will have his chance," Molly said, and guided her son to her breast.

Colony of New York

He would not tell them that he understood their fear, or that he felt fear himself. But nothing he could say or do would prevent them from leaving. They had been on the warpaths since spring; they had followed him and believed in him—and in Sganyodaiyo and his power over the spirits. Something had interfered with his last and greatest summoning, one that had scared Guyasuta himself—the *Gâ-oh*, the spirits of the four winds. It wasn't clear what he had been trying to do—the spirits of the winds were fickle and unpredictable.

The cost of that last summoning—the loss of the remaining Dry-Hands and ten hands of warriors, now summoned to the spirit lands by *Ciinkwia*—was the deciding factor. Whatever loyalty they felt for the cause had melted away.

As for Sganyodaiyo—he was gone, not in his tent, not among the warriors that remained. He might have left on his own, except that the mare he had ridden remained in the camp. If Sganyodaiyo had gone, he had gone on foot.

Guyasuta did not know what to feel and did not know what might await him back in Logstown. For a spring and summer, he had made the whites feel real fear, and had commanded the loyalty of many warriors who felt the same anger and resentment.

Uncertainty and insecurity were not sensations he enjoyed. But he told himself, this was simply a setback—a pause before the next steps in a campaign to remove the whites from the lands of the Great Spirit. It would come to pass: not this season, but another.

Chapter 62

We must learn to live together

Colony of New York

It had been nearly twenty years since Henri-Marie Dubreil de Pontbriand, Archbishop of Québec, had come to the New World aboard *Rubis*. It was a trip he would rather forget. Tossed on the waves of the Atlantic, he had been sick most of the way and praying to the Lord Almighty for his life to be spared in nearly every waking hour. When the ship finally reached calm waters in the Gulf of Saint Lawrence, he had held a thanksgiving Mass that had been more heartfelt and more moving than any mass he had performed in Paris, or Saint-Malo, or anywhere else. His arrival in his own see could not have been less auspicious.

But that had been two decades and two wars ago. He flattered himself to think that the land, and the Church, had prospered in that time. There had not been much progress in bringing the light of the True Faith to the *Anglais*, but he believed that there would be plenty of time for that.

The last few months had been trying. Récher had told him of what he had seen upriver, and there were other tidings—troubling ones—from all over. And now, it seemed, they were on their own. No word from the king, or from the Holy Father. He didn't know what that could mean. The sacred Word had not changed, the message of the Gospel had not changed, but the rest of the world seemingly had.

As if he had needed any confirmation of the nature of the *terra incognita* the world had become, a courier had come to Québec bearing a letter written on fine parchment, with a wax seal embedded with a royal signet.

By the royal command of Prince Edward Augustus, it read, *your presence is requested for the consecration and confirmation of His Royal Highness as King of North America.*

There had been another letter from the Marquis de Montcalm explaining that as the senior clergyman on the continent, the archbishop would be called upon to place a crown on the head of an Englishman—and in return the French, at least the *habitants* of New France, would acknowledge him as king. There were no other kings available; the world had been sundered, and there were people and forces that wanted to destroy Christian civilization on the continent.

What was more—if there needed to be any more!—this coronation would take place at the center of the native confederation—the Onondaga place they called the Council Fire. In this way, French and English and even some of the natives, would be bound together in a new confederation. Royal dignity would be reposed in the body of a young English prince of the blood. And Montcalm's letter, as polite and deferential as it had been, made it clear that this was not a request—it was a settled *arrangement*, in which Pontbriand would be expected to play his part.

With all the dignity and ceremony he could muster, Pontbriand directed his vicar-general, Jean-Olivier de Briand, to prepare his household for a trip into the heart of darkness; native land surrounded by English land. He could have demanded that all parties come to him—but it was clearly not part of the *arrangement*.

It took a full week for the archbishop's entourage to travel the distance from Québec to Onondaga. Pontbriand thought it might take longer but the paths through the forest seemed unusually clear for his mounted party, as if some effort had been made to move debris out of the way. They were straighter and more direct than he had expected them to be. Even the weather seemed to be cooperating.

A few days from Québec an honor guard met up with the episcopal party, led by the young officer, Olivier D'Egremont. They were attired in their best uniforms, and though Pontbriand had felt himself adequately escorted, he was relieved when the officer and his six guards joined the southward-moving party.

D'Egremont dismounted and kissed the archbishop's ring, then returned to his horse. Pontbriand gestured for the young man to ride alongside him.

"Tell me, my son. Have you met the prince?"

"Oh, yes, Your Grace. He is . . . an impressive man."

"For an Englishman."

"I didn't say that," D'Egremont answered. "And I'm not sure that distinction means anything anymore, Your Grace. When we fought the natives, he was as brave as anyone on the field."

"Is he strong in the faith?"

"He is not a part of Mother Church, of course, nor has he indicated that he would convert."

"So he does not intend to accept it. I'm curious why he was eager to have me crown him."

"He made the offer to Montcalm, because he wanted to honor our people."

"There is no clergyman of comparable rank in the English plantations."

"While that is true, Your Grace . . . I think he made the gesture consciously and intentionally."

"Even though I am a Frenchman." Pontbriand was silent for a few moments, looking down at his hands holding the reins of his horse as they rode along. "I still find that curious."

"I should like to speak freely, if I may."

"Of course, my son. You may say whatever you need to say."

"The world has fundamentally changed. Whatever distinction existed between Frenchman and Englishman is gone now; we are one people or shall be in due time. Language and—perhaps—even color may cease to be matters of distinction, and we must learn to live together."

"Our loyalty—"

"Is to each other, Your Grace."

"My loyalty is to the Holy Father in Rome, my son."

"If the events of comet-fall are permanent, Your Grace, the Holy Father and Rome itself are forever inaccessible to us. As far as the Holy Church is concerned, Monsieur, you are the head of it; and it will be up to you to decide what that means, and what you will do with the authority that God has invested in you. Indeed, if I may say so—and you might be offended, but I must say it—your loyalty is to your flock."

"I am not accustomed to being lectured by a young—"

He paused, and D'Egremont waited to see how the archbishop would finish the sentence.

"—lay person. You presume much, my son."

"I do, Your Grace."

It was not the response that Pontbriand had expected: polite, but direct and not the least bit humble.

"I shall have to take the matter under advisement."

"I would be disappointed, Your Grace, if you did not."

Onondaga Council Fire

The troops were accommodated some distance from the Onondaga village. Skenadoa took charge of the encampment, making sure that the troops did not completely ravage the countryside—an almost impossible task, but neither General Amherst nor the Marquis de Montcalm had any intention of coming west without their armies. Guyasuta was still at large, and still a threat.

Amherst elected to remain with his command, and detailed General Wolfe to accompany Montcalm into the village, several hundred yards from the encampment. Wolfe appeared to want to object but thought better of it.

"I have been thinking about all of this," Montcalm said as they made their way into Onondaga village.

"I think about it all the time."

"Really."

"Truly," Wolfe said. "Six months ago, when the comet fell, I was on the way to New France to finish what we'd started a year ago."

"You mean the vain attempt to conquer New France."

"Vain!" Wolfe laughed, an annoying habit that set Montcalm's teeth on edge. "For every Frenchman in the New World, there are ten Englishmen. How did you expect this to turn out?"

"Do you know the problem with you English?"

"Tell me," Wolfe said. "I can scarcely contain my excitement."

"English and French colonists, and dissidents, and troops have been on this continent for nearly two hundred years. In all those years the great numbers of English have never managed to conquer the small numbers of French. Wars and campaigns and Indian wars, religious strife—all of it, and we're still here, and you are still here as well. What makes you think that 1759 would have been any different?"

"Because 1758 was different, Marquis. We were winning in 1758. We took Louisbourg. We had everything ready for the next campaign—"

"Until the comet fell."

"Your point?"

"My point? My point, Wolfe, is this: *until the comet fell* is exactly the point. There was a 1759 campaign coming—and if what I heard is true, you and the troops you commanded, and the troops Amherst commanded, were ready to do what you claimed: conquer New France. At some point you might have even drawn us out to battle. Who can say? Perhaps we would both have died."

"That seems vanishingly unlikely. A battle where both commanders die? Who could even conceive of that?"

"I have a vivid imagination," Montcalm said. "But it is not a world that exists. We are, remarkably, no longer at war. There was no great battle. We are alive."

"Indeed, we are." They stopped walking. Wolfe looked around the clearing. Ahead of them was a great native house, with doors at each end. "And we are here. For better or worse."

"You don't like the idea."

"I do not understand why this ceremony is not taking place in Québec, or Albany, or New York. Why does it have to happen *here*?"

"I believe that Monsieur le Prince feels that this ceremony should involve the natives. As we are seeking to bind together so that your people and my people are united, he feels that those of the Iroquois who did not follow Guyasuta and his shaman should be included as well, if they so choose."

"Will they consider His Highness their king?"

"I don't know."

"My dear Marquis, if they do not consider Prince Edward their king, then they are intruders on this ceremony. Or, to put a finer point on it, our ceremony intrudes on *them*. It should not be here. We should not be here."

"You dismiss this so easily, General Wolfe. You resent that you never had the chance to try and conquer New France. You are disdainful of the people your prince—*your prince!*—is willing to take by the hand. And you find no place for the natives.

"What do you want, Monsieur? What is the world you would rather live in? The one where you conquer New France? The one where you and I might die in battle? How is that a better world than this?"

"This is a 'better world'? Where London and Paris and all the rest of the world is gone? This is not what I expected when we came across the Atlantic."

Montcalm stared at Wolfe, and after a moment he began to laugh. It was not simply a snicker—it was a full-throated laugh, erupting from his chest and his throat and shaking his shoulders.

"Marquis?"

Montcalm continued to laugh, holding his hand out and looking away from Wolfe, who was reddening as he did so.

"Monsieur *Marquis*," Wolfe said assertively.

"*Pardon*," Montcalm said, finally composing himself. "I'm sorry, General. I could not help myself."

"You will give me the courtesy of an explanation."

"General Wolfe, this world—the world we have—is what you must come to terms with. You did not expect this? Who *could* have expected this? A world with stone soldiers and one-handed shamans and, Blessed Mother of God, native divinities who intervene and stop a battle? A world in which French and English fight together? We are not mortal enemies, General. In another world we might well have been. But not in this world.

"Within a few days, the head of my Church will place a crown on the prince of your country, and he will be my king as well, so long as he gives assurances that my Church and your—varieties of faith— can live in harmony. This is the world we have. You must accept that or go mad. And you must cease troubling yourself about what you *expected* or what you *might have done*. You must stop, or I shall die of laughter."

✦ ✦ ✦

In due course a pavilion was erected in the clearing, bearing the flags of both Great Britain and France at the same height. To it, an escort of British regulars in dress uniform led Prince Edward, unarmed and on foot with bare head, from the encampment. Revere walked behind him, carrying his hat and sword. He was met at the entry by Montcalm, Wolfe and the *Tadodaho* of the Iroquois; the two European generals offered formal salutes, and the native, without a word, presented the prince with a length of woven shells the width of two hands, two feet in length. Edward accepted the gift with a bow, and then entered the pavilion. Wolfe and Montcalm exchanged glances, and then Wolfe followed the prince inside.

Edward's pavilion was spacious and already well appointed; he handed the gift to a subaltern and stripped off his gloves, handing them to Revere, then settled onto a stool.

"The chief made a great ceremony of that," he said, gesturing toward the gift.

"It is called *wampum*, Your Highness. They do you honor by presenting it to you—a demonstration of wealth, I believe."

"Shells?"

"Their currency. I am told that the purple ones are particularly valuable."

"What should I do with it? Display it somewhere?"

"It is intended to be worn, I believe. The chief had a similar one he wore as a sort of sash."

"I shall wear it then. Tell me, General; has the archbishop arrived?"

"I believe so. He has been situated near the military camp."

"Should I have him escorted here? Should I send for him?"

"I would think so. He is—he will be—your subject."

"I would not want to offend him. He is a prince of their church, if I recall the appellation. I think perhaps a polite invitation to join me—"

"To *attend* you, Highness."

"To *join* me," Edward repeated. "We will have to change our view of protocol to get along in this new world, General Wolfe. I know I shall have to make clear to him that I will not be embracing his version of faith, but I shall respect it—both in New France and elsewhere. I shall invite him to join me."

"Your Highness, I . . . "

"You may speak freely, General."

"I hope this is wise. It was Catholics who tore our country apart, who tried to overthrow your grandfather, and his father before him. Whatever they say, their loyalty will always be to their so-called universal church."

"You would think that their outlook might have changed, given that the seat of that church is—well, is no longer accessible."

"I would not presume to guess."

"You presume all that and more, General Wolfe," Edward said, standing up. "I don't know what you want from them. We cannot afford to have the French as enemies, not anymore.

"Go to the archbishop with General Montcalm and present my compliments and ask him to attend me at a time of his convenience."

"Highness, I—"

"Would you rather I send Colonel Revere instead?" He gestured to his aide, who looked surprised at the suggestion.

Wolfe hesitated a moment, but he said, "No, of course not, Your Highness. I shall attend to it immediately." He saluted and gave a bow, then backed out of the tent.

"We must learn to live together," Edward said. "I pray that we all believe that."

Chapter 63

An unbroken circle

Onondaga Council Fire

With all the dignity he could muster, the archbishop of Québec walked slowly up the aisle between two groups of people standing to his left and right. French and British officers and men in dress uniforms, Colonials in their homespun, native warriors in multicolored finery; men and women and children, watching him walk in full episcopal regalia including crook and miter, with a small canopy held over his head by two acolytes, and his vicar-general, Monseigneur Briand, following in his wake. Carpets had been laid down along the path, but the setting was decidedly rustic: in an open-air clearing, under a bright September sun and a brisk September breeze. There was not the comfort of a well-appointed and decorated church—there was not even a roof over the heads of the congregants.

Though he would never admit it, Pontbriand was nervous about what was to come.

There had been an extended formal discussion with the prince the previous day. His Highness had received him in a sort of camp tent, as if it had been a council of war—which, upon consideration, was not a bad analogy. It was a campaign for peace, a war against bias and resentment and all the things that had kept all peoples apart for so many years.

The prince had been clear. There would be no celebratory Mass; he was not a part of the Universal Church, and neither were many of the congregants. Blessings would be Christian, but nondenominational; and while deference would be shown to the Christian faith in the ceremony, the prince would not promise to uphold it as a part of his oath of kingship, and courtesy would be extended to the natives with respect for their beliefs.

In short, it would be like no coronation ceremony Pontbriand had ever seen or heard of. It almost begged the question of why he was being asked to perform it.

Because, Prince Edward had said to him, *I made a promise to accept a crown from your hands, as a token of my good faith to the subjects in New France.*

What of the Catholic faith? Pontbriand had asked.

All Catholics may practice their faith without hindrance, Edward had answered. *Wherever they reside. And, Your Grace*, he had added, *I suspect that when they seek Christ's Vicar upon Earth, they will look to you.*

When he reached the dais, the acolytes turned and faced inward. Pontbriand turned to face the assembly; his vicar-general stepped past to take a position behind him and slightly to his left. On either side of the dais stood a tall native in colorful dress. On his right was a man, with a bow strapped over his back and his hand resting lightly on a tomahawk at his belt, while on his left was a comely woman who held a stalk of wheat in her hand.

They will all look to you, he thought.

"'I have lifted up my eyes to the mountains, from whence help shall come to me,'" he began, spreading his hands. It seemed strange to speak the words in anything but Latin: *Levavi oculos meos in montes unde veniet auxilium mihi* . . . but he knew that not everyone would understand it in the proper tongue, and the Protestants in particular would find it jarring, *Popish*, as they would say. But Psalm 121 was as nondenominational as he was willing to be.

"'My help is from the Lord, who made heaven and earth. May he not suffer thy foot to be moved; neither let him slumber that keepeth thee. Behold he shall neither slumber nor sleep, that keepeth Israel.'

"Dearly beloved in the Lord—and in the Great Spirit—we are gathered in this place under the dome of Heaven to mark an event of great moment—to mark a beginning of something new, something that marks us as one people. It is a serious matter, which commands our attention and requires our earnest consent; the crowning and consecration of a king.

"This ceremony is one that has been performed in many lands and in many eras. It is attended by custom and tradition, protocol and formality . . . and yet in this land, at this time, it is being performed in a manner unlike any other."

He lowered his hands to his sides and took a breath. The audience was expectant, waiting for his next words; but they seemed a long time in coming.

"I will confess," the archbishop said before continuing, "if this were a French prince, called to rule over the provinces of New France, the formalities and the ceremonies would be familiar and customary. But this ceremony must include everyone, for this prince will be a king for all the people: French and British and native, all who would dwell within his domain.

"This is the peril of such an uncharted land, and the promise of an uncertain, but hopeful, future. Peril and promise interlinked; that will be our challenge and our hope. His are young shoulders to bear such a heavy burden—but they are strong ones, and we trust in the Lord"—he looked to his right and left at the natives who stood, unmoving, looking directly at him—"and the Great Spirit to protect, enrich and empower him to do right, to rule carefully, to administer with justice and mercy. He shall take up the crown alone, but he shall not rule alone.

"'My help,' says the Psalm, 'is from the Lord, who made heaven and earth . . . he shall not slumber or sleep, that keepeth Israel.' The eye that sees all pervades our innermost heart: and the One in Heaven will protect us in this time of change, and reward us by our merits.

"Is the prince ready to be made king?" he asked his vicar-general, without turning.

"Edward Augustus Hanover, son of Prince Frederick Louis Hanover, grandson of George Augustus Hanover, second of his name, King of Great Britain," the vicar-general intoned. "If His Highness is disposed to take up the crown of this land, may he deign to approach at this time."

From behind the audience, a soldier blew a single, sharp, clear note on a trumpet. Prince Edward stepped out of his pavilion, wearing his Royal Navy dress uniform, draped with the wampum belt that the *Tadodaho* had presented to him. At his neck, in place of the gorget, he wore a powder-blue ribbon from which was suspended a single silver *fleur-de-lys*.

General Amherst stood behind him holding a small pillow on which rested an unadorned gold circlet, which shone in the sun. It had been fashioned by Revere, whose skill as a silver- and goldsmith had been brought to the prince's attention; a more elaborate crown was in contemplation, but this simple diadem would serve for the ceremony.

Without a word, Edward walked slowly along the path that the archbishop had trod a few minutes earlier. When he reached the dais, Pontbriand extended his hand—it would have been customary for a Catholic to kiss his ring; but instead Edward took the hand in his own, knelt, and guided the hand to the top of his bare head. It was done so smoothly that neither Frenchmen, who might have found it an affront, nor Englishmen, who might have thought it a demeaning gesture, had time to react; it was what Edward and Pontbriand had agreed upon during their brief interview.

Humility but not subservience, Edward had said, and Pontbriand remembered the young man's serious words.

"Your Highness," Pontbriand said, looking down at the young man upon whose head he laid his hand, "if you would take upon yourself the burden of kingship, you will please swear the following oath.

"I, Edward Augustus Hanover do, of my own will—"

He continued through the rest of the oath, with Edward echoing his words, and concluded with:

"I swear that I shall."

Pontbriand felt the absence of a religious oath in the ceremony, but Edward had demanded that no such condition be included. Instead, he simply said:

"Your Highness, it is my duty and honor to invest you with the symbols of your royal status." He nodded to Amherst, who stepped forward, extending the pillow. Pontbriand took up the simple crown and laid it upon Edward's head; it had been made for him and fit perfectly.

"This crown is in the form of an unbroken circle, denoting the universality of your oath, and the unending commitment you have made to your people by taking up the authority which it represents."

From a pocket in his cassock, Briand took out a polished wooden rod, which looked like a tomahawk handle; but instead of an axe-head, it bore an equally polished white stone set in the top. A small band of wampum encircled the place where stone and wood joined.

"I place in your hands this scepter, which represents the mace of justice. May you wield this with dread and duty, a king and judge to all your people." He handed it to Edward, who took it in his left hand.

"Rise, King," he said, and Edward did so. "Behold your people."

Edward now turned to face the assembly. He tried to assume the greatest dignity he could muster, but could not keep a smile from his face.

"People of the land," the archbishop said. "Behold your king."

Then, with a spontaneity born of joy, shouts of acclamation rang out from the assembly—men and women, British and French, white and red, proclaiming Edward as king in the new world.

Almost unnoticed, the eyes of the two natives flanking the dais glowed for just a moment, signaling—perhaps—some kind of approbation.

Part VII: Salutation

September, 1759

He who reigns within himself and rules passions, desires, and fears is more than a king.

—John Milton

Chapter 64

King of something

New York City

The combined British/French/native army was the first to acclaim King Edward, but the formal welcome would take place in New York. On the morning following the ceremony at the Council Fire, arrangements were made for him to travel there.

Both Montcalm and Wolfe remained with the army, while General Amherst prepared to accompany the king. As one of his first royal acts, Edward had designated Lord Boscawen as his First Lord of the Admiralty, and Amherst as Field Marshal, in command of all the armed forces on land. His first task would be to handle relations with the colonial militias. The threats from emerging supernatural elements were likely not over, and there would have to be some coordination among the colonies. Over the objection of Wolfe, Edward had directed Amherst to offer the militia commanders the opportunity to take up regular army commissions—and all the responsibilities and honors that came with them. There would be a need for training, and there would be costs—but there would have to be an army. Something similar would be needed for the French colonies: and that too would take time. Not all of them had bent the knee to the new king; most didn't even know about it yet.

The procession moved slowly and included both riders and carriages. The concatenator was loaded into its wagon, but Mademoiselle LaGèndiere and Doctor Messier rode with the new king—a public demonstration of his gratitude for their help in the great battle just past, but also an obvious indication of personal affection.

Paul Revere traveled with the king, though Edward gave him the opportunity to withdraw and return with the Massachusetts militia. They still had work to do pacifying Salem, among other places; but Revere refused to leave his king's side, indicating that he was planning to send for his wife and children to join him in New York. Edward found his loyalty admirable, though he felt that it was an imposition.

But the world had changed, and men chose new roles depending on the way in which that change affected them.

It took eight days to reach the city, though riders were sent ahead well in advance. The last part of their journey was on the Hudson River on a flatboat. The weather had turned slightly chilly, as was so often the case in this part of the continent, the memory of summer seemed altogether too recent for it to have disappeared so suddenly. But the scenery on the journey was stunning: leaves beginning to turn color were a revelation for those new to the continent.

On a sunny autumn afternoon, they reached the outskirts of Greenwich. As they disembarked, they were met by a troop of New York militia, who looked anxious and tense.

Amherst approached the older man in command of the troop, who offered a casual salute.

"Report."

The officer—or whatever he was—paused a moment, as if trying to decide what sort of duty he owed to Amherst. Then he said, "You are on your way to New York? Sir?"

"The king is on his way there, yes."

"King?"

"King Edward. Your king, and mine."

The officer scowled. "I don't know anything about that, sir. But this isn't the best time to be visiting New York City."

"Why would that be?"

"The recent troubles," the officer answered. "The monsters."

"We had not heard. What sort of monsters?"

"Some slave conjured up monsters that attacked all over the city. Took some doing to put them down. Lots of damage all over. Who knows whether it might all come back."

"Are you saying there was a slave revolt?"

"Something like that, sir. Governor De Lancey called out the militia, and the admiral—"

"Admiral Boscawen."

"Yes, sir. The admiral had his men on the streets too."

Amherst looked over his shoulder at the escort for King Edward: twenty regular British soldiers. He wasn't sure whether they could deal with monsters, but they were equal to anything short of it.

"I think we'll be safe enough."

"Well, sir, it's up to you. But . . . can I ask a question?"

"Please do."

"The only king I know about is George, back in England. Who's this king you're talking about?"

The scenery on the high road that followed the Hudson River from Greenwich to New York showed more and more signs of civilization: windmills, a large iron foundry, and a sprawling brewery from which rose a wheaty, earthy smell that made the soldiers smile. They gathered a following as they traveled, first a group of young boys leaving their chores, then a group of blacksmiths from the foundry who decided they'd go along to see what things were about.

At last the road turned away from the river and joined the wide street called the Broad Way that led into the heart of the city. They found the makeshift gate in the palisade heavily guarded; and as well, awaiting their arrival, was Governor James De Lancey. The governor was astride a fine horse and attired in an elaborate uniform that Amherst took to be militia; as the royal party approached, De Lancey dismounted and removed his hat.

As they reached the palisade, Edward dismounted as well. He wore a tricorn, but he removed it to reveal the circlet that served as his crown. He approached De Lancey, who offered a bow.

"Rise, Governor," Edward said. "I will enter this city on foot and at your side."

"You honor me, Your Majesty. We received word of your coronation with great joy."

Edward smiled. "It won't be an easy task, sir, but with God's help I will do my best."

"I'm sure you will," De Lancey said.

"Walk with me," Edward said, and the king entered New York walking next to James De Lancey, who stepped to his left as they came down Broad Way, with a crowd visible in the distance. Even from where they were, they could hear the cheers.

The young king was accompanied by a cheering crowd all the way to the Admiralty building, where members of his escort took up positions outside as he, Revere and Boscawen entered. A tall young officer wearing some military uniform—militia, Edward thought—was waiting for them.

It was almost a relief to have the door closed and the cheering muted.

"Your Majesty," Boscawen said, "may I present Colonel George Washington, my aide. Colonel, please see we are not disturbed."

Washington bowed.

"Colonel Revere, perhaps you can keep Colonel Washington company. I suspect the admiral wants a private conversation."

Boscawen and the king ascended the stairs together, leaving their aides behind.

In his upstairs office, with the door closed, Boscawen gestured to a settle. He remained standing.

"Admiral—"

"I beg Your Majesty's pardon, but I'm going to take advantage of my one opportunity to speak plainly with you. When I am done, you may use your authority and your discretion to dismiss me from your service; but until then, you will listen to what I have to say."

"I have been king for ten days, Admiral. I think I have enough humility to accept a dressing down from such a distinguished officer."

"We will see what you think when I am done," Boscawen said. "It has been assumed for some time that you would become king of— well, of something here in the New World. But that should have been accomplished here in New York, at an assembly of the principal men of your kingdom.

"I am informed by your letters, and by other information, that you have received this *crown*—" he gestured to the circlet on Edward's brow, with a tone that conveyed exactly what he thought of it—"in some patch of woods. What's more, the man who placed it on your head is a Catholic prelate.

"So tell me; *what in God's name do you think you are doing*?"

Edward did not reply for a moment, and Boscawen could see that the king was surprised at his tone; perhaps too surprised to be angry.

"You have heard about the battle we fought somewhat east of that patch of wood, my Lord. We had the help of a fair number of French regulars."

"So I understand."

"That participation was made possible because I promised to have a Catholic prelate place the crown on my head. If I am to be king of—of *something*, as you say, I intend that it should include New France as well. It was the only way to gain their trust and their aid."

"The ceremony could have been performed in New York."

"I do not think that the archbishop of Québec would have found it at all comfortable traveling here or performing the coronation ceremony here. The Iroquois *Tadodaho* would not have been in attendance either—and I daresay the natives will have to be part of the *something* as well. Many of them fought at our side."

"Why do you believe that either the French or the natives are either willing or suitable as your subjects?"

"Because this is the world we live in, and because the French have no king either. Our enemy is not the French, Admiral Boscawen; our enemy is hostile nature, and the natives who seek to command it."

"The French accept you?"

"Those at the battle do. The Marquis de Montcalm does. He will need to convince his fellows, but I have confidence that he will be successful."

Boscawen did not answer, but paced back and forth a few times.

"Your actions are precipitate, I think. But they cannot be undone. And clearly the people, at least the people of New York, seem to approve. They want a king, and they want you to be that king."

"I am blessed to be so well received," Edward said.

"I daresay you are," Boscawen answered. He sighed and made a minute adjustment to one sleeve of his uniform coat. "I had hoped to accomplish a few more things before we reached that point, but what is done is done.

"Your Majesty, if you are not prepared to dismiss me, then I have something to ask of you. You are aware of what happened while you were absent; a black man used some sort of African ritual to summon monsters. I can't believe I am saying these words, but there is no better way to describe it.

"When the situation was resolved—after a considerable amount of destruction, I may add, evidence of which you can see wherever you look—I determined that the pernicious practice of slavery must be brought to an end here in New York at least, and I think eventually all across your realm."

"That is a rather dramatic turn," Edward said.

"What you said about the French and the natives applies equally well to the black people of this realm," Boscawen said. "I have a young black boy aboard *Namur* whom I have asked to be manumitted. There are brave negroes here in New York, free and slave, who need to be assured that they have a future in your realm. Some of them played a critical role in suppressing the monsters. I am not sure we would have prevailed without them."

"I see. Do you have something in mind?"

"I do." Boscawen went to his desk and picked up a sheet of parchment. "I had hoped that this might accompany, or occur subsequent, to your coronation. Now, if you choose to endorse it, you can make it your first true official act."

"Say on."

"I propose the following." Boscawen held the document at an angle to catch the sunlight through the window. "Any slave under the age of ten is to be freed at once with no compensation to the owner. One between the age of ten and twenty-five would sign an indenture contract of some length, and would be freed at latest at age twenty-five. Any other slave would have a shorter indenture, and would be freed at its conclusion.

"No families would be broken up in any way.

"Any owner choosing to sell a slave directly to the Royal Navy would be compensated at a higher rate; we would in turn manumit the slave and enlist him if male, and find other employment for her if female.

"What is more, all free blacks would have the right to petition in cases of grievance, to serve on juries, and to sue and enter into contracts without bias."

"Can they not do these things already?"

"Not in the colony of New York, and in most cases not in other colonies either. New York City is particularly difficult. Two decades ago there was a violent backlash against blacks in the city. The repercussions of that event are still felt today. We must be sure that it never happens again."

Edward stood and walked to the window, which overlooked an inner courtyard. He could still hear the cheers from outside.

"If I am not mistaken, Admiral," he said without turning, "there are colonies that rely exclusively on the labor of their black slaves to maintain their economy. Sugar and cotton and tobacco are all grown by slave labor. Are you prepared to give them this proclamation?"

"Ultimately, yes. But it would start here, Your Majesty. It would be an indication to the other colonies that this change would be coming."

"It seems like a rather radical—"

"Dispensation, yes. But I, too, made a promise. I am disinclined to go back on my word."

There was a long silence. Boscawen remembered that pause for years to come, wondering what the young king might say, and whether his stridency had caused irredeemable offense.

Finally, King Edward turned to face Boscawen. "Admiral, you have had strong words for me, and each of us has dealt with situations we could hardly imagine when we left our homes months ago. But we must work together if we want anything to survive.

"We will undertake this dispensation you propose. And you will be my First Lord of the Admiralty. I could not find a more capable man to command the Royal Navy."

"It's not much of a navy."

"It is what we have, sir. And it will be greater in the future. In the meanwhile, we have a proclamation to make."

Chapter 65

Common cause

New York City

At the southernmost berth of the docks on the East River, *HMS Neptune* stood ready to set sail, just a few days after returning from Halifax. Four other vessels rode at anchor out in Long Island Sound, waiting for a signal from the flagship. On the main deck, rows of regulars, in their best dress uniforms, stood at rigid attention.

Admiral Sir Charles Saunders also stood at attention before his commander, Admiral Boscawen. Just behind him, his adjutant stood holding the dispatch bag that Boscawen had just presented to him.

"I'm not giving you the easiest assignment, Charles. Truly, I don't know if you can accomplish half of what I'm asking you to do."

"The appointment will help, My Lord."

"Admiral of the White? Yes, well. We need someone to hold that title. But you're right; it grants you authority over people like Pinfold, and Admiral Coates will respect it. But having said that, I don't know what you'll encounter there. Jamaica might be the most disturbed, if the *obeah*-men have risen again."

"You mentioned that."

"My letters to the governors and commanders should explain everything. But you'll be the man on the spot."

"And we'll get these vessels away before the weather sets in."

"It's been a very strange few months, Charles—we don't know if the weather has abated down south." Vessels on station in North

America traditionally avoided heavy weather in the north and hurricane season in the south; but the comet's fall could very well have upset those patterns.

"We'll know soon enough, My Lord. I'll have word sent from Charles Town."

"If it's not in revolt, or under attack by who knows what. Your first goal is to protect this squadron, for it's the only squadron we have."

"I understand, sir."

"Then fair winds to you, Charles. Until we meet again."

"My Lord." Saunders and his aide saluted, and then they turned and went up the gangplank and aboard *Neptune*.

A few minutes later, with anchor raised and sails set, *Neptune* moved out into the channel, with the other ships following. Boscawen stood and watched, turning slightly away from the brisk wind, until the five ships passed Staten Island.

Rumor outran fact on the streets of New York, as it always did. Among black residents it ran even faster; that the new king would be freeing all the slaves; that he would be buying all the slaves and *then* freeing them; that all the male slaves in New York would be freed and made sailors and soldiers. There was so much talk of freedom, or—among those who knew the word—manumission, that it was assumed that there had to be some truth to it.

Governor De Lancey's militia was still on the streets, patrolling against anything strange or extraordinary. The spiders were all gone, and the elephant-creatures had left as well: but the black people seemed to be moving with confidence, not keeping their heads low. Among the militiamen it was said that De Lancey was furious—about the new king, about the departure of the naval squadron, or about something else that no one wanted to mention.

Change was in the air.

Minerva was busier than ever, and scarcely ever left alone. It didn't trouble her; she was used to having folks around, not just Absalom or Coffey, but anyone who needed comforting or advice or healing in one form or another.

On a late afternoon in mid-September, Coffey arrived just at tea-time with York in tow. The young man, now a manumitted freedman working at the Admiralty office for Admiral Boscawen, looked like a devoted puppy.

Sweet on that girl, Minerva thought, and it made her smile. Coffey smiled as well, as did York, though it was clear he wasn't sure why he was doing so.

"Tea is in the pot," Minerva said. "And I gathered up a few biscuits. Sit, sit. La, you two look like you're joined at the hip."

The two young people found spots on the settle, and Minerva took her customary place near the fire. Coffey sprung right up and poured the tea before Minerva could stop her, and soon they were all comfortable again.

"What news, then?"

"Oh, everyone is saying everything, Mercy." Coffey looked at York. "They say that the new king is going to free all the peoples."

"Have you heard him say this, child?"

"I haven't heard him say anything, Mercy. He doesn't talk to the likes of me."

"But you've seen him, up close."

"Oh, yes." She smiled. "Handsome man." She patted her young man's hand. "But not like you," she added.

"Even a cat can look at a king," Minerva said, and laughed. A ray of late-afternoon sunlight pierced the clouds and passed through the window and into the sitting-room. "Young kings are always handsome. What else do you see in him, girl?"

"I can't see more clearly than anyone else, Mercy," she said.

"What your normal eyes see is good enough."

"Well," Coffey said, "he's getting used to his place. But he doesn't let anyone scare him, not the admiral, or the governor neither. He's acting like a king." She smiled, a bit slyly. "And he's in love."

"In love? With whom?"

"He's in love with a French woman, the one who came on the admiral's ship. Ever since they came back from the battle, he can't take eyes off her whenever she's around."

"A French woman," mused Minerva. "And a French priest put that crown on his head. I wonder what that all means."

"Not our place to worry," York said, the first words he'd spoken as he listened to the two women's conversation.

Minerva set her teacup down carefully on the little table next to her and smoothed her skirts around her.

"That is what a slave says, child," she said to York. "But you are not a slave, you are a freedman, no matter your indenture. *Of course,* it is your place to worry. What is it the admiral said to us: a new *dispensation.* Our people have a stake in what happens, and it is of course our place. The world has changed, York."

"The governor's militia have all the guns, Mercy. So long as they do, they will do all the worrying for everyone."

"You're afraid," Minerva said. "I know you are. So am I."

"You are, Miss Mercy?"

"Of course I am. But I will not show it, and neither should you. The admiral is a good man; I can see it. He is in pain, which he won't admit, but he believes in the right things. He sees us not just as black people, but as *people.*"

"Governor thinks different," York said. "Admiral isn't the governor."

"The king—" Coffey began, but York cut her off.

"King isn't the governor neither. Governor thinks that every black man is Jupiter waiting to happen. He's scared of us, all of us, and scared folks with guns are dangerous. All the blacks that were held to account in 1741 were put to death, but Judge Horsmanden is still judge. You ask your parents, girl," he said to Coffey. "What happened in their day could happen in ours."

"York is right," Minerva said. "We have a chance for change now because the world is changed. But it's all promises. Anyone willing to make common cause with the black folks of New York is taking a risk.

"But we can hope. We can always hope."

Two days after arriving in New York, King Edward and Catherine LaGèndiere found time to walk in the gardens at James De Lancey's estate. The leaves were beginning to turn, and the quiet, pastoral place seemed the nearest thing to an English country estate. Still, for Edward at least, it was the most poignant reminder of where he was, and where he was not.

Catherine had long since recovered from her exhaustion, but still looked careworn. Anne De Lancey, the governor's wife, had arranged with her own dressmaker to fit Catherine for some new clothing—more plain than what might be found at the Court, perhaps, but enough to enhance her natural beauty. Anna, her unmarried daughter, had been offered as a companion, which Catherine gladly accepted. The young woman and Colonel Revere were present at a polite distance as the king and the Frenchwoman enjoyed the autumn sunlight.

After a time, they settled on a bench, side by side.

"I have been thinking quite a bit about what you told me," Edward said. "I want you to know . . . while it makes things more acceptable to others, it really makes no difference to me."

"I had never intended to deceive you, Your Majesty."

"Edward. Please."

"I am not accustomed to address a king by his Christian name."

"I think such a privilege can be waived in private, Catherine. Or would you prefer I now address you as Louise?"

She took a fold of fabric from her sleeve in her hand, examining it. "I have worn Catherine LaGèndiere like a suit of clothes for so many months now, I've grown quite used to it. I think I prefer it."

"There is no one to gainsay you. Out of curiosity, then; is there a real person who bears that name?"

"There was. Henri LaGèndiere's daughter was a particular friend of mine, and served as an assistant to Doctor Messier in Paris. She fell ill with cholera and died a month before we set sail. It was not well known in Paris, and it was a simple matter to take her place."

"Then I am moved to ask why you did so."

"It is difficult to discuss."

"If it troubles you so—"

"No, no." She smiled faintly, as if she wanted to make light of it. "It is something you must learn, sooner or later. I was betrothed at age twelve. Louis was fifteen at the time, already being fitted for the army. It was a good match in the eyes of his parents and mine, but I would be lying if I said that there was any love in it. He was . . . unkind, unthinking."

"The cad."

"Well, just so—Edward. But he had his career, and since last year he had his own regiment; he was, shall I say, a rising star, settled in his marital affairs. But he did not see me as anything but a decoration. It did not trouble me at all to find my own diversions and interests, just as he found his."

"A man of poor taste."

"Aristocrats can afford to have poor taste," she answered. "Or poor judgment. And I mean no offense to you personally, of course."

"My judgment has been questioned; very recently, in fact. No offense is taken, I assure you."

"The cad," she said, smiling. "Who would dare?"

"Admiral Boscawen. He was disturbed that I took matters into my own hands regarding the coronation." He removed his hat and touched the circlet on his head. "Apparently that was a political decision he would have preferred to make for me."

"It is not his decision to make."

"I believe that he knows that, Catherine," Edward said. "But it is a delicate matter, and as I am a callow youth—"

Catherine laughed, and covered her mouth. "I'm sorry," she said. "I don't mean to make light of it."

"We *should* make light of it. He—and Field Marshal Amherst, I think—had originally thought that I would be elevated from prince to king in some manner that the English colonies could accept easily."

"What about the French colonies?"

"Their acceptance was not a matter under discussion. I have made it complicated because I chose to make common cause with them, and offered to be crowned by the Catholic prelate of Québec. It remains to be seen what the rest of the English colonies will think of that."

"I don't see as they have any choice, Edward. You are the king."

"Spoken like a true Frenchwoman. That isn't how the British Empire is run."

"Still, you *are* the king."

"In this environment, my dear, I am king if the people decide to accept me as such. English or French or native, they will need to conclude that a king is needed and then if I qualify."

"To be certain, no one else qualifies."

"To be certain. However, the colonies of New England have managed very well without royal attention since Cromwell's time. New York and Pennsylvania and Virginia have always been independent and headstrong; and the others are likely indifferent.

The French and the Iroquois have their own traditions and customs. What we have is not so much a kingdom as three kingdoms united under a single crown—and each of those kingdoms will develop along their own lines, at least for a time. We—I, especially—will need to be patient."

He smiled. "You may think of our new kingdom as a work in progress. The one thing that unites us all and binds us together is a strong bond; our common struggle against the new perverse forces of nature and those who seek to wield them against us."

Catherine shuddered slightly and looked away.

"I'm sorry," Edward said. "I spoke carelessly and without thinking. I . . . don't know what that battle must have been like from your perspective. I confess that I don't understand much of what you were doing—but your effort was absolutely indispensable. If you were a man, I'd give you a title."

"I already have a title, for what it's worth."

"Then I shall do the next best thing."

"Oh?" She turned to look at him. "What would that be?"

"If you will have me," he said, "I will make you my queen."

The words hung between them for several seconds, as a series of expressions crossed Catherine's face: surprise, joy, worry, some fear as well. It was hard to tease them all apart.

Finally she said, "And what would Admiral Boscawen or Field Marshal Amherst make of that?"

"I have not consulted them. And they don't have any idea that you are Louise, Duchesse de Mazarin. In fact, I believe they are somewhat at a loss to determine who might be suitable in the role. But I don't care; what I witnessed at that battle made it clear that no other would do.

"Catherine. My lady. I cannot command—I can only beseech. Would you consent to become my wife?"

"I . . . am a married woman, Your Ma—. Edward."

"But there was no issue. I trust that the archbishop could put that marriage aside, particularly given the circumstances. For all practical purposes, after all, you are now a widow. And you have my solemn word and bond that your stature would be far beyond that of a *decoration*."

"Still, it is beyond my power to accept."

"And it is beyond my authority to compel. But at least you do not reject my suit out of hand."

"Reject . . . ? You think . . . you fear that I might reject you? After your demonstration of bravery and gallantry on the field in the face of . . . what opposed us? No, no. Certainly not. I am honored that you would ask me to marry you, and I am flattered that you would do so given the many obstacles that face the proposition.

"I cannot accept at this moment—but if it becomes possible, then of course. Yes. *Certainement.* I can think of nothing I would rather do."

Chapter 66

No one is alone in the world

Johnson Hall

"I don't want to leave my home," Molly said. The infant in her lap shifted a little in its sleep; she stroked her son's head gently, but her face was serious and determined.

"No one can make you go," Skenadoa said. "The *Tadodaho* knows he cannot compel. The clan mothers cannot compel. They *ask*, Degonwadonti."

"What do they want of me?"

"I think you know the answer," Skenadoa responded. "They see how you have protected this place; they want you to protect *their* place."

"I could not protect any place before the broom-star fell, and before . . . " She looked down at her son, and at last said, ". . . before William disappeared. There is no way to know whether I can do anything at all if I leave here, or whether this place itself is the defense they credit to me."

"They believe otherwise."

"And I am to give up my home and my safety because of what they *believe*? Please, Elder Brother. They believed that the League of the Longhouse would prevail forever, and that it would remain together as long as the Council Fire burned. But the Floating Heads put out the fire and the League has been broken. What is more, Skenadoa, we of the Longhouse always counted on the two white confederations to be balanced against each other—and now they are allied. Olivier—"

462

"Olivier?"

"Olivier D'Egremont. A French officer," Molly continued. "He told me that the French and British now call each other friends."

"He speaks truth," Skenadoa said.

"Tell me," Molly said. "With the French and English yoked together, what role is left for the People of the Longhouse? What is it that the *Tadodaho* wants me to protect? No, I wish to stay in my own home, with my family and the people I am protecting."

"That is not the answer they want to hear."

"But it is the answer you will give them."

"Actually," Skenadoa said, "you may have to do that yourself; you must tell the clan-mothers who have come to ask for your protection."

"You did not say that the clan-mothers were here."

"You did not ask," Skenadoa answered. "They are ready to see you . . . " he looked from Molly to the baby in her lap. "Whenever your time permits."

With her baby settled in a nap, Molly left the house and walked down the hill to the refugee camp. There was a crispness in the air, a hint of fall; she felt the presence of all four of the forms of *Ga'oh*, the wind spirits, but they were subdued and quiet, as if they did not want to enter here. As she passed them, both men and women greeted her with a word or a glance. She still felt somewhat uneasy with the attention and respect, but knew that she had earned it with her newfound powers.

She found the clan mothers sitting with a large group of refugee women in a flat area some distance from the enclosing wall. The women were in close conversation, but they fell silent as Molly approached.

"Degonwadonti," one of the visiting clan mothers said. "We had thought to come up to the great house." She gestured toward the house on the hill.

"There is no need. The baby sleeps. Best to talk in public."

"You know why we are here."

"Skenadoa told me. Did he tell you about my reluctance?"

"He has not spoken to us."

"I'm not surprised." Molly stepped forward and sat in a place that had been left empty. "Let me explain it to you.

"I do not know why the Great Spirit has given me any power, or what I am to do with it—other than to protect my people." She spread her hands, gesturing toward the refugee camp all around her. "But I do not know whether I am bound to this place, or whether the power is bound to this place."

"It is in you," the leading clan mother said.

"How do you know that?"

"We see it in you," the woman answered. "You have the power wherever you go."

"You see it."

"Yes."

"Is this a power brought by the broom-star? You know this to be true?"

"Not all power came from the broom-star, Degonwadonti," the clan mother said. "I, Osha, have led the Heron clan for many seasons, and the Great Spirit gave me the eyes to see from a young age. I can see the mantle of power on your shoulders, Degonwadonti, and it will serve you wherever you go."

"This is my home."

"The world is your home, Younger Sister. You owe—"

"I *owe*," Molly interrupted, "I owe my duty to my family and my clan. I owe respect to the memory of Sir William Johnson and the son he left me. I did not choose to be where I am, and I am ready to return to quiet."

"The world has changed, Degonwadonti. You must—"

"I *must*?"

Osha sighed. "No one is alone in the world," she said. "You are right to say that the world has changed. Of course, it has. The whites have lost their world and are here to stay. They will make better friends than enemies now that they are not at war with each other.

"When they come to treat with the People of the Longhouse, Degonwadonti, they will come to the Longhouse itself—to the Council Fire."

"Which was extinguished."

"Which has been relit."

"It means nothing, Elder Sister. Not anymore."

"That is not true."

"Of course, it is. I watched when Guyasuta's messenger came here and tossed down the bundle of broken arrows. The Covenant Chain is broken; the tribes are no longer in the same longhouse. The Council Fire is no more important than . . . " Molly gestured toward the wisps of smoke rising from cookfires around her. "Than any of these fires."

"The Council Fire has whatever power we invest in it."

"So does my home."

Osha tugged on the sleeves on her shirt and adjusted the headband that held her hair out of her face.

"You are right, Degonwadonti. I cannot compel you to quit this place and come to Onondaga. I can only beseech you to come. And as for the Covenant, the shape and size of the Longhouse has changed over the seasons, and it has changed again. The Cayuga may have gone their own way, and the Seneca as well, but the Covenant will survive. Even if you do not protect the Council Fire, or believe that you can protect it, your presence is a symbol. You may not realize it, but who you are, and what you represent, is known far beyond the low stone wall of your home. We *need* you, Degonwadonti. Even your young French admirer will tell you that."

"Olivier is not my admirer, Elder Sister. I do not have time for such things, and I am in mourning."

"You will have time. And you will not always be in mourning."

Québec

Montcalm never thought of himself as an especially religious man. He had never failed to be present when required, or requested, but he had spent far more of his time astride a horse, or in court dress attending his king, than on his knees. But since the comet's fall, and especially since the trip upriver when he had been confronted with the natives' spirits—the ones who had reappeared in the battle so recently won—he had been more inclined to seek the solace and peace of a church.

It was in the modest Basilica of Notre-Dame where Jean-Félix Récher found him; not kneeling, exactly, but contemplating a large bas-relief on the side of the nave depicting one of the Stations of the Cross.

"I hope I'm not disturbing you."

"Ah, *Père*. No, not at all. I'm just waiting for His Grace. He is at the Governor's Palace."

"Is he. I assume Monsieur de Vaudreuil is not happy."

"We have scarcely spoken since we returned from New York. But I am inclined to agree."

"The archbishop's mood seemed more sunny."

"Once the ceremony was complete, yes. I still think he's in a state of shock to be asked, particularly since certain bounds were placed on what he might say and do, how the consecration and coronation would be arranged so that everyone was satisfied."

"Except Monsieur de Vaudreuil."

"He was not consulted in the matter."

"I imagine that contributes to his dissatisfaction," Récher said. "But you have no regrets on that subject."

"None at all—and certainly none for which I require absolution. As for the archbishop . . . well, perhaps we should let him speak for himself." Montcalm turned to face Henri-Marie de Pontbriand, who had just come into the nave, and was in the process of handing off his crook and episcopal headgear to an acolyte. He seemed in no hurry to divest himself of his robes of office—whether that was for effect, or to ward off the cold September draft that chilled the building, Montcalm was not sure. When the archbishop came before them, both he and Récher bowed and kissed the episcopal ring.

"Your Grace," Montcalm said.

"Monsieur. And Father Récher."

"If Your Grace will excuse me—"

"Yes, by all means. Unless you'd like to stay," the archbishop said, smiling. "I believe the Marquis and I will simply be making impolite comments about the governor."

"Your Grace . . . ?"

"Monsieur de Vaudreuil summoned me. If you can imagine it, he *summoned* me, when we arrived in Québec yesterday. I pled fatigue, of course, and arrived when I pleased. Properly attired, I might add, to make sure he was aware with whom he was dealing."

"Christ's Vicar on Earth," Montcalm said.

"I didn't try to suggest that, and I trust you will forbear in thus promoting me, Monsieur," Pontbriand answered. "But likely, eventually, yes. He was having none of it: not the peace with the British, not the king, not the coronation. '*Not my king*,' he insisted," the archbishop added, in a tone reminiscent of the governor that almost made Montcalm laugh. "'*And not your king either, Your Grace*.' He seemed quite insistent on that point."

"You told him that it was Prince—King—Edward's idea."

"I did, and that seemed to make little difference. He refuses to recognize the authority you were so willing to delegate, as he put it. I think that if he thought there was a ship to take it home he would have dashed off an indignant letter to Versailles."

"I know of no ship that travels that route, at least at present," Montcalm answered. "Or to London either."

"Or Rome," the archbishop added.

"When he—or Bigot—could write to the King's ministers, they had power. Now they will have to come to terms with the world the way it actually is. As for the rest of the *habitants* . . . I think that they will be glad to have a king again. I think this king will actually care about them as well."

"Amen," Father Récher said.

"Amen," the archbishop agreed. "But a great deal of prayer is ahead of us, I think."

"Don't let me keep you from it."

"You won't," the archbishop answered. "I expect you will be praying along with us, Monsieur."

New York

"Which one?" Absalom asked.

Looking out of the window of her apartment in the boarding house, Minerva smiled. "You would think that a man so bound up with chance would not assume things are simple and straightforward."

Absalom's jaws tightened for a moment. "It matters, woman. Which one?"

Her smile stayed in place. "Which *ones*, you would do better to ask."

"Dear Lord." He wiped his face. "I speak of the Christian one.

Such a simple god, he is. One son—one only—and something called the Holy Spirit. So, which *ones*, Minerva? Dare I hope that Nana Buluku is among them?"

Minerva shook her head. "Not she herself. I am hardly so mighty, even now. But if it makes you feel better, I can sense Ayizan stirring within me."

"Well, that's something." Absalom cocked his head a little, giving her a look that was both quizzical and skeptical. "Although you're not an ancient grandmother—not even a mother—and your skin is brown, not black. I will grant that you are a splendid herbalist."

The smile left Minerva's face. "Oya is there also, Absalom. So is Gledi and Musso Koroni. Some others."

Absalom took a deep breath and glanced at the door, as if contemplating an escape route. But, instead, he came to stand beside her at the window.

The street below was packed with people, this time of day. Almost all of them were black.

"Well," he said. "At least we won't need to fear that the white folk will inflict another slaughter upon us."

Minerva's face, normally warm and friendly, became grim. "They may *begin*." The room was suddenly filled with the image of a great snake, followed by that of a huge woman with wild hair and wild eyes. She held a machete in her hand. "They will not finish."

Absalom grunted, with a bit of humor. "At least I am not your consort. As I recall the legends, it went badly for some of them."

That broke the mood. Minerva laughed. "Oh, la! Very badly indeed."